The step on the stair

Anna Katharine Green

The step on the stair

The present edition is a reproduction of previous publication of this classic work. Minor typographical errors may have been corrected without note; however, for an authentic reading experience the spelling, punctuation, and capitalization have been retained from the original text.

ISBN: 979-8-88942-540-3

CONTENTS

Book I   The Three Edgars 1
Book II   Hidden 47
Book III   Which of Us Two? 97
Book IV   Love 140

BOOK I

THE THREE EDGARS

CHAPTER 1

I had turned the corner at Thirty-fifth Street and was halfway down the block in my search for a number I had just taken from the telephone book when my attention was suddenly diverted by the quick movements and peculiar aspect of a man whom I saw plunging from the doorway of a large office-building some fifty feet or so ahead of me.

Though to all appearance in a desperate hurry to take the taxi-cab waiting for him at the curb, he was so under the influence of some other anxiety almost equally pressing that he stopped before he reached it to give one searching look down the street which, to my amazement, presently centered on myself.

The man was a stranger to me, but evidently I was not so to him, for his expression changed at once as our eyes met and, without waiting for me to advance, he stepped hastily towards me, saying as we came together:

"Mr. Bartholomew, is it not?"

I bowed. He had spoken my name.

"I have been waiting for you many interminable minutes," he hurriedly continued. "I have had bad news from home—a child hurt—and must go at once. So, if you will pardon the informality, I will hand over to you here and now the letter about which I telephoned you, together with a key which I am assured you will find very useful. I am sorry I cannot stop for further explanations; but you will pardon me, I know. You can have nothing to ask which will not keep till to-morrow?"

"No; but—"

I got no further, something in my tone or something in my look seemed to alarm him for he took an immediate advantage of my hesitation to repeat anxiously:

"You are Mr. Bartholomew, are you not? Edgar Quenton Bartholomew?"

I smiled a polite acquiescence and, taking a card from my pocketbook, handed it to him.

He gave it one glance and passed it back. The name corresponded exactly with the one he had just uttered.

With a muttered apology and a hasty nod, he turned and fairly ran to the waiting taxi-cab. Had he looked back—

But he did not, and I had the doubtful satisfaction of seeing him ride off before I could summon my wits or pocket the articles which had been so unceremoniously thrust upon me.

For what had seemed so right to him seemed anything but right to me. I was Edgar Q. Bartholomew without question, but I was very sure that I was not the Edgar Quenton Bartholomew he thought he was addressing. This I had more than suspected when he first accosted me. But when, after consulting my card, he handed me the letter and its accompanying parcel, all doubt vanished. He had given into my keeping articles meant for another man.

And I knew the man.

Yet I had let this stranger go without an attempt to rid him of his misapprehension. Had seen him hasten away to his injured child without uttering the one word which would have saved him from an error the consequences of which no one, not even myself, could at that moment foresee.

Why did I do this? I call myself a gentleman; moreover I believe myself to be universally considered as such. Why, then—

Let events tell. Follow my next move and look for explanations later.

The man who had accosted me was a lawyer by the name of Miller. Of that I felt assured. Also that he had been coming from his own office when he first rushed into view. Of that office I should be glad to have a momentary glimpse; also I should certainly be much more composed in mind and ready to meet the possible results of my inexcusable action if I knew whether or not the man for whom I had been taken—the other Edgar Q. Bartholomew, would come for that letter and parcel of which I had myself become the guilty possessor.

The first matter could be settled in no time. The directory just inside the building from which I had seen Mr. Miller emerge would give me the number of his office. But to determine just how I might satisfy myself on the other point was not so easy. To take up my stand somewhere in the vicinity—in a doorway, let us say—from which I could watch all who entered the building in which I had located Mr. Miller's office seemed the natural and moreover the safest way. For the passers-by were many and I could easily slip amongst them and so disappear from view if by chance I perceived the other man of my name approaching. Whereas, if once inside, I should find it difficult to avoid him in case of an encounter.

Policy called for a watch from the street, but who listens to policy at the age of twenty-three; and after a moment of two of indecision, I hurried forward and, entering the building, was soon at a door on the third floor bearing the name of

John E. Miller
ATTORNEY AT LAW

Satisfied from the results of my short meeting with Mr. Miller in the street below that he neither knew my person nor that of the other Bartholomew (strange as this latter may seem when one considers the character of the business linking them together), I felt that I had no reason to fear being recognized by any of his clerks; and taking the knob of the door in hand, I boldly sought to enter. But I found the door locked, nor did I receive any response to my knock. Evidently Mr. Miller kept no clerks or they had all left the building when he did.

Annoyed as I was at the mischance, for I had really hoped to come upon some one there of sufficient responsibility to be of assistance to me in my perplexity, I yet derived some gratification from the thought that when the other Bartholomew came, he would meet with the same disappointment.

But would he come? There seemed to be the best of reasons why he should. The appointment made for him by Mr. Miller was one, which, judging from what had just taken place between that gentleman and myself, was of too great importance to be heedlessly ignored. Perhaps in another moment—at the next stop of the elevator—I should behold his gay and careless figure step into sight within twenty feet of me. Did I wish him to find me standing in hesitation before the lawyer's closed door? No, anything but that, especially as I was by

3

no means sure what I might be led into doing if we thus came eye to eye. The letter in my pocket—the key of whose usefulness I had been assured —was it or was it not in me to hand them over without a fuller knowledge of what I might lose in doing so?

Honestly, I did not know. I should have to see his face—the far from handsome face which nevertheless won all hearts as mine had never done, good-looking though I was said to be even by those who liked me least. If that face wore a smile—I had reason to dread that smile—I might waver and succumb to its peculiar fascination. If on the contrary its expression was dubious or betrayed an undue anxiety, the temptation to leave him in ignorance of what I held would be great and I should probably pass the coming night in secret debate with my own conscience over the untoward situation in which I found myself, himself and one other thus unexpectedly involved.

It would be no more than just, or so I blindly decided as I hastily withdrew into a short hall which providentially opened just opposite the spot where I stood lingering in my indecision.

It was an unnecessary precaution. Strangers and strangers only met my eye as I gazed in anxious scrutiny at the various persons hurrying by in every direction.

Five minutes—ten went by—and still a rush of strangers, none of whom paused even for a moment at Mr. Miller's door.

Should I waste any more time on such an uncertainty, or should I linger a little while longer in the hope that the other Quenton Bartholomew would yet turn up? I was not surprised at his being late. If ever a man was a slave to his own temperament, that man was he, and what would make most of us hasten, often caused him a needless delay.

I would wait ten, fifteen minutes longer; for petty as the wish may seem to you who as yet have been given no clew to my motives or my reason for them, I felt that it would be a solace for many a bitter hour in the past if I might be the secret witness of this man's disappointment at having through some freak or a culpable indifference as to time, missed the interview which might mean everything to him.

I should not have to use my eyes to take all this in; hearing would be sufficient. But then if he should chance to turn and glance my way he would not need to see my face in order to recognize me; and the ensuing conversation would not be without its embarrassments for the one hiding the other's booty in his breast.

No, I would go, notwithstanding the uncertainty it would leave in my mind; and impetuously wheeling about, I was on the point of carrying out this purpose when I noticed for the first time that there was an opening at the extreme end of this short hall, leading to a staircase running down to the one beneath.

This offered me an advantage of which I was not slow to avail myself. Slipping from the open hall on to the platform heading this staircase, I listened without further fear of being seen for any movement which might take place at door 322.

But without results. Though I remained where I was for a full half hour, I heard nothing which betrayed the near-by presence of the man for whom I waited. If a step seemed to halt before the office-door upon which my attention was centered it went speedily on. He whom I half hoped, half dreaded to see failed to appear.

Why should I have expected anything different? Was he not always himself and no other? He keep an appointment?—remember that time is money to most men if not to his own easy self? Hardly, if some present whim, or promising diversion stood in the way. Yet business of this nature, involving— But there! what did it involve? That I did not know—could not know till what lay concealed in my pocket should open up its secrets. My heart jumped at the thought. I was not indifferent if he was. If I left the building now, the letter containing these secrets would have to go with me. The idea of leaving it in the hands of a third party, be he who he may, was an intolerable one. For this night at least, it must remain in my keeping. Perhaps on the morrow I should see my way to some other disposition of the same. At all events, such an opportunity to end a great perplexity seldom comes to any man. I should be a fool to let it slip without a due balancing of the pros and cons incident to all serious dilemmas.

So thinking, I left the building and in twenty minutes was closeted with my problem in a room I had taken that morning at the Marie Antoinette.

For hours I busied myself with it, in an effort to determine whether I should open the letter bearing my name but which I was certain was not intended for me, or to let it lie untampered with till I could communicate with the man who had a legal right to it.

It was not the simple question that it seems. Read on, and I think you will ultimately agree with me that I was right in giving the matter some thought before yielding to the instinctive impulse of an honest man.

CHAPTER 2

My Uncle, Edgar Quenton Bartholomew, was a man in a thousand. In everything he was remarkable. Physically little short of a giant, but handsome as few are handsome, he had a mind and heart measuring up to his other advantages.

Had fortune placed him differently—had he lived where talent is recognized and a man's faculties are given full play—he might have been numbered among the country's greatest instead of being the boast of a small town which only half appreciated the personality it so ignorantly exalted. His early life, even his middle age I leave to your imagination. It is of his latter days I would speak; days full of a quiet tragedy for which the hitherto even tenor of his life had poorly prepared him.

Though I was one of the only two male relatives left to him, I had grown to manhood before Fate brought us face to face and his troubles as well as mine began. I was the son of his next younger brother and had been brought up abroad where my father had married. I was given my uncle's name but this led to little beyond an acknowledgment of our relationship in the shape of a generous gift each year on my birthday, until by the death of my mother who had outlived my father twenty years, I was left free to follow my natural spirit of adventure and to make the acquaintance of one whom I had been brought up to consider as a man of unbounded wealth and decided consequence.

That in doing this I was to quit a safe and quiet life, and enter upon personal hazard and many a disturbing problem,

I little realized. But had it been given me to foresee this I probably would have taken passage just the same and perhaps with even more youthful gusto. Have I not said that my temperament was naturally adventurous?

I arrived in New York, had my three weeks of pleasure in town, then started north for the small city from which my uncle's letters had invariably been postmarked. I had not advised him of my coming. With the unconscious egotism of youth I wanted to surprise him and his lovely young daughter about whom I had had many a dream.

Edgar Quenton Bartholomew sending up his card to Edgar Quenton Bartholomew tickled my fancy. I had forgotten or rather ignored the fact that there was still another of our name, the son of a yet younger brother whom I had not seen and of whom I had heard so little that he was really a negligible factor in the plans I had laid out for myself.

This third Edgar was still a negligible factor when on reaching C— I stepped from the train and made my way into the station where I proposed to get some information as to the location of my uncle's home. It was while thus engaged that I was startled and almost thrown off my balance by seeing in the hand of a liveried chauffeur awaiting his turn at the ticket office, a large gripsack bearing the initials E. Q. B.—which you will remember were not only mine but those of my unknown cousin.

There was but one conclusion to be drawn from this circumstance. My uncle's second namesake—the nephew who possibly lived with him—was on the point of leaving town; and whether I welcomed the fact or not, must at that very moment be somewhere in the crowd surrounding me or on the platform outside.

More startled than gratified by this discovery, I impulsively reversed the bag I was carrying so as to effectively conceal from view the initials which gave away my own identity.

Why? Most any other man in my position would have rejoiced at such an opportunity to make himself known to one so closely allied to himself before the fast coming train had carried him away. But I had my own conception of how and where my introduction to my American relatives should take place. It had been my dream for weeks, and I was in no mood to see it changed simply because my uncle's second namesake chose to take a journey just as I was entering the town. He was young and I was young; we could both afford to wait. It was not about his image that my fancies lingered.

Here the crowd of outgoing passengers caught me up and I was soon on the outside platform looking about, though with a feeling of inner revulsion of which I should have been ashamed and was not, for the face and figure of a young man answering to my preconceived idea of what my famous uncle's nephew should be. But I saw no one near or far with whom I could associate in any way the initials I have mentioned, and relieved in mind that the hurrying minutes left me no time for further effort in this direction. I was searching for some one to whom I might properly address my inquiries, when I heard a deep voice from somewhere over my head remark to the chauffeur whom I now saw standing directly in front of me, "Is everything all right? Train on time?" and turned, realizing in an instant upon whom my gaze would fall. Tones so deliberate and so rich with the mellowness of years never could have come from a young man's throat. It was my uncle, and not my cousin, who stood at my back awaiting the coming train. One glance at his face and figure made any other conclusion impossible.

Here then, in the hurry of departure from town where I had foolishly looked upon him as a fixture, our meeting was to come off. The surprise I had planned had turned into an embarrassment for myself. Instead of a fit setting such as I had often imagined (how the dream came back to me at that incongruous moment! The grand old parlor, of the elegance of which strange stories had come to my ears—my waiting figure, expectant, with eyes on the door opening to admit uncle and cousin, he stately but kind, she curious but shy)—instead of all this, with its glamour of hope and uncertainty, a station platform, with but three minutes in which to state my claim and receive his welcome.

Could any circumstances have been more prejudicial to my high hopes? Yet must I make my attempt. If I let this opportunity slip, I might never have another. Who knows! He might be going away for weeks, perhaps for months. Danger lurks in long delays. I dared not remain silent.

Meantime, I had been taking in his imposing personality. Though anticipating much, I found myself in no wise disappointed. He was all and more than my fancy had painted. If the grandeur of his proportions aroused a feeling of awe, the geniality of his expression softened that feeling into one of a more pleasing nature. He was gifted with the power to win as well as to command; and as I noted this and yielded to an influence such as never before had entered my life, the hardihood with which I had contemplated this meeting received a shock; and a warmth to which my breast was more or less a stranger took the place of the pretense with which I had expected to carry off a situation I was hardly experienced enough in social amenities to handle with suitable propriety.

While this new and unusual feeling lightened my heart and made it easy for my lips to smile, I touched him lightly on the arm (for he was not noticing me at all), and quietly spoke his name.

Now I am by no means a short man, but at the sound of my voice he looked down and meeting the glance of a stranger, nodded and waited for me to speak, which I did with the least circumlocution possible.

Begging him to pardon me for intruding myself upon him at such a moment, I smilingly remarked:

"From the initials I see on the bag in the hand of your chauffeur, I judge that you will not be devoid of all interest in mine, if only because they are so strangely familiar to you." And with a repetition of my smile which sprang quite unbidden at his look of quick astonishment, I turned my own bag about and let him see the E. Q. B. hitherto hidden from view.

He gave a start, and laying his hand on my shoulder, gazed at me for a moment with an earnestness I would have found it hard to meet five minutes before, and then drew me slightly aside with the remark:

"You are James' son?"

I nodded.

"You have crossed the ocean and found your way here to see me?"

I nodded again; words did not come with their usual alacrity.

"I do not see your father in your face."

"No, I favor my mother."

"She must have been a handsome woman."

I flushed, not with displeasure, but because I had hoped that he would find something of himself or at least of his family in my personal traits.

"She was the belle of her village, when my father married her," I nevertheless answered. "She died six weeks ago. That is why I am here; to make your acquaintance and that of my two cousins who up till now have been little more than names to me."

"I am glad to see you,"—and though the rumble of the approaching train was every moment becoming more audible, he made no move, unless the gesture with which he summoned his chauffeur could be called one. "I was going to Albany, but that city won't run away, while I am not so sure that you will not, if I left you thus unceremoniously at the first moment of our acquaintance. Bliss, take us back home and tell Wealthy to order the fatted calf." Then, with a merry glance my way, "We shall have to do our celebrating in peaceful contemplation of each other's enjoyment. Both Edgar and Orpha are away. But do not be concerned. A man of my build can do wonders in an emergency; and so, I have no doubt, can you. Together, we should be able to make the occasion a memorable one."

The laugh with which I replied was gay with hope. No premonition of mischief or of any deeper evil disturbed that first exhilaration. We were like boys. He sixty-seven and I twenty-three.

It is an hour I love to look back upon.

CHAPTER 3

I had always been told that my uncle's home was one of unusual magnificence but placed in such an undesirable quarter of the city as to occasion surprise that so much money should have been lavished in embellishing a site which in itself was comparatively worthless. And yet while I was thus in a measure prepared for what I was to see, I found the magnificence of the house as well as the unattractiveness of the surroundings much greater than anything my imagination had presumed to picture.

The fact that this man of many millions lived not only in the business section but in the least prosperous portion of it was what I noted first. I could hardly believe that the street we entered was his street until I saw that its name was the one to which our letters had been uniformly addressed. Old fashioned houses, all decent but of the humbler sort, with here and there a sprinkling of shops, lined the way which led up to the huge area of park and dwelling which owned him for its master. Beyond, more street and rows of even humbler dwellings. Why, the choice of this spot for a palace? I tried to keep this question out of my countenance, as we turned into the driveway, and the beauties of the Bartholomew home burst upon me.

I shall find it a difficult house to describe. It is so absolutely the product of a dominant mind bound by no architectural conventions that a mere observer like myself could only wonder, admire and remain silent.

It is built of stone with a curious admixture of wood at one end for which there seems to be no artistic reason. However, one forgets this when once the picturesque effect of the whole mass has seized upon the imagination. To what this effect is due I have never been able to decide. Perhaps the exact proportion of part to part may explain it, or the peculiar grouping of its many chimneys each of individual design, or more likely still, the way its separate roofs slope into each other, insuring a continuous line of beauty. Whatever the cause, the result is as pleasing as it is startling, and with this expression of delight in its general features, I will proceed to give such details of its scope and arrangement as are necessary to a full understanding of my story.

Approached by a double driveway, its great door of entrance opened into what I afterwards found to be a covered court taking the place of an ordinary hall.

Beyond this court, with its elaborate dome of glass sparkling in the sunlight, rose the main facade with its two projecting wings flanking the court on either side; the one on the right to the height of three stories and the one on the left to two, thus leaving to view in the latter case a row of mullioned windows in line with the facade already mentioned.

It was here that wood became predominate, allowing a display of ornamentation, beautiful in itself, but oddly out of keeping with the adjoining stone-work.

Hemming this all in, but not too closely, was a group of wonderful old trees concealing, as I afterwards learned, stables and a collection of outhouses. The whole worthy of its owner and like him in its generous proportions, its unconventionality and a sense of something elusive and perplexing, suggestive of mystery, which same may or may not have been in the builder's mind when he fashioned this strange structure in his dreams.

Uncle was watching me. Evidently I was not as successful in hiding my feelings as I had supposed. As we stepped from the auto on to the platform leading to the front door—which I noticed as a minor detail, was being held open to us by a man in waiting quite in baronial style —he remarked:

"You have many fine homes in England, but none I dare say, built on the same model as this. There is a reason for the eccentricities you notice. Not all of this house is new. A certain portion dates back a hundred years. I did not wish to demolish this; so the new part, such as you see it, had to be fashioned around it. But you will find it a home both comfortable and hospitable. Welcome to Quenton Court."

Here he ushered me inside.

Was I prepared for what I saw?

Hardly. I had looked for splendor but not for such a dream of beauty as recalled the wonders of old Granada.

Moorish pillars! Moorish arches in a continuous colonnade extending around three sides of the large square! Above, a dome of amber-tinted glass through which the sunbeams of a cloudless day poured down upon a central fountain tossing aloft its bejeweled sprays from a miracle of carven stonework. Encircling the last a tesselated pavement covered with rugs such as I had never seen in my limited experience of interior furnishings. No couches, no moveables of any sort here, but color—color everywhere, not glaring, but harmonized to an exquisite degree. Through the arches on either side highly appointed rooms could be seen; but to one entering from the front, all that met the eye was the fountain at play backed by a flight of marble steps curving up to a gallery which, like the steps themselves, supported a screen pierced by arches and cut to the fineness of lace-work.

And it was enough; artistry could go no further.

"You like it?"

The hearty tone called me from my dreams.

"There is but one thing lacking," I smiled; "the figure of my cousin Orpha descending those wonderful stairs."

For an instant his eyes narrowed. Then he assumed what was probably his business air and said kindly enough but in a way to stop all questioning:

"Orpha is in the Berkshires." Then laughingly, as we proceeded to enter one of the rooms, "Orpha does look well coming down those stairs."

She was not mentioned again between us for many days, and then only casually. Yet his heart was full of her. I knew this from the way he talked about her to others.

CHAPTER 4

I was given a spacious apartment on the third story. It was here that my uncle had his suite and, as I was afterwards told, my cousin Edgar also whenever he chose to make use of it, which was not very often. Mine overlooked the grounds on the east side of the building, and was approached from the main staircase by a winding passageway, and from a rear one by a dozen narrow steps down which I was lucky never to fall. The second story I soon learned was devoted to Orpha and the many guests she was in the habit of entertaining. In her absence, all the rooms on this floor remained closed. During my whole stay I failed to see a single one of its many doors opened.

I met my uncle at table and in the library opening off the court and for a week we got on beautifully together. He seemed to enjoy my companionship and to welcome every effort on my part towards mutual trust and understanding. But the next week saw us no further advanced either in confidence or warmth of affection, and this notwithstanding an ever increasing regard on my part both for his character and attainments. Was the fault, then, in me that he was not able to give me the full response I so ardently desired? Or was it that the strength of his attachment for the second bearer of his name was such as to preclude too hearty a reception of one who might possibly look upon himself as possessing a corresponding claim upon his consideration?

I tried to flatter myself that this and not any real lack in myself was the cause of the slight but quite perceptible break in our mutual understanding. For whenever my cousin's name came up, which was oftener than was altogether pleasing to me, the light in my uncle's eye brightened and the richness in his tone grew more marked. Yet when I once ventured to ask him if my cousin had any special bent or predominate taste, he turned sharply aside, with the carefully modulated remark:

"If he has, neither he nor ourselves have ever been able as yet to discover it."

But he loved him; of that I grew more and more assured as I noted that there was not a room in the great mansion, no, nor a nook, so far as I could see, without a picture of him somewhere on desk, table or mantel. There was even one in my room. Photographs all, but taken at different times of his life from childhood up, and framed every one with that careful taste and lavishness of expense which we only bestow on what is most precious.

I spent a great deal of time studying these pictures. I may have been seen doing so and I may not, having no premonition as to what was in store for me. My interest in them sprang from a different source than a casual onlooker would be apt to conjecture. I was searching for what gave him such a hold on the affections of every sort of person with whom he came in contact. There was no beauty in his countenance nor in so far as I could judge from the various poses in which these photographs had been taken, any distinction in his build or bearing. His expression even lacked that haunting quality which sometimes makes an otherwise ordinary countenance unforgetable. Yet during the fortnight of my first stay under my uncle's roof I never heard this cousin of mine mentioned in the house or out of it, that I did not observe that quiet illumination of the features on the part of the one speaking which betrays lively admiration if not love.

Was I generous enough to be glad of the favor so unconsciously shown him by those who knew him best? I fear I must acknowledge to the contrary in spite of the prejudice it may arouse against me. For I mean to be frank in these pages and to present myself as I am, faults and all, that you may rate at their full value the difficulties which afterwards beset me.

I was not pleased to find my cousin, unknown quantity though he was, held so firmly in my uncle's regard, especially as—but here let me cry a moment's halt while I speak of one who, if hitherto simply alluded to, was much in my thoughts through these half pleasant, half trying days of my early introduction into this family. Orpha did not return, nor was I so happy as to come across her picture anywhere in the house; which, considering the many that were to be seen of Edgar, struck me as extremely odd till I heard that there was a wonderful full length portrait of her in Uncle's study, which fact afforded an explanation, perhaps, of why I was never asked to accompany him there.

This reticence of his concerning one who must be exceptionally dear to him, taken with the assurances I received from more than one source of the many delightful qualities distinguishing this heiress to many millions, roused in me a curiosity which I saw no immediate prospect of satisfying.

Her father would not talk of her and as soon as I was really convinced that this was no passing whim but a positive determination on his part, I encouraged no one else to do so, out of a feeling of loyalty upon which I fear I prided myself a little too much. For the better part of my stay, then, she held her place in my imagination as a romantic mystery which some day it would be given me to solve. At present she was away on a visit, but visits are not interminable and when she did come back her father would not be able to keep her shut away from all eyes as he did her picture. But the complacency with which I looked forward to this event received a shock when one morning, while still in my room, I overheard a couple of sentences which passed between two of the maids as they went tripping down the walk under my open window.

One was to the effect that their young mistress was to have been home the previous week but for some reason had changed her plans.

"Or her father changed them for her," laughed a merry voice. "The handsome cousin might put the other out."

"Oh, no, don't you think it," was the quick retort. "No one could put our Mr. Edgar out."

That was all. Mere servants' gossip, but it set me thinking, and the more I brooded over it, the more deeply I flushed in shame and dissatisfaction. What if there were some truth in these idle words! What if I were keeping my young cousin from her home! What if this were the secret of that slight decrease in cordiality which my uncle had shown or I felt that he had shown me these last few days. It might well be so, if he had already planned as these chattering girls had intimated in the few sentences I had overheard, a match between his child and his best known, best loved nephew. The pang of extreme dissatisfaction which this thought brought me roused my good sense and sent me to bed that night in a state of self-derision which should have made a man of me. Certainly it was not without some effect, for early the next morning I sought an interview with my uncle in which I thanked him for his hospitality and announced my intention of speedily bidding him good-by as I had come to this country to stay and must be on the look-out for a suitable situation.

He looked pleased; commended me, and gave me half his morning in a discussion of my capabilities and the best plan for utilizing them. When I left him the next day, it was with a feeling of gratitude strangely mingled with sentiments not quite so worthy. He had made me understand without words or any display of coldness that I had come too late upon the scene to alter in any manner his intentions towards his youngest nephew. I should have his aid and sympathy to a reasonable degree but beyond that I need hope for little more unless I should prove myself a man of exceptional probity and talent which same I perceived very plainly he did not in the least expect.

Nor did I blame him.

And so ends the first act of my little drama. You must acknowledge that it gives small promise of a second one of more or less dramatic intensity.

CHAPTER 5

Two months from that day I was given a desk of my own in a brokerage office in New York city and as the saying is was soon making good. This favorable start in the world of finance I owed entirely to my uncle, without whose influence, and I dare say, without whose money, I could never have got so far in so short a space of time. Was I pleased with my good fortune? Was I even properly grateful for the prospects it offered? In my heart of hearts I suppose I was. But visions would come of the free and easy life of the man I envied, beloved if not approved and looking forward to a continuance of these joys without the sting of doubt to mar his outlook. I had seen my uncle several times but not my cousins. They had remained in C—, happy, as I could well believe, in each other's companionship.

With this conviction in mind it was certainly wise to forget them. But I was never wise, and moreover I was a very selfish man in those days, as you have already discovered—selfish and self-centered. Was I to remain so? You will have to read further to find out.

Thus things were, when suddenly and without the least warning, a startling change took place in my life and social condition. It happened in this wise. I was dining at a restaurant which I habitually patronized, and being alone, which was my wont also, I was amusing myself by imagining that the young man seated at a neighboring table and also alone was my cousin. Though only a part of his profile was visible, there was that in his general outline highly suggestive of the man whose photographs I had so carefully studied. What might not happen if it were really he! My imagination was hard at work, when he impetuously rose and faced me, and I saw that I had made no mistake; that the two Bartholomews, Edgar Quentons both, were at last confronting each other; and that he as surely recognized me as I did him.

In another moment we had shaken hands and I was acknowledging to myself that a man does not need to have exceptionally good looks to be absolutely pleasing. Though quite assured that he did not cherish any very amiable feelings towards myself, one would never have known it from his smile or from the seemingly spontaneous warmth with which he introduced himself and laughingly added:

"I was told that I should be sure to find you here. I have been entrusted with a message from those at home."

I motioned him to sit down beside me, which he did with sufficient grace. Then before I could speak, he burst out in a matter-of-fact tone:

"We are to have a ball. You are to come." His hand was already fumbling in one of his pockets. "Here is the formal invitation. Uncle thought—in fact we both thought —that you would be more likely to accept it if it were accompanied by some preliminary acquaintance between us two. Say, cousin, I think it is quite fortunate that you are a dark man and I a light one; for people can now say the dark Mr. E. Q. Bartholomew or the light one, which will quite preclude any mistakes being made."

I laughed, so did he, but there was an easy confidence in his laugh which was not in mine. Somehow his remark did not please me. Nor do I flatter myself that the impression I made upon him was any too favorable.

But we continued outwardly cordial. Likewise, I accepted the invitation he had taken so long a trip to deliver and would have offered him a bed in my bachelor apartment had he not already informed me that it was his intention to return home that night.

"Uncle did not seem quite as well as usual this morning," he explained, "and Orpha made me promise to come back at once. Just a trifling indisposition," he continued, a little carelessly. "He has always been so robust that the slightest change in him is a source of worry to his devoted daughter."

It was the first time he had mentioned her, and I may have betrayed my interest, carefully as I sought to hide it; for his smile took on meaning as he lightly remarked:

"This ball is in celebration of an event you will be the first to congratulate me upon when you see our pretty cousin."

"I am told that she is more than pretty; that she is very lovely," I observed somewhat coldly.

His gesture was eloquent; yet to me his manner was not that of a supremely happy man. Nor did I like the way he looked me over when we parted as we did after a half hour of desultory conversation. But then it would have been hard for me to find him wholly agreeable after the announcement he had just made, little reason as I had to concern myself over a marriage between one long ago chosen for that honor and a woman I had not even seen.

CHAPTER 6

Whether I was not over and above eager to attend this ball or whether I was really the victim of several mischances which delayed me over more than one train, I did not arrive in C— till the entertainment at Quenton Court was in full swing. This I knew from the animation observable in the streets leading to my uncle's home, and in the music I heard as I entered the gate which, for no reason good enough to mention, I had approached on foot.

But though fond of dancing and quite used to scenes of this nature, I felt little or no chagrin over the hour or two of pleasure thus lost. The night was long and I should probably see all, if not too much, of a celebration in which I seemed likely to play an altogether secondary part. Which shows how little we know of what really confronts us; upon what thresholds we stand,—or to use another simile,—how sudden may be the tide which slips us from our moorings.

I had barely stepped from under the awning into the vestibule guarding the side entrance, when I found myself face to face with my uncle's butler. He was an undemonstrative man but there was something in his countenance as he drew me aside, which disturbed, if it did not alarm me.

"I have been waiting for you, sir," he said in a tone of suppressed haste. "Mr. Bartholomew wishes to have a few words with you before you enter the ball-room. Will you go straight up to his room?"

"Most assuredly," I replied, bounding up the narrow staircase used on such occasions.

He did not follow me. I knew the house and the exact location of my uncle's room. But imperative as my duty was to hasten there without the least delay, a strong temptation came and I lingered on the way for how many minutes I never knew.

The cause was this. The room in which I had rid myself of my great-coat and hat was on the opposite side of the hall from the stair-case running up to the third story. In crossing over to it the lure of the brilliant scene below drew me to the gallery overlooking the court where most of the dancing was taking place.

Once there, I stopped to look, and looking once, I looked again and yet again, and with this last look, my life with its selfish wishes and sordid plans took a turn from which it has never swerved from that day to this.

There is but one factor in life potent enough to work a miracle of this nature. Love!

I had seen the woman who was to make or unmake me; the only one who had ever roused in me anything more than a pleasing emotion.

It was no mere fancy. Fancy does not remold a man in a moment. Fancy has its ups and downs, its hot minutes and its cold. This was a steady inspiration; an enlargement of the soul such as I had hitherto been a stranger to, and which I knew then, as plainly as I do now, would serve to make my happiness or my misery as Fortune lent her aid or passed me coldly by.

I have called her a woman, but she was hardly that yet. Just a girl rejoicing in the dance. Had she been older I should not have had the temerity to associate her in this blind fashion with my future. But young and care free—a blossom opening to the sun—what wonder that I put no curb on my imagination, but watched her every step and every smile with a delight in which self if assertive triumphed more in its power to give than in its expectation of reward.

It was a wonderful five minutes to come into any man's life and the experience must have left its impress upon me even if at this culminating point of high feeling I had gone my way to see her face no more.

But Fate was in an impish mood that night. While I still lingered, watching her swaying figure as it floated in and out of the pillared arcade, the whirl of the dance brought her face to face with me, and whether from the attraction of my fixed gaze or from one of those chances which make or mar life, she raised her eyes to the latticed gallery and our glances met.

Was it possible—could it be—that hers rested for an instant longer on mine than the occasion naturally called for? I blushed as I found myself cherishing the thought, —I who had never blushed in all my memory before—and forced myself to look elsewhere and to listen with attention to the music just then rising in a bewildering crash.

I have taken time to relate this, but the minutes of my lingering could not have been many. However, as I have already acknowledged, I have never known the sum of them, and when, at last, struck by a sudden pang of remembrance, I started back from the gallery-railing and made my way up a second flight of stairs to my uncle's room, I was still so lost to the realities of life that it was with a distinct sense of shock I heard the sound of my own knock on my uncle's door.

But that threshold once passed, all thought of self—I will not say of her—vanished in a great confusion. For my uncle, as I saw him now, had little in common with my uncle as I saw him last.

Sitting with face turned my way but with head lowered on his breast and all force gone from his great body, he had the appearance of a very sick man or of one engulfed beyond his own control in human misery. Which of the two was it? Sickness I could understand; even the prostration, under some insidious disease, of so powerful a physical organism as that of the once strong man before me. But misery, no; not while my own heart beat so high and the very walls shook with the thrum, thrum of the violin and cello. It was too incongruous.

But if sickness, why did I find him, the master of so many hearts, alone in his room looking for help from one who was little more than a stranger to him? It must be misery, and Edgar, my cousin, the cause. For who but he could inflict a pang capable of working such havoc as this in our uncle's inflexible nature. Nor was I wrong; for when at some movement I made he lifted his head and our eyes met, he asked abruptly and without any word of welcome, this question:

"Have you seen Edgar? Does he know that you are here?"

I shook my head, in secret wonder that I had given him a thought since setting foot in the house.

"I have had no opportunity of seeing him," I hastened In explain. "He is doubtless with the dancers."

"Is he with the dancers?" It was said somewhat bitterly; but not in a way which called for reply. Then with, feverish abruptness, "Sit down, I want to talk to you."

I took the first chair which offered and as I did so, became aware of a hitherto unobserved presence at the farther end of the room. He was not alone, then, it seemed. Some one was keeping watch. Who? I was soon to know for he turned almost immediately in the direction I have named and in a tone as far removed as possible from the ringing one to which I was accustomed, he spoke the name of Wealthy, saying, as a middle-aged woman came forward, that he would like to be alone for a little while with this nephew who was such a stranger.

She passed me in going out—a wholesome, kindly looking woman whom I faintly remembered to have seen once or twice during my former visit. As she stopped to lift the portiere guarding the passage-way leading to the door, she cast me a glance over her shoulder. It was full of anxious doubt.

I answered it with a nod of understanding, then turned to my uncle whose countenance was now lit with a purpose which made it more familiar.

"I shall not waste words." Thus he began. "I have been a strong man, but that day is over. I can even foresee my end. But it is not of that I wish to speak now. Quenton—"

It was the first time he had used this name in addressing me and I greeted it with a smile, recognizing immediately how it would not only prevent confusion in the household but give me here and elsewhere an individual standing.

He saw I was pleased and so spoke the name again but this time with a gravity which secured my earnest attention.

"Quenton, (I am glad you like the name) I will not ask you to excuse my abruptness. My condition demands it. Do you think you could ever love my daughter, your cousin Orpha?"

I was too amazed—too shaken in body and soul to answer him. This, within fifteen minutes of an experience which had sealed my emotions from all thought of love save for the one woman who had awakened my indifferent nature to the real meaning of love. An hour before, my heart would have leaped at the question. Now it was cold and unresponsive as stone.

"You do not answer."

It was not harshly said but very anxiously.

"I—I thought," was my feeble reply, "that Edgar, my cousin, was to have that happiness. That this dance—this ball—was in celebration of an engagement between them. Surely I was given to understand this."

"By him?"

I nodded; the room was whirling about me.

"Did he tell you like a man in love?"

I flushed. What a question from him to me! How could I answer it? I had no objection now to Edgar marrying her; but how could I be true to my uncle or to myself, and answer this question affirmatively.

"Your countenance speaks for you," he declared, and dropped the subject with the remark, "There will be no such announcement to-night. If Edgar's hopes appear to stand in the way of any you might naturally cherish, you may eliminate them from your thoughts. And so I ask again, do you think you could love my Orpha; really love her for herself and not for her fortune? Love her as if she were the one woman in the world for you?"

He had grown easier; the flush and sparkle of health were returning to his countenance. It smote my heart to say him nay; yet how could I be worthy of her if I misled him for an instant in so important a matter.

"Uncle," I cried, "you forget that I have never seen my cousin Orpha, But even if I had and found her to be all that the most exacting heart could desire, I could not give her my love; for that has gone out to another—and irrevocably if I know my own nature."

He laughed, snapping his finger and thumb, in his recovered spirits. "That," he sung out, "for any other love when you have once seen Orpha! I had forgotten that I kept her from you when you were here before. You see I am not the man I was. But I may find myself again if—"

He paused, tried to rise, a strange light suddenly illuminating his countenance. "Come with me," he said, taking the arm I hastened to hold out to him.

Steadying myself, for I quickly divined his purpose, I led him toward the door he had indicated by a quick gesture. It was that of his so-called den from which I had always been excluded—the small room opening off his larger one, containing, as I had been told, Orpha's portrait.

"So," thought I to myself, "shut from me when my heart was free to love, to be shown now when all my being is filled with another." It was the beginning of a series of ironies which, while I recognized them as such, did not cause me a moment of indecision. No, though his laugh was yet ringing in my ears.

"Open," he cried, as we reached the door. "But wait. Go back and put out all the lights. I can stand alone. And now," as I did his bidding, marveling at the strength of his purpose which did not shun a theatrical effect to insure its success, "return and give me your hand that I may lead you to the spot where I wish you to stand."

What could I do but obey? Tremulous with sympathy, but resolved, as before, not to succumb to the allurement he was evidently preparing for me, I yielded myself to his wishes and let him put me where he would in the darkness of that small chamber. A click and—

You have guessed it. In the sudden burst of light, I saw before me in glorious portraiture the vision of her with whom my mind was filled.

The idol of my thoughts was she, whose father had just asked me if I could love her enough to marry her.

CHAPTER 7

I had never until now considered myself as a man of sentiment. Indeed, a few hours before I would have scoffed at the thought that any surprise, however dear, could have occasioned in me a display of emotion.

But that moment was too much for me. As the face and form of her whom to see was to love, started into view before me with a vividness almost of a living presence, springs were touched within my breast which I had never known existed there, and my eyes moistened and my heart leapt in thankfulness that the appeal of so exquisite a womanhood had found response in my indifferent nature.

For in the portrait there was to be seen a sweetness drawn from deeper sources than that which had bewitched me in the smile of the dancer: a richness of promise in pose and look which satisfied the reason as well as charmed the eye. I had not done ill in choosing such a one as this to lavish love upon.

"Ha, my boy, what did I say?" The words came from my uncle and I felt the pressure of his hand on my arm. "This is no common admiration I see; it is something deeper, bigger. So you have forgotten the other already? My little girl has put out all lesser lights."

"There is no other. She is the one, she only."

And I told him my story.

He listened, gaining strength with every word I uttered.

"So for a mere hope which might never have developed, you were ready to give up a fortune," was all he said.

"It was not that which troubled me," was my reply, uttered in all candor. "It was the thought that I must disappoint you in a matter you seem to have taken to heart."

"Yes, yes," he muttered as if to himself.

And I stood wondering, lost in surprise at this change in his wishes and asking myself over and over as I turned on the lights and helped him back to his easy chair in the big room, what had occasioned this change, and whether it would be a permanent one or pass with the possible hallucinations of his present fevered condition.

To clear up this point and make sure that I should not be led to play the fool in a situation of such unexpected difficulty, I ventured to ask him what he wished me to do now—whether I should remain where I was or go down and make my young cousin's acquaintance.

"She seemed very happy," I assured him. "Evidently she does not know that you are upstairs and ill."

"I do not want her to know it. Not till a half hour before supper-time. Then she may come up. I will allow you to carry her this message; but she must come up alone."

"Shall I call Wealthy?" I asked, for his temporary excitement was fast giving away to a renewed lassitude.

"She will come when you are gone. She must not know what has been said here to-night. No one must know. Promise me, Quenton."

"No one shall know." I was as anxious as he for silence. How could I face her, or return Edgar's handshake if my secret were known to either?

"Go, then; Orpha will be wondering where you are. Naturally, she is curious. If you ever win her love, be gentle with her. She is used to gentleness."

"If I ever win her love," I returned with some solemnity, "I will remember this hour and what I owe to you."

He made a slight gesture and taking it for dismissal I turned to go.

But the sigh I heard drew me back.

"Is there nothing I can do for you before I go?"

"Keep him below if you have the wit to do it. I do not feel as if I could see him to-night. But no hints; no cousinly innuendoes. Remember that you have no knowledge of any displeasure I may feel. I can trust you?"

"Implicitly in this."

He made another gesture and I opened the door.

"And don't forget that I am to see Orpha half an hour before supper." In another moment he was on his feet. "How? What?" he cried, his face, his voice, his whole appearance changed.

And I knew why. Edgar was in the hall; Edgar was coming our way and in haste; he was almost running.

"Uncle!" was on his lips; and in another instant he was in the room. "I heard you were ill," he cried, passing by me without ceremony and flinging himself on his knees at the sick man's side.

I did not stay to mark the other's reception of this outburst. There could be but one. Loving Edgar as he did in spite of any displeasure he may have felt he could not but yield to the charm of his voice and manner never perhaps more fully exercised than now. I was myself affected by it and from that moment understood why he had got such a hold on that great heart and why any dereliction of his or fancied slight should have produced such an overwhelming effect. To-morrow would see him the favored heir again; and with this belief and in this mood I went below.

CHAPTER 8

I have thought many times since that I was fortunate rather than otherwise to have received this decided set-back to my hopes before I came into the presence of my lovely young cousin. It at least served to steady me and give to our first meeting a wholesome restraint which it might have lacked if no shadowing doubt had fallen upon my spirits. As it was, there was a moment of self-consciousness, as our hands touched, which made the instant a thrilling one. That she should show surprise at identifying me, her cousin from a far-off land, with a stranger who half an hour before had held her gaze from the gallery above, was to be expected. But any hope that her falling lids and tremulous smile meant more than this was a folly of which I hope I was not guilty. Had I not just seen Edgar under circumstances which showed the power he possessed over the hearts of men? What then must it be over the hearts of women! Orpha could not help but love him and I had been a madman to suppose that even with the encouragement of her father I could dream for a moment of supplanting him in her affections. To emphasize the effect of this conclusion I recalled what I had heard said by one of the two servant-maids who had had countless opportunities of seeing him and Orpha together, "Oh, nobody could put our Mr. Edgar out" and calmed myself into a decent composure of mind and manner, for which she seemed grateful. Why, I did not dare ask myself.

A few minutes later we were whirling in the dance.

I will not dwell on that dance or on the many introductions which followed. The welcome accorded me was a cordial one and had I been free to make full use of my opportunities I might have made a more lasting impression upon my uncle's friends. But my mind was diverted by my anxiety as to what was going on in the room above, and the question of how soon, if at all, Edgar would reappear upon the scene. It was sufficiently evident from the expression of those about me that his absence had been noted, and I could not keep my eyes from the gallery through which he must pass on his way down.

At last he came into view, but too far back in the gallery for me to determine whether he came as conqueror or conquered from our uncle's room. Nor was I given a chance to form any immediate conclusion on this important matter, though I passed him more than once in the dance into which he had thrown himself with a fervor which might have most any sentiment for its basis.

But fortune favored me later and in a way I was far from expecting. Having some difficulty in finding my partner for the coming dance, I strolled into one of the smaller rooms leading, as I knew, to a certain favorite nook in the conservatory. On the wall at my left was a mirror and chancing to glance that way, I paused and went no further.

For reflected there, from the hidden nook of which I have spoken, I saw Edgar's face and figure at a moment when the soul speaks rather than the body, thus leaving its choicest secret no longer to surmise.

He was bending to assist a young lady to rise from the seat which they had evidently been occupying together. But the courtesy was that of love and of love at its highest pitch—love at the brink of fate, of loss, of wordless despair.

There was no mistaking his look, the grasp of his hand, the trembling of his whole body; and as I muttered to myself, "This is a farewell," my heart stood still in my breast and my mind lost itself for the instant in infinite confusion.

For the lady was not Orpha, but a tall superb brunette whose countenance was a mirror of his in its tenderness and desolation. Was this the cause of Uncle's sudden reversal of opinion as to the desirability of a union between the two cousins? Had some unexpected discovery of the state of Edgar's feelings towards another woman, wrought such a change in his own that he could ask me, me, whether I could love his daughter warmly enough to marry her? If so, I could easily understand the passion with which he had watched the effect of this question upon the only other man whom his pride of blood would allow him to consider as the heir of his hard gotten fortune.

All this was plain enough to me now, but what drove me backward from that mirror and into a spot where I could regain some hold upon myself was the certainty which these conclusions brought of the end of my hopes.

For the scene of which I had just been the inadvertent witness was one of renunciation. Edgar had yielded to his uncle's exactions and if I were not mistaken in him as well as in my uncle, the announcement would yet be made for which this ball had been given.

How was I to bear it knowing what I did and loving her as I did! How were any of us to endure a situation which left a sting in every heart? It was for Orpha only to dance on untroubled. She had seen nothing—heard nothing to disturb her joy. Might never hear or see anything if we were all true to her and conscientiously masked our unhappiness and despair. Edgar would play his part,—would have to with Uncle's eye upon him; and Uncle himself—

This inner mention of his name brought me up standing. I owed a duty to that uncle. He had entrusted me with a message. The time to deliver it had come. Orpha must be told and at once that her father wished to see her in his room upstairs. For what purpose he had not said nor was it for me to conjecture. All that I had to do was to fulfill his request. I was glad that I had no choice in the matter.

Leaving my quiet corner I reentered the court where the dance was at its height. Round and round in a mystic circle the joyous couples swept, to a tune entrancing in melody and rhythm. From their midst the fountain sent up its spray of dazzling drops a-glitter with the colors flashed upon them from the half hidden lights overhead. A fairy scene to the eye of untroubled youth; but to me a maddening one, masking the grief of many hearts with its show of pleasure.

What Orpha thought of me as I finally came upon her at the end of the dance, I have often wondered. She appeared startled, possibly because I was looking anything but natural myself. But she smiled in response to my greeting, only to grow sober again, as I quietly informed her that her father was a trifle indisposed and would be glad to see her for a few minutes in his own room.

"Papa, ill? I don't understand," she murmured. "He is never ill." Then suddenly, "Where is Edgar?"

The question as she uttered it struck me keenly. However I managed to reply in a purposely careless tone:

"In the library, I think, where they are practicing some new steps. Shall I take you to him?"

She shook her head, but accepted my arm after a show of hesitation quite unconscious I was sure. "No, I will go right up."

Without further words I led her to the foot of the great staircase. As she withdrew her arm from mine she turned her face towards me. Its look of trouble smote sorely on my heart.

"Shall I go up with you?" I asked.

She shook her head as before, and with a strange wavering smile I found it hard to interpret, sped lightly upward.

A few minutes later I had located my missing partner and was dancing with seeming gayety; but almost lost my step as Edgar brushed by me with a girl whom I had not seen before on his arm. He was as pale as a man well could be who was not ill and though his lips wore a forced smile the girl was doing all the talking.

What was in the air? What would the next half hour bring to him—to me—to all of us?

I tried to do my duty by my partner, but it was not easy and I hardly think she carried away a very favorable impression of me. When released, I sought to hide myself behind a wall of flowering shrubs as near the foot of the stairs as possible. Much can be read from the human countenance, and if I could catch a glimpse of Orpha's face as she rejoined her guests, some of my doubts might be confirmed or, as I secretly hoped, eliminated.

That Edgar had the same idea was soon apparent; for the first figure I saw approaching the stairs was his, and while he did not go up, he took his stand where he would be sure to see her the moment she became visible in the gallery.

There was, however, a reason for this, aside from any personal anxiety he may have had. They two, as acting host and hostess, were to lead the procession to the supper-room.

I was to take in a Miss Barton and while I kept this young lady in sight, I remained where I was, watching Edgar and those empty stairs for the coming of that fairy figure whose aspect might reveal my future fate. Nothing could be so important as this hoped-for freeing of my mind from its heavy doubts.

Fortunately I had not long to wait. She presently appeared, and with my first view of her face, doubt became certainty in my bewildered mind. For she came with a joyful rush, and there was but one thing which could so wing her feet and give such breeziness to her every movement. The desire of her heart was still hers. Nothing that her father had said had robbed her of that. Then as Edgar advanced, I perceived that her feelings were complex and quite evenly balanced between opposite emotions. Happiness lay before her, but so did trouble, and I could not feel at ease until I knew just what this trouble was. Then I remembered; she had found her father ill. That was certainly enough to account for the secret care battling with her joy. And so all was clear again to my mind. But not to my heart. For by the way Edgar received her and the quiet manner in which they interchanged a few words, I saw that they understood each other. That was what disturbed me and gave to my hopes their final blow. They understood each other.

Whenever I think of the next half hour it is with astonishment that I can remember so little of it. I probably spoke and answered questions and conducted myself on the whole as a gentleman is expected to do on a festive occasion. But I have no memory of it—none whatever. When I came to myself, the supper was half over and the merriment, to which I had probably added my full quota, at its height. With quick glances here and there I took in the whole situation, and from that moment on was quite conscious of how frequently my attention wandered from my ingenuous little partner to where Orpha sat with Edgar, lovely as youth and happiness could make her, but with never a look for me, much as I longed for it.

That he should fail to see and appreciate this loveliness, was no longer a matter of surprise to me who had seen him under the complete domination of his secret passion for Miss Colfax. But the fear that others might note it and wonder, was strong within me. For while he offered her no slight, his glances like mine would seek the face of the woman he loved, who to my amazement occupied the seat at his right. What a juxtaposition for him! But she did not seem to be affected by it, but chatted and smiled with a composure startling to see in one who to my unhappy knowledge had just passed through one of the really great crises in life. How could she look just that way, smile just that way, with a breaking heart beneath her silks and laces? It was incomprehensible to me till I suddenly awoke to the fact that I was smiling too and quite broadly at some remark made by my friendly little partner.

Meantime the moment was approaching which I was anticipating with so much dread. If the announcement of Edgar and Orpha's engagement was to be made, it would be during, or immediately after, the dessert and that was on the point of being served. Edgar, I could see was nerving himself for the ordeal, and as Orpha's eyes sought her plate, I prepared myself to hear what would end my evanescent dream and take away all charm from life.

CHAPTER 9

"Friends!"

Was that Edgar speaking? Surely this was not his voice I heard.

But it was. Through the mist which had suddenly clouded everything in that long room, I could see him standing at his full height, with his glass held high in hand.

The hush was instantaneous. This seemed to unnerve him for I saw a drop or two of wine escape from that overfilled glass. But he quickly recovered the gay sang-froid which habitually distinguished him, and with the aspect and bearing which made him the most fascinating man I had ever met, went on to say:

"I have a word to speak for my uncle who I am sorry to say is detained in his room by a passing indisposition. First, he bids me extend to you his hearty greetings and best wishes for your very good health."

He drank—we all drank—and joy ran high.

"Secondly:"—a forced emphasis, for all his strong command over himself breaking in upon the suavity of his tone, "he bids me say that this bringing together of his best friends is in celebration of an event dear to his heart and as he hopes of interest to yourselves. It is my pleasure, good friends, to announce to you the engagement of my uncle's ward, Miss Colfax, to one whom you all know, Dr. Hunter. Harry, stand up. I drink to your future happiness, and—hers." Oh, that slight, slight pause!

Was I dreaming? Were we all dreaming? From the blank looks I espied on every side, it was evident that the surprise was not confined to myself, but, was in the minds of every one present. Miss Colfax and Dr. Hunter! when the understanding was that we were here in celebration of his own engagement to Orpha! It took a full minute for the commotion to subside, then the whole crowd rose, I with the rest, and glasses were clinking and shouts of good feeling rising in merry chorus from one end of the room to the other.

Dr. Hunter spoke in response and Orpha smiled and I believe I uttered some words myself when they all looked my way; but there was no reality in any of it for me; instead, I seemed to be isolated from the whole scene, in a rush of joy and wonder; seeing everything as through a mist and really hearing nothing but the pounding of my own heart reiterating with every throb, "All is not over for me. There is yet hope! There is yet hope!"

But a doubt which came all too soon for my comfort drove much of this mist away. What if we had heard but half of what our young host had to say? What if his next words were those which I for one most dreaded? Uncle was too just and kind a man to exact so painful a service from one he so deeply loved, without the intention of seeing him made happy in the end. And what to his mind, could so insure that blessing as a final union between the two most dear to him?

In secret trepidation I waited for the second and still more profound hush which would follow another high lifting of the glass in Edgar's hand. But it did not come. The ceremony, or whatever you might call it, was over, and Orpha sat there, beaming and serene and so far as appearances went, free to be loved and courted.

And then it came to me with sudden and strong conviction that Uncle would never have countenanced such a blow to my hopes (hopes which he had himself roused as well as greatly encouraged)—without giving me some warning that his mind had again changed. He did not love me,— not with a hundredth part of the fervor with which he regarded Edgar—but he respected our relationship and must, unless he were a very different man from what I believed him to be, have an equal respect for the attachment I had professed for his daughter. He had sent me no warning, therefore I need fear no further move this night.

But to-morrow? Well, I would let to-morrow take care of itself. For this night I would be happy; and under the inspiration of this resolve, I felt a lightness of spirit which for the first time that evening allowed me to be my full and natural self. Perhaps the grave almost inquiring look I received from Orpha as chance brought us for a moment together gave substance to this cheer. I did not understand it and I dared not give much weight to it, but from that time on the hours dragged less slowly.

At four o'clock precisely we three stood in an empty parlor.

"Now for Father!" cried Orpha. And with a kindly good-night to Edgar and an equally kindly one to me, she sped away and vanished upstairs leaving Edgar and myself alone together for the first time that evening.

It was an awkward moment for us both. I had no means of knowing what was in his mind and was equally ignorant of how much he knew of what was in mine. One thing alone was evident. The excitement of doing a difficult thing, possibly a heart-breaking thing, had ebbed with the disappearance of Orpha. He looked five years older, and blind as I was to his motives or the secret springs of the action which had left him a desolate man, I could not but admire the nerve with which he had carried off his bitter, self-sacrificing task. If he loved this stunning brunette as I loved Orpha he had my sympathy, whatever his motives, for the manner in which he had yielded her thus openly to another. But, by this time, I knew him well enough to recognize his mercurial, joy-seeking nature. In a month he would be the careless, happy-go-lucky fellow in whom everybody delighted.

And Uncle? And Orpha? What of them? Reminded thus of other sufferings than my own, I asked, with what calmness I could:

"Have you had any further news from upstairs? I thought our uncle looked far from well when I saw him in the early evening."

"Wealthy sent for a doctor. I have not heard his report," was the somewhat curt answer I received. "I am going up now," he added. Then with continued restraint in his manner, he looked me full in the face and remarked, "Of course you know that you are to remain here till Uncle considers himself well enough for you to go. You will explain the situation to your firm. I am but repeating Uncle's wishes."

I nodded and he stepped to the foot of the stairs. But there he turned.

"If you will make yourself comfortable in your old room," he said, "I will see that you receive that report as soon as I know it myself."

This ended our interview.

* * * * * * * *

Fifteen minutes later Wealthy appeared at my door. She did not need to speak for me to foresee that dark days confronted us. But what she said was this:

"Miss Orpha is not to know the worst. Mr. Bartholomew is in no immediate danger; but he will never be a strong man again."

CHAPTER 10

Of the next few days there is little to record. They might be called non-betrayal days, leading nowhere unless it was to a growth of self-control in us all which made for easier companionship and a more equable feeling throughout the house.

Of the couple whose engagement had been thus publicly proclaimed, I learned some further facts from Orpha, who showed no embarrassment in speaking of them.

Miss Colfax had been a ward of my uncle from early childhood. She was an orphan and an heiress in a small way, which in itself gave her but little prestige. It was her beauty which distinguished her; that and a composed nature of great dignity. Though much admired, especially by men, she had none of the whims of an acknowledged belle. Amiable but decided, she gave her lovers short shrift. She would have none of them until one fine day the sole admirer who would not take no for an answer, renewed his importunities with such spirit that she finally yielded, though not with any show of passion or apparent loss of the dignity which was an essential part of her.

"Yet," Orpha confided to me, "I was more astonished than I can say when Father told me on the night of the ball that the two were really engaged and that it was his wish that a public acknowledgment of it should be made at the supper-table. And I don't understand it yet; for Lucy never has shown any preference for Dr. Hunter. But she is a girl of strong character and however this match may turn out you will never know from her that it is not a perfect success."

No word of herself or Edgar; no hint of any knowledge on her part of what I felt to be the true explanation of Miss Colfax's cold treatment of her various lovers. Was this plain ignorance, or just the effort of a proud heart to hide its own humiliation? If the former, what a story it told of secret affections developing unseen and unknown in a circle of intimates whose lives were supposed to be open as the day. I marveled at Edgar, I marveled at Orpha, I marveled at Lucy Colfax. Then I gave a little thought to myself and marveled that I, unsuspected by all, should have been given an insight into a situation which placed me on a level with those who thought their secret hidden. The day might come when this knowledge would be of some importance to me. But till that day arrived, it was for me to hold their secret sacred. Of that there could be no question. So what I had to say in response to these cousinly confidences left everything where it was. Those were days of non-betrayal, as I have already remarked; and they remained so until Uncle was again on his feet and the time seemed ripe for me to return to New York.

Convinced of this I sought an interview with him. Though constantly in the house I had not seen him since that fateful night.

He received me kindly but with little enthusiasm, while I exerted all my self-control to keep from showing by look or manner how shocked I was at his changed appearance. He confronted me from his invalid's chair, an old man; he who a month ago, was regarded by all as a most notable specimen of physical strength and brilliant mentality.

* * * * * * * *

The blow which had thus laid low this veritable king of men must indeed have been a heavy one. As I took in this fact more fully I questioned whether I had been correct in ascribing it to nothing more serious than the discovery, at the last minute, of Edgar's passion for another woman than Orpha.

But I kept these doubts to myself and studiously avoided betraying any curiosity, anxious as I was to know how matters stood with him, what his present feelings were towards Edgar and what they were towards myself. That he had not sent for me during these days of serious illness, while his door had been constantly open to Edgar, might not mean quite as much as appeared. He was used to Edgar and quite unused to myself. Besides, his special attendants, those whose business it was to care for him, would be more likely to balk than assist the intrusion into his presence of one who might consider himself as a possible rival to their old time favorite.

Unless it was Orpha.

But why should I except Orpha? Had I any reason whatever for doing so? No; a thousand times, no. Yet—

I was still astonished at my own persistence in formulating in my mind that word yet when my uncle spoke.

"You must pardon me, Quenton, for leaving it to you to remind me of our relationship. I was too ill to see any other faces about me than those to which I am accustomed. I could not bear—"

We were alone and as he hesitated, he, the strong man, I put out my hand with a momentary show of my real feelings.

"I understand. No apologies from you, Uncle. You have allowed me to remain in the house with you. That in itself showed a consideration for which I am truly grateful. But the time has now come for me to return to my work. You are better—"

But here he stopped me.

"You are right; I am better, but I am on the down grade, Quenton, I who till now have never known one sick day. I shall need attendance—companionship—a man at my side—some one to write my letters—to keep track of my affairs—you or—or Edgar. I cannot have him here always. His temperament is such that it would be almost impossible for him to bear for any length of time the constraint of a sick room. Nor would I impose too much of the same on you. I have a proposition to make," he proceeded with a drop in his tone which bespoke a sudden access of feeling. "What do you say to an equal sharing of this duty, pleasure or whatever you may call it; a week of attendance from each in turn, the off week of either being one of complete freedom from all obligations and to be spent wherever you or Edgar may wish so that it is not in this house? I will make it all right for you in New York. Edgar will not need my help." Then as I hesitated to reply he added with a touch of pride, "An unusual proceeding, no doubt, but I have always been master of the unusual and in this case my heart and honor are both involved."

He did not explain how or in what way, nor did I ask him, for I saw that he had not finished with what he had to say, and I wished to hear all that was in his mind.

"It will not be for long." (How certain he was!) "Consequently, it will not be hard for you to assure me that whether here or elsewhere, you will not disturb the present condition of affairs by any revelation of purpose or desire beyond the one common to you all to see me slip happily and as easily as possible out of life. Cousins, do you hear? cousins all three, whatever the temptation to overstep the mark; cousins, until I speak or am dead."

I rose, and advanced to his side. I even ventured to take him by the hand.

"You may rely on my honor," I quietly assured him, glad to see his eye brighten and a smile reminiscent of his old hearty gladness, brighten his worn countenance.

What more was said is of no consequence to my story.

CHAPTER 11

During the weeks which followed we all, so far as I know, kept scrupulously to the line of conduct so arbitrarily laid out for us. Surface smiles; surface looks; surface courtesies. The only topic which called out full sincerity on the part of any of us was my uncle's steadily failing health.

Edgar and I saw little of each other save at the week's end and then only for a passing moment. As the one entered the front door the other stepped out. The automobile which brought the one carried away the other. As we met, we invariably bowed and spoke. Sometimes we shook hands and just as invariably exchanged glances of inquiry seemingly casual, but in reality, penetrating.

I doubt if he ever saw anything in me to awaken his alarm. But I saw much in him to awaken mine. Though the control he had over his features was remarkable, it is easy for the discerning eye to mark the difference between what is forced and what is spontaneous. The restlessness of an uneasy heart was rapidly giving way in him to more cheerful emotions. His mercurial nature was reasserting itself and the charm he had for a short time lost was to be felt again in all he did and said.

This was what I had expected to happen, but not so soon; and my heart grew more and more heavy as the month advanced. The recurring breaks in his courtship of Orpha, and the presence in his absence of a possible rival with opportunities of unspoken devotion equal to his own, had given zest to a situation somewhat too tame before. From indifference to the game or to what he may have looked upon as such, he began to show a growing interest in it. A great fortune linked with a woman he felt free to court under his rival's eyes did not look quite so undesirable after all.

I may have done him injustice. Jealousy is not apt to be fair. But, if I read him aright, he was just the man to be swayed by the influences I have mentioned, and loving Orpha as I did, I found it hard to maintain even a show of equanimity at what was fast becoming for me a hopeless mystery. It was during these days that the monotony of my thoughts was broken by my hearing for the first time of the Presence said to haunt this house. I do not think my uncle had meant me to receive any intimation of it, at least, not yet. He may have given command and he may simply have expressed a wish, or he may have trusted to the good sense of his entourage to keep silence where speaking would do no good. But, let that be as it may, I had come and gone through the house to this day without an idea that its many wonders were not confined to its unusual architecture, its sumptuous appointments and the almost baronial character of its service and generous housekeeping, but extended to that crowning glory of so many historic structures in my own country, of—I will not say a ghost, but a presence, for by that name it was known and sometimes spoken of not only where its influence was felt, but by the gossips of the town, to the delight of the young and the disdain of the old; for the supernatural makes small appeal to the American mind when once it has entered into full acquaintanceship with the realities of life.

Personally I am not superstitious and I smiled when told of this impalpable something which was neither seen nor heard but strangely felt at odd times by one person or another moving about the halls. But it was less a smile of disdain than of amusement, at the thought of this special luxury imported from the old world being added to the many others by which I was surrounded.

But the person telling me did not smile.

My introduction to this incongruous feature of a building purely modern happened through an accident. I was coming up the stairs connecting the second floor with the one on which my own room was situated when a sudden noise quite sharp and arresting in one of the rooms below, stopped me short and caused me to look back over my shoulder in what was a perfectly natural way.

But it did not so strike Bliss the chauffeur who was passing the head of the stairs on his way from Uncle's room. He was comparatively a new comer, having occupied his present position but a few months, and this may have been the reason both for his curiosity and his lack of self-control. Seeing me stop in this way, he took a step down, involuntarily no doubt, and gurgled out:

"Did—did you feel it? They say that it catches you by the hair and—and—just in this very spot."

I stared up at him in amazement.

"Feel it? Feel what?" And joining him I surveyed him with some attention to see if he were intoxicated.

He was not; only a little ashamed of himself; and drawing back to let me pass, he stammered apologetically:

"Oh, nothing. Just nonsense, sir; girls will talk, you know, and they told me some queer stories about—about— Will you excuse me, sir; I feel like a fool talking to a man of—"

"Of what? Speak it."

He looked behind him, and very carefully in the direction of the short passage-way leading to Uncle's room; then whispered:

"Ask the girls, Mr. Bartholomew, or—or—Miss Wealthy. They'll tell you." And was gone before I could hold him back for another word.

And that night I did ask Miss Wealthy, as he called her; and she, probably thinking that since I knew a little of this matter I might better know more, told me all there was to tell about this childish superstition. She had never had any experience herself with the thing—this is the way she spoke of it,—but others had and so the gossip had got about. It did no harm. It never kept any capable girl or man from working in the house or from staying in it year after year, and it need not bother me.

It was then I smiled.

CHAPTER 12

I had some intention at the time of speaking to Uncle about this matter, but I did not until the day he himself broached the subject. But that comes later. I must first relate an occurrence of much more importance which took place very soon after this interchange of words with Wealthy.

I was still in C—. Everything had been going on as usual and I thought nothing of being summoned to my Uncle's room one morning at an earlier hour than usual. Nor did I especially notice any decided change in him though he certainly looked a little brighter than he had the day before.

Orpha was with him. She was sitting in the great bay window which opened upon the lawn; he by the fireside where a few logs were smouldering, the day being damp rather than cold.

He started and looked up with his kindly smile as I approached with the morning papers, then spoke quickly:

"No reading this morning, Quenton. I have an errand for you. One which only you can do to my satisfaction." And thereupon he told me what it was, and how it might take me some hours, as it could only be accomplished in a town some fifty miles distant. "The car is ready," said he, "and I would be glad to have you take it now as I want you to be home in time for dinner."

I turned impulsively, casting one glance at Orpha.

"You may take Orpha."

But she would not go. In a flurry of excitement and with every sign of subdued agitation, she hurriedly rose and came our way.

"I cannot leave you, Father. I should worry every minute. Quenton will pardon my discourtesy, but with him gone and Edgar not yet here my place is with you."

I could not dispute it, nor could he. With a smile half apologetic, half grateful, he let me go, and the only consolation which the moment brought me was the fact that her eyes were still on mine when I turned to close the door.

But intoxicating as the pleasure would have been to have had her with me during this hundred mile ride, my thoughts during that long flight through a most uninteresting country, dwelt much less upon my disappointment than on the purpose actuating my uncle in thus disposing of my presence for so many hours on this especial day.

In itself, the errand was one of no importance. I knew enough of his business affairs to be quite sure of that. Why, then, this long trip on a day so unpropitious as to be positively forbidding?

The question agitated me all the way there and was not settled to my mind at the hour of my return. Something had been going on in my absence which he had thought it undesirable for me to witness. The proof of this I saw in every face I met. Even the maids cast uneasy glances at me whenever I chanced to run upon one of them in my passage through the hall. It was different with Uncle. He wore a look of relief, for which he gave no explanation then or later.

And Orpha? She was a riddle to me, too, that night. Abstracted by fits and by fits interested and alert as though she sought to make up to me for the many moments in which she hardly heard anything I said.

The tears were in her eyes more than once when she impulsively turned my way. And no explanation followed, nor did she allude in any manner to my ride or to what had taken place in my absence until we came to say goodnight, when she remarked:

"I don't know why I feel so troubled and as if I must speak to some one who loves my father. You have seen how much brighter he is to-night. That makes me happy, but the cause worries me. Something strange happened here to-day. Mr. Dunn, who has attended to papa's law business for years, came to see him shortly after you left. There was nothing strange about that and we thought little of it till Clarke and Wealthy were sent for to witness Father's signature to what they insist must have been a new will. You see they had gone through an experience of this kind before. It must have been five years or so ago, and both feel sure that to-day's business is but a repetition of the former one. And a new will at this time would be quite proper," she went on, with her glance turned carefully aside. "It is not that which has upset me and upset them. It is that in an hour or so after Mr. Dunn left another lawyer came in whom I know only by name; a Mr. Jackson, who is well thought of, but whom I have never chanced to meet. He brought two clerks with him and stayed quite a time with Father and when he was gone, Wealthy came rushing into my room to tell me what Haines had heard one of the clerks say to the other when going out of the front door. It was this. 'Well, I call that mighty quick work, considering the size of his fortune.' To which the other answered, 'The instructions were minute; and all written out in his own hand. He may be a sick man, but he knows what he wants. A will in a thousand—' Here the door shut and Haines heard nothing more. But Quenton, what can it mean? Two lawyers and two wills! Do you think father can be all right when he can do a thing like that? It has frightened me and I don't know whether or not I ought to tell Dr. Cameron. What do you advise?"

I was as ignorant as herself as to our duty in a matter about which we knew so little, but I certainly was not going to let her go to bed in this disturbed condition of mind; so I said:

"You may trust your father to be all right in all that concerns business. His mental powers are as great as ever. If we do not understand all he does it is because we do not know what lies back of his action." Then as her face brightened, I added: "Edgar and I have often been surprised at the clearness of his perceptions and the excellence of his judgment in all matters which have come up since we have taken the place of his former stenographers. For nearly a month we in turn have done his typewriting and never has he faltered in his dictation or seemed to lack decision as to what he wanted done. You may rest easy about his employing two lawyers even in one day. With so many interests and such complicated affairs to manipulate and care for I only wonder that he does not feel the need of a dozen."

A little quivering smile answered this; and it was the hardest thing I was ever called upon to do, not to take her sweet, appealing figure in my arms and comfort her as my heart prompted me to do.

"I hardly think Dr. Cameron would say any different. You can put the question to him when he comes in."

But when she had flitted from my side and disappeared in the hall above, I asked myself with some misgiving whether in encouraging her in this fashion, I had quite convinced myself of the naturalness of her father's conduct or of my own explanation of the same.

Had he not sent me out of the house and on a long enough trip to cover the time likely to be consumed by these two visits I might not have concerned myself beyond the obvious need of sustaining her in her surprise and anxiety. For as I told her, his interests were large and he must often feel the need of legal advice. But with this circumstance in mind it was but natural for me to wonder what connection I had with this matter. Lawyers! And two of them! One if not both of them there in connection with a will! Was he indeed in full possession of his faculties? Or was some strange event brooding in this house beyond my power to discern?

Alas! I was not to know that day, nor for many, many others. What I was to know was this. Why, I had frequently seen Martha and, yes, I will admit it, Clarke—the hard-headed, unimaginative Clarke—always step more quickly when they came to the flight of stairs leading to the third floor.

I was on this flight myself that night and about half way up, when I was stopped,—not by any unexpected sound as at the time before—but by a prickle of my scalp and a sense of being pulled back by some unseen hand. I shook the fancy off and rushed pell-mell to the top with a laugh on my lips which however never reached my ears. Then reason reasserted itself and I went straight on in the direction of my room, and was just turning aside from Wealthy's cosy corner when I saw the screen which hemmed it in move aside and reveal her standing there.

She had seen me through a slit in the screen and for some purpose or other showed a disposition to speak.

Of course, I paused to hear what she had to say.

It was nothing important in itself; but to her devotion everything was important which had any connection with her sick master.

"It is late," she said. "Clarke is out and I have been waiting for Mr. Bartholomew's bell. It does not ring. Would you mind— Oh, there it is," she cried, as a sharp tinkle sounded in our ears. "You will excuse me, sir," releasing me with a gesture of relief.

An episode of small moment and hardly worth relating; but it is part—a final part, so far as I am concerned—of that day's story.

CHAPTER 13

The following one was less troublesome, and so was the next; then came the week of my sojourn elsewhere and of Edgar's dominance in the house we all felt would soon be his own. Whether Orpha confided to him her latest trouble I never heard. When his week was up and I replaced him again in the daily care of our uncle, I sought to learn if help or disappointment had come to her in my absence. But beyond a graver bearing and a manifest determination not to be alone with me even for a few moments in any of the rooms on the ground floor, I received no answer to my question. Orpha could be very inscrutable when she liked.

It was during the seven happy days of this week that three rather important conversations took place between Uncle and myself, portions of which I now propose to relate. I will not try your patience by repeating the preamble to any one of them or the after remarks. Just the bits necessary to make this story of the three Edgars understandable.

* * * * * * * * *

Uncle is speaking.

"I have been criticised very severely by my lawyer and less openly but fully as earnestly by both men and women of my acquaintance, for my well-known determination to leave the main portion of my property to a man—the man who is to marry my daughter. My answer has always been that no woman should be trusted with the responsibilities and conduct of very large interests. She has not the nerve, the experience, nor the acquaintanceship with other large holders, requisite for conducting affairs of wide scope successfully. She would have to employ an agent which in this case would of course be her husband. Then why not give him full control from the start?"

I was silent, what could I say?

"Quenton?"

His tone was so strange, so different from any I had ever heard pass his lips, that I looked up at him in amazement. I was still more amazed when I noted his aspect. His expression which until now had impressed me as fundamentally stern however he might mask it with the smile of sympathy or indulgence, had lost every attribute suggestive of strength or domination. Gone the steady look of power which made his glance so remarkable. Even the set of his lips had given way to a tremulous line full of tenderness and indefinable sorrow.

"Quenton," he repeated, "there are griefs and remembrances of which a man never speaks until the sands of life are running low; and not even then save for a purpose. I loved my wife." My heart leaped. I knew from his tone why he had understood me that night of the ball and taken instantly and at its full value the love I had expressed for Orpha. "Orpha was only two years old when her mother died. A babe with no memories of what has made my life! For me, the wife of my youth lives yet. This house which has been constructed so as to incorporate within its walls the old inn where I first met her, is redolent of her presence. Her tread is on the stairs. Her beauty makes more beautiful every object I have bought of worth or value to adorn her dwelling-place. Yet were she really living and I had no other inheritor, I should not consider that I was doing right by her or right by the world to leave her in full possession of means so hardly accumulated and interests so complicated and burdensome. She was tested once with the temporary charge of my affairs and, poor darling, broke under it. Orpha is her child. She has the same temperament, the same gentleness, the same strictness of conscience, to offend which is an active and all-absorbing pain. If this burden fell upon her—"

When he had finished I wondered if he had ever spoken of his wife to Edgar as he spoke of her to me that hour.

* * * * * * * *

33

"You have heard the gossip about this house. Some one must have told you of unaccountable sounds heard at odd moments on the stairs or elsewhere—steps other than your own keeping pace with you as you went up or down."

"Yes, uncle, I have been told of this. I heard something of the kind once myself."

"You did? When?" The glance he shot at me was quick and searching.

I told him and for a long time he sat very still gazing with retrospective eyes into the fire.

"More than that," I whispered after a while, "I heard a cough. It came from no one in sight. It sounded smothered. It seemed to come from the wall at my left, but that was impossible of course."

"Impossible, of course. The whole thing is foolishness —not to be thought of for a moment. The harmless result of some defect in carpentry. I smile when people speak of it. So do my servants. I keep them all, you see."

"Uncle, if this house needed a finishing touch to make it the most romantic in the world, this suggestion of mystery supplies it."

I shall never forget his quick bend forward or the long, long look he gave me. It emboldened me to ask almost seriously:

"Uncle, have you ever felt this presence yourself?"

He laughed a long, hearty, amused laugh, then a strange expression crossed his face unlike any I had ever seen on it before. "There's romance in these old fancies,— romance," he murmured—"romance."

No lover's voice could have been more tender; no poet's eye more dreamy.

I locked the remembrance away in my mind, for I doubted if I ever should see him in just such a mood again.

* * * * * * * *

"Your eyes are very often on Orpha's picture. I do not wonder at it; so are mine. It has a peculiar power to draw and then hold the attention. I chose an artist of penetrating intelligence; one who believes in the soul of his sitter and impresses you more with that than with the beauty of a woman or the mind of a man. I wanted her painted thus. Shall I tell you why? I think I will. It may steady you as it has steadied me and so serve a double purpose. Wealth has its charms; it also has its temptations. To keep me clean in the getting, the saving, and the spending, I had this picture painted and hung where I could not fail to see it when sitting at my desk. If a business proposition was presented to me which I could not consider under that clear, direct gaze so like her mother's, I knew what to do with it. You will have the same guardianship. The souls of two women will protect you from yourself; Orpha's mother's and Orpha's own."

I felt a thrill. Something more than wealth, more even than love, was to be my portion. The living of a clean life in sight of God and man.

CHAPTER 14

This gave me a great lift for the time. He had not changed his mind, then. He still meant me to marry Orpha; and some of the mystery of the last lawyer's visit was revealed. That connected with the one which preceded it might rest. I needed to know nothing about that. The great question had been answered; and I trod on air.

Meanwhile Uncle seemed better and life in the great house resumed some of its usual formality. But this did not last. The time soon came when it became evident to every eye that this man of infinite force was rapidly losing his once strong hold on life. From rising at ten, it grew to be noon before he would put foot to floor. Then three o'clock; then five; then only in time to eat the dinner spread before him on a small table near the fireplace. Then came the day when he refused to get up at all but showed great pleasure at our presence in the room and even chatted with us on every conceivable topic. Then came a period of great gloom when all his strength was given to a mental struggle which soon absorbed all his faculties and endangered his life. In vain we exerted ourselves to distract him. He would smile at our sallies, appear to listen to his favorite authors, ask for music— (Orpha could play the violin with touching effect and Edgar had a voice which like all his other gifts was exceptional) but not for long, nor to the point of real relief. While we were hoping that we had at last secured his interest, he would turn his head away and the struggle of his thoughts would recommence, all the stronger and more unendurable because of this momentary break.

Orpha's spirits were now at as low an ebb as his. She had sat for weeks under the shadow of his going but now this shadow had entered her soul. Her beauty once marked for its piquancy took on graver lines and moved the hearts of all by its appeal. It was hard to look at her and keep back all show of sympathy but such as was allowable between cousins engaged in the mutual tasks which brought us together at a sick man's bedside. If the discipline was good for my too selfish nature, the suffering was real, and in some of those trying hours I would have given all my chance in life to know if Orpha realized the turmoil of mind and heart raging under my quiet exterior.

Meantime, a change had been made in our arrangements. Edgar and I were no longer allowed to leave town though we continued to keep religiously to our practice of spending alternate weeks in attendance on the invalid.

This, in these latter days included sleeping in the den opening off Uncle's room. The portrait of Orpha which had made this room a hallowed one to me, had been removed from its wall and now hung in glowing beauty between the two windows facing the street, and so in full sight from Uncle's bed. His desk also, with all its appurtenances had been in a corner directly under his eye, and as I often noted, it was upon one or other of these two objects his gaze remained fixed unless Orpha was in the room, when he seemed to see nothing but her.

He had been under the care of a highly trained nurse during the more violent stages of his illness, but he had found it so difficult to accommodate himself to her presence and ministrations that she had finally been replaced by Wealthy, who had herself been a professional nurse before she came to

Quenton Court. This he had insisted upon and his will was law in that household. He ruled from his sick bed as authoritatively as he had ever done from the head of his own table. But so kindly that we would have yielded from love had we not done so from a sense of propriety.

His gloom was at its height and his strength at its lowest ebb when an experience befell me, the effects of which I was far from foreseeing at the time.

Edgar's week was up and the hour had come for me to take his place in the sick room. Usually he was ready to leave before the evening was too old for him to enjoy a few hours in less dismal surroundings. But this evening I found him still chatting and in a most engaging way to our seemingly delighted uncle, and taking the shrug he made at my appearance as a signal that they were not yet ready for my presence, I stepped back into the hall to wait till the story was finished which he was relating with so much spirit.

It took a long time, and I was growing quite weary of my humiliating position, when the door finally opened and he came out. With every feature animated and head held high he was a picture of confident manhood. This should not have displeased me and perhaps would not have done so had I not caught, as I thought, a gleam of sinister meaning in his eye quite startling from its rarity.

It also, to my prejudiced mind, tinged his smile, as slipping by me, he remarked:

"I think I had the good fortune to amuse him to-night. He is asleep now and I doubt if he wakes before dawn. Lower his light as you pass by his bed. Poor old Uncle!"

I had no answer for this beyond a slight nod, at which, with an air I found it difficult to dissociate with a sense of triumph, he uttered a short good-night and flew past me down the stairs.

"He has won some unexpected boon from "Uncle," I muttered in dismay as the sound of his footsteps died out in the great rooms below. "Is it fortune? Is it Orpha?" I could bear the loss of the first. But Orpha? Rather than yield her up I would struggle with every power with which I had been endowed. I would—

But here I entered the room and coming under the direct influence of the masterly portraiture of her who was so dear to me, better feelings prevailed.

To see her happy should and must be my chief aim in life. If union with myself would ensure her that and I came to know it, then it would be time for me to exert my prowess and hold to my own in face of all opposition. But if her heart was his—truly and irrevocably his, then my very love should lead me to step aside and leave them to each other. For that would be their right and one with which it would be presumptuous in me to meddle.

The light which I had been told to extinguish was near my uncle's hand as he lay in bed.

Seeing that he was, as Edgar said, peacefully asleep, I carefully pulled the chain attached to the flaming bulb.

Instantly the common-places of life vanished and the room was given over to mystery and magic. All that was garish or simply plain to the view was gone, for wherever there was light there were also shadows, and shadows of that shifting and half-revealing kind which can only be gotten by the fitful leaping of a few expiring flames on a hearth-stone.

Uncle's fire never went out. Night or day there was always a blaze. It was his company, he said, and never more so than when he woke in the wee small hours with the moon shut out and silence through all the house. It would be my task before I left him for the night to pile on fresh fuel and put up the screen, which being made of glass, allowed the full play of the dancing flames to be seen.

Reveling in the mystic sight, I drew up a chair and sat before Orpha's portrait. Edgar was below stairs and doubtless in her company. Why, then, should I not have my hour with her here? The beauty of her pictured countenance which was apparent enough by day, was well nigh unearthly in the soft orange glow which vivified the brown of her hair and heightened the expression of eye and lip, only to leave them again in mystery as the flame died down and the shadows fell.

I could talk to her thus, and as I sat there looking and longing, words fell from my lips which happily there was no one to hear. It was my hour of delight snatched in an unguarded hour from the hands of Fate.

She herself might never listen, but this semblance of herself could not choose but do so. In this presence I could urge my plea and exhaust myself in loving speeches, and no displeasure could she show and even at times must she smile as the shadows again shifted. It was a hollow amends for many a dreary hour in which I got nothing but the same sweet show of patience she gave to all about her. But a man welcomes dream food if he can get no other and for a full hour I sat there talking to my love and catching from time to time in my presumptuous fancy faint whispers in response which were for no other ears than mine.

At last, fancy prevailed utterly, and rising, I flung out my arms in inappeasable longing towards her image, when, simultaneously with this action I felt my attention drawn irresistibly aside and my head turn slowly and without my volition more and more away from her, as if in response to some call at my back which I felt forced to heed.

Yet I had heard no sound and had no real expectation of seeing any one behind me unless it was my uncle who had wakened and needed me.

And this was what had happened. In the shadow made by the curtains hanging straight down from the headboard on either side of his bed, I saw the gleam of two burning eye-balls. But did I? When I looked again there was nothing to be seen there but the shadowy outlines of a sleeping man. My fancy had betrayed me as in the hour of secret converse I had just held with the lady of my dreams.

Yet anxious to be assured that I had made no mistake, I crossed over to the bedside and, pushing aside the curtains, listened to his breathing. It was far from equable, but there was every other evidence of his being asleep. I had only imagined those burning eye-balls looking hungrily into mine.

Startled, not so much by this freak of my imagination as by the effect which it had had upon me, I left the bed and reluctantly sought my room. But before entering it —while still on its threshold—I was again startled at feeling my head turning automatically about under the uncanny influence working upon me from behind, and wheeling quickly, I searched with hasty glances the great room I was leaving for what thus continued to disturb me.

Orpha's picture—the great bed—the desk, pathetic to the eye from the absence before it of its accompanying chair—books—tables—Orpha's pet rocker with the little stand beside it—each and every object to which we had accustomed ourselves for many weeks, lit to the point of weirdness, now brightly, now faintly and in spots by the dancing firelight! But no one thing any more than before to account for the emotion I felt. Yet I remember saying to myself as I softly closed my door upon it all:

"Something impends!"

But what that something was, was very far from my thoughts as are all spiritual upheavals when we are looking for material disaster.

I had been asleep, but how long I had no means of knowing, when with a thrill such as seizes us at an unexpected summons, I found myself leaning on my elbow and staring with fascinated if not apprehensive gaze at the door leading into my uncle's room left as I always left it on retiring, slightly ajar.

I had heard no sound, I was conscious of no movement in my room or in his, yet there I was looking—looking— and expecting—what? I had no answer for this question and soon would not need one, for the line of ruddy light running upward from the floor upon which my eyes were fixed was slowly widening, and presently I should see whose hesitating foot made these long pauses yet showed such determination to enter where no foot should come thus stealthily on any errand.

Again! a furtive push and I caught the narrowest of glimpses into the room beyond. At which a sudden thought came, piercing me like a dart. Whoever this was, he must have crossed my uncle's room to reach this door—may have stood at the sick man's side—may have— Fear seized me and I sprang up alert but sank back in infinite astonishment and dismay as the door finally swung in and I beheld dimly outlined in the doorway the great frame of Uncle himself standing steadily and alone, he, who for days now had hardly moved in his bed.

Ignorant of the cause which had impelled him to an action for which he was so unfit; not even being able to judge in the darkness in which I lay whether he was conscious of his movements or whether he was in that dangerous state where any surprise or interference might cause in him a fatal collapse, I assumed a semblance of sleep while covertly watching him through half shut lids.

A moment thus, then I felt rather than saw his broad chest heave and his shaking limbs move bringing him step by step to my side. Had he fallen face downward on to my narrow couch I should not have wondered. But he came painfully on and paused, his heart beating so that I could hear it above my own though that was throbbing far louder than its wont.

Next moment he was on his knees, with his arms thrown over my breast and clinging there in convulsive embrace as he whispered words such as had never been uttered into my ears before; words of infinite affection laden with self-reproaches it filled me with a great compassion to hear.

For I knew that these words were not meant for me; that he had been misled by the events of the evening and believed it to be in Edgar's ear he was laying bare his soul.

"I cannot do it." These were the words I heard. "I have tried to and the struggle is killing me. Forgive me, Edgar, for thinking of punishing you for what was the result of my own shortsighted affection."

I stirred and started up. I had no right to listen further.

But his hold on me tightened till the pressure became almost unendurable. The fever in his veins made him not only strong but oblivious to all but the passion of the moment,—the desire to right himself with the well-beloved one who was as a son to him.

"I should have known better." Thus he went on. "I had risen through hardship, but I would make it easy for my boy. Mistake! mistake! I see it now. The other is the better man, but my old heart clings to its own and I cannot go back on the love of many years. You must marry Orpha and her gentle heart will—"

A sob, a sudden failing of his fictitious strength, and I was able to rise and help him to rise, though he was almost a dead weight in my arms.

Should I be able alone and unassisted to guide him back to his bed without his discovering the mistake he had made and thus shocking him into delirium? The light was dim where we stood and rapidly failing in the other room as the great log which had been blazing on the hearth-stone crumbled into coals. Could I have spoken, the task might have been an easier one; but my accent, always emphasized under agitation, would have betrayed me.

Other means must be taken to reassure him and make him amenable to my guidance. Remembering an action of Edgar's which I had lately seen, I drew the old man's arm about my shoulder and led him back into his room. He yielded easily. He had passed the limit of acute perception and all his desire was for rest. With simple, little soothing touches, I got him to his bed and saw his head sink gratefully into his pillow.

Much relieved and believing the paroxysm quite past, I was turning softly away when he reached out his hand and, grasping me by the arm, said with an authority as great as I had ever seen him display even on important occasions:

"Another log, Edgar. The fire is low; it mustn't go out. Whatever happens, it must never go out."

And he, burning up with fever!

Though this desire for heat or the cheer of the leaping blaze might be regarded as one of the eccentricities of illness, it was with a strange and doubtful feeling that I turned to obey him—a feeling which did not leave me in the watchful hour which followed. Though I had much to brood over of a more serious character than the mending or keeping up of a fire, the sense of something lying back of this constant desire for heat would come again and again to my mind mingling with the great theme now filling my breast with turmoil and shaping out new channels for my course in life. Mystery, though of the smallest, has a persistent prick. We want to know, even if the matter is inconsequent.

I had no further sleep that night, but Uncle did not move again till late morning. When he did and saw me standing over him, he mentioned my name and smiled almost with pleasure and gave me the welcoming hand.

He had forgotten what had passed, or regarded it, if it came to his mind at all, as a dream to be ignored or cherished according to his mood, which varied now, as it had before, from one extreme to the other.

But my mood had no ups and downs. It had been given me to penetrate the depths of my uncle's heart and mind. I knew his passionate wish—it was one in which I had little part—but nothing must ever make me forget it.

However, I uttered no promises myself. I would wait till my judgment sanctioned them; and the time for that had not yet come.

CHAPTER 15

Nevertheless it was approaching. One day Orpha came to me with the report that her father was worse—that the doctor was looking very sober and that Edgar, whose week it was to give what aid and comfort he could in the sick room, complained that for the first time during his uncle's illness he had failed to find any means of diverting him even for a moment.

As she said this her look wandered anywhere but to my face.

"It is growing to be very hard for Edgar," she added in a tone full of feeling.

"And for you," I answered, with careful attention to voice and manner.

She shuddered, and crept from my side lest she should be tempted to say how hard.

When an hour or two later I went up to Uncle's room, I found him where I had never expected to see him again, up and seated close to the fire. His indomitable will was working with some of its by-gone force. It was so hot that I noted when I took the seat he pointed out to me, that the perspiration stood on his forehead, but he would not be moved back.

He had on a voluminous dressing gown and his hands, were hidden in its folds in what I thought was an unnatural manner. But I soon forgot this in watching his expression, which was more fixed and harder in its aspect than I had supposed it could be, and again I felt ready to say, "Something impends!"

Wealthy was present; consequently my visit was a brief one. It might have been such had she not been there, for he showed very little desire for my company and indeed virtually dismissed me in the following words:

"I may have need of you this evening and I may not. May I ask you to be so good as to stay indoors till you receive a message from me?"

My answer was a cheerful acquiescence, but as I left, I cast one long, lingering look at Orpha's picture. Might it not be my last? The doubt was in my mind, for Edgar's foot was on the stair; there would be a talk between him and Uncle, and if as a result of that talk Uncle failed to send for me, my place at his bedside would be lost. He would have no further use for my presence.

I had begun to understand his mind.

I have no doubt that I was helped to this conclusion by something I saw in passing his bedside on my way out. Wealthy was rearranging the pillows and in doing so gave me for the first time a full glimpse of the usually half-hidden head-board. To my amazement I perceived that it held a drawer, cunningly inserted by a master hand.

A drawer! Within his own reach—at all times—by night and day! It must contain—

Well, I had no difficulty in deciding what. But the mystery of his present action troubled me. A few hours might make it plain. A few hours! If only they might be spent with Orpha!

With beating heart I went rapidly below, passing Edgar on my way. We said nothing. He was in as tense a mood as I was. For him as well as for myself the event was at hand. Ah! where was Orpha?

Not where I sought her. The living rooms as well as the court and halls were all empty. For a half hour I waited in the library alone, then the door opened and my uncle's man showed himself:

"Am I wanted?" I asked, unable to control my impatience.

He answered with a respectful affirmative, but there was a lack of warmth in his manner which brought a cynical smile to my lips. Nothing would ever change the attitude of these old servants towards myself, or make Edgar anything less in their eyes than the best, kindest and most pleasing of masters. Should I allow this to disturb me or send me to the fate awaiting me in the room above in any other frame of mind than the one which would best prepare me for the dreaded ordeal?

No. I would be master of myself if not of my fate. By the time I had reached my uncle's door I was calm enough. Confident that some experience awaited me there which would try me as it had tried Edgar, I walked steadily in. He had not come out of his ordeal in full triumph, or why the look I had seen on every face I had encountered in coming up? Wealthy at the end of the long hall, with a newspaper falling from her lap, had turned at my step. Her aspect as she did so I shall not soon forget. The suspicious nods and whispers of the two maids I had surprised peering at me from over the banisters, were all of a character to warn me that I was at that moment less popular in the house than I had ever been before. Was I to perceive the like in the greeting I was about to receive from the one on whom my fortunes as well as those of Orpha hung?

I trembled at the prospect, and it was not till I had crossed the floor to where he was seated in his usual seat at the fire-place, that I ventured to look up. When I did so it was to meet a countenance showing neither pleasure nor pain.

When he spoke it was hurriedly as though he felt his time was short.

"Quenton, sit down and listen to what I have to say. I have put off from day to day this hour of final understanding between us in the hopes that my duty would become plain to me without any positive act on my part. But it has failed to do so and I must ask your help in a decision vital to the happiness of the two beings nearest if not dearest to me in this world I am so soon to leave. I mean my daughter and the man she is to marry."

This took my breath away but he did not seem to notice either my agitation or the effort I made to control it. He was too intent upon what he had yet to say, to mark the effect of the words he had already spoken.

"You know what my wishes are,—the wishes which have been expectations since Edgar and Orpha stood no higher than my knee. The fortune I have accumulated is too large to be given into the hands of a girl no older than Orpha, I do not believe in a woman holding the reins when she has a man beside her. I may be wrong, but that is the way I feel, as truly to-day as when she was a wee tot babbling in my ear. The inheritor of the millions I perhaps unfortunately possess must be a man. But that man must marry my daughter, and to marry her he must love her, sincerely and devotedly love her or my money will prove a curse to her, to him and, God pardon the thought, to me in my grave, if the dead can still feel and know.

"Until a little while ago,—until you came, in fact,—I was content, thinking that all was well and everything going to my mind. But presently a word was dropped in my ear,—from whose lips it does not matter,—which shook my equanimity and made me look for the first time with critical eyes on one I had hitherto felt to be above criticism; and once my attention was called that way, I saw much that did not quite satisfy me in the future dispenser of a fortune which in wise hands could he made productive of great good but in indifferent ones of incalculable mischief.

"But I thought he loved Orpha, and rating her, as we all must, as a woman of generous nature with a mind bound to develop as her happiness grows and her responsibilities increase, I rested in the hope that with her for a wife, his easy-going nature would strengthen and the love he universally inspires would soon have a firmer basis than his charming smile and his invariable good nature.

"But one day something happened—do not ask me what, I cannot talk about it; it has been the struggle of my life since that day to forget it—which shook my trust even in this hope. The love capable of accomplishing so much must be a disinterested one, and I saw—saw with my own eyes—what gave me reason to doubt both the purity and depth of his feeling for Orpha.

"You remember the day, the hour. The ball which was to have ended all uncertainty by a public recognition of their engagement saw me a well man at ten, and a broken down one at eleven. You know, for you were here, and saw me while I was still suffering from the. shock. I had to speak to some one and I would not disturb Orpha, and so I thought of you. You pleased me in that hour and the trust I then felt in your honor I have never lost. For in whatever trial I have made of the character of you two boys you have always stood the test better than Edgar. I acknowledge it, but, whether from weakness or strength I leave you to decide, I cannot forget the years in which Edgar shared with Orpha my fatherly affection. You shall not be forgotten or ungenerously dealt with—I owe you too much for that—but I ask you to release me from the ill-considered promise I made to you that night of the ball. I cannot cut him off from the great hopes I have always fostered in him. I want you to—"

He did not conclude, but, shifting nervously in his seat, brought into view the hands hidden from sight under the folds of his dressing-gown. In each was a long envelope apparently enclosing a legal document. He laid them, one on each knee and drooped his head a little as he remarked, with a hasty glance first at one document and then at the other:

"Here, Quenton, you see what a man who once thought very well of himself has come to through physical weakness and mental suffering. Here are two wills, one made largely in his favor and one equally largely in yours. They were drawn up the same day by different men, each ignorant of the other's doing. One of these it is my wish to destroy but I have not yet had the courage to do so; for my reason battles with my affection and I dare not slight the one nor disappoint the other."

"And you ask me to aid you in your dilemma," I prompted, for I saw that he was greatly distressed. "I will do so, but first let me ask one question. How does Orpha feel? Is she not the one to decide a matter affecting her so deeply?"

"Oh! She is devoted to Edgar," he made haste to assert. "I have never doubted her feeling for him."

"Uncle, have you asked her to aid your decision?"

He shook his head and muttered sadly:

"I dare not show myself in such colors to my only child. She would lose her respect for me, and that I could never endure."

My heart was sad, my future lost in shadows, but there was only one course for me to take. Pointing to the two documents lying in his lap, I asked, with as little show of feeling as I could command:

"Which is the one in my favor? Give it to me and I will fling it into the fire with my own hand. I cannot endure seeing your old age so heavily saddened."

He rose to his feet—rose suddenly and without any seeming effort, letting the two wills fall unheeded to the floor.

"Quenton!" he cried, "You are the man! If Orpha does not love you she must learn to do so. And she will when she knows you." This in a burst; then as he saw me stumble back, dazed and uncomprehending like one struck forcibly between the eyes, "This was my final test, boy, my last effort to ascertain what lay at the root of your manhood. Edgar failed me. You—"

His lip quivered, and grasping blindly at the high back of the chair from which he had risen, he turned slightly aside in an effort to hide his failing self-control. The sight affected me even in the midst of the storm of personal feeling he had aroused within me by this astounding change of front. Stooping for the two documents lying on the floor between us, I handed them to him, then offered my arm to aid him in reseating himself. But I said nothing. Silence and silence only befitted such a moment.

* * * * * * * *

He seemed to appreciate both the extent of my emotion and my reticence under it. It gave him the opportunity to regain his own poise. When I finally moved, as I involuntarily did at the loud striking of the clock, he spoke in his own quiet way which nevertheless carried with it so much authority.

"I have deceived you; not greatly, but to a certain necessary degree. You must forgive this and forget." He did not say how he had deceived me and for months I did not know. "To-morrow we will talk as a present master confers with a future one. I am tired now, but I will listen if there is anything you want me to hear before you call in Clarke."

Then I found voice. I must utter the one protest which the situation called for or despise myself forever. Turning softly about, I looked up at Orpha's picture, never more beautiful in my eyes, never more potent in its influence than at this critical instant in our two lives.

Then addressing him while pointing to the picture, I said:

"Your goodness to me, and the trust you have avowed in me, is beyond all words. But Orpha! Still, Orpha! You say she must learn to love me. What if she cannot? I am lacking in many things; perhaps in the very thing she naturally would look for in the man she would accept as her husband."

His lips took a firm line; never had he shown himself more the master of himself and of every one about him, than when he rejoined in a way to end the conversation: "We will not talk of that. You are free to sound her mind when opportunity offers. But quietly, and with due consideration for Edgar, who will lose enough without too great humiliation to his pride. Now you may summon Clarke."

I did so; and left thus for a little while to myself, strove to balance the wild instinctive joy making havoc in my breast, with fears just as instinctive that Orpha's heart would never be won by me completely enough for me to benefit by the present wishes of her father. It was with the step of a guilty man I crept from the sight of Edgar's door down to the floor below. At Orpha's I paused a moment. I could hear her light step within, and listening, thought I heard her sigh.

"God bless my darling!" leaped from heart to lip in a whisper too low for even my own ears to hear. And I believed—and left that door in the belief—that I was willing it should be in His way, not mine, so long as it was a blessing in very truth.

But once on the verandah below, whither I went for a cooling draught of the keen night air, I stopped short in my even pacing as though caught by a detaining hand.

A thought had come to me. He had two wills in his hand, yet he had destroyed neither though the flames were leaping and beckoning on the hearth-stone at his feet. Let him say this or let him say that, the ordeal was not over. Under these circumstances dare I do as he suggested and show my heart to Orpha?

Suppose he changed his mind again!

The mere suggestion of such a possibility was so unsettling that it kept me below in an unquiet mood for hours. I walked the court, and when Haines came to put out the lights, paced the library floor till I was exhausted. The house was still and well nigh dark when I finally went upstairs, and after a little further wandering through the halls entered my own room.

Three o'clock! and as wide awake as ever. Throwing myself into the Morris chair which had been given me for my comfort, I shut my eyes in the hope of becoming drowsy and was just feeling a lessening of the tense activity which was keeping my brain in a whirl when there came a quick knock at my door followed by the hurried word:

"Mr. Bartholomew is worse, come quickly."

I was on my feet in an instant, my heart cold in my breast but every sense alert. Had I feared such a summons? Had some premonition of sudden disaster been the cause of the intolerable restlessness which had kept my feet moving in the rooms below?

Useless to wonder; the sounds of hurrying steps all over the house warned me to hasten also. Rushing from my room I encountered Wealthy awaiting me at the turn of the hall. She was shaking from head to foot and her voice broke as she said:

"A sudden change. Mr. Edgar and Orpha are coming. Mr. Bartholomew wants to see you all, while he has the power to speak and embrace you for the last time."

I saw her eyes leave my face and pass rapidly over my person. I was fully dressed.

44

"There they are," she whispered, as Edgar emerged from his room far down the hall just as Orpha, trembling and shaken with sobs, appeared at the top of the staircase. Both were in hastily donned clothing. I alone presented the same appearance as at dinner.

As we met, Edgar took the lead, supporting Orpha, weakened both by her grief and sudden arousal from sleep. I followed after, never feeling more lonely or more isolated from them all. And in this manner we entered the room.

Then, as always on crossing this threshold my first glance was given to the picture which held such sway over my heart. The living Orpha was but a step ahead of me, but the Orpha most real to me, most in accord with me, was the one in whose imaginary ear I had breathed my vows of love and from whose imaginary lips I had sometimes heard with fond self-deception those vows returned.

To-day, the picture was in shadow and my eyes turned quickly towards the fireplace. Shadow there, too. No leaping flame or smouldering coals. For the first time in months the fire had been allowed to die out. The ominous fact struck like ice to my heart and a secret shudder shook me. But it passed almost instantly, for on turning towards the bed I saw preparations made which assured me that my uncle's mind was clear to the duty of the hour and that we had not been called to his side simply for his final embrace.

He was lying high on his pillow, his eyes blazing as if the fire which had gone out of the hearth had left its reflection on his blazing eye-balls. He had not seen us come in and he did not see us now.

At his side was a table on which stood a large bowl and a lighted candle. They told their own story. His hands were stretched out over the coverlid. They held in feverish grasp the two documents I knew so well, one in one hand and one in the other just as I had seen them the evening before. Edgar recognized them too, as I saw by the imperturbability of his look as his glance fell on them. But Orpha stood amazed, the color leaving her cheeks till she was as pale as I had ever seen a woman.

"What does that mean?" She whispered or rather uttered with throat half closed in fear and trepidation.

"Shall we explain?" I asked, with a quick turn towards Edgar.

"Leave it to him," was the low, undisturbed reply. "He has heard her voice, and is going to speak."

It was true. Slowly and with effort her father's glance sought her out and love again became animate in his features. "Come here, Orpha," he said and uttered murmuring words of affection as she knelt at his side. "I am going to make you happy. You have been a good girl. Do you see the two long envelopes I am holding, one in each hand?''

"Yes, Father."

"Look at them. No, do not take them, just look at them where they lie and tell me if in the corner of one you see a cross drawn in red?"

"Yes, Father."

"In which hand do you see it?"

"In this one,—the one nearest me."

"You are sure?"

"Very sure. Edgar, look too, and tell him that I am right."

"I will take your word, my darling child. Now pull that envelope,—the one with the mark on it, from under my hand."

"I have it, Father."

A moment's silence. Edgar's breath stopped on his lips; mine had come haltingly from my breast ever since I entered the room.

"Now, burn it."

Instinctively she shrank back, but he repeated the command with a force which startled us all and made Orpha's hand shake as she thrust the document into the flame and then, as it caught fire, dropped it into the gaping bowl.

As it flared up and the scent of burning paper filled the room, he made a mighty effort and sat almost erect, watching the flaming edges curl and drop away till all was consumed.

"A will made a few weeks ago of which I have repented," he declared quite steadily. "It had a twin, drawn up on the same day. That is the one I desire to stand. It is not in the envelope I hold in this other hand. This envelope is empty but you will find the will itself in—"

A choke—a gasp. The exertion had been too much for him. With a look of consummate fear distorting his features, he centered his gaze on his child, then sought to turn it on—which of us? On Edgar, or on me?

We never knew. The light in his eye went out before his glance reached its goal.

Edgar Quenton Bartholomew was dead, and we, his two namesakes—the lesser and the greater—stood staring the one upon the other, not knowing to which that term of greater rightfully belonged.

BOOK II

HIDDEN

CHAPTER 16

"Dead?"

The word was spoken in such astonishment that it had almost the emphasis of unbelief.

From whose lips had it come?

I turned to see. We were all still grouped near or about the bed, but this voice was strange, or so it seemed to me at the moment.

But it was strange only from emotion. It was that of Dr. Cameron, who had come quietly in, in response to the summons sent him at the first sign of change seen in his patient.

"I did not anticipate this," he was now saying. "Yesterday he had strength enough for a fortnight or more of life. What was his trouble? He must have excited him self."

Looking round upon our faces as we failed to reply, he let his fingers rest on the bowl from which little whiffs of smoke were still going up. "This is an odd thing to have where disinfection is not necessary. Something of a most unusual nature has taken place here. What was it? Did I not tell you to keep him quiet?"

It was Edgar who answered.

"Doctor, you knew my uncle. Knew him in health and knew him in illness. Do you think that any one could have kept him quiet if he had the will to act even if it were to please simply a momentary whim? What then if he felt himself called upon to risk his life in the performance of a duty? Could you or I or even his well loved daughter have prevented him?" And looking very noble, Edgar met the doctor's eye unflinchingly.

"Ah, a duty!" The doctor's voice had grown milder. "No, I do not think that any of us could have stopped him in that case."

Turning towards the bed, he stood a moment gazing at the rigid countenance which but a few minutes before had been so expressive of emotion. Then, raising his hand, he pointed directly at it, saying with a gravity which shook every heart:

"The performance of duty brings relief to both mind and body. Then why this look of alarm with which he met his end—"

"Because he felt it coming before that duty was fully accomplished. If you must know, doctor, I am willing to tell you what occasioned this sudden collapse. Shall I not, Orpha? Shall I not, Quenton? It is his right, as our physician. We shall save ourselves nothing by silence."

"Tell."

That was all Orpha seemed to have power to utter, and I attempted little more. I was willing the doctor should know—that all the world should know— my part in this grievous tragedy. Even if I had wished for silence, the sting of Edgar's tone as he mentioned my name would have been enough to make me speak.

"I have no wish to keep anything from the doctor," I affirmed as quickly and evenly as if the matter were of ordinary purport. "Only tell him all; keep nothing back."

And Edgar did so with a simplicity and fairness which did him credit. If he had shown a tinge of sarcasm when he addressed me directly, it was not heard in the relation he now gave of the drawing up of the two wills and our uncle's final act in destroying one. "He loved me—it was a life-long affection—and when Quenton came, he loved him." This was said with a certain display of hardihood. —"Not wishing to divide his fortune but to leave it largely in favor of one, he wavered for a time between us, but finally, at the conscious approach of death, made up his mind and acted as you have seen. Only," he finished with naivete peculiar to his temperament and nature, "we do not know which of us he has chosen to bless or curse with his great fortune. You see the remains of one will. But of the other one or of its contents we have as yet no knowledge."

The doctor, who had followed Edgar's words with great intentness, opened his lips as though to address him, but failed to do so, turning his attention towards me instead. Then, still without speaking, he drew up the sheet over the face once so instinct with every generous emotion, and quietly left our presence. As the door closed upon him Orpha burst into sobs, and it was Edgar's arm, not mine, which fell about her shoulders.

CHAPTER 17

No attempt was made during those first few grief-stricken hours to settle the question alluded to above. Of course it would be an easy matter to find the will which he from sheer physical weakness could not have put very far away. But Edgar showed no anxiety to find it and I studiously refrained from showing any; while Orpha seemed to have forgotten everything but her loss.

But at nightfall Edgar came to where I was pacing the verandah and, halting in the open French window, said without preamble and quite brusquely for him:

"The will of which Uncle spoke as having been taken from the other envelope and concealed in some drawer or other, cannot be found. It is not in the cubby-hole at the back of his bed or in any of the drawers or subdivisions of his desk. You were with him later than I last night. Did he intimate to you in any way where he intended to put it?"

"I left him while the two wills, or at least the two envelopes, still remained in his hands. But Clarke ought to be able to tell you. He is the one most likely to have gone in immediately upon my departure."

"Clarke says that he no sooner entered Uncle's presence than he was ordered out, with an injunction not to come back or to allow any one else to approach the room for a full half hour. My uncle wished to be alone."

"And was he obeyed?"

"Clarke says that he was. Wealthy was sitting in her usual place in the hall as he went by to his room; and answered with a quiet nod when he told her what

Uncle's wishes were. She is the last person to disobey them. Yet Uncle had been so emphatic that more than once he stole about the corner to see if she were still sitting where he had left her. And she was. Neither he nor she disturbed him until the time was up. Then Clarke went in. Uncle was sitting in his great chair looking very tired. The envelopes were in his hand but he allowed Clarke to add them to a pile of other documents lying on the stand by his bed where they still were when Wealthy came in. She says she was astonished to see so many valuable papers lying there, for he usually kept everything of the kind in the little cubby-hole let into the head of his bed. But when she offered to put them there he said 'No,' and was very peremptory indeed in his demand that she should go down to Orpha's room on an errand, which while of no especial moment, would keep her from the room for fifteen minutes if not longer. She went and when she came back the envelopes as well as all the other papers were still lying on the stand. Later, at his request, she put them all back in the drawer."

"Looking at them as she did so?"

"No."

"Who got them out this morning? The two envelopes, I mean."

"She, and it was not till then that she noticed that one of them was empty. She says, and the plausibility of her surmise you must acknowledge, that it was during the time she was below with Orpha, that Uncle took out the will now missing from its envelope and hid it away. Where, we cannot conceive."

"What do you know of this woman?"

"Nothing but what is good. She has had the confidence of many people for years."

"It is an extraordinary situation in which we find ourselves," I commented, approaching him where he still stood in the open window. "But there cannot be any real difficulty ahead of us. The hiding-places which in his feeble state he could reach, are few. To-morrow will see this necessary document in hand. Meanwhile, you are the master."

I said it to try him. Though my tone was a matter-of-fact one he could not but feel the sting of such a declaration from me.

And he did, and fully as much as I expected.

"You seem to think," he said, with a dilation of the nostril and a sudden straightening of his lips which while it lasted made him look years older than his age, "that there is such a thing as the possibility of some other person taking that place upon the finding and probating of the remaining will."

"I have reason to, Edgar."

"How much reason, Quenton?"

"Only my uncle's word."

"Ah!" He was very still, but the shot went home. "And what did he say?" he asked after a moment of silent communion with himself.

"That I was the man."

I repeated these words with as little offense as possible. I felt that no advantage should be taken of his ignorance if indeed he were as ignorant as he seemed. Nor did I feel like wounding his feelings. I simply wanted no misunderstandings to arise.

"You the man! He said that?"

"Those were his exact words."

50

"The man to administer his wealth? To take his place in this community? To—" his voice sank lower, there was even an air of apology in his manner—"to wed his daughter?"

"Yes. And to my mind,"—I said it fervently—"this last honor out-weighs all the rest. I love Orpha deeply and devotedly. I have never told her so, but few women are loved as I love her."

"You dare?" The word escaped him almost without his volition. "Didn't you know that there at least I have the precedence? That she and I are engaged—"

"Truly, Edgar?"

He looked down at my hand which I had laid in honest appeal on his arm and as he did so he flushed ever so slightly.

"I regard myself as engaged to her."

"Yet you do not love her. Not as I do," I hastened to add. "She is my past, my present and my future; she is my whole life. Otherwise my conduct would be inexcusable. There is no reason why I should take precedence of you in other ways than that."

He was taken aback. He had not expected any such an avowal from me. I had kept my secret well. It had not escaped the father's eye but it had that of the lukewarm lover.

"You have some excuse for your presumption," he admitted at last. "There has been no public recognition of our intentions, nor have we made any display of our affection. But you know it now, and must eliminate from your program that hope which you say is your whole life. As for the rest, I might as well tell you, now as later, that nothing but the sight of the lost will, made out as you have the hardihood to declare, will ever convince me that Uncle, even in the throes of approaching dissolution, would so far forget the affection of years as to give into the hands of my betrothed wife for public destruction the will he had made while under the stress of that affection. The one we all saw reduced to ashes was the one in which your name figured the largest. That I shall always believe and act upon till you can show me in black and white the absolute proof that I have made a mistake."

He spoke with an air of dignity and yet with an air of detachment also, not looking me in the eye. The sympathy I had felt for him in his unfortunate position left me and I became boldly critical of everything he said. In every matter in which we, creatures of an hour, are concerned, there are depths which are never fully sounded. The present one was not likely to prove an exception. But the time had not come for me to show any positive distrust, so I let him go, with what I tried to make a dispassionate parting.

"Neither of us wish to take advantage of the other. That is why we are both disposed to be frank. I shall stand on my rights, too, Edgar, if events prove that I am legally entitled to them. You cannot expect me to do otherwise. I am a man like yourself and I love Orpha."

Like a flash he wheeled at that and came hastily back.

"Do you mean that according to your ideas she goes absolutely with the fortune, in these days of woman's independence? You will have to change your ideas. Uncle would never bind her to his wishes like that."

He spoke with a conviction not observable in anything he had said before. He was not surmising now but speaking from what looked very much like knowledge.

"Then you saw those two wills—read them—became acquainted with their contents before I knew of their existence?"

"Fortunately, yes," he allowed.

"There you have the advantage of me. I have only a general knowledge of the same. They were not unfolded before my eyes."

He did not respond to this suggestion as I had some hope that he would, but stood in silence, drumming nervously with his fingers on the framework of the window standing open at his side. My heart, always sensitive to changes of emotion, began pounding in my breast. He was meditating some action or formulating some disclosure, the character of which I could not even guess at. I saw resolution climaxing in the expression of his eye.

"Quenton, there is something you don't know." These words came with slow intensity; he was looking fairly at me now. "There is another will, a former one, drawn up and attested to previous to those which made a nightmare of our uncle's final days. That one I have also seen, and what is more to the point, I believe it to be still in existence, either in some drawer of my uncle's desk or in the hands of Mr. Dunn, our legal adviser, and consequently producible at any time. I will tell you on my honor that by the terms of this first will—the only one which will stand—I am given everything, over and above certain legacies, which were alike in all three wills."

"No mention of Orpha?"

"Yes. He leaves her a stated sum and with such expressions of confidence and affection that no one can doubt he did what he did from a conception, mistaken perhaps but sincere, that he was taking the best course to secure her happiness."

"Was this will made previous to my coming or after?"

"Before."

"How long before, Edgar? You cannot question my right to know."

"I question nothing but the good taste of this conversation on the part of both of us, while Uncle lies cold in the house!"

"You are right; we will defer it. Take my hand, Edgar. I have not from the beginning to the end played you false in this matter. Nor have I made any effort beyond being at all times responsive to Uncle's goodness, to influence him in any unfair way against you. We are cousins and should be friends."

He took a long breath, smiled faintly and reached out his hand to mine. "You have the more solid virtues," he laughed, "and I ought to envy you. But I don't. The lighter ones will win and when they do—not if mind you, but when—then we will talk of friendship."

Not the sort of harangue calculated to calm my spirits or to make this day of mourning lose any of its gloom.

CHAPTER 18

That night I slept but little. I had much to grieve over; much to think about. I had lost my best friend. Of that I was sure. His place would never again be filled in my heart or in my imagination. Without him the house seemed a barren shell save for the dim unseen corner where my darling mourned in her own way the man we both loved.

Might we but have shared each other's suffering!

But under the existing state of things, that could not be. Our relations, one to the other, were too unsettled. Which thought brought me at once face to face with the most hopeless of all my perplexities. How were Orpha and I to know—and when, if ever—what Uncle's wishes were or what his final intentions? The will which would have made everything plain, as well as fixed the status of everybody in the house, had not been found; and among the disadvantages in which this placed me was the fact that he, as the present acknowledged head of the house, had rights which it would have been most unbecoming in me to infringe upon. If he wished a door to be closed against me, I could not, as a mere resident under his roof, ask to have it opened. For days—possibly for weeks,—at all events until he saw fit to pursue the search he had declared to be at present so hopeless, it was for me to remain quiescent—a man apart—anxious for my rights but unable as a gentleman. and a guest to make a move towards obtaining them.

And unhappily for us, instantaneous action was what the conditions called for. An immediate and exhaustive inquiry, conducted by Edgar in the presence of every occupant of the house, offered the only hope of arriving speedily at the truth of what it was not to the interests of any of us to leave much longer in doubt.

For some one of the few persons admitted to Uncle's presence after Edgar and I had left it, must have aided him in the disposal of this missing document. He was far too feeble to have taken it from the room himself, nor could he, without a helping hand, have made any extraordinary effort within it which would have necessitated the displacing of furniture or the opening of drawers or other receptacles not plainly in sight and within easy access.

If the will which his sudden death prevented him from definitely locating was not found within twenty-four hours, it would never be found. The one helping him will have suppressed it; and this is what I believed had already occurred. For every servant in the house from his man Clarke to a shy little sewing girl who from time to time scurried on timid feet through the halls, favored Edgar to the point of self-effacing devotion.

And Edgar knew it.

Recognizing this fact at its full value, but not as yet questioning his probity, I asked myself who was the first person to enter my uncle's room immediately after my departure on the evening before.

I did not know.

Did Edgar? Had he taken any pains to find out?

Fruitless to conjecture. Impertinent to inquire.

I had left Uncle sitting by the fire. He had bidden me call Wealthy, and it was just possible that in the interim elapsing between my going out and the entrance of nurse or servant, he had found the nervous strength to hide the missing paper where no one as yet had thought to look for it.

It did not seem possible, and I gave but little credence to this theory; yet such is the activity of the mind when once thoroughly aroused, that all through the long night I was in fancy searching the dark corners of my uncle's room and tabulating the secret spots and unsuspected crevices in which the document so important to myself might lie hidden.

Beginning with the bed, I asked myself if there could be anywhere in it an undiscovered hiding-place other than the drawer I have already mentioned as having been let into the headboard. I decided to the contrary since this piece of furniture upon which he had been found lying, would have received the closest attention of the searchers. If Edgar had called in the services of Wealthy, as it would be natural for him to do, she would never have left the mattresses and pillows unexamined; while he would have ransacked the little drawer and sounded the wood of the bedstead for hollow posts or convenient slits. I could safely trust that the bed could tell no tales beyond those associated with our uncle's sufferings. Leaving it, then, in my imaginary circuit of the room, I followed the wall running parallel with the main hall, till I came to the door opening at the southern end of the room into a short passageway communicating with that hall.

Here I paused a moment, for built into this passageway was a cabinet which during his illness had been used for the safeguarding of medicine bottles, etc. Could a folded paper of the size of the will find any place among the boxes and phials with which every one of its shelves were filled? I knew the place well enough to come to the quick decision that I should lose nothing by passing them quickly by.

Turning the corner which had nothing to show but another shelf—this time a hanging one—on which there was never anything kept but a jar or two and a small photograph of Edgar, I concentrated my attention on the south wall made beautiful by the full length portrait of Orpha concerning which I have said so much.

It had not always hung there. It had been brought from the den, as you will remember, when Uncle's illness had become pronounced, taking the place of a painting which had been hung elsewhere. Flanked by windows on either side, it filled the wall-space up to where a table stood of size sufficient to answer for the serving of a meal. There were chairs here too and Orpha's little basket standing on its three slender legs. The document might have been put under her work. But no, the woman would have found it there; or in the table drawer, or among the cushions of the couch filling the space between this corner and the fireplace. There were rugs all over the room but they must have been lifted; and as for the fireplace itself, not having had the sifting of the ashes, I must leave it unconsidered.

But not so the mantel or the winged chair dedicated solely to my Uncle's use and always kept near the hearth. This was where I had last seen him, sitting in this chair close to the fire-dogs. The two wills were in his hands. Could one have fallen from its envelope and so into the flames,—the one he had meant to preserve,—the one which was not marked with a hastily scrawled cross? Mad questions to which there was no answer. Would that I might have been the man to sift those ashes! Or that I might yet be given the opportunity of looking behind the ancient painting which filled the large square above the mantel. I did not see how anything like a folded paper could have been lodged there; but not an inch from floor to ceiling would have escaped my inspection had I been fortunate enough or my claims been considered important enough to have entitled me to assist in the search.

Should I end this folly of a disturbed imagination? Forget the room for to-night and the whole gruesome tragedy? Could I, in reality, do this before I had only half circled the room? There was the desk,—the place of all others where he would naturally lock up a paper of value. But this was so obvious that probably not another article in the room had been more thoroughly overhauled or its contents more rigidly examined. If any of its drawers or compartments contained false backs or double bottoms, Edgar would be likely to know it. Up to the night of the ball, when in some way he forfeited a portion of our uncle's regard, he had been, according to his own story, in his benefactor's full confidence, even in matters connected with business and his most private transactions. The desk was negligible, if, as I sincerely believed, he had sought to conceal the will from Edgar, as temporarily from every one else.

But back of the desk there was a bookcase, and books offer an excellent hiding place. But that bookcase was always locked, and the key to it, linked with that of the desk, kept safely to hand in the drawer inserted in his bed-head. The desk key, of course, had come into use at the first moment of the search, but had that of the bookcase? Possibly not.

I made a note of this doubt; and in my fancy moved on to the two rooms which completed my uncle's suite towards the north. The study and a dressing closet! I say study and I say closet but both were large enough to merit the name of rooms. The dressing closet was under the combined care of Wealthy and Clarke. They must be acquainted with every nook and corner of it. Wealthy had undoubtedly been consulted as to its contents, but had Clarke?

The study, since the time when Uncle's condition became serious enough to have a nurse within call, had been occupied by Wealthy. Certainly he would have hidden nothing in her room which he wished kept from Edgar.

The fourth corner was negligible; so was the wall between it and a second passageway which, like the one already described, led to a door opening into the main hall. Only, this one, necessitated like the other by the curious break between the old house and the new, held no cabinet or any place of concealment. It was the way of entrance most used by uncle when in health and by all the rest of us both then and later. Had he made use of it that night, for reaching the hall and some place beyond?

Hardly; but if he had, where would he have found a cubbyhole for the will, short of Edgar's room or mine?

The closet indicated in the diagram of this room as offering another break in this eastern wall, was the next thing to engage my attention.

I had often seen it open and it held, according to my recollection, nothing but clothes. He had always been very methodical in his ways and each coat had its hook and every hat, not in constant use, its own box. The hooks ran along the back and along one of the sides; the other side was given up to shelves only wide enough to hold the boxes just alluded to and the long row of shoes, the number and similarity of which I found it hard to account for till I heard some one in speaking of petty economies and of how we all have them, mentioned this peculiar one of my uncle's, which was to wear a different pair of shoes every day in the week.

Had Edgar, or whoever conducted the search, gone through all the pockets of the many suits lining these simple walls? Had they lifted the shoes?

The only object to be seen between the door of this closet and the alcove sunk in the wall for the accommodation of the bed-head, was the small stand holding his night-lamp and the various articles for use and ornament which one usually sees at an invalid's bedside. I remembered the whole collection. There was not a box there nor a book, not even a tablet nor a dish large enough to hold the will folded as I had seen it. Had the stand a drawer? Yes, but this drawer had no lock. Its contents were open to all. Edgar must have handled them. I had come back to my starting-point. And what had I gained in knowledge or in hope by my foolish imaginary quest? Nothing. I had but proved to myself that I was no more exempt than the next man from an insatiable, if hitherto unrecognized desire for this world's goods and this world's honors. Nothing less could have kept my thoughts so long in this especial groove at a time of such loss and so much personal sorrow.

My shame was great and to its salutary effect upon my mind I attribute a certain lessening of interest in things material which I date from this day.

My hour of humiliation over, my thoughts reverted to Orpha, I had not seen her all day nor had I any hope of seeing her on the morrow. She had not shown herself at meals, nor were we to expect her to leave her room—or so I was told—until the day of the funeral.

Whether this isolation of hers was to be complete, shutting out Edgar as well as myself, I had no means of determining. Probably not, if what uncle had told me was true and they were secretly engaged.

When I fell asleep at dawn it was with the resolution fixed in my mind, that with the first opportunity which offered I would make a desperate endeavor to explain myself to her. As my pride was such that I could only do this in Edgar's presence, the risk was great. So would be the test made of her feelings by the story I had to relate. If she listened, hope, shadowy but existent, might still be mine. If not, then I must bear her displeasure as best I could. Possibly I should suffer less under it than from the uncertainty which kept every nerve quivering.

CHAPTER 19

The next day was without incident save such as were connected with the sad event which had thrown the house into mourning, Orpha did not appear and Edgar was visible only momentarily and that at long intervals.

When he did show himself it was with an air of quiet restraint which caused me some thought. The suspicion he had shown—or was it just a natural revulsion at my attitude and pretensions,—seemed to have left him. He was friendly in aspect and when he spoke, as he did now and then, there was apology in his tone, almost commiseration, which showed how assured he felt that nothing I could do or say would ever alter the position he was maintaining amongst us with so much grace and calm determination.

Had he found the will and had it proved to be the one favorable to his interests and not to mine? I doubted this and with cause, for the faces of those about him did not reflect his composure, but wore a look of anxious suspense quite distinct from that of sorrow, sincerely as my uncle was mourned by every member of his devoted household. I noticed this first in Clarke, who had taken his stand near his dead master's door and could not be induced to leave it. No sentinel on watch ever showed a sadder or a more resolute countenance.

It was the same with Wealthy. Every time I passed through the hall I found her hovering near one door or the other of her former master's room, the great tears rolling down her cheeks and her mouth set with a firmness which altered her whole appearance. Usually mild of countenance, she reminded me that day of some wild animal guarding her den, especially when her eye met mine. If the will favoring Edgar had been found, she would have faced me with a very different aspect and cared little what I did or where I stayed. But no such will had been found; and what was, perhaps, of almost equal importance, neither had the original one—the one made before I came to C—, and which Edgar had so confidently stated was still in the house. Both were gone and— Here a thought struck me which stopped me short as I was descending the stairs. If the original one had been destroyed—as would have been natural upon or immediately after the signing of the other two, and no other should ever come to light—in other words, if Uncle, so far as all practical purposes went, had died intestate, then in the course of time Orpha would inherit the whole estate (I knew enough of law to be sure of that) and if engaged to Edgar, he would have little in the end to complain of. Was this the source of his composure, so unnatural to one of his temperament and headlong impulses?

I would not have it so. With every downward step which I took after that I repeated to myself, "No! no!" and when I passed within sight of Orpha's door somehow the feeling rose within me that she was repeating with me that same vigorous "No! no!"

A lover's fancy founded on—well, on nothing. A dream, light as air, to be dispelled the next time I saw her. For struggle against it as I would, both reason and experience assured me only too plainly that women of her age choose for their heart's mate, not the man whose love is the deepest and most sincere, but the one whose pleasing personality has fired their imagination and filled their minds with dreams.

And Edgar, in spite of his irregular features possessed this appeal to the imagination above and beyond any other man I have ever met.

I shall never forget this seemingly commonplace descent of mine down these two flights of stairs. In those few minutes I seemed to myself to run the whole gamut of human emotions; to exhaust the sorrows and perplexities of a life-time.

And it was nothing; mere child's play. Before another twenty-four hours had passed how happy would I have been if this experience had expressed the full sum of grief and trial I should be called upon to endure.

I had other experiences that day confirmatory of the conclusion I had come to. Hostile glances everywhere except as I have said from Edgar. Attention to my wants, respectful replies to my questions, which I assure you were very limited, but no display of sympathy or kind feeling from any one indoors or out. To each and all I was an unwelcome stranger, with hand stretched out to steal the morsel from another man's dish.

I bore it. I stood the day out bravely, as was becoming in one conscious of no evil intentions; and when evening came, retired to my room, in the hope that sleep would soon bring me the relief my exhausted condition demanded.

So little are we able to foresee one hour, nay, one minute into the future.

I read a little, or tried to, then I sank into a reverie which did not last long, for they had chosen this hour to carry down the casket into the court.

My room, of which you will hear more later, was in the rear of the house and consequently somewhat removed from the quarter where all this was taking place. But imagination came to the aid of my hearing, intensifying every sound. When I could stand no more I threw up my window and leaned out into the night. There was consolation in the darkness, and for a few fleeting minutes I felt a surcease of care and a lightening of the load weighing upon my spirits. The face of heaven was not unkind to me and I had one treasure of memory with which to meet whatever humiliation the future might bring. My uncle had been his full vigorous self at the moment he rose up before me and said, with an air of triumph, "You are the man!" For that one thrilling instant I was the man, however the people of his house chose to regard me.

Soothed by the remembrance, I drew in my head and softly closed the window. God! how still it was! Not a sound to be heard anywhere. My uncle's body had been carried below and this whole upper floor was desolate. So was his room! The room which had witnessed such misery; the room from which I had felt myself excluded; where, if it still existed, the missing will lay hidden; the will which I must see—handle—show to the world—show to Orpha.

Was there any one there now,—watching as they had watched, at door or bedside while his body still lay in the great bed and the mystery of his last act was still a mystery unsolved?

A few steps and the question would be answered. But should I take those steps? Brain and heart said no. But man is not always governed by his brain or by his heart, or by both combined. Before I knew it and quite without conscious volition I had my hand on the knob of my door. I had no remembrance of having crossed the floor. I felt the knob of the door turning in my hand and that was the sum of my consciousness. Thus started on the way, I could not stop. The hall as I stepped into it lay bare and quiet before me. So did the main one when I had circled the bend and stood in sight of my uncle's door. But nothing would have made me believe at that moment that there was no sentinel behind it. Yet I hurried on, listening and looking back like a guilty man, for brain and heart were yet crying out "No."

There was no one to mark my quickly moving figure, for the doors, whichever way I looked, were all shut. Nor would any one near or far be likely to hear my footsteps, for I was softly shod. But when I reached his door, it was as impossible for me to touch it as if I had known that the spirit of my uncle would meet me on the threshold.

Sick at heart, I staggered backwards. There should be no attempt made by me to surprise, in any underhanded way, the secrets of this room. What I might yet be called upon to do, should be done openly and with Orpha's consent. She was the mistress of this home. However our fortunes turned, she was now, and always would be, its moral head. This was my one glad thought.

To waft her a good-night message I leaned over the balustrade and was so leaning, when suddenly, sharply, frightfully, a cry rang up from below rousing every echo in the wide, many-roomed house. It was from a woman's lips, but not from Orpha's, thank God; and after that first instant of dismay, I ran forward to the stair-head and was on the point of plunging recklessly below, when the door of Uncle's room opened and the pale and alarmed face of Wealthy confronted me.

"What is it?" she cried. "What has happened?"

Before I could answer Clarke rushed by me, appearing from I never knew where. He flew pell-mell down the stairs and I followed, scarcely less heedless of my feet than he. As we reached the bottom, I almost on top of him, a hardly audible click came from the hall above. I recognized the sound, possibly because I was in a measure listening for it. Wealthy was about to follow us, but not until she had locked the door she was leaving without a watcher. As we all crowded in line at the foot of the first flight, the door of Orpha's room opened and she stepped out and faced us.

"What is it? Who is hurt?" were her first words. "Somebody cried out. The voice sounded like Martha's."

Martha was the name of one of the girls.

"We don't know," replied Clarke. "We are going to see."

She made as if to follow us.

"Don't," I prayed, beseeching her with look and hand. "Let us find out first whether it is anything but a woman's hysterical outcry."

She paused for a moment then pressed hastily on.

"I must see for myself," she declared; and I forebore to urge her further. Nor did I offer her my arm. For my heart was very sore. She had not looked my way once, no, not even when I spoke.

So she too doubted me. Oh, God! my lot was indeed a hard one.

CHAPTER 20

The scene which met our view as we halted in one of the arches overlooking the court was one for which we sought in vain for full explanation.

The casket had been placed and a man stood near it, holding the lid which he had evidently just taken off, probably at some one's request. But it was not upon the casket or the man that our glances became instantly focused. Grief has its call but terror dominates grief, and terror stood embodied before us in the figure of the girl Martha, who with staring eyes and pointing finger bade us "Look! look!" crouching as the words left her lips and edging fearfully away.

Look? look at what? She had appeared to indicate the silent form in the casket. But that could not be. The death of the old is sad but not terrible; she must have meant something else, something which we could not perceive from where we stood.

Leaning further forward, I forced my gaze to follow hers and speedily became aware that the others were doing the same and that it was inside the casket itself that they were all peering and with much the same appearance of consternation Martha herself had shown.

Something was wrong there; and alive to the effect which this scene must have upon Orpha, I turned her way just in time to catch her as she fell back from the marble balustrade she had been clutching in her terror.

"Oh, what is it? what is it?" she moaned, her eyes meeting mine for the first time in days.

"I will go and see, if you think you can stand alone."

"Wealthy will take care of me," she murmured, as another arm than mine drew her forcibly away.

But I did not go on the instant for just then Martha spoke again and we heard in tones which set every heart beating tumultuously:

"Spots! Black spots on his forehead and cheek! I have seen them before— seen them on my dead brother's face and he died from poison!"

"Wretch!" I shouted down from the gallery where I stood, in irrepressible wrath and consternation, as Orpha, escaping from Wealthy's grasp, fell insensible at my feet. "Would you kill your young mistress?" And I stooped to lift Orpha, but an arm thrust across her pushed me inexorably back.

"Would you blame the girl for what you yourself have brought upon us?" came in a hiss to my ear.

And staring into Wealthy's face I saw with a chill as of the grave what awaited me at the hands of Hate if no succor came from Love.

CHAPTER 21

In another moment I had left the gallery. Whether it was from pride or conscious innocence or just the daring of youth in the face of sudden danger, the hot blood within me drove me to add myself to the group of friends and relatives circling my uncle's casket, where I belonged as certainly and truly as Edgar did. Not for me to hide my head or hold myself back at a crisis so momentous as this. Even the shudder which passed from man to man at my sudden appearance did not repel me; and, when after an instant of hesitation one person after another began to sidle away till I was left there alone with the man still holding the lid in his trembling fingers, I did not move from my position or lift the hand which I had laid in reverent love upon the edge of the casket.

That every tongue was stilled and many a breath held in check I need not say. It was a moment calling for a man's utmost courage. For the snake of suspicion whose hiss I had heard above was rearing its crest against me here, and not a friendly eye did I meet.

But perhaps I should have, if Edgar's face had been turned my way; but it was not. Miss Colfax was one of the group watching us from the other side of the fountain, and his eyes were on her and not on me. I stood in silent observation of him for a minute, then I spoke.

"Edgar, if there is anything in the appearance of our uncle's body which suggests foul play though it be only to an ignorant servant, why do you not send for the doctor?"

He started and, turning very slowly, gave me look for look.

"Do you advise that?" he asked.

With a glance at the dear features which were hardly recognizable, I said:

"I not only advise it, but as one who believes himself entitled to full authority here, I demand it."

A murmur from every lip varying in tone but all hostile was followed by a silence which bitterly tried my composure. It was broken by a movement of the undertaker's man. Stepping forward, he silently replaced the lid he had been holding.

This forced a word from Edgar.

"We will not dispute authority in this presence or disagree as to the action you propose. Let some one call Dr. Cameron."

"It is not necessary," announced a voice from the staircase. "That has already been done." And Orpha, erect, and showing none of the weakness which had so nearly laid her at my feet a few minutes before, stepped into our midst.

CHAPTER 22

Such transformations are not common, and can only occur in strong natures under the stress of a sudden emergency. With what rejoicing I hailed this new Orpha, and marked the surprise on every face as she bent over the casket and imprinted a kiss upon the cold wood which shut in the heart which had so loved her. When she faced them again, not an eye but showed a tear; only her own were dry. But ah, how steady!

Edgar, who had started forward, stopped stock-still as she raised her hand. No statue of even-handed Justice could have shown a calmer front. I could have worshiped her, and did in my inmost heart; for I saw with a feeling of awe which I am sure was shared by many others there, that she whom we had seen blossom from girl to womanhood in a moment, was to be trusted, and that she would do what was right because it was right and not from any less elevated motive.

That she was beautiful thus, with a beauty which put her girlhood's charms to blush, did not detract from her power.

Eagerly we waited for what she had to say. When it came it was very simple.

"I can understand," said she, "the shock you have all sustained. But I ask you to wait before you accept the awful suggestion conveyed by my poor Martha's words. She had a dreadful experience once and naturally was thrown off her balance by anything which brought it to mind. But the phenomenon which she once witnessed in her brother—under very different circumstances I am sure—is no proof that a like cause is answerable for what we see disfiguring the face we so much love. Let us hear what Dr. Cameron has to say before we associate evil with a death which in itself is hard enough to bear. Edgar, will you bring me a chair. I shall not leave my father's side till Dr. Cameron bids me do so."

He did not hear her; that is, not attentively enough to do her bidding. He was looking again at Miss Colfax, who was speaking in whispers to the man she was engaged to; and in the pride of my devotion it was I who brought a chair and saw my dear one seated.

Her "Thank you," was even and not unkind but it held no warmth. Nor did the same words afterwards addressed to Edgar at some trifling service he showed her. She was holding the balance of her favor at rest between us; and so she would continue to hold it till her duty became clear and Providence itself tipped the scale.

Thus far it was given me to penetrate her mind. Was it through my love for her or because the rectitude of her nature was so apparent in that high hour?

Dr. Cameron not being able to come immediately upon call, the few outsiders who were present took their leave after a voluntary promise by each and all to preserve a rigid silence concerning the events of the evening until released by official authority.

The grace with which Edgar accepted this token of friendship showed him at his best. But when they were gone it was quite another Edgar who faced us in the great court. With hasty glance, he took in all our faces, then turned his attention upward to the gallery where Clarke and Wealthy still stood.

"No one is to stir from his place while I am gone," said he. "If the doctor's ring is heard, let him in. But I am in serious earnest when I say that I expect to see on my return every man and woman now present in the precise place in which I leave them."

His voice was stern, his manner troubled. He was anything but his usual self. Nor was it with his usual suavity he suddenly turned upon me and said:

"Quenton, do you consent?"

"To remain here?" I asked. "Certainly." Indeed, I had no other wish.

But Orpha was not of my mind. With a glance at Edgar as firm as it was considerate, she quietly said:

"You should allow yourself no privilege which you deny to Quenton. If for any reason you choose to leave us for purposes you do not wish to communicate, you must take him with you."

The flush which this brought to his cheek was the first hint of color I had seen there since the evening began.

"This from you, Orpha?" he muttered. "You would place this stranger—"

"Where my father put him,—on a level with yourself. But why leave us, Edgar? Why not wait till the doctor comes?"

They were standing near each other but they now stepped closer.

Instinctively I turned my back. I even walked away from them. When I wheeled about again, I saw that they were both approaching me.

"I am going up with Edgar," said she. "Will you sit in my place till I come back?"

"Gladly, Orpha." But I wondered what took them above—something important I knew—and watched them with jealous eyes as in their ascent their bright heads came into view, now through one arch and now through another, till they finally emerged, he leading, she following, upon the gallery.

Here they paused to speak to Clarke and Wealthy. A word, and Clarke stepped back, allowing Wealthy to slip up ahead of them to the third floor.

They were going to Uncle's room of which Wealthy had the key.

Deliberately I wheeled about; deliberately I forebore to follow their movements any further, even in fancy. Prudence forbade such waste of emotion. I would simply forget everything but my present duty, which was to hold every lesser inmate of the house in view, till these two had returned or the doctor arrived.

But when I heard them coming, no exercise of my own will was strong enough to prevent me from concentrating my attention on the gallery to which they must soon descend. They reached it as they had left it, Edgar to the fore and Orpha and Wealthy following slowly after. A momentary interchange of words and Wealthy rejoined Clarke, and Edgar and Orpha came steadily down. There was nothing to be learned from their countenances; but I had a feeling that their errand had brought them no relief; that the situation had not been bettered and that what we all needed was courage to meet the developments awaiting us.

I was agreeably disappointed therefore, when the doctor, having arrived, met the first hasty words uttered by Edgar with an incredulous shrug. Nor did he show alarm or even surprise when after lifting the lid from the casket he took a prolonged look at the august countenance thus exposed. It was not until he had replaced this lid and paused for a moment in thoughtful silence that I experienced a fresh thrill of doubt and alarm. This however passed when the doctor finally said:

"Discolorations such as you see here, however soon they appear, are in themselves no proof that poison has entered the stomach. There are other causes which might easily induce them. But, since the question has been raised—since, in the course of my treatment poison in careful doses has been administered to Mr. Bartholomew, of which poison there probably remained sufficient to have hastened death, if inadvertently given by an inexperienced hand, it might be well to look into the matter. It would certainly be a comfort to you all to know that no such accident has taken place."

Here his eyes, which had been fixed upon the casket, suddenly rose. I knew—perhaps others did—where his glance would fall first. Though an excellent man and undoubtedly a just one, he could not fail to have been influenced by what he must have heard in town of the two wills and the part I had played in unsettling my uncle's mind in regard to his testamentary intentions. If under the doctor's casual manner there existed anything which might be called doubt, it would be—must be—centered upon the man who was a stranger, unloved and evidently distrusted by all in this house.

Convinced as I was of this, I could not prevent the cold perspiration from starting out on my forehead, nor Orpha from seeing it, or, seeing it, drawing a step or two further off. Fate and my temperament—the susceptibility of which I had never realized till now,—were playing me false. Physical weakness added to all the rest! I was in sorry case.

As I nerved myself to meet the strain awaiting me, it came. The doctor's gaze met mine, his keen with questioning, mine firm to meet and defy his or any other man's misjudgment.

No word was spoken nor was any attempt at greeting made by him or by myself. But when I saw those honest eyes shift their glance from my face to whomever it was who stood beside me, I breathed as a man breathes who, submerged to the point of exhaustion, suddenly finds himself tossed again into the light of day and God's free air.

The relief I felt added to my self-scorn. Then I forgot my own sensations in wondering how others would hold up against this ordeal and what my thoughts would be—remembering how nearly I had come to losing my own self-possession—if I beheld another man's lids droop under a soul search so earnest and so prolonged.

Shrinking from so stringent a test of my own generosity I turned aside, not wishing to see anything further, only to hear.

Had I looked—looked in the right place, this story might never have been written; but I only listened—held my breath and listened for a break—any break—in the too heavy silence.

It came just as my endurance had reached the breaking point. Dr. Cameron spoke, addressing Edgar.

"The funeral I understand is to be held to-morrow. At what hour, may I ask?"

"At eleven in the morning."

"It will have to be postponed. Though there is little probability of any change being necessary in the wording of the death certificate; yet it is possible and I must have time to consider."

CHAPTER 23

It was just and proper. But only Orpha had the courage to speak—to seek to probe his mind—to sound the depths of this household's misery. Orpha! whom to guard from the mere disagreabilities of life were a man's coveted delight! She our leader? The one to take her stand in the breach yawning between the old life and the new?

"You mean," she forced herself to say, "that what had happened to Martha's brother may have happened to my beloved father?"

"I doubt it, but we must make sure. A poison capable of producing death was in this house. You know that; others knew it. I had warned you all concerning it. I made it plain, I thought, that small doses taken according to prescription were helpful, but that increased beyond a certain point, they meant death. You remember, Orpha?" She bowed her head.

"And you, Edgar and Quenton?"

We did, alas!

"And his nurses, and the man Clarke, all who were at liberty to enter his room?"

"They knew." It was Orpha who spoke. "I called their attention to what you had said more than once."

"Is the phial containing that poison still in the house? I have not ordered it lately."

"It is. Edgar and I have just been up to see. We found it among the other bottles in the medicine cabinet."

"When did he receive the last dose of it under my instructions?"

"Wealthy can tell you. She kept very close watch of that bottle."

"Wealthy," he called, with a glance towards the gallery, "come down. I have a question or two to put to you." She obeyed him quickly, almost eagerly.

The other servants, Clarke alone excepted, came creeping from their corner as they saw her enter amongst us and stand in her quiet respectful way before the doctor.

He greeted her kindly; she had always been a favorite of his; then spoke up quickly:

"Mr. Bartholomew died too soon, Wealthy. We should have had him with us for another fortnight. What was the cause of it, do you know? A wrong dose? A repeated dose? One bottle mistaken for another?"

Her eyes, filled with tears, rose slowly to his face.

"I cannot say. The last time I saw that bottle it was at the very back of the shelf where I had pushed it after you had said he was to have no more of it at present. It was in the same place when we went up just now to see if it had been taken from the cabinet. It did not look as though it had been moved."

"Holding the same amount as when you saw it last?"

"To all appearance, yes, sir."

What was there in her tone or in the little choke which followed these few words which made the doctor stare a moment, then open his lips to speak and then desist with a hasty glance at Edgar? I had myself felt the shiver of some new fear at her manner and the unconscious emphasis she had given to that word appearance. But was it the same fear which held him back from pursuing his inquiries, and led him to say instead:

"I should like to see that bottle. No," he remonstrated, as Orpha started to accompany him. "You are a brave girl, but it is not for your physician to abuse that bravery. Wealthy will go up with me. Meantime, let Edgar take you away to some spot where you can rest till I come back."

It was kindly meant but oh, how hard I felt it to see these two draw off like accepted lovers; and with what joy I beheld them stop, evidently at a word from her, and seat themselves on one of the leather-covered lounges drawn up against the wall well within the sight of every one there.

I could rest, with these two sitting thus in full view—rest in the present; the future must take care of itself.

The result of the doctor's visit to the room above was evident in the increased gravity he showed on his return. He had little to say beyond enjoining upon Edgar and Orpha the necessity for a delay in the funeral services and a suggestion that we separate at once for the night and get what sleep we could. He would send a man to sit by the dead and if we would control ourselves sufficiently not to discuss this unhappy event all might yet be well.

The picture he made with Orpha as he took his leave of her at the door remains warm in my memory. She had begun to droop and he saw it. To comfort her he took her two hands in his and drew them to his breast while he talked to her, softly but firmly. As I saw the confidence with which she finally received his admonitions, I blessed him in my heart; though with a man's knowledge of men I perceived that his endeavor to give comfort sprang from sympathy rather than conviction. Tragedy was in the house, veiled and partially hidden, but waiting—waiting for the full recognition which the morrow must bring. A shadow with a monstrous substance behind it we would be called upon to face!

For one wild instant I wished that I had never left my native land; never seen the great Bartholomew; never felt the welcoming touch of Orpha's little hand on mine. As I knelt again in my open window a half hour later, the star which had shone in upon me two hours before had vanished in clouds.

Darkness was in the sky, darkness was in the house, darkness was in my own soul, and saddest of all, darkness was in that of our lovely and innocent Orpha.

CHAPTER 24

The next day was one of almost unendurable apprehension. Edgar, Orpha and myself could not face each other. The servants could not face us. If we moved from our rooms and by chance met in any of the halls we gazed at each other like specters and like specters flitted by without a word.

Orpha had a friend with her or I could not have stood it. For a long time I did not know who this friend was; then from some whisper I heard echoing up my convenient little stairway I learned that it was Lucy Colfax, Edgar's real love and Dr. Hunter's fiancée.

I did not like it. Such companionship was incongruous and unnatural; an insult to Orpha, though the dear child did not know it; but if she found relief in the presence of the one woman who, next to herself, stood in the closest relation to him who was gone, why should I complain so long as I myself could do nothing to comfort her or assuage her intolerable grief and the suspense of this terrible day.

I did not fear that Edgar would make a third. Neither he nor Orpha were ready for talk. None of us were till the doctor's report was known and the fearful question settled. I heard afterwards that Edgar had spent most of the time in the great room upstairs staring into the corners and seeming to ask from the walls the secret they refused to give.

I did the same in mine, only I paced the floor counting the slow hours as they went by. I am always restless under suspense and movement was my only solace.

What if the report should be one of which I dared not think—dared not mention to myself. What then? What if the roof of the house in which I stood should thunder in and the great stones of the walls fall to the ground and desolation ravish the spot where life, light and beauty reigned in such triumph. I would go down with it, that I knew; but would others? Would that one other whom to save—

Was it coming? The whole house had been so still that the least sound shook me. And it was a least sound. A low but persistent knocking at my door.

I was at the other end of the room and the distance from where I stood to the door looked interminable. I must know—know instantly; I could not wait another moment. Raising my voice, or endeavoring to, I called out:

"Come in."

It was a mere whisper; ghostly hands were about my throat. But that whisper was heard. I saw the door open and a quiet appearing man,—a complete stranger to me—stepped softly in.

I knew him for what he was before he spoke a word.

The police were in the house. There was no need to ask what the doctor's report had been.

CHAPTER 25

It is not my intention, and I am sure it is not your wish, that I should give all the details leading up to the inevitable inquest which followed the discoveries of the physicians and the action of the police.

In the first place my pride, possibly my self-respect held me back from any open attempt to acquaint myself with them. My interview with the Inspector of which I have just made mention, added much to his knowledge but very little to mine. To his questions I gave replies as truthful as they were terse. When I could, I confined myself to facts and never obtruded sentiment unless pressed as it were to the wall. He was calm, reasonable and not without consideration; but he got everything from me that he really wanted and at times forced me to lay my soul bare. In return, I caught, as I thought, faint glimmers now and then of how the mind of the police was working, only to find myself very soon in a fog where I could see nothing distinctly. When he left, the strongest impression which remained with me was that in the terrible hours I saw before me my greatest need would be courage and my best weapon under attack the truth as I knew it. In this conclusion I rested.

But not without a feeling which was as new to me as it was disturbing. I could not leave my room without sensing that somewhere, unseen and unheard, there lingered a presence from whose watchfulness I could not hope to escape. If in passing towards the main hall, I paused at the little circular staircase outside my door for one look down at the marble-floored pavement beneath, it was with the consciousness that an ear was somewhere near which recognized the cessation of my steps and waited to hear them recommence.

So in the big halls. Every door was closed, so slight the movement, so unfrequent any passing to and fro in the great house during the two days which elapsed before the funeral. But to heave a sigh or show in any way the character or trend of my emotions was just as impossible to me as though the walls were lined with spectators and every blank panel I passed was a sounding-board to some listener beyond.

Once only did I allow myself the freedom natural to a mourner in the house of the dead. Undeterred by an imaginary or even an actual encounter with unsympathetic servant or interested police operative, I left my room on the second day and went below; my goal, the court, my purpose, to stand once more by the remains of all that was left to me of my great-hearted uncle.

If I met any one on the way I have no memory of it. Had Orpha flitted by, or Edgar stumbled upon me at the turn of a corner, I might have stayed my step for an instant in outward deference to a grief which I recognized though I was not supposed to share it. But of others I took no account nor do I think I so much as lifted my eyes or glanced to right or left, when having crossed the tessellated pavement of the court, I paused by the huge mound of flowers beneath which lay what I sought, and thrusting my hand among these tokens of love and respect till I touched the wood beneath, swore that whatever the future held for me of shame or its reverse, I would act according to what I believed to be the will of him now dead but who for me was still a living entity.

This done I returned as I had come, only with a lighter step, for some portion of the peace for which I longed had fallen upon me with the utterance of that solemn promise.

I shall give but one incident in connection with the funeral. To my amazement I was allotted a seat in the carriage with Edgar. Orpha rode with some relatives of her mother—people I had never seen.

Though there was every chance for Edgar and myself to talk, nothing more than a nod passed between us. It was better so; I was glad to be left to my own thoughts. In the church I noted no one; but at the grave I became aware of an influence which caused me to turn my head a trifle aside and meet the steady look of a middle-aged man who was contemplating me very gravely.

Taking in his lineaments with a steady look of my own, I waited till I had the opportunity to point him out to one of the undertaker's men when I learned that he was a well known lawyer by the name of Jackson, and instantly became assured that he was no other than the man who had drawn up the second will—the will which I had been led to believe was strongly in my favor.

As his interest in me was to all appearance of a kindly sort untinged by suspicion, I felt that perhaps the odds after all, were not so greatly against me. Here was a man ready to help me, and should I need a friend, Providence had certainly shown me in what direction to look.

That night I slept the best of any night since the shock which had unhinged the nerves of every one in the house. I had ascertained that the full name of the lawyer who had been instrumental in drawing up the second will was Frederick W. Jackson, and while uttering this name more than once to myself, I fell into a dreamless slumber.

CHAPTER 26

You may recall that my first thought in contemplating the coil in which we had all been caught by the alleged disappearance of the will supposed to contain my uncle's final instructions, was that an inquiry including every person then in the house, should be made by some one in authority—Edgar, for instance—for the purpose of determining who was responsible for the same by a close investigation into the circumstances which made this crime possible. Little did I foresee at the time that such an inquiry, though shirked when it might have resulted in good, lay before us backed by the law and presided over by a public official.

But this fact was the first one to strike me, as convened in one of the large rooms in the City Hall, we faced the Coroner, in ignorance, most of us, of what such an inquiry portended and how much or how little of the truth it would bring to light.

I knew what I had to fear from my own story. I had told it once before and witnessed its effect. But how about Orpha's? And Edgar's? and that of the long row of servants, uneasy in body and perplexed in mind, from whose unwitting, if not unwilling lips some statement might fall which would fix suspicion or so shift it as to lead us into new lines of thought.

I had never been in a court-room before and though I knew that the formality as well as the seriousness of a trial would be lacking in a coroner's inquest, I shivered at the prospect, for some one of the witnesses soon to be heard had something to hide and whether the discovery of the same or its successful suppression was most to be desired who could tell.

The testimony of the doctors, as well as much of general interest in connection with the case, fell on deaf ears so far as I was concerned. Orpha, clad in her mourning garments and heavily veiled, held all my thoughts. Even the elaborate questioning of the two lawyers who drew up the wills, the similarity and dissimilarity of which undoubtedly lay at the bottom of the dreadful crime we were assembled to inquire into, left me cold. In a way I heard what had passed between each of these men and the testator on the day of the signing. How Mr. Dunn, who had attended to my uncle's law business for years, had recognized the desirability of his client making a new will under the changed conditions brought about by the reception into his family of a second nephew of whose claims upon a certain portion of his property he must wish to make some acknowledgment, received the detailed instructions sent him, with no surprise and followed them out to the letter, bringing the document with him for signature on the day and at the hour designated in the notes he had received from his client. The result was so satisfactory that no delay was made in calling in the witnesses to his signature and the signing of all three. What delay there was was caused by a little controversy in regard to his former will whose provisions differed in many respects from this one. Mr. Bartholomew wished to retain it,—the lawyer advised its destruction, the lawyer finally gaining the day. It being in Mr. Bartholomew's possession at the time, the witness expected it to be brought out and burned before his eyes; but it was not, Mr. Bartholomew merely promising that this should be done before the day ended. Whether or not he kept his word, the lawyer could not say from any personal knowledge.

Mr. Jackson had much the same story to tell. He too had received a letter from Mr. Bartholomew, asking his assistance in the making of a new will, together with instructions for the same, scrupulously written out in full detail by the testator's own hand on bits of paper carefully numbered. Asked to show these instructions, they were handed over and laid side by side with those already passed up by Mr. Dunn. I think they were both read; I hardly noticed; I only know that they were found to be exactly similar, with the one notable exception I need not mention. Of course the names of the witnesses differed.

What did reach my ear was a sentence uttered by Mr. Jackson as coming from my uncle when the will brought for his signature was unfolded before him. "You may be surprised," Uncle had said, "at the tenor of my bequests and the man I have chosen to bear the heavy burden of a complicated heritage. I know what I am doing and all I ask of you and the two witnesses you have been kind enough to bring here from your office is silence till the hour comes when it will be your business to speak."

This created a small hubbub among the people assembled, to many of whom it was probably the first word they had ever heard in my favor. During it and the sounding of the gavel calling them to order, my attention naturally was drawn in the direction of these men and women to whom my affairs seemed to be of so much importance. Alas! egotist that I was! They were not interested in me but in the case; and especially in anything which suggested an undue influence on my part over an enfeebled old man. Their antagonism to me was very evident, being heightened rather than lessened by the words just heard.

But there was one face I encountered which told a different story. Mr. Jackson had his own ideas and they were favorable to me. With a sigh of relief I turned my attention back to the heavily veiled figure of Orpha.

What was she thinking? How was she feeling? What interpretation might I reasonably put upon her movements, seeing that I lacked the key to her inmost mind. Witnesses came and went; but only as she swayed forward in her interest, or sank back in disappointment, did I take heed of their testimony or weigh in the scales of my own judgment the value or non-value of what they said.

For truth to say, I had heard nothing so far that was really new to me; nothing to solve certain points raised in my own mind; nothing that vied in interest with the slightest gesture or the least turn of the head of her who bore so patiently this marshalling before her in heavy phalanx facts so hideous as to bar out all sweeter memories.

But when in the midst of a sudden silence I heard my own name called, I started in dismay, all unprepared as I was to face this hostile throng. But it was not I whom they wanted, but Edgar. No one had glanced my way.

To the people of C— there was but one Edgar Quenton Bartholomew now that their chief citizen was gone.

The moment was a bitter one to me and I fear I showed it. But my good sense soon reasserted itself. Edgar was answering questions and I as well as others was there to learn; and to learn, I must listen.

"Your father and mother?"

"Both dead before I was five years old. Uncle Edgar then took me into his home."

"Adopted you?"

"Not legally. But in every other respect he was a father to me, and I hope I was a son to him. But no papers were ever drawn up."

"Did he ever call you Son?"

"I have no remembrance of his ever having done so. His favorite way of addressing me was Boy."

A slight tremulousness in speaking this endearing name added to its effect. I gripped at my heart beneath my coat. Our uncle had used the same word in speaking to me—once.

"Did he ever talk to you of his intentions in regard to his property, and if so when?"

"Often, before I became of age."

"And not since?"

"Oh, yes, since. But not so often. It did not seem necessary, we understood each other."

"Mr. Bartholomew, did it never strike you as peculiar that your uncle, having a daughter, should have chosen his brother's son as his heir?"

"No, sir. You see, as I said before, we understood each other."

"Understood? How?"

"We never meant, he nor I, that his daughter should lose anything by my inheritance of his money."

It was modestly, almost delicately said and had he loved her I could not but have admired him at that moment. But he did not love her, and to save my soul I could not help sending a glance her way. Would her head rise in proud acknowledgment of his worth or would it fall in shame at his hypocrisy? It fell, but then, I was honest enough to realize that the shame this bespoke might be that of a loving woman troubled at hearing her soul's most sacred secrets thus bared before the public.

Anxious for her as well as for myself, I turned my eyes upon the crowd confronting us, and wondered at the softened looks I saw there. He had touched a chord of fine emotion in the breasts of these curiosity-mongers. It was no new story to them. It had been common gossip for years that he was to marry Orpha and so make her and himself equal heirs of this great fortune. But his bearing as he spoke,—the magnetism which carried home his lightest word—gave to the well-known romance a present charm which melted every heart.

I felt how impotent any words of mine would be to stem the tide of sympathy that was bearing him on and soon would sweep me out of sight.

But as, overwhelmed by this prospect, I cowered low in my seat, the thought came that these men and women whose dictum I feared were not the arbiters of my destiny. And I took a look at the jury and straightened in my seat. Surely I saw more than one honest face among the twelve and two or three that were more than ordinarily intelligent. I should stand some chance with them.

Meanwhile another question had been put.

"Did your uncle at any time ever suggest to you that under a change of circumstances he might change his mind?"

"Never, till the day before he died."

"There was no break between you? No quarrel?"

"We did not always agree. I am not perfect—" With a smile he said this—"and it was only natural that he should express himself as not always satisfied with my conduct. But break? No. He loved me better than I deserved."

"You have a cousin, a gentleman of the same name, now a resident in your house. Did the difference of opinion between yourself and uncle to which you acknowledge occur since or prior to this cousin's entrance into the family?"

"Oh, I have memories of childish escapades not always approved of by my uncle. Nor have I always pleased him since I became a man. But the differences of opinion to which you probably allude became more frequent after the introduction amongst us of this second nephew; why, I hardly know. I do not blame my cousin for them."

The subtle inflection with which this last was said was worthy of a master of innuendo. It may have been unconscious; it likely was, for Edgar is naturally open in his attacks rather than subtle. But conscious or unconscious it caused heads to wag and sly looks to pass from one to another with many a knowing wink. The interloper was to blame of course though young Mr. Bartholomew was too good to say so!

The Coroner probably had his own private opinions on this subject, for taking no notice of these wordless suggestions he proceeded to ask:

"Was your cousin ever present when these not altogether agreeable discussions occurred between yourself and uncle?"

"He was not. Uncle was not the kind of man to upbraid me in the presence of a relative. He thought I showed a growing love of money without much recognition of what it was really good for."

"Ah! I see. Then that was the topic of these unfortunate conversations between you, and not the virtues or vices of your cousin."

"We had one, perhaps two conversations on that subject; but many, many others on matters far from personal in which there was nothing but what was agreeable and delightful to us both."

"Doubtless; what I want to bring out is whether from anything your uncle ever said to you, you had any reason to fear that you had been or might be supplanted in your uncle's regard by this other man of his and your name. In other words whether your uncle ever intimated that he and not you might be made the chief beneficiary in a new will."

"He never said it previous to the time I have mentioned." There was a fiery look in Edgar's eye as he emphasized this statement by a sharpness of tone strangely in contrast to the one he had hitherto used. "What he may have thought, I have no means of knowing. It was for him to judge between us. "

"Then, there has always existed the possibility of such a change? You must have known this even if you failed to talk on the subject."

"Yes, I sometimes thought my uncle was moved by a passing impulse to make such a change; but I never believed it to be more than a passing impulse. He showed me too much affection. He spoke too frequently of days when I studied under his eye and took my pleasure in his company."

"You acknowledge, then, that lately you yourself began to doubt his constancy to the old idea. Will you say what first led you to think that what you had regarded as a momentary impulse was strengthening into a positive determination?"

"Mr. Coroner, if you will pardon me I must take exception to that word positive. He could never have been positive at any time as to what he would finally do. Else why two wills? It was what I heard the servants say on my return from one of my absences which first made me question whether I had given sufficient weight to the possibility of my cousin's influence over Uncle being strong and persistent enough to drive him into active measures. I allude of course to the visit paid him by his lawyer and the witnessing on the part of his man Clarke and his nurse Wealthy to a document they felt sure was a will. As it was well known throughout the house that one had already been drawn up in full accordance with the promises so often made me, they showed considerable feeling, and it was only natural that this should arouse mine, especially as that whole day's proceedings, the coming of a second lawyer with two men whom nobody knew, was never explained or even alluded to in any conversation I afterwards held with my uncle. I thought it all slightly alarming but still I held to my faith in him. He was a sick man and might have crotchets."

"At what time and from whom did you definitely hear the truth about that day's proceedings—that two wills had been drawn up, alike in all respects save that in one you were named as the chief beneficiary and in the other your cousin from England?"

At this question, which evidently had power to trouble him, Edgar lost for the first time his air of easy confidence. Did he fear that he was about to incur some diminution of the good feeling which had hitherto upheld him in any statement he chose to make? I watched him very closely to see. But his answer hardly enlightened me.

The question, if you will remember, was when and where he received definite confirmation of what had been told him concerning two wills.

"In my uncle's room the night before he died," was his reply, uttered with a gloom wholly unnatural to him even in a time of trouble. "He had wished to see me and we were talking pleasantly enough, when he suddenly changed his tone and I heard what he had done and how my future hung on the whim of a moment."

"Can you repeat his words?"

"I cannot. The impression they made is all that is left me. I was too agitated—too much taken aback—for my brain to work clearly or my memory to take in more than the great fact. You see it was not only my position as heir to an immense fortune I saw threatened; but the dearer hope it involved and what was as precious as all the rest, the loss of my past as I had conceived it, for I had truly believed that I stood next to his daughter in my uncle's affections; too close indeed for any such tampering with my future prospects."

He was himself again; shaken with feeling but winsome in voice, manner and speech. And it was the sincerity of his feeling which made him so. He had truly loved his uncle. No one could doubt that, not even myself who had truly loved him also.

"On what terms did you leave him? Surely you can remember that?"

Edgar's eye flashed. As I noted it and the resolution which was fast overcoming the sadness which had distinguished his features up till now, I held my breath in apprehension, for here was something to fear.

"When I left him it was with a mind much more at ease than when he first showed me these two wills. For my faith in him had come back. He would burn one of those wills before he died, but it would not be the one which would put to shame by its destruction, him who had been as a child to him from the day of his early orphanage."

The Coroner himself was startled by the effect made by these words upon the crowd, and probably blamed his own leniency in allowing this engaging witness to express himself so fully.

In a tone which sounded sharp enough in contrast to the mellow one which had preceded it, he said:

"That is what you thought. We had rather listen to facts."

Edgar bowed, still gracious, still the darling of the men and women ranged before him, many of whom remembered his boyhood; while I sat rigid, realizing how fully I was at the mercy of his attractions and would continue to be till I had an opportunity to speak, and possibly afterwards, for prejudice raises a wall which nothing but time can batter down.

And Orpha? What of her? How was she taking all this? In my anxiety, I cast one look in her direction. To my astonishment she sat unveiled and was gazing at Edgar with an intentness which slowly but surely forced his head to turn and his eye to seek hers. An instant thus, then she pulled down her veil, and the flush just rising to his cheek was lost again in pallor.

Unconsciously the muscles of my hands relaxed; for some reason life had lost some of the poignant terror it had held for me a moment before. A drowning man will catch at straws; so will a lover; and I was both.

In the absorption which followed this glimpse of Orpha's face so many days denied me, I lost the trend of the next few questions, and only realized that we were approaching the crux of the situation when I heard:

"You did not visit him again?"

"No."

"Where did you go?"

"To my room."

"Will you state to the jury just where your room is located?"

"On the same floor as Uncle's, only further front and on the opposite side of the hall."

"We have here a chart of that floor. Will you be good enough to step to it and indicate the two rooms you mention?"

Here, at a gesture from the Coroner, an official drew a string attached to a roll suspended on one of the walls and a rudely drawn diagram, large enough to he seen from all parts of the court-room, fell into view.[1]

Edgar was handed a stick with which he pointed out the two doors of his uncle's room and those of his own.

What was coming?

"Mr. Bartholomew, will you now tell the jury what you did on returning to your room?"

"Nothing. I threw myself into a chair and just waited."

"Waited for what?"

---

[1] A reduced copy of the plan will be found facing the title page of this book.

"To hear my cousin enter my uncle's room."

The bitterness with which he said this was so deftly hidden under an assumption of casual rejoinder, as only to be detected by one who was acquainted with every modulation of his fine voice.

"And did you hear this?"

"Very soon; as soon as he could come up from the lower hall where Clarke, my uncle's man, had been sent to summon him."

"If you heard this, you must also have heard when he left your uncle's room."

"I did."

"Was the interview a long one?"

"I was sitting in front of the clock on my mantel-piece. He was in there just twenty minutes."

I felt my breast heave, and straightening myself instinctively I met the concentrated gaze of a hundred pair of eyes leveled like one against me.

Did I smile? I felt like it; but if I did it must have expressed the irony with which I felt the meshes of the net in which I was caught tighten with every word which this man spoke.

The Coroner, who was the only person in the room who had not looked my way, went undeviatingly on.

"In what part of the house does this gentleman of whom we are speaking have his room?"

"On the same floor as mine; but further back at the end of a short hall."

"Will you take the pointer from the officer and show the location of the second Mr. Bartholomew's room?"

The witness did so.

"Did you hear in which direction your cousin went on leaving your uncle? Did he go immediately to his room?"

"He may have done so, but if he did, he did not stay long, for very soon I heard him return and proceed directly down stairs."

"How long was he below?"

"A long time. I had moved from my seat and my eye was no longer on the clock so I cannot say how long."

"Did you hear him when he came up for a second time?"

"Yes; he is not a light stepper."

"Where did he go? Directly to his room?"

"No, he stopped on the way."

"How, stopped on the way?"

"When he reached the top of the stairs he paused like one hesitating. But not for long. Soon I heard him coming in the direction of my room, pass it by and proceed to our uncle's door—the one in front so little-used as to be negligible—where he lingered so long that I finally got up and peered from my own doorway to see what he was doing?"

"Was the hall dark?"

"Very."

"Darker than usual?"

"Yes, much."

"How was that? What had happened?"

"The electric light usually kept burning at my end of the hall had been switched off."

"When? Before your cousin came up or after?"

"I do not know. It simply was not burning when I opened my door."

"Will you say from which of the doors in your suite you were looking?"

"From the one marked C on the chart."

"That, as the jury can see if they will look, is diagonally opposite the one at which the witness had heard his cousin pause. Will the witness now state if the hall was too dark at the time he looked out for him to see whether or not any one stood at his uncle's door?"

"No, it was not too dark for that, owing to the light which shone in from the street through the large window you see there."

"Enough, you say, to make your uncle's door visible?"

"Quite enough."

"And what did you see there? Your cousin standing?"

"No; he was gone."

"How gone? Could he not have been in your uncle's room?"

"Not then."

"Why do you say 'not then'?"

"Because while I looked I could hear his footsteps at the other end of the house rounding the corner where the main hall meets the little one in which his room is situated."

My God! I had forgotten all this. I had been very anxious to know how Uncle had fared since I left him in such a state of excitement; whether he were sleeping or awake, and hoped by listening I should hear Wealthy's step and so judge how matters were within. But a meaning sinister if not definite had been given to this natural impulse by the way Edgar's voice fell as he uttered that word stopped; and from that moment I recognized him for my enemy, either believing in my guilt or wishing others to; in which latter case, it was for me to fight my battle with every weapon my need called for. But the conflict was not yet and "Patience" must still be my watch-word. But I held my breath as I waited for the next question.

"You say that you heard him moving down the hall. You did not see him at your uncle's door?"

"No, I did not."

"But you are confident he was there, previous to your looking out?"

"I am very sure that he was; my ear seldom deceives me."

"Mr. Bartholomew, will you think carefully before you answer the following question. Was there any circumstance connected with this matter which will enable you to locate the hour at which you heard your cousin pass down the hall?"

He hesitated; he did not want to answer. Why? I would have given all that I possessed to know; but he only said:

"I did not look at my watch; I did not need to. The clock was striking three."

"Three! The jury will note the hour."

Why did he say that?—the jury will note the hour? My action was harmless. Everything I did that night was harmless. What did he mean then by the hour? The mystery of it troubled me—a mystery he was careful to leave for the present just where it was.

Returning to his direct investigation, the coroner led the witness back to the time preceding his entrance into the hall. "You were listening from your room; that room was dark, you were no longer watching the clock which had not yet struck; yet perhaps you can give us some idea of how long your cousin lingered at your uncle's door before starting down the hall."

"No, I should not like to do that."

"Five minutes?"

"I cannot say."

"Long enough to have entered that room and come out again?"

"You ask too much. I am not ready to swear to that."

"Very good; I will not press you!" But the suggestion had been made. And for a purpose—a purpose linked with the mystery of which I have just spoken. Glancing at Mr. Jackson, I saw him writing in his little book. He had noted this too. I was not alone in my apprehension which, like a giant shadow thrown from some unknown quarter, was reaching slowly over to envelop me. When I was ready to listen again, it was to hear:

"What did you do then?"

"I went to bed."

"Did you see or hear anything more of your cousin that night?"

"No, not till the early morning when we were all roused by the news which Wealthy brought to every door, that Uncle was very much worse and that the doctor should be sent for."

"Tell us where it was you met him then."

"In the hall near Uncle's door—the one marked 2 on the chart."

"How did he look? Was there anything peculiar in his appearance or manner?"

"He was fully dressed."

"And you?"

"I had had no time to do more than wrap a dressing gown about me."

"At what time was this? You remember the hour no doubt?"

"Half past four in the morning; any one can tell you that."

"And he was fully dressed. In morning clothes or evening?"

"In the ones he wore to dinner the night before."

It was true; I had not gone to bed that night. There was too much on my mind. But to them it would look as if I had sat up ready for the expected alarm.

"Was he in these same clothes when you finally entered your uncle's room?"

"Certainly; there was no time then for changing."

These questions might have been addressed to me instead of to him. They would have been answered with as much truth; but the suggestiveness would have been lacking and in this I recognized my second enemy. I now knew that the Coroner was against me.

A few persons there may have recognized this fact also. But they were all too much in sympathy with Edgar to resent it. I made no show of doing so nor did I glance again at Orpha to see the effect on her of these attacks leveled at me with so much subtlety. I felt, in the humiliation of the moment, that unless I stood cleared of every suspicion, I could never look her again in the face.

Meanwhile the inquiry had reached the event for which all were waiting—

the destruction of the one will and the acknowledgment by the dying man that the envelope which held the other was empty.

"Were you near enough to see the red mark on the one he had ordered burned?"

"Yes; I took note of it."

"Had you seen it before?"

"Yes; when, in the interview of which I have spoken, my uncle showed me the two envelopes and informed me of their several contents."

"Did he tell you or did you learn in any way which will was in the one marked with red?"

"No. I did not ask him and he did not say."

"So when you saw it burning you did not know with certainty whether it was the will making you or your cousin his chief heir?"

"I did not."

He said it firmly, but he said it with effort. Again, why?

The time to consider this was not now, for at this reply, expected though it was, a universal sigh swept through the house, carrying my thoughts with it. Emotion must have its outlet. The echo in my own breast was a silent one, springing from sources beyond the ken of the simple onlooker. We were approaching a critical part of the inquiry. The whereabouts of the missing document must soon come up. Should I be obliged to listen to further insinuations such as had just been made? Was it his plan to show that I was party to a fraud and knew where the missing will lay secreted,—where it would always lie secreted because it was in his favor and not in mine? It was possible; anything was possible. If I were really wise I would prepare myself for the unexpected; for the unexpected was what I probably should be called upon to face.

Yet it was not so, or I did not think it so, in the beginning.

Asked to describe his uncle's last moments he did so shortly, simply, feelingly.

Then came the question for which I waited.

"Your uncle died, then, without a sign as to where the remaining will was to be found?"

"He did not have time. Death came instantly, leaving the words unsaid. It was a great misfortune."

With a gesture of reproof, for he would not have it seem that he liked these comments, the Coroner pressed eagerly on:

"What of his looks? Did his features betray any emotion when he found that he could no longer speak?"

Edgar hesitated. It was the first time we had seen him do so and my heart beat in anticipation of a lie.

But again I did him an injustice. He did not want to answer—that we could all see—but when he did, he spoke the truth.

"He looked frightened, or so I interpreted his expression; and his head moved a little. Then all was over."

In the silence which followed, a stifled sob was heard. We all knew from whom it came and every eye turned to the patient little figure in black who up till now had kept such strong control over her feelings.

"If Miss Bartholomew would like to retire into the adjoining room she is at liberty to do so," came from the Coroner's seat.

But she shook her head, murmuring quietly:

"Thank you, I will stay."

I blessed her in my heart. Still neutral. Still resolute to hear and know all. The inquiry went on.

"Mr. Bartholomew, did you search for that will?"

"Thoroughly. In a haphazard way at first, expecting to find it in some of the many drawers in his room. But when I did not, I went more carefully to work, I and my two faithful servants, who having been in personal attendance upon him all through his illness, knew his habits and knew the room. But even then we found nothing in any way suggestive of the document we were looking for."

"And since?"

"The room has been in the hands of the police. I have not heard that they have been any more successful."

There were more questions and more answers but I paid little attention to them. I was thinking of what had passed between the Inspector and myself at the time he visited me in my room. I have said little about it because a man is not proud of such an experience; but in the quiet way in which this especial official worked, he had made himself very sure before he left me that this document was neither on my person nor within the four walls of the room itself. This had been a part of the search. I tingled yet whenever I recalled the humiliation of that hour. I tingled at this moment; but rebuked myself as the mystery of the whole proceeding got a stronger hold upon my mind. Not with me, not with him, but somewhere! When would they reach the point where perhaps the solution lay? Five hours had elapsed between the time I left uncle and the rousing of the house at Wealthy's hurried call. What had happened during those hours? Who could tell the tale—the whole tale, since manifestly that had never been fully related. Clarke? Wealthy? I knew what they had told the police, what they had confided to each other concerning their experience in the sickroom; but under oath, and with the shadow of crime falling across the lesser mystery what might not come to light under the probe of this prejudiced but undoubtedly honest Coroner?

CHAPTER 27

My impatience grew with every passing moment, but fortunately it was not to be tried much longer, for I soon had the satisfaction of seeing Edgar leave the witness chair and Clarke, as we called him, take his seat there.

This old and tried servant of a man exacting as he was friendly and generous as he was just, had always inspired me with admiration, far as I was from being in his good books. Had he liked me I would have felt myself strong in what was now a doubtful position. But devoted as he was to Edgar, I could not hope for any help from him save of the most grudging kind. I therefore sat unmoved and unexpectant while he took his oath and answered the few opening questions. They pertained mostly to the signing of the first will to which he had added his signature as witness. As nothing new was elicited this matter was soon dropped.

Other points of interest shared the same fate. He could substantiate the testimony of others, but he had nothing of his own to impart. Would it be the same when we got to his final attendance on his master—the last words uttered between them—the final good-night?

The Coroner himself seemed to be awake to the full importance of what this witness might have to disclose, for he scrutinized him earnestly before saying:

"We will now hear, as nearly as you can recall, what passed between you and your sick master on the night which proved to be his last? Begin at the beginning—that is, when you were sent to summon one or other of his two nephews to Mr. Bartholomew's room."

"Pardon, sir, but that was not the beginning. The beginning was when Mr. Bartholomew, who to our astonishment had eaten his supper in his chair by the fireside, drew a small key from the pocket in his dressing-gown and, handing it to me, bade me unlock the drawer let into the back of his bedstead and bring him the two big envelopes I should find there."

"You are right, that is the beginning. Go on with your story."

"I had never been asked to unlock this drawer before; he had always managed to do it himself; but I had no difficulty in doing it or in bringing him the papers he had asked for. I just lifted out the whole batch, and laying them down in his lap, asked him to pick out the ones he wanted."

"Did he do it?"

"Yes, immediately."

"Before you moved away?"

"Yes, sir."

"Then you caught a glimpse of the papers he selected?"

"I did, sir. I could not help it. I had to wait, for he wished me to relieve him of the ones he didn't want."

"And you did this?"

"Yes; I took them from his hand and laid them on the table to which he pointed."

"Now for the ones he kept. Describe them."

"Two large envelopes, sir, larger than the usual legal size, brown in color, I should say, and thick with the papers that were in them."

"Had you ever seen any envelopes like these before?"

"Yes, on Mr. Bartholomew's desk the day I was called in to witness his signature."

"Very good. There were two of them, you say?"

"Yes, sir, two."

"Were they alike?"

"Exactly, I should say."

"Any mark on either one?"

"Not that I observed, sir. But I only saw the face of one of them and that was absolutely blank."

"No red marks on either."

"Not that I saw, sir."

"Very good. Proceed, Mr. Clarke. What did Mr. Bartholomew say, after you had laid the other papers aside?"

"He bade me look for Mr. Edgar; said he was in a hurry and wanted to see him at once."

"Was that all?"

"Yes, sir, he was not a man of many words. Besides, I left the room immediately and did not enter it again till Mr. Edgar left him."

"Where were you when he did this?"

"At the end of the hall talking to Wealthy. There is a little cozy corner there where she sits and where I sometimes waited when I was expecting Mr. Bartholomew's ring."

"Did you see Mr. Edgar, as you call him, when he came out?"

"Yes, sir; crossing over to his room."

"And what did you do after that?"

"Went immediately to Mr. Bartholomew to see if he was wishing to go to bed. But he was not. On the contrary, he had another errand for me. He wanted to see his other nephew. So I went below searching for him."

"Was Mr. Bartholomew still sitting by the fire when you went in?"

"He was."

"With the two big envelopes in his hands?"

"Not that I noted, sir; but he had pockets in his gown large enough to hold them and they might have been in one of these."

"Never mind the might have beens; just the plain answer, Mr. Clarke."

"Yes, sir. Excuse me, sir. Feeling afraid that he would get very tired sitting up so long, I hurried downstairs, found Mr. Quenton, as we call him, in the library and brought him straight up. Then I went back to Wealthy."

"Is there a clock in the cozy corner?"

"There is, sir."

"Did you look at it as you came and went?"

"I did this time."

"Why this time?"

"First, because I was anxious for Mr. Bartholomew not to tire himself too much and—and—"

"Go on; we want the whole truth, Mr. Clarke."

"I was curious to see whether Mr. Bartholomew would keep Mr. Quenton any longer than he did Mr. Edgar."

"And did he?"

"A little, sir."

"Did you and the woman Wealthy exchange remarks upon this?"

"We—we did, sir."

At this admission, I took a quick look at Mr. Jackson and was relieved to see him make another entry in his little book. He had detected, here, as well as I, an opening for future investigation. I heard him, as it were in advance, putting this suggestive query to the present witness: "What had you and Wealthy been saying on this subject?" I know very little of courts or the usages of court procedure, but I know that I should have put this question if I had been conducting this examination.

The Coroner evidently was not of my mind, which certainly was not strange, seeing where his sympathies were.

"What do you mean by little?"

"Ten minutes."

"By the clock?"

"Yes, sir," said rather sheepishly.

"Proceed; what happened next?"

"I went immediately to Mr. Bartholomew's room, thinking that of course he would be ready for me now. But he was not. Instead, he bade me leave him and not come back for a full half hour, and not to allow any one else to disturb him. I was to give the same order to Wealthy."

"And did you?"

"Yes, sir; and left her on the watch."

"And where did you go?"

"To my room for a smoke."

"Were you concerned at leaving Mr. Bartholomew alone for so long a time?"

"Yes, sir; we never liked to do that. He had grown to be too feeble. But he was not a man you could disobey even for his own good."

"Did you spend the whole half hour in smoking?"

"Yes, sir."

"Not leaving your room at all?"

"Oh, I left my room several times, going no further, though, than the end of my small hall."

"Why did you do this?"

"Because Mr. Bartholomew had been so very peremptory about anybody coming to his room. I had every confidence in Wealthy, but I could not help going now and then to see if she was still on the watch."

"With what result?"

"She was always there. I did not speak to her, not wishing her to know that I was keeping tabs on her. But each time I went I could see the hem of her dress protruding from behind the screen and knew that she, like myself, was waiting for the half hour to be up. As soon as it was, I stepped boldly down the hall, telling Wealthy as I passed that I should make short work of putting the old gentleman to bed and for her to be ready to follow me in a very few minutes. And I kept my word. Mr. Bartholomew was still sitting in his chair when I went in. He had the two documents in his hand and asked me to place them, together with the other papers, on the small stand at the side of the bed. And there they stayed up to the time I gave place to Wealthy. This is all I have to tell about that night. I went from his room to mine and slept till we were all wakened by the ill news that Mr. Bartholomew had been taken worse and was rapidly sinking."

There was an instant's lull during which I realized my own disappointment. I had heard nothing that I had not known before. Then the Coroner said:

"Did your duties in Mr. Bartholomew's room during these months of illness include at any time the handling of his medicines?"

"No, sir."

"Did you ever visit his medicine cabinet, or take anything from its shelves?"

"No, sir."

"You must often have poured him out a glass of water?"

"Oh, yes, I have done that."

"Did you do so on that night? Think carefully before you answer."

"I do not need to, for I am very sure that I handed him nothing. I do not even remember seeing the usual pitcher and glass anywhere in the room."

"Not on the stand at his side?"

"No, sir."

'Nothing of the kind near him?"

"Not that I saw, sir."

"Very good; you may step down."

CHAPTER 28

Wealthy was the next witness summoned, and her appearance on the stand caused a flutter of excitement to pass from end to end of the well packed room. All knew that from her, if from anybody, enlightenment must come as to what had taken place in the few fatal hours which had elapsed after Clarke's departure from the room. Would she respond to our hopes? Would she respond to mine? Or would she leave the veil half raised from sheer inability to lift it higher?

Conscious that the blood was leaving my cheeks and fearful that she could not hold the attention of the crowd from myself, I sought for relief in the face of Edgar. He must know her whole story. Also whom it threatened. Would I be able to read in his lip and eye, ordinarily so expressive, what we had to expect?

No. He was giving nothing away. He was not even looking with anything like attention at anybody; not even my way as I had half expected. The mobile lip was straight; the eye, usually sparkling with intelligence, fixed to the point of glassiness.

I took in that look well; the time might come when I should find it wise to recall it.

Wealthy is a good-looking woman, with that kind of comeliness which speaks of a warm heart and motherly instincts. Seen in the home, whether at work or at rest, she was the embodiment of all that insured comfort and ease to those under her care. She was more than a servant, more than nurse, and as such was regarded with favor by every one in the house, even by my poor unappreciated self.

In public and before the eyes of this mixed assemblage she showed the same pleasing characteristics. I began to breathe more easily. Surely she might be trusted not to be swayed sufficiently by malice, either to evade or color the truth. For all her love for Edgar, she will be true to herself. She cannot help it with that face and demeanor.

The Coroner showed her every consideration. This was but due to the grief she so resolutely endeavored to keep under. All through the opening questions and answers which were mainly corroborative of much that had gone before, he let her sometimes garrulous replies pass without comment, though the spectators frequently evinced impatience in their anxiety to reach the point upon which the real mystery hung.

It came at last and was welcomed by a long drawn breath from many an overburdened breast.

"Mr. Clarke has said that on leaving Mr. Bartholomew's room for the last time that night, he saw the two envelopes about which so much has been said still lying on the little stand drawn up by the bedside. Were they there when you went into the room?"

"Yes, sir; I noticed them immediately. The stand is very near the door by which I usually enter, and it was a matter of habit with me to take a look at my patient before busying myself with making my final preparations for the night. As I did this, I observed some documents lying there and as it was never his custom to leave business papers lying about I asked him if he would not like to have me put them away for him. But he answered no, not to bother, for there was something he wanted me to get for him which would take me down into Miss Orpha's room, and as it was growing late I had better go at once. 'Mind you,' he said, 'she is but a girl and may not remember where she has put it; but, if so, she must look for it and you are not to come back until she has found it, if you have to stay an hour.'

"As the thing he wanted was a little white silk shawl which had been her mother's, and as the dear child did not know exactly in which of two or three chests she had hidden it, it did take time to find it, and it was with a heart panting with anxiety that I finally started to go back, knowing what a hard evening he had had and how often the doctor had told us that he was to be kept quiet and above all never to be left very long alone. But I was more frightened yet when I got about halfway upstairs, for, for the first time since I have lived in the house, though I have been up and down that flight hundreds of times, I felt the Presence—"

"You may cut that out," came kindly but peremptorily from the Coroner, probably to the immense disappointment of half the people there.

The Presence on that night!

I myself felt a superstitious thrill at the thought, though I had laughed a dozen times at this old wives' tale.

"Tell your story straight," admonished the Coroner.

"I will, sir. I mean to, sir. I only wanted to explain how I came to stumble in rushing up those stairs and yet how quick I was to stop when I heard something on reaching the top which frightened me more than any foolish fancy. This was the sound of a click in the hall towards the front. Some one was turning the key in Mr. Bartholomew's door—the one nearest the street. As this door is only used on occasion it startled me. Besides, who would do such a thing? There was no one in the hall, for I ran quickly the length of it to see. So it must have been done from the inside and by whom then but by Mr. Bartholomew himself. But I had left him in bed! Here was a coil; and strong as I am I found myself catching at the banisters for support, for I did not understand his locking the door when he was in the room alone. However, he may have had his reasons, and rather ashamed of my agitation I was hurrying back to the other door when I heard a click there, and realized that the doors were being unlocked and not locked; —that he was expecting me and was making the way open for me to come in. Had I arrived a few minutes sooner I should not have been able to enter. It gave me a turn. My sick master shut up there alone! Locked in by himself! I had never known him to do such a thing all the time he was ill, and I had to quiet myself a bit before I dared go in. When I did, he was lying in bed looking very white but peaceful enough; more peaceful indeed than he had at any time that day. 'Is that you, Wealthy?' he asked. 'Where is the little shawl? Give it to me.' I handed it to him and he laid it, folded as it was, against his cheek. I felt troubled, I hardly knew why and stood looking at him. He smiled and glancing at the little pile of documents lying on the stand told me that I could put them away now. 'Here is the key,' he said; I took it from his hand after seeing him draw it from under the pillow. I had often used it for him. Unlocking the drawer which was set into the headboard of his bed where it jutted into the alcove, I reached for the papers and locked them up in the drawer and handed him back the key. 'Thank you,' he said and turned his face from the light. It was the signal for me to drop the curtain hanging at that side of the bed. This I did—"

"One moment. In handling the papers you speak of did you notice them particularly?"

"Not very, sir. I remember that the top one was in a dark brown envelope and bulky."

"Which side was up?"

"The flap side."

"Sealed?"

"No, open; that is loose, not fastened down."

"You noticed that?"

"I couldn't help it. It was right under my eyes."

"Did you notice anything else? That there was a second envelope in the pile similar to the one on top."

"I cannot say that I did. The papers were all hunched, you see, and I just lifted them quickly and put them in the drawer."

"Why quickly?"

"Mr. Bartholomew was looking at me, sir."

"Then you did not note that there was another envelope in that pile, just like the top one, only empty?"

"I did not, sir."

"Very good. You may go on now. You dropped the curtain. What did you do next?"

"I prepared his soothing medicine." Her voice fell and an expression of great trouble crossed her countenance. "I always had this ready in case he should grow restless in the night."

"A soothing medicine! Where was that kept?"

"With the rest of the medicines in the cabinet built into the small passageway leading to the upper door."

"And you went there for the soothing medicine. At about what time?"

"Not far from eleven o'clock, sir: I remember thinking as I passed by the mantel clock how displeased Dr. Cameron would be if he knew that Mr. Bartholomew's light was not yet out."

"Go on; what about the medicine? Did you give it to him every night?"

"Not every night, but frequently. I always had it ready."

"Will you step down a minute? I want to ask Dr. Cameron a few questions about this soothing medicine."

The interruption was welcome; we all needed a moment's respite. Dr.

Cameron was again sworn. He had given his testimony at length earlier in the day but it had been mainly in reference to a very different sort of medicine, and it was of this simpler and supposedly very innocent mixture that the Coroner wished to learn a few facts.

Dr. Cameron was very frank with his replies. Told just what it was; what the dose consisted of and how harmless it was when given according to directions. "I have never known," he added, "of Mrs. Starr ever making any mistake in preparing or administering it. The other medicine of which I have already given a detailed account I have always prepared myself."

"It is of that other medicine taken in connection with this one of which I wish to ask. Say the two were mixed what would be the result?"

"The powerful one would act, whatever it was mixed with."

"How about the color? Would one affect the other?"

"If plenty of water were used, the change in color would hardly be perceptible."

"Thank you, doctor; we can release you now."

The doctor stepped down, whereupon a recess was called, to the disappointment and evident chagrin of a great many.

CHAPTER 29

The mood of the Coroner changed with the afternoon session. He was curter in speech and less patient with the garrulity of his witnesses. Perhaps he dreaded the struggle which he foresaw awaited him.

He plunged at once into the topic he had left unfinished and at the precise point where he had left off. Wealthy had resumed her place on the stand.

"And where did you put this soothing mixture after you had prepared it?"

"Where I always did—on the shelf hanging in the corner on the further side of the bed—the side towards the windows. I did this so that it would not be picked up by mistake for a glass of water left on his stand."

"Tell that to the jury again, Mrs. Starr. That the soothing medicine of which you speak was in a glass on the shelf we all can see indicated on the chart above your head, and plain water in a glass standing on the table on the near side of the bed."

"Excuse me, Doctor Jones, I did not mean to say that there was any glass of water on the small stand that night. There was not. He did not seem to want it, so I left the water in a pitcher on the table by the hearth. I only meant that it being my usual custom to have it there I got in the habit of putting anything in the way of medicine as far removed from it as possible."

"Mrs. Starr, when did you prepare this soothing medicine as you call it?"

"Soon after I entered the room."

"Before Mr. Bartholomew slept?"

"Oh, yes, sir."

"Tell how you did it, where you did it and what Mr. Bartholomew said while you were doing it—that is, if he said anything at all."

"The bottle holding this medicine was kept, as I have already said, with all the other medicines, in the cabinet hanging in the upper passageway." Every eye rose to the chart. "The water in a pitcher on the large table to the left of the fire-place. Filling a glass with this water which I had drawn myself, I went to the medicine cabinet and got the bottle containing the drops the doctor had ordered for this purpose, and carrying it over to the table, together with the medicine-dropper, added the customary ten drops to the water and put the bottle back in the cabinet and the glass with the medicine in it on the shelf. Mr. Bartholomew's face was turned my way and he naturally followed my movements as I passed to and fro; but he showed no especial interest in them, nor did he speak."

"Was this before or after you dropped the curtain on the other side of the bed."

"After."

"The bed, I have been given to understand, is surrounded on all sides by heavy curtains which can be pulled to at will. Was the one you speak of the only one to be dropped or pulled at night?"

"Usually. You see Miss Orpha's picture hangs between the windows and was company for him if he chanced to wake in the night."

Again that sob, but fainter than before and to me very far off. Or was it that I felt so far removed myself— pushed aside and back from the grief and sufferings of this family?

The heads which turned at this low but pathetic sound were soon turned back again as the steady questioning went on: "You speak of going to the medicine cabinet. It was your business, no doubt, to go there often."

"Very often; I was his nurse, you see."

"There was another bottle of medicine kept there—the one labeled 'Dangerous'?"

"Yes, sir."

"Did you see that bottle when you went for the soothing mixture you speak of?"

"No, sir." This was very firmly said. "I wasn't thinking of it, and the bottle I wanted being in front I just pulled it out and never looked at any other."

"This other bottle—the dangerous one—where was that kept?''

"Way back behind several others. I had put it there when the doctor told us that we were not to give him any more of that especial medicine without his orders."

"If you went to this cabinet so often you must have a very good idea of just how it looked inside."

"I have, sir," her voice falling a trifle—at least, I thought I detected a slight change in it as if the emotion she had so bravely kept under up to this moment was beginning to make itself felt.

"Then tell us if everything looked natural to you when you went to it this time; everything in order,—nothing displaced."

"I did not notice. I was too intent on what I was after. Besides, if I had—"

"Well, go on."

Her brows puckered in distress; and I thought I saw her hand tremble where it showed amid the folds of her dress. If no other man held his breath at that short interim in which not a sound was heard, I did. Something was about to fall from her lips—

But she was speaking.

"If I had observed any disorder such as you mention I should not have thought it at all strange. I am not the only one who had access to that cabinet. His daughter often went to it, and—and the young gentlemen, too."

"Both of them?"

"Yes, sir."

"What should take them there?"

Her head lifted, her voice steadied, she looked the capable, kindly person of a few moments ago. That thrill of emotion was gone; perhaps I have overemphasized it.

"We all worked together, sir. The young gentlemen, that is one or the other of them, often took my place in the room, especially at night, and Mr. Bartholomew, used to being waited on and having many wants, they had learned how to take care of him and give him what he called for."

"And this took them to the cabinet?"

"Undoubtedly; it held a great variety of things besides his medicines."

The Coroner paused. During the most trying moment of my life every eye in the room turned on me, not one on Edgar.

I bore it stoically; a feeling I endeavored to crush making havoc in my heart.

Then the command came:

"Continue with your story. You have given us the incidents of the night such as you observed them before Mr. Bartholomew slept; you will now relate what happened after."

Again I watched her hand. It had clenched itself tightly and then loosened as these words rang out from the seat of authority. The preparation for what she had to tell had been made; the time had now come for its relation. She began quietly, but who could tell how she would end.

"For an hour I kept my watch on the curtained side of the bed. It was very still in the room, so deathly still that after awhile I fell asleep in my chair. When I woke it was suddenly and with a start of fear. I was too confused at first to move and as I sat listening, I heard a slight sound on the other side of the bed, followed by the unmistakable one of a softly closing door. My first thought, of course, was for my patient and throwing the curtains aside, I looked through. The room was light enough, for one of the logs on the hearth had just broken apart, and the glow it made lit up Mr. Bartholomew's face and showed me that he was sleeping. Relieved at the sight, I next asked myself who could have been in the room at an hour so late, and what this person wanted. I was not frightened, now that I was fully awake, and being curious, nothing more, I drew the portiere from before the passage-way at my back and, stepping to the door beyond, opened it and looked out."

Here she became suddenly silent, and so intent were we all in anticipation of what her next words would reveal, that the shock caused by this unexpected break in her story, vented itself in a sort of gasp from the parched lips and throats of the more excitable persons present. It was a sound not often heard save on the theatrical stage at a moment of great suspense, and the effect upon the witness was so strange that I forgot my own emotion in watching her as she opened her lips to continue and then closed them again, with a pitiful glance at the Coroner.

He seemed to understand her and made a kindly effort to help her in this sudden crisis of feeling.

"Take your time, Mrs. Starr," he said. "We are well aware that testimony of this nature must be painful to you, but it is necessary and must be given. You opened the door and looked out. What did you see?"

"A man—or, rather, the shadow of a man outlined very dimly on the further wall of the hall."

"What man?"

"I do not know, sir."

She did; the woman was lying. No one ever looked as she did who was in doubt as to what she saw. But the Coroner intentionally or unintentionally blind to this very decided betrayal of her secret, still showed a disposition to help her.

"Was it so dark?"

"Yes, sir. The electrolier at the stair-head had been put out probably by him as he passed, for—"

It was a slip. I saw it in the way her face changed and her voice faltered as with one accord every eye in the assemblage before her turned quickly towards the chart.

I did not need to look. I knew that hall by heart. The electrolier she spoke of was nearer the back than the front; to put it out in passing, meant that the person stopping to extinguish it was heading towards the rear end of the hall. In other words, Clarke or myself. As it was not myself— But she must have thought it was, for when the Coroner, drawing the same conclusion, pressed her to describe the shadow and, annoyed at her vague replies, asked her point blank if it could be that of Clarke, she shook her head and finally acknowledged that it was much too slim.

"A man's, though?"

"Certainly, a man's."

"And what became of this shadow?"

"It was gone in a minute; disappeared at the turn of the wall."

She had the grace to droop her head, as if she realized what she was doing and took but little pleasure in it. My estimation of her rose on the instant; for she did not like me, was jealous of every kindness my uncle had shown me, and yet felt compunction over what she was thus forced into saying.

"If she knew! Ah, if she knew!" passed in tumult through my brain; and I bore the stare of an hundred eyes as I could not have borne the stare of one if that one had been Orpha's. Thank God, her veil was so thick.

Further questions brought out little more concerning this incident. She had not followed the shadow, she had not looked at the clock, she had not even gone around the bed to see what had occasioned the peculiar noise she had heard. She had not thought it of sufficient importance. Indeed, she had not attached any importance to the incident at the time, since her patient had not been wakened and late visits were not uncommon in that sickroom where the interest of everybody in the house centered, night as well as day.

But, when Mr. Bartholomew at last grew restless and she went for the medicine she had prepared, she saw with some astonishment that it was not in the exact place on the shelf where she had placed it,—or, at least, in the exact place where she felt sure that she had placed it. But even this did not alarm her or arouse her suspicion. How could it when everybody in the house was devoted to its master—or at all events gave every evidence of being so. Besides, she might have been mistaken as to where she had set down the glass. Her memory was not what it was,—and so on and so on till the Coroner stopped her with the query:

"And what did you do? Did you give him the dose his condition seemed to call for?"

"I did; and my heart is broken at the thought." She showed it. Tears were welling from her eyes and her whole body shook with the sob she strove to suppress. "I can never forgive myself that I did not suspect—mix a fresh draught—do anything but put that spoon filled with doubtful liquor between his lips. But how could I imagine that any one would tamper with the medicines in that cabinet. That any one would—"

Here she was stopped again, peremptorily this time, and her testimony switched to the moment when she saw the first signs of anything in Mr. Bartholomew's condition approaching collapse and how long it was after she gave him the medicine.

"Some little time. I was not watching the clock. Perhaps I slept again—I shall never know, but if I did, it was the sound of a sudden gasp from behind the curtains which started me to my feet. It was like a knife going through me, for I had a long experience with the sick before I came to C— and knew that it foretold the end.

"I was still surer of this when I bent over to look at him. He was awake, but I shall never forget his eye. 'Wealthy,' he whispered, exerting himself to speak plainly, 'call the children—call all of them—bid them come without delay—all is over with me—I shall not live out the coming day. But first, the bowl—the one in the bathroom—bring it here—put it on the stand—and two candles— lighted— don't look; act!' It was the master ordering a slave. There was nothing to do but to obey. I went to the bathroom, found the bowl he wanted, brought it, brought the candles, lighted them, turned on the electricity, for the candles were mere specks in that great room and then started for the door. But he called me back. 'I want the two envelopes,' he cried. 'Open the drawer and get them. Now put them in my hands, one in my right, the other in my left, and hasten, for I fear to—to lose my speech.'

"I rushed—I was terrified to leave him alone even for an instant but to cross him in his least wish might mean his death, so I fled like a wild woman through the halls, first to Mr. Edgar's room, then downstairs to Miss Orpha and later—not till after I had seen these two on their way to Mr. Bartholomew's room, to the rear hall and Mr. Quenton's door."

"What did you do there?"

"I both knocked and called."

"What did you say?"

"That his uncle was worse, and for him to come immediately. That Mr. Bartholomew found difficulty in speaking and wanted to see them all before his power to do so failed."

"Did he answer?"

"Instantly; opening the door and coming out. He was in Mr. Bartholomew's room almost as soon as the others."

"How could that be? Did he not stop to dress?"

"He was already dressed, just as he rose from dinner." What followed has already been told; I will not enlarge upon it. The burning of the one will in the presence of Orpha, Edgar and myself, with Wealthy Starr standing in the background. Uncle's sudden death before he could tell us where the will containing his last wishes could be found, and the shock we had all received at the astonishment shown by the doctor at his patient having succumbed so suddenly when he had fully expected him to live another fortnight.

The excitement which had been worked up to fever-point gradually subsided after this and, the hour being late, the inquiry was adjourned, to be continued the next day.

CHAPTER 30

In my haste to be through with the record of a testimony which so unmistakably gave the impression that I was the man who had tampered with the medicine which prematurely ended my uncle's fast failing life, I omitted to state Wealthy's eager admission that notwithstanding the doctor's surprise at the sudden passing of his patient and her own knowledge that the room contained a previously used medicine which had been pronounced dangerous to him at this stage of his illness, she did not connect these two facts in her mind even then as cause and effect. Not till the dreadful night in which she heard the word poison uttered over Mr. Bartholomew's casket, did she realize what the peculiar sound which had roused her from her nap beside the sick-bed really was. It was the setting down of the glass on the shelf from which it had been previously lifted.

This was where the proceedings had ended; and it was at this point they were taken up the next day.

I say nothing of the night between; I have tried to forget it. God grant the day will come when I may. Nor shall I enter into any description of the people who filled the room on this occasion or of the change in Orpha's appearance or in that of such persons towards whom my eyes, hot with the lack of sleep, wandered during the first half hour. I am eager to go on; eager to tell the worst and have done with this part of my story.

To return then to Wealthy's testimony as continued from the day before. The casket in which Mr. Bartholomew's body had been laid on the morning of the second day had been taken in the early evening down into the court. She had not accompanied it. When asked why, she said that Mr. Edgar had asked her to remain in the room, and on no account to leave it without locking both doors. So she had stayed until she heard a scream ringing up through the house, and convinced from its hysterical sound that it came from one of the maids, she hastened to lock the one door which had been left unfastened, and go below. As in company with Mr. Quenton and Clarke she reached the balcony on the second floor, she could see that there were several persons in the court, so she stopped where she was, and simply looked down at what was going on. It was then she got the shock of her life. The girl who had uttered the scream was pointing at her dead master's face and shouting the word poison. One can imagine what passed through her mind as the clouds cleared away from it and she realized to what in her ignorance she had been made a party to.

She certainly made the jury feel it, though she was less garrulous and simpler in her manners than on the previous day; and hardly knowing what to expect from her peculiar sense of duty, I was in dread anticipation of hearing her relate the few words which had passed between us as Orpha fell into my arms,—words in which she accused me of being the cause of all this trouble.

But she spared me that, either because she did not know how to obtrude it without help from the Coroner, or because she had enough right feeling not to emphasize the suspicion already roused against me by her previous testimony.

Grateful for this much grace, I restrained my own anxieties and listened intently for what else she had to say, in the old hope that some word would yet fall from her lips or some glance escape from her eye which would give me the clew to the hand which had really lifted that glass and set it down a little further along the shelf.

I thought I was on its track when she came to the visit she had paid to the room above in the company of Edgar and Orpha. But I heard little new. The facts elicited were well-known ones. They had approached the cabinet together, looked into it together, and, pushing the bottles about, brought out the one for which they were seeking from the very place in the rear of the shelf where she had put it herself when told that it would not be required any longer.

"Yes, that is the bottle," she declared, as the Coroner lifted a small phial from the table before him and held it up in her sight and in that of the jury. As he did this, I could scarcely hide the sickening thrill which for a moment caused everything to turn black around me. For the label was written large and the word Poison had a ghastly look to one who had loved Edgar Quenton Bartholomew. When I could see and hear again, Wealthy was saying:

"A few drops wouldn't be missed. My memory isn't good enough for me to be sure of a fact like that."

Evidently she had been asked if on taking the phial from the shelf she had noticed any diminution of its contents since she had last handled it.

"You say that you pushed the bottles aside in order to get at this one. Was that necessary? Could you not have reached in over them and lifted it out?"

"I never thought of doing that; none of us did. We were all anxious to satisfy ourselves as to whether or not the bottle was there and just took the quickest way we knew of finding out."

"But you could have got hold of it in the way I suggested? Reached in, I mean, and pulled it out without disarranging the other bottles?"

She stopped to think; contracting her brows and stealing what I felt sure was a look at Edgar.

"It would have been difficult," she finally conceded: "but a person with long fingers might have got hold of it all right. The bottles in front and around it were not very large. Much of the same size as the one you just showed us."

"Then in your opinion this could have been done?"

(I heard afterwards that it had been done by one of the police operatives.)

"It could have been done."

Almost doggedly she said it.

"Without making much noise?"

"Without making any if the person doing it knew exactly where the phial was to be found."

Not doggedly now, but incisively.

"And how many of the household, to your definite knowledge, did?"

"Three, besides myself. Miss Orpha, Mr. Edgar and Mr. Quenton, all of whom shared my nursing."

The warmth with which she uttered the first two names, the coldness with which she uttered mine! Was it intentional, or just the natural expression of her feelings? Whatever prompted this distinction in tone, the effect was to signal me out as definitely as though a brand had left its scorching mark upon my forehead.

And I innocent!

Why I did not leap to my feet I do not know. I thought I did, shouting a wild disclaimer. If men stared and women shrieked that was nothing to me. All that I cared for was Orpha sitting there listening to this hellish accusation. So maddened was I, so dead to all human conditions that I doubt if I should have been surprised had the ghostly figure of my uncle evolved itself from air and taken its place on the witness-stand in revolt against this horror. Anything was possible, but to let the world—by which I meant Orpha—believe this thing for a moment.

All this tumult in brain and heart, and my body quiet, fixed, with not a muscle so much as quivering. By what force was I thus withheld? Possibly by some hypnotic influence exerted by Mr. Jackson, for when I looked in his direction I found him gazing very earnestly in mine. I smiled. It must have been a very dreary smile and ironic in the extreme; for my heart was filled with bitterness and could express itself in no other way.

The decided shake of the head which he gave me in return had its effect, however, and digging my nails into my palm, I listened to what followed with all the stoicism the situation called for.

I was still in a state of rigid self-control when I heard my name spoken loudly and with command and woke to the fact that Wealthy had been dismissed from the stand and that I was to be the next witness.

Was I ready for it? I must be; and to test my strength, I cast one straight look at Orpha. She had lifted her veil and met my gaze fairly. Had there been guilt in my heart—

But I could pass her without shame; and sustained by this fact, I took my place on the stand with a calmness I had hardly expected to show in the face of this prejudiced throng.

CHAPTER 31

As my story, sometimes allowed to take the form of an uninterrupted narrative, differed in no essential from the one already given in these pages, I see no reason for recapitulating it here any more than I did the one I told days before to the Inspector. Fixed in my determination to be honest in all I said but not to say any more than was required, I was able to hear unmoved the low murmurs which now and then rose from the center of the room as I made some unexpected reply or revealed, as I could not help doing, the strength of the tie which united me to my deceased uncle. No one believed in that and consequently attributed any assertion of the kind to hypocrisy; and with this I had to contend from the beginning to the end, softened perhaps a little towards the last, but still active enough to make my position a very trying one.

The result of my examination must be given, however, even if I have to indulge in some repetition.

My testimony, if accepted as truth, established certain facts.

They were these:

That Mr. Bartholomew had changed his mind more than once as to which of us two nephews he would leave the bulk of his fortune:

That he had shown positive decision only on the night preceding his death, declaring to me that I was his final choice:

That, notwithstanding this, he had not then and there destroyed the will antagonistic to this decision, as would seem natural if his mind had been really settled in its resolve; but had kept them both in hand up to the time of my departure from the room:

That late in the night after a long seance with myself in the library on the lower floor, I had come upstairs, and in my anxiety to know whether my uncle were awake or resting quietly after so disturbing an evening, had stopped to listen first at one of his doors and then at the other; but had refrained from going in, or even seeing my uncle again until summoned with the rest of the family to hear his dying wishes:

That when he handed one of the wills to his daughter and bade her burn it in the large bowl he had ordered placed at his bedside, I believed it to be the one I had expected to see him burn the night before, and that I just as confidently believed that the one which had been taken from the other envelope and put away in some spot not yet discovered was the one designating me as his chief heir according to his promise, and should so believe until it was found and I was shown to the contrary. (This in justification of my confidence in him and also to refute the idea in so far as I was able, that I had been so fearful of his changing his mind again that I was willing to cut his life short rather than run the risk of losing my inheritance.)

For I was sensible enough to see that to minds so prejudiced, the fact that the will favoring myself having been the last one drawn, afforded them sufficient excuse for a supposition which seemed the only explanation possible for the mystery they were facing.

A few were undoubtedly influenced either by my earnestness or the dignity which innocence gives to the suspected man, but the many, not; and when at the conclusion of my testimony I was forced to repass Orpha on my way back to my seat, I found that I no longer had the courage to meet her eye, lest I should see pity there or, what was worse, an attempt to accept what I had to say against reason and possibly against her own judgment.

But when her name was called and with a quick unveiling of her face she took her place upon the stand, I could not keep my glances back, for I was thinking now, not of myself but of her and the suffering which she must undergo if her examination was to be of any help in disentangling the threads of this involved inquiry.

That I was justified in my fears was at once apparent, for the first question which attracted attention and drew every head forward in breathless interest and undisguised curiosity was this:

"Miss Bartholomew, I regret that I must trespass upon matters which in my respect for yourself and family I should be glad to leave untouched. But conditions force me to ask if the rumor is correct that you are engaged to marry your cousin, Edgar, with whom you have been brought up."

"No," she answered at once, with that clear ring to her voice which carried it without effort to the remotest corners of the room. "I am engaged to no one. But am under an obligation, gladly entered into because it was my father's wish, to marry the man—if the gentleman so pleases—to whom my father has willed the greater portion of his money."

The Coroner raised his gavel, but laid it down again, for the excitement called forth by the calm dignity of this answer, was of that deep and absorbing kind which shrinks from noisy demonstration.

"Miss Bartholomew, do you know or have you any suspicion as to where your father concealed the will which will settle this question?"

"None whatever."

And now, the sweet voice wavered.

"You know your father's room well?"

"Every inch of it."

"And can imagine no place in it where he might have thrust this document on taking it out of the envelope?"

"None."

"Miss Bartholomew, you have heard the last witness state that your father distinctly told him on the night before his death that he had decided to make him his chief inheritor. Did your father ever make the same declaration to you?"

"He has said that he found my foreign cousin admirable."

"That hardly answers my question, Miss Bartholomew." The pink came out on her cheeks. Ah; how lovely she was! But in what trouble also.

"He once asked me if I could rely on his judgment in the choice of my future husband?" came reluctantly from her lips. "Up till then I had not been aware that there was to be any choice."

"You mean—"

"That I had never been given reason to think that there was any man living whom he could prefer for a real son to the nephew who lived like a son in the family."

"Can you remember just when this occurred? Was it before or after the ball held in your house?"

"It was after; some weeks after."

"After he had been ill for some little time, then?"

"Yes, sir."

The Coroner glanced at the jury; and the jurymen at each other. She must have observed this, for a subtle change passed over her face which revealed the steadfast woman without taking from the winsomeness of her girlishness so well known to all.

She was yet in the glow of whatever sentiment had been aroused within her, when she was called upon to reply to a series of questions concerning this ball, leading up, as I knew they must, to one which had been in my own mind ever since that event. What had passed between her and her father when, on hearing he was ill, she went up to see him in his own room.

"I found him ailing but indisposed to say much about it. What he wanted was to tell me that on account of not feeling quite himself, he had decided not to have any public announcement made of his plans for Edgar and myself. That would keep. But lest our friends who had expected something of the kind might feel aggrieved, he proposed that as a substitute for it, another announcement should be made which would give them almost equal pleasure,—that of the engagement of his ward, Miss Colfax, to Dr. Hunter. And this was done."

"And was this all which passed between you at this time? No hint of a quarrel between himself and the nephew for whom he had contemplated such honor?"

"He said nothing that would either alarm or sadden me. He was very cheerful, almost gay, all the time I was in the room. Alas! how little we knew!"

It was the spontaneous outburst of a bereaved child and the Coroner let it pass. Would he could have spared her the next question. But his fixed idea of my guilt would not allow this and I had to sit there and hear him say:

"In the days which followed, during which you doubtless had many opportunities of seeing both of your cousins, did the attentions of the one you call Quenton savor at all of those of courtship?"

"No, sir. We were all too absorbed in caring for my sick father to think of anything of that kind."

It was firmly but sweetly said, and such was the impression she made on the crowd before her, that I saw a man who was lounging against the rear wall, unconsciously bow his head in token of his respect for her womanliness.

The Coroner, a little impressed himself perhaps, sat in momentary silence and when he was ready to proceed, chose a less embarrassing subject. What it was I do not remember now, nor is it of importance that I should enlarge any further on an examination which left things very much as they were and had been from the beginning. By the masses convened there I was considered guilty, but by a few, not; and as the few had more than one representative in the jury, the verdict which was finally given was the usual one where certainty is not attained.

Murder by poison administered by a person unknown.

BOOK III

WHICH OF US TWO?

CHAPTER 32

Solitude! How do we picture it?

A man alone on a raft in the midst of a boundless sea. A figure against a graying sky, with chasms beneath and ice peaks above. Such a derelict between life and death I felt myself to be, as on leaving the courthouse, I stepped again into the street and faced my desperate future. I almost wished that I might feel a hand upon my shoulder and hear a voice in my ear saying: "Here is my warrant. I arrest you for murder in the name of the law;" for then I should know where my head would be laid for the night. Now I knew nothing.

Had Edgar joined me— But that would have been asking too much. I stood alone; I walked alone; and heads fell and eyes turned aside as I threaded my slow way down the street.

Where should I go? Suddenly it came to me that Orpha would expect me to return home. I had no reason for thinking so; but the impression once yielded to, I was sure of her expectancy and sure of the grave welcome I should receive. But how could I face them all with that brand between my eyes! To see Clarke's accusing face and Wealthy's attempt not to show her hatred of me too plainly! It would take a man with a heart of adamant to endure that. I had no such heart. Yet if I failed to go, it might look to some persons like an acknowledgment of guilt. And that would be worse. I would go, but for the night only. To-morrow should see me far on my way to other quarters—that is, if the police would allow it. The police! Well, why not see the Inspector! He had visited me; why should I not visit him?

An objective was found. I turned towards the Police Station. But before I reached it I met Mr. Jackson. He never admitted it, but I think he had been dogging me, having perhaps some inkling as to my mood. The straightforward way in which he held out his hand gave me the first gleam of comfort I had had that day.

Could it be that he was sincere in this show of confidence? That he had not been influenced by Wealthy's story, or his judgment palsied by the fact patent to all, that with the exception of myself there was not a person among those admitted to my uncle's room who had not lived in the house for years and given always and under all circumstances evidences of the most devoted attachment to him?

Or did he simply look upon me as the millionaire client who would yet come into his own and whose favor it would be well to secure in this hour of present trial?

A close study of his face satisfied me that he was really the friend he seemed, and, yielding to his guidance, I allowed him to lead me to his office where we sat down together and had our first serious talk.

He did believe me and would stand by me if I so desired it. Edgar Bartholomew was a favorite everywhere, but if his uncle who had loved him and reared him in the hope of uniting him with his daughter, could be moved from that position to the point of having a second will of an opposing nature drawn up and signed by another lawyer on the same day, it must have been because he felt he had found a better man to inherit his fortune and to marry his daughter. It was a fact well enough known that Edgar was beginning to show a streak of recklessness in his demeanor which could not have been pleasing to his staid and highly respectable uncle. There was another man near by of characteristics more trustworthy; and his conscience favored this man.

"A strong nature, that of our late friend. He had but one weakness—an inordinate partiality for this irresponsible, delightful nephew. That is how I see the matter. If you will put your affairs in my hands, I think I can make it lively for those who may oppose you."

"But Wealthy's testimony, linking my presence at the upper door of uncle's room with the person she heard tampering with the glass believed by all to have held the draught which was the cause of his death?"

"Mr. Bartholomew, are you sure she saw your figure fleeing down the hall?"

I was on the point of saying, "Whose else? I did rush down the hall," when he sharply interrupted me.

"What we want to know and must endeavor to find out is whether, under the conditions, she could see your shadow or that of any other person who might be passing from front to rear sufficiently well to identify it."

Greatly excited, I stared at him.

"How can that be done?"

"Well, Mr. Bartholomew, fortunately for us we have a friend at court. If we had not, I judge that you would have been arrested on leaving the courthouse."

"Who? Who?" My heart beat to suffocation; I could hardly articulate. Did I hope to hear a name which would clear my sky of every cloud, and make the present, doubtful as it seemed, a joy instead of a menace? If I did, I was doomed to disappointment.

"The Inspector who was the first to examine you does not believe in your guilt."

Disappointment! but a great—a hopeful surprise also! I rose to my feet in my elation, this unexpected news coming with such a shock on the heels of my despair. But sat again with a gesture of apology as I met his steady look.

"I know this, because he is a friend of mine," he averred by way of explanation.

"And will help us?"

"He will see that the experiment I mention is made. Poison could not have got into that glass without hands. Those hands must be located. The Police will not cease their activities."

"Mr. Jackson, I give you the case. Do what you can for me; but—"

I had risen again, and was walking restlessly away from him as I came to this quick halt in what I was about to say. He was watching me, carefully, thoughtfully, out of the corner of his eye. I was aware of this and, as I turned to face him again, I took pains to finish my sentence with quite a different ending from that which had almost slipped from my unwary tongue.

"But first, I want your advice. Shall I return to the house, or go to the hotel and send for my clothes?"

"Return to the house, by all means. You need not stay there more than the one night. You are innocent. You believe that the house and much more are

yours by your uncle's will. Why should you not return to your own? You are
not the man to display any bravado; neither are you the man to accept the
opinion of servants and underlings."

"But—but—my cousin, Orpha? The real owner, as I look at it, of everything
there?"

"Miss Bartholomew has a just mind. She will accept your point of view—for
the present, at least."

I dared not say more. I was never quite myself when I had to speak her
name.

He seemed to respect my reticence and after some further talk, I left him
and betook myself to the house which held for me everything I loved and
everything I feared in the world I had made for myself.

CHAPTER 33

During the first portion of this walk I forced my mind to dwell on the
astonishing fact that the Inspector whom I had regarded as holding me in
suspicion was the one man most convinced of my innocence. He had certainly
shown no leaning that way in the memorable interview we had held together.
What had changed him? Or had I simply misunderstood his attitude, natural
enough to an amateur who finds himself for the first time in his life subject to
the machinations of the police.

As I had no means of answering this query, I gradually allowed the matter,
great as it was, to slip from my mind, and another and more present interest
to fill it.

I was approaching the Bartholomew mansion, and its spell was already
upon me. An embodiment of beauty and of mystery! A glorious pile of
masonry, hiding a secret on the solution of which my honor as a man and my
hope as a lover seemed absolutely to depend.

There was a mob at either gate, dispersing slowly under the efforts of the
police. To force my way through a crowd of irritated, antagonistic men and
women collected perhaps for the purpose of intercepting me, required not
courage, but a fool's bravado. Between me and it I saw an open door. It
belonged to a small shop where I had sometimes traded. I ventured to look in.
The woman who usually stood behind the counter was not there, but her
husband was and gave me a sharp look as I entered.

"I want nothing but a refuge," I hastily announced. "The crowd below there
will soon be gone. Will it incommode you if I remain here till the street is
clear?"

"Yes, it will," he rejoined abruptly, but with a twinkle of interest in his eye
showing that his feelings were kindlier than his manner. "The better part of
the crowd, you see, are coming this way and some of them are in a mood far
from Christian."

By "some of them," I gathered that he meant his wife, and I stepped back.

"People have such a way of making up their minds before they see a thing out," he muttered, slipping from behind the counter and shutting the door she had probably left open. "If you will come with me," he added more cheerfully, "I will show you the only thing you can do if you don't want a dozen women's hands in your hair."

And, crossing to the rear, he opened another door leading into the yard, where he pointed out a small garage, empty, as it chanced, of his Ford. "Step in there and when all is quiet yonder, you can slip into the street without difficulty. I shall know nothing about it."

And with this ignominious episode associated with my return, I finally approached the house I had entered so often under very different auspices.

I had a latch-key in my pocket, but I did not choose to use it. I rang, instead. When the door opened I took a look at the man who held the knob in hand. Though he occupied the position of butler in the great establishment, and was therefore continually to be seen at meals, I did not know him very well—did not know him at all; for he was one of the machine-made kind whose perfect service left nothing to be desired, but of whose thoughts and wishes he gave no intimation unless it was to those he had known much longer than he had me.

Would he reveal himself in face of my intrusion? I was fully as curious as I was anxious to see. No; he was still the perfect servant and opened the door wide, without a gleam of hostility in his eye or any change in his usual manner.

Passing him, I stepped into the court. The fountain was playing. The house was again a home, but would it be a home to me? I resolved to put the question to an immediate test upstairs. Hearing Haines' steps passing behind me on his way to the rear, I turned and asked him if Mr. Bartholomew had returned. Then I saw a change in the man's face—a flash of feeling gone as quickly as it came. It had always been, "Does Mr. Edgar want this or Mr. Edgar want that?" The use of his uncle's name in designating him, seemed to seal that uncle forever in his tomb.

"You will find him in the library," was Haines' reply as he passed on; and looking up, I saw Edgar standing in the doorway awaiting me.

Without any hesitation I approached him, but stopped before I was too near. I was resolved to speak very plainly and I did.

"Edgar, I can understand why with this hideous doubt still unsettled as to the exact person who, through accident we hope, was unfortunate enough to be responsible for our uncle's death, you should find it very unpleasant to see me here. I have not come to stay, though it might be better all around if I were to remain for this one night. I loved Uncle. I am innocent of doing him any harm. I believe him to have made me the heir to this estate in the will thus unhappily lost to sight, but I shall not press my claim and am willing to drop it if you will drop yours, leaving Orpha to inherit."

"That would be all right if the loss of the will were all." —Was this Edgar speaking?—"But you know and I know that the loss of the will is of small moment in comparison to the real question you mentioned first. The verdict was murder. There is no murder without an active hand. Whose hand? You say that it was not yours. I—I want to believe you, but—"

"You do not."

His set expression gave way; it was an unnatural one for him; but in the quick play of feature which took its place I could not read his mind, one emotion blotting out another so rapidly that neither heart nor reason could seize satisfactorily upon any.

"You do not?" I repeated.

"I know nothing about it. It is all a damnable mystery."

"Edgar, shall I pack up my belongings and go?"

He controlled himself.

"Stay the night," he said, and, turning on his heel, went back into the library.

Then it was that I became aware of the dim figure of a man sitting quietly in an inconspicuous corner near the stairway.

It needed no perspicacity on my part to recognize in him a police detective.

I found another on the second floor and my heart misgave me for Orpha. Verily, the police were in occupation! When I reached the third, I found two more stationed like sentinels at the two doors of my departed Uncle's room. This I did not wonder at and I was able to ignore them as I hurried by to my own room where I locked myself in.

I was thankful to be allowed to do this. I had reached the point where I felt the necessity of absolute rest from questioning or any thought of the present trouble. I would amuse myself; I would smoke and gradually pack. The darkness ahead was not impenetrable. I had a friend in the Inspector. Edgar had not treated me ill—not positively ill. It would be possible for me to appear at the dinner-table; possibly to face Orpha if she found strength to come. Yet were it not well for her to be warned that I was in the house? Would Edgar think of this? Yes, I felt positive that he would and then if she did not come—

But nothing must keep her from the table. I would not go myself unless summoned. I stood in no need of a meal. In those days I was scarcely aware of what I ate. On this night it seemed simply unbelievable that I should ever again crave food.

But a smoke was different. Sitting down by the window, I opened my favorite box. It was nearly empty. Only a part of the lower layer remained. Taking out a cigar, I was about to reach for a match when I caught sight of a loose piece of paper protruding from under the few cigars which remained. It had an odd, out-of-the-way look and I hastened to pull it forth. Great Heaven! it appeared to be a note. The end of a sheet of paper taken from my own desk had been folded once and, on opening it, I saw this:

No signature; the letters, as shown above, had been cut carefully from some magazine or journal. Was it a trap laid by the police; or the well meant message of a friend? Alas! here was matter for fresh questioning and I was wearied to the last point of human endurance. I sat dazed, my brain in confusion, my faculties refusing to work. One thing only remained clear—that I was to burn this scrawl as soon as read. Well, I could do that. There was a fireplace in my room, sometimes used but oftener not. It had not been used that day, which had been a mild one. But that did not matter. The draught was good and would easily carry up and out of sight a shred of paper like this. But my hand shook as I set fire to it and watched it fly in one quick blaze up the chimney. As it disappeared and the last spark was lost in the blackness of the empty shaft, I seemed to have wakened from a dream in which I was myself a shadow amongst shadows, so remote was this incident and all the rest of this astounding drama from my natural self and the life I had hoped to live when I crossed the ocean to make my home in rich but commonplace America.

CHAPTER 34

"Miss Bartholomew wishes me to say that she would be glad to see you at dinner."

I stared stupidly from the open doorway at Haines standing respectfully before me. I was wondering if the note I had just burned had come from him. He had shown feeling and he had not shown me any antagonism. But the feeling was not for me, but for the master he had served almost as long as I was years old. So I ended in accepting his formality with an equal show of the same; and determined to be done with questions for this one night if no longer, I prepared myself for dinner and went down.

I found Orpha pacing slowly to and fro under the glow of the colored lamps which illuminated the fountain. Older but lovelier and nobler in the carriage of her body and in the steady look with which she met my advance.

Suddenly I stopped dead short. It was the first time I had entered her presence without a vivid sense of the barrier raised between us by the understanding under which we all met, that we were cousins and nothing more, till the word was given which should release us to be our natural selves again.

But the lift of one of her fingers, scarcely perceptible save to a lover's eye, brought me back to reason. This was no time for breaking down that barrier, even if we were alone, which I now felt open to doubt, and my greeting had just that hesitation in it which one in my position would be likely to show to one in hers. Her attitude was kindly, nothing more, and Edgar presently relieved me of the embarrassment of further conversation by sauntering in from the conservatory side by side with Miss Colfax.

Remembering the scene between them to which I had been a witness on the night of the ball, I wondered at seeing them thus together; but perceiving by the bearing of all three that she was domiciled here as a permanent guest, this wonder was lost in another: why Orpha should not sense the secret with which, as I watched them, the whole air seemed to palpitate.

But then she had not had my opportunities for enlightenment.

A little old lady whom I had not seen before but who was evidently a much esteemed relative of the family made the fifth at the dinner table. Formality reigned. It was our only refuge from an embarrassment which would have made speech impossible. As it was, Miss Colfax was the only one who talked and what she said was of too little moment to be remembered. I was glad when the meal was at an end and I could with propriety withdraw.

Better the loneliest of rooms in the dreariest of hotels than this. Better a cell— Ah, no, no! my very soul recoiled. Not that! not that! I am afraid that I was just a little mad as I paused at the foot of the great staircase on my way up.

But I was sane enough the next moment. The front door had opened, admitting the Inspector. I immediately crossed the court to meet him. Accosting him, I said in explanation of my presence, "You see me here, Inspector; but if not detained, I shall seek other quarters to-morrow. I was very anxious to get back to my desk in New York, if the firm are willing to receive me. But whether there or here, I am always at your call till this dreadful matter is settled. Now if you have no questions to ask, I am going to my room, where I can be found at any minute."

"Very good," was his sole reply, uttered without any display of feeling; and, seeing that he wished nothing from me, I left him and went quickly upstairs.

I always dreaded the passage from the second floor to the third,—to-night more than ever. Not that I was affected by the superstitious idea connected by many with that especial flight of steps—certainly I was too sensible a man for that, though I had had my own experience too— but the dread of the acute memories associated with the doors I must pass was strong upon me, and it was with relief that I found myself at last in my own little hall, even if I had yet to hurry by the small winding staircase at the bottom of which was a listening ear acquainted with my every footfall.

Briskly as I had taken the turn from the main hall, I had had time to note the quiet figure of Wealthy seated in her old place—hands in lap—face turned my way—a figure of stone with all the wonted good humor and kindliness of former days stricken from it, making it to my eyes one of deliberate accusation. Was not this exactly what I had feared and dreaded to encounter? Yes, and the experience was not an agreeable one. But for all that it was not without its compensations. Any idea I may have had of her being the one to warn me that the key invariably carried by my uncle on his person was not to be found there at his death, was now definitely eliminated from my mind. She could not have shown this sympathy for me in my anomalous position and then eye me as she had just done with such implacable hostility.

My attention thus brought back to a subject which, if it had seemed to lie passive in my mind, had yet made its own atmosphere there during every distraction of the past hour, I decided to have it out with myself as to what this communication had meant and from whom it had come.

That it was no trap but an honest hint from some person, who, while not interested enough to show himself openly as my friend but who was nevertheless desirous of affording me what help he could in my present extremity, I was ready to accept as a self-evident truth. The difficulty—and it was no mean one, I assure you—was to settle upon the man or woman willing to take this secret stand.

Was it Clarke? I smiled grimly at the very thought.

Was it Orpha? I held my breath for a moment as I contemplated this possibility—the incredible possibility that this made-up, patched-up line of printed letters could have been the work of her hands. It was too difficult to believe this, and I passed on.

The undertaker's man? That could easily be found out. But why such effort at concealment from an outsider? No, it was not the undertaker's man. But who else was there in all the house who would have knowledge of the fact thus communicated to me in this mysterious fashion? Martha? Eliza? Haines? Bliss? The chef who never left his kitchen, all orders being conveyed to him by Wealthy or by telephone from the sick room?

No, no.

There was but one name left—the most unlikely of all— Edgar's. Could it be possible—

I did not smile this time, grimly or otherwise, as I turned away from this supposition also. I laughed; and, startled by the sound which was such as had never left my lips before, I rose with a bound from my chair, resolved to drop the whole matter from my mind and calm myself by returning to my task of looking over and sorting out my effects. Otherwise I should get no sleep.

CHAPTER 35

What was it? It was hardly a noise, yet somebody was astir in the house and not very far from my door. Listening, I caught the sound of heavy breathing in the hall outside, and, slipping out of bed, crossed to the door and suddenly pulled it wide open.

A face confronted me, every feature distinct in the flood of moonlight pouring into the room from the opposite window. Alarm and repugnance made it almost unrecognizable, but it was the face of Edgar and no other, and, as in my astonishment I started backward, he spoke.

"I was told—they said—that you were ill—that groans were heard coming from this room. I—I am glad it is not so. Pardon me for waking you." And he was gone, staggering slightly as he disappeared down the hall. A moment later I heard his voice raised further on, then a door slam and after that, quiet.

Confounded, for the man was shaken by emotion, I sat down on the edge of the bed and tried to compose my faculties sufficiently to understand the meaning of this surprising episode.

Automatically, I looked at my watch. It was just three. I had associations with that hour. What were they? Suddenly I remembered. It was the hour I visited my uncle's door the night before his death, when Wealthy—

The name steadied the rush and counter-rush of swirling, not-to-be-controlled thoughts. Mr. Jackson had spoken of an experiment to be made by the police for the purpose of determining whether the shadow Wealthy professed to have seen about that time flitting by on the wall further down would be visible from the place where she stood.

Had they been trying this?

Had he been the one—

There was no thoroughfare in this direction. And wearied to death, I sank back on my pillow and after a few restless minutes fell into a heavy sleep.

CHAPTER 36

Next day the Thunderbolt fell. Entering Mr. Jackson's office, I found him quite alone and waiting for me. Though the man was almost a stranger to me and I had very little knowledge of his face or its play of expression, I felt sure that the look with which he greeted me was not common to him and that so far as he was concerned, my cause had rather gained than lost in interest since our last meeting.

"You did not telephone me last night," were his first words.

"No," I said, "there was really no occasion."

"Yet something very important happened in your house between three and four in the morning."

"I thought so; I hoped so; but I knew so little what, that I dared not call you up for anything so indefinite. This morning life seems normal again, but in the night—"

"Go on, I want to hear."

"My cousin, Edgar, came to my door in a state of extreme agitation. He had been told that I was ill. I was not; but say that I had been, I do not see why he should have been so affected by the news. I am a trial to him; an incubus; a rival whom he must hate. Why should he shiver at sight of me and whirl away to his room?"

"It was odd. You had heard nothing previously, then?"

"No, I was fortunate enough to be asleep."

"And this being a silent drama you did not wake."

"Not till the time I said."

He was very slow, and I very eager, but I restrained myself. The peculiarity observable in his manner had increased rather than diminished. He seemed on fire to speak, yet unaccountably hesitated, turning away from my direct gaze and busying himself with some little thing on his desk. I began to feel hesitant also and inclined to shirk the interview.

And now for a confession. There was something in my own mind which I had refused to bare even to my own perceptions. Something from which I shrank and yet which would obtrude itself at moments like these. Could it be that I was about to hear, put in words, what I had never so much as whispered to myself?

It was several minutes later and after much had been said before I learned. He began with explanations.

"A woman is the victim of her own emotions. On that night Wealthy had been on the watch for hours either in the hall or in the sick room. She had seen you and another come and go under circumstances very agitating to one so devoted to the family. She was, therefore, not in a purely normal condition when she started up from her nap to settle a question upon which the life of a man might possibly hang.

"At least this was how the police reasoned. So they put off the experiment upon which they were resolved to an hour approximately the same in which the occurrence took place which they were planning to reproduce, keeping her, in the meantime, on watch for what interested her most. Pardon me, it was in connection with yourself," he commented, flashing me a look from under his shaggy brows. "She has very strong beliefs on that point—strong enough to blind her or—" he broke off suddenly and as suddenly went on with his story. "Not till in apparent solitude she had worked herself up to a fine state of excitement did the Inspector show himself, and with a fine tale of the uselessness of expecting anything of a secret nature to take place in the house while her light was still burning and her figure guarded the hall, induced her to enter the room from which she might hope to see a repetition of what had happened on that fatal night. I honor the police. We could not do without them;—but their methods are sometimes—well, sometimes a little misleading.

After another half hour of keen expectancy, during which she had not dozed, I warrant, there came the almost inaudible sound of the knob turning in the upper door. Had she been alone, she would have screamed, but the Inspector's hand was on her arm and he made his presence felt to such a purpose that she simply shuddered, but that so violently that her teeth chattered. A fire had been lit on the hearth, for it was by the light thus given that she had seen what she said she had seen that night. Also, the curtains of the bed had been drawn back as they had not been then but must be now for her to see through to the shelf where the glass of medicine had been standing. Her face, as she waited for whomever might appear there, was one of bewilderment mingled with horror. But no one appeared. The door had been locked and all that answered that look was the impression she received of some one endeavoring to open it.

"As shaken by these terrors, she turned to face the Inspector, he pressed her arm again and drew her towards the door by which they had entered and from which she had seen the shadow she had testified to before the Coroner. Stepping the length of the passage-way intervening between the room and the door itself, he waited a moment, then threw the latter open just as the shadow of a man shot through the semi-darkness across the opposite wall.

" 'Do you recognize it?' the Inspector whispered in her ear. 'Is it the same?'

"She nodded wildly and drew back, suppressing the sob which gurgled in her throat.

" 'The Englishman?' he asked again.

"Again she nodded.

"Carefully he closed the door; he was himself a trifle affected. The figure which had fled down the hall was that of the man who had just been told that you were ill in your room. I need not name him."

CHAPTER 37

Slowly I rose to my feet. The agitation caused by these words was uncontrollable. How much did he mean by them and why should I be so much more moved by hearing them spoken than by the suppressed thought?

He made no move to enlighten me, and, walking again to the window, I affected to look out. When I turned back it was to ask:

"What do you make of it, Mr. Jackson? This seems to place me on a very different footing; but—"

"The woman spoke at random. She saw no shadow. Her whole story was a fabrication."

"A fabrication?"

"Yes, that is how we look at it. She may have heard some one in the room—she may even have heard the setting down of the glass on the shelf, but she did not see your shadow, or if she did, she did not recognize it as such; for the light was the same and so was every other condition as on the previous night, yet the Inspector standing at her side and knowing well who was passing, says there was nothing to be seen on the wall but a blur; no positive outline by which any true conclusion could be drawn."

"Does she hate me so much as that? So honest a woman fabricate a story in order to involve me in anything so serious as crime?" I could not believe this myself.

"No, it was not through hate of you; rather through her great love for another. Don't you see what lies at the bottom of her whole conduct? She thinks—"

"Don't!" The word burst from me unawares. "Don't put it into words. Let us leave some things to be understood, not said." Then as his lips started to open and a cynical gleam came into his eyes, I hurriedly added: "I want to tell you something. On the night when the question of poison was first raised by the girl Martha's ignorant outbreak over her master's casket, I was standing with Miss Bartholomew in the balcony; Wealthy was on her other side. As that word rang up from the court, Miss Bartholomew fainted, and as I shrieked out some invective against the girl for speaking so in her mistress' presence, I heard these words hissed into my ear. 'Would you blame the girl for what you yourself have brought upon us?' It was Wealthy speaking, and she certainly hated me then. And," I added, perhaps with unnecessary candor, "with what she evidently thought very good reason."

At this Mr. Jackson's face broke into a smile half quizzical and half kindly:

"You believe in telling the truth," said he. "So do I, but not all of it. You may feel yourself exonerated in the eyes of the police, but remember the public. It will be uphill work exonerating yourself with them."

"I know it; and no man could feel the sting of his position more keenly. But you must admit that it is my duty to be as just to Edgar as to myself. Nay, more so. I know how much my uncle loved this last and dearest namesake of his. I know—no man better—that if what we do not say and must not say were true, and Uncle could rise from his grave to meet it, it would be with shielding hands and a forgiveness which would demand this and this only from the beloved ingrate, that he should not marry Orpha. Uncle was my benefactor and in honor to his memory I must hold the man he loved innocent unless forced to find him otherwise. Even for Orpha's sake—"

"Does she love him?"

The question came too quickly and the hot flush would rise. But I answered him.

"He is loved by all who know him. It would be strange if his lifelong playmate should be the only one who did not."

"Deuce take it!" burst from the irate lawyer's lips, "I was speaking of a very different love from that."

And I was thinking of a very different one.

The embarrassment this caused to both of us made a break in the conversation. But it was presently resumed by my asking what he thought the police were likely to do under the circumstances.

He shot out one word at me.

"Nothing."

"Nothing?" My face brightened, but my heart sank.

"That is, as I feel bound to inform you, this is one of those cases where a premature move would be fatal to official prestige. The Bartholomews are held in much too high esteem in this town for thoughtless attack. The old gentleman was the czar of this community. No one more respected and no one more loved. Had his death been attributed to the carelessness or aggression of an outsider, no one but the Governor of the state could have held the people in cheek. But the story of the two wills having got about, suspicion took its natural course; the family itself became involved—an enormity which would have been inconceivable had it not been that the one suspected was the one least known and—you will pardon me if I speak plainly, even if I touch the raw—the one least liked: a foreigner, moreover, come, as all thought, from England on purpose to gather in this wealth. You felt their animosity at the inquest and you also must have felt their restraint; but had any one dared to say of Edgar what was said of you, either a great shout of derisive laughter would have gone up or hell would have broken loose in that court-room. With very few exceptions, no one there could have imagined him playing any such part. And they cannot to-day. They have known him too long, admired him too long, seen him too many times in loving companionship with the man now dead to weigh any testimony or be moved by any circumstance suggestive of anything so flagrant as guilt of this nature. The proof must be absolute before the bravest among us would dare assail his name to this extent. And the proof is not absolute. On the contrary, it is very defective; for so far as any of us can see, the crime, if perpetrated by him, lacks motive. Shall I explain?"

"Pray do. Since we have gone thus far, let us go the full length. Light is what I want; light on every angle of this affair. If it serves to clear him as it now seems it has served to clear me, I shall rejoice."

Mr. Jackson, with a quick motion, held out his hand. I took it. We were friends from that hour.

"First, then," continued the lawyer, "you must understand that Edgar has undergone a rigid examination at the hands of the police. This may not have appeared at the inquest but nevertheless what I say is true. Now taking his story as a basis, we have this much to go upon:

"He has always been led to believe that his future had been cut out for him according to the schedule universally understood and accepted. He was not only to marry Orpha, but to inherit personally the vast fortune which was to support her in the way to which she is entitled. No doubt as to this being his uncle's intention—an intention already embodied in a will drawn up by Mr. Dunn— ever crossed his mind till you came upon the scene; and not then immediately. Even the misunderstanding with his uncle, occasioned, as I am told, by Mr. Bartholomew learning of some obligations he had entered into of which he was himself ashamed, failed to awaken the least fear in his mind of any change in his uncle's testamentary intentions, or any real lessening of the affection which had prompted these intentions. Indeed, so much confidence did he have in his place in his uncle's heart that he consented, almost with a smile, to defer the announcement of what he considered a definite engagement with Orpha, because he saw signs of illness in his uncle and could not think of crossing him. But he had no fear, as I have said, that all would not come right in time and the end be what it should be.

"Nor did his mind change with the sudden signs of favor shown by his uncle towards yourself. The odd scheme of sharing with you, by a definite arrangement, the care which your uncle's invalid condition soon called for, he accepted without question, as he did every other whim of his autocratic relative. But when the servants began to talk to him of how much writing his uncle did while lying in his bed, and whispers of a new will, drawn up in your absence as well as in his began to circulate through the house, he grew sufficiently alarmed to call on Mr. Dunn at his office and propound a few inquiries. The result was a complete restoration of his tranquillity; for Mr. Dunn, having been kept in ignorance of another lawyer having visited Quenton Court immediately upon his departure, and supposing that the will he had prepared and seen attested was the last expression of Mr. Bartholomew's wishes, gave Edgar such unqualified assurances of a secured future that he naturally was thrown completely off his balance when on the night which proved to be Mr. Bartholomew's last, he was summoned to his uncle's presence and was shown not only one new will but two, alike in all respects save in the essential point with which we are both acquainted. Now, as I am as anxious as you are to do justice to the young man, I will say that if your uncle was looking for any wonderful display of generosity from one who saw in a moment the hopes of a lifetime threatened with total disaster, then he was expecting too much. Of course, Edgar rebelled and said words which hurt the old gentleman. He would not have been normal otherwise. But what I want to impress upon you in connection with this interview is this. He left the room with these words ringing in his ears, 'Now we will see what your cousin has to say. When he quits me, but one of these two wills will remain, and that one you must make up your mind to recognize.' Therefore," and here Mr. Jackson leaned towards me in his desire to hold my full attention, "he went from that room with every reason to fear that the will to be destroyed was the one favoring himself, and the one to be retained that which made you chief heir and the probable husband of Orpha. Have we heard of anything having occurred between then and early morning to reverse the conclusions of that moment? No. Then why should he resort to crime in order to shorten the few remaining days of his uncle's life when he had every reason to believe that his death would only hasten the triumph of his rival?"

I was speechless, dazed by a fact that may have visited my mind, but which had never before been clearly formulated there! Seeing this, the lawyer went on to say: "That is why our hands are held."

Still I did not speak. I was thinking. What I had said we would not do had been done. The word crime had been used in connection with Edgar, and I had let it pass. The veil was torn aside. There was no use in asking to have it drawn to again. I would serve him better by looking the thing squarely in the face and meeting it as I had met the attack against myself, with honesty and high purpose. But first I must make some acknowledgment of the conclusion to which this all pointed, and I did it in these words.

"You see! The boy is innocent."

"I have not said that."

"But I have said it."

"Very good, you have said it; now go on."

This was not so easy. But the lawyer was waiting and watching me and I finally stammered forth:

"There is some small fact thus far successfully suppressed which when known will change the trend of public opinion and clarify the whole situation."

"Exactly, and till it is, we will continue the search for the will which I honestly believe lies hidden somewhere in that mysterious house. Had he destroyed it during that interval in which he was left alone, there would have been some signs left in the ashes on the hearth; and Wealthy denies seeing anything of the sort when she stooped to replenish the fire that night, and so does Clarke, who, at Edgar's instigation, took up the ashes after their first failure to find the will and carefully sifted them in the cellar."

"I have been wondering if they did that."

"Well, they did, or so I have been told. Besides, you must remember the look of consternation, if not of horror, which crossed your uncle's face as he felt that death was upon him and he could no longer speak. If he had destroyed both wills, the one when alone, the other in the face of you all, he would have shown no such emotion. He had simply been eliminating every contestant save his daughter—something which should have given him peace."

"You are right. And as for myself I propose to keep quiet, hoping that the mystery will soon end. Do you think that the police will allow me to leave town?"

"Where do you want to go?"

"Back to work; to my desk at Meadows & Waite in New York."

"I don't think that I would do that. You will meet with much unpleasantness."

"I must learn to endure cold looks and hypocritical smiles."

"But not unnecessarily. I would advise you to take a room at the Sheldon; live quietly and wait. If you wish to write a suitable explanation to your firm, do so. There can be no harm in that."

My heart leaped. His advice was good. I should at least be in the same town as Orpha.

"There is just one thing more," I observed, as we were standing near his office door preparatory to my departure. "Did Edgar say whether he saw the wills themselves or, like myself, only the two envelopes presumably holding them?"

"He was shown them open. Mr. Bartholomew took them one after the other from their envelopes and, spreading them out on the desk, pointed out the name of Edgar Quenton, the son of my brother, Frederick, on the one, and Edgar Quenton, the son of my brother, James, on the other, and so stood with his finger pressed on the latter while they had their little scene. When that was over, he folded the two wills up again and put them back in their several envelopes, all without help, Edgar looking on, as I have no doubt, in a white heat of perfectly justifiable indignation. Can't you see the picture?"

I could and did, but I had no disposition to dwell on it. A question had risen in my mind to which I must have an answer.

"You speak of Edgar looking on. At what, may I ask? At Uncle's handling of the wills or in a general way at Uncle himself?"

"He said that he kept his eye on the two wills."

"Oh! and did he note into which envelope the one went in which he was most interested,—the one favoring himself?"

"Yes, but the envelopes were alike, neither being marked at that time, and as his uncle jumbled them together in his hands, this did not help him or us."

"Ah, the red mark was put on later?"

"Yes. The pencil with which he did it was found on the floor."

I tried to find a way through these shadows,—to spur my memory into recalling the one essential thing which would settle a very vexing question—but I was obliged to give it up with the acknowledgment:

"That mark was in the corner of one of the envelopes at the time I saw them; but I do not know which will it covered. God! what a complication!"

"Yes. No daylight yet, my boy. But it will come. Some trivial matter, unseen as yet, or if seen regarded as of no account, will provide us with a clew, leading straight to the very heart of this mystery. I believe this, and you must, too; otherwise you will find your life a little hard to bear."

I braced myself. I shrank unaccountably from what I felt it to be my present duty to communicate. I always did when there was any possibility of Orpha's name coming up.

"Some trivial matter? An unexpected clew?" I repeated. "Mr. Jackson, I have been keeping back a trivial matter which may yet prove to be a clew."

And I told him of the note made up of printed letters which I had found in my box of cigars.

He was much interested in it and regretted exceedingly that I had obeyed the injunction to burn it.

"From whom did this communication come?"

That I could not answer. I had my own thoughts. Much thinking and perhaps much hoping had led me to believe that it was from Orpha; but I could not say this to him. Happily his own thoughts had turned to the servants and I foresaw that sooner or later they were likely to have a strenuous time with him. As his brows puckered and he seemed in imagination to have them already under examination, I took a sudden resolution.

"Mr. Jackson, I have heard—I have read—of a means now in use in police investigation which sometimes leads to astonishing results." I spoke hesitatingly, for I felt the absurdity of my offering any suggestion to this able lawyer. "The phial which held the poison was handled—must have been handled. Wouldn't it show finger-prints—"

The lawyer threw back his head with a good-natured snort and I stopped confused.

"I know that it is ridiculous for me," I began—

But he cut me short very quickly.

"No, it's not ridiculous. I was just pleased; that's all. Of course the police made use of this new method of detection. Looked about for finger-prints and all that and found some, I have been told. But you must remember that two days at least elapsed between Mr. Bartholomew's death and any suspicion of foul play. That such things as the glass and other small matters had all been removed and—here is the important point; the most important of all,—that the cabinet which held the medicines had been visited and the bottle labeled dangerous touched, if not lifted entirely out, and that by more than one person. Of course, they found finger-prints on it and on the woodwork of the cabinet, but they were those of Orpha, Edgar and Wealthy who rushed up to examine the same at the first intimation that your uncle's death might have been due to the use of this deadly drug. And now you will see why I felt something like pleasure at your naive mention of finger-prints. Of all the persons who knew of the location and harmful nature of this medicine, you only failed to leave upon the phial this irrefutable proof of having had it in your hand. Now you know the main reason why the police have had the courage to dare public opinion. Your finger-prints were not to be found on anything connected with that cabinet."

"My finger-prints? What do they know of my fingerprints. I never had them taken."

Again that characteristic snort.

"You have had a personal visit, I am told, from the Inspector. What do you think of him? Don't you judge him to be quite capable of securing an impression of your finger-tips, if he so desired, during the course of an interview lasting over two hours?"

I remembered his holding out to me a cigarette case and urging me to smoke. Did I do so? Yes. Did I touch the case? Yes, I took it in hand. Well, as it had done me no harm, I could afford to smile and I did.

"Yes, he is quite capable of putting over a little thing like that. Bless him for it."

"Yes, you are a fortunate lad to have won his good will."

I thought of Edgar and of the power which, seemingly without effort, he exercised over every kind of person with whom he came in contact, and was grateful that in my extremity I had found one man, if not two, who trusted me.

Just a little buoyed up by my success in this venture, I attempted another.

"There is just one thing more, Mr. Jackson. There is a name which we have not mentioned—that is, in any serious connection,—but which, if we stop to think, may suggest something to our minds worthy of discussion. I mean— Clarke's. Can it be that under his straightforward and devoted manner he has held concealed jealousies or animosities which demanded revenge?"

"I have no acquaintance with the man; but I heard the Inspector say that he wished every one he had talked to about this crime had the simple candor and quiet understanding of Luke Clarke. Though broken-hearted over his loss, he stands ready to answer any and all questions; declaring that life will be worth nothing to him till he knows who killed the man he has served for fifteen years. I don't think there is anything further to be got out of Clarke. The Inspector is positive that there is not."

But was I? By no means. I was not sure of anything but Orpha's beauty and worth and the love I felt for her; and vented my dissatisfaction in the querulous cry:

"Why should I waste your time any longer? I have nothing to offer; nothing more to suggest. To tell the truth, Mr. Jackson, I am all at sea."

And he, being, I suspect, somewhat at sea himself, accepted my "Good day," and allowed me to go.

CHAPTER 38

"There is some small fact thus far successfully suppressed, which, when known, will alter the trend of public opinion and clarify the whole situation."

A sentence almost fatuous in its expression of a self- evident truth. One, too, which had been uttered by myself. But foolish and fatuous as it was, it kept ringing on in my brain all that day and far into the night, until I formulated for myself another one less general and more likely to lead to a definite conclusion:

"Something occurred between the hour I left Uncle's room and my visit to his door at three o'clock in the morning which from its nature was calculated to make Edgar indifferent to the destruction of the will marked with red and Wealthy so apprehensive of harm to him that to save him from the attention of the police she was willing to sacrifice me and perjure herself before the Coroner." What was it?

You see from declining to connect Edgar with this crime, I had come to the point of not only admitting the possibility of his guilt, but of arguing for and against it in my own mind. I had almost rather have died than do this; but the word having once passed between me and Mr. Jackson, every instinct within me clamored for a confutation of my doubt or a confirmation of it so strong that my duty would be plain and the future of Orpha settled as her father would have it.

To repeat then: to understand this crime and to locate the guilty hand which dropped poison into the sick man's soothing mixture it was necessary to discover what had happened somewhere in the house between the hours I have mentioned, of sufficient moment to account for Edgar's attitude and that of the faithful Wealthy.

But one conjecture suggested itself after hours of thought. Was it not possible that while I was below, Clarke in his room, and Wealthy in Orpha's, that Edgar had made his way for the second time into his uncle's presence, persuaded him to revoke his decision and even gone so far as to obtain from him the will adverse to his own hopes?

Thus fortified, but still fearful of further vacillation on part of one whose mind, once so strong, seemed now to veer this way or that with every influence brought to bear upon it, what more natural than, given a criminal's heart, he should think of the one and only way of ending this indecision and making himself safe from this very hour.

A glass of water—a drop of medicine from the bottle labeled dangerous—a quick good-night—and a hasty departure!

It made the hair stir on my forehead to conceive of all this in connection with a man like Edgar. But my thoughts, once allowed to enter this groove, would run on.

The deed is done; now to regain his room. That room is near. He has but to cross the hall. A few steps and he is at the stair-head,—has passed it, when a noise from below startles him, and peering down, he sees Wealthy coming up from the lower floor.

Wealthy! ready to tell any story when confronted as she soon would be by the fact that death had followed his visit—death which in this case meant murder.

It was base beyond belief: hardly to be thought of, but did it not explain every fact?

I would see.

First, it accounted for the empty envelope and the disappearance of the will which it had held. Also for the fact that this will could not be found in any place accessible to a man too feeble to leave his own room. It had been given to Edgar and he had carried it away.

(Had they searched his room for it? They had searched mine and they had searched me. Had they been fair enough to search his room and to search him?)

Secondly: Edgar's restlessness on that fatal night. The watch he kept on Uncle's door. The interest he had shown at seeing me there and possibly his reluctance to incriminate me by any absolute assertion which would link me to a crime which he, above all others, knew that I had not committed.

Thirdly: the comparative calmness with which he saw his uncle, still undecided, or what was fully as probable, confused in mind by his sufferings and the near approach of death, order the destruction of the remaining will, to preserve which and make it operative he had risked the remorse of a lifetime. He knew that with both wills gone, the third and original one which at that time he believed to be still in existence would secure for him even more than the one he saw being consumed before his eyes, viz.: the undisputed possession of the Bartholomew estate.

So much for the time preceding the discovery that crime and not the hazard of disease had caused our uncle's sudden death. How about Edgar's conduct since? Was there anything in that to dispute this theory?

Not absolutely. Emotion, under circumstances so tragic, would be expected from him; and with his quick mind and knowledge of the worshipful affection felt for him by every member of the household, he must have had little fear of any unfortunate results to himself and a most lively recognition of where the blame would fall if he acted his part with the skill of which he was the undoubted master.

There was but one remote possibility which might turn the tables. Perhaps, it came across him like a flash; perhaps, he had thought of it before, but considered it of no consequence so long as it was the universally accepted belief that Uncle had died at natural death.

And this brings us to Fourthly:

Was it in accordance with my theory or the reverse, for him, immediately and before the doctor could appear, to rush upstairs in company with Orpha and Nurse Wealthy to inspect the cabinet where the medicines were kept?

In full accordance with my theory. Knowing that he must have left finger-marks there on bottle or shelf, he takes the one way to confound suspicion: adds more of his own, and passes the phial into the hands of the two who accompanied him on this very excusable errand.

Was there any other fact which I could remember which might tip the scale, so heavily weighted, even a trifle the other way?

Yes, one—a big one. The impossibility for me even now to attribute such deviltry to a man who had certainly loved the victim of this monstrous crime.

As I rose from this effort to sound the murky depths into which my thoughts had groveled in spite of myself and all the proprieties, I found by the strong feeling of revulsion which made the memory of the past hour hateful to me, that I could never pursue the road which I had thus carefully mapped out for myself. That, innocent or guilty, Edgar Quenton Bartholomew, beloved by our uncle, was sacred in my eyes because of that love, and that whatever might be done by others to fix this crime upon him, I could do nothing—would do nothing to help them even if I must continue to bear to the very end the opprobrium under which I now labored.

And Orpha! Had I forgotten my fears for her—the duty I had felt to preserve her from a step which might mean more than unhappiness—might mean shame?

No; but in that moment of decision made for me by my own nature, the conviction had come that I need not be apprehensive of Orpha marrying Edgar or marrying me while this question between us remained unsettled.

She would be neutral to the end, aye, even if her heart broke. I knew my darling.

In this mood and in this determination I remained for two weeks. I tried to divert myself by reading, and I think my love for books which presently grew into a passion had its inception in that monotonous succession of day after day without a break in the suspense which held me like a hand upon my throat.

I was not treated ill, I was simply boycotted. This made it unpleasant for me to walk the streets, though I never hesitated to do so when I had a purpose in view.

Of Orpha I heard little, though now and then some whiff of gossip from Quenton Court would reach me. She had filled the house with guests, but there was no gayety. The only young person among them was Lucy Colfax, who was preparing for her wedding. The rest were relatives of humble means and few pleasures to whom life amid the comforts and splendors of Quenton Court was like a visit to fairyland. Edgar had followed my example and taken up his abode in one of the hotels. But he spent most of his evenings at the house where he soon became the idol of the various aunts and cousins who possibly would never have honored me with anything beyond a certain civility.

Ere long I heard of his intention to leave town. With his position no better defined than it was, he found C— intolerable.

I wondered if they would let him go! By they I meant the police. If they did, I meant to go too, or at least to make an effort to do so. I wanted to work. I wanted to feel my manhood once again active. I wrote to the firm in whose offices I had a desk.

This is my letter robbed of its heading and signature.

I am well aware in what light I have been held up to the public by the New York press. No one accuses me, yet there are many who think me capable of a great crime. If this were true I should be the most despicable of men. For my uncle was my good friend and made a man of me out of very indifferent material. I revered him and as my wish was to please him while he was living so it is my present desire to do as he would have me do now that he is gone.

If on the receipt of this you advise me not to come, I shall not take it as an expression of disbelief in what I have said but as a result of your kindly judgment that my place is in my home town so long as there is any doubt of the innocency of my relations towards my uncle.

This dispatched, I waited three days for a response. Then I received this telegram:

> Come.

Going immediately to Headquarters, I sought out the Inspector and showed him this message.

"Shall I go or shall I not?" I asked.

He did not answer at once; seemed to hesitate and finally left the room for a few minutes. When he came back he smiled and said:

"My answer is yes. You are young. If you wait for full justification in this case, you may have to wait a lifetime. And then again you may not."

I wrung his hand and for the next hour forgot everything but the manner in which I would make the attempt to see Orpha. I could not leave without a word of farewell to the one being for whose sake I kept my soul from despair.

I dared not call without permission. I feared a rebuff at the front door; Orpha would certainly be out. Again, I might write and she might get the letter, but I could not be sure. Bliss handled the mail and—and— Of course I was unreasonably suspicious, but it was so important for me to reach her very self, or to know that any refusal or inability to see me came from her very self, that I wished to take every precaution. In pursuance of this idea I ran over the list of servants to see if there was one who in my estimation could be trusted to hand her a note. From Wealthy down I named them one by one and shook my head over each. Discouraged, I rose and went out and almost at the first corner I ran upon Clarke.

What came over me at the sight of his uncompromising countenance I do not know, but I stopped him and threw myself upon his mercy. It was an act more in keeping with Edgar's character than with mine, and I cannot account for it save by the certainty I possessed that if he did not want to do what I requested, he would say so. He might be blunt, even accusing, but he would not be insincere or play me false.

"Clarke, well met." Thus I accosted him. "I am going to leave town. I may come back and I may not. Will you do me this favor? I am very anxious to have Miss Bartholomew know that I greatly desire to say good-by to her, but hardly feel at liberty to telephone. If she is willing to see me I shall feel honored."

"I have left Quenton Court for the present," he objected. "I hope to return when it has a master."

If he noticed my emotion at this straightforward if crude statement, he gave no sign of having done so. He simply remained standing like a man awaiting orders, and I hastened to remark:

"But you will be going there to see your old friends, to-day possibly, to-night at latest if you have any good reason for it."

"Yes, I have still a trunk or two there. I will call for them to-night, and I will give Miss Orpha your message. Where shall I bring the reply?"

I told him and he walked off, erect, unmoved, and to all appearance totally unconscious of the fact—or if conscious of it totally unaffected by it—that he had thrown a ray of light into a cavern of gloom, and helped a man to face life again who had almost preferred death.

Evening came and with it a telephone message.

"She will see you to-morrow morning at eleven."

CHAPTER 39

What should I say to her? How begin? How keep the poise due to her and due to myself, with her dear face turned up to mine and possibly her hand responding to my clasp?

Futile questions. When I entered her presence it was to find that my course was properly marked out. She was not alone. Lucy Colfax was with her and the greeting I received from the one was dutifully repeated by the other. I was caught as in a trap; but pride came to my rescue, coupled with a recognition of the real service she was doing me in restraining me to the formalities of a friendly call.

But I would not be restrained too far. What in my colder moments I had planned to say, I would say, even with Lucy Colfax standing by and listening. Lucy Colfax! whose story I knew much better than she did mine.

"Cousin Orpha," I began, with a side glance at Miss Colfax which that brilliant brunette did not take amiss, "I am going almost immediately to New York to take up again the business in which I was occupied when all was well here and my duty seemed plain. Inspector Redding has my address and I will always be at his call. And at that of any one else who wants me for any service worth the journey. If you—" a little catch in my voice warned me to be brief. "If you have need of me, though it be but a question you want answered, I will come as readily as though it were a peremptory summons. I am your cousin and there is no reason in the world why I should not do a cousin's duty by you."

"None," she answered. But she did not reach out her hand. Only stood there, a sweet, sane woman, bidding good-by to a friend.

I honored her for her attitude; but my heart bade me begone. Bowing to

Miss Colfax whose eyes I felt positive had never left my face, I tried to show the same deference to Orpha. Perhaps I succeeded but somehow I think I failed, for when I was in the street again all I could remember was the surprised look in her eyes which yet were the sweetest it had ever been my good fortune to meet.

CHAPTER 40

It was a dream,—nothing else—but it made a very strong impression upon me. I could not forget it, though I was much occupied the next morning and for several days afterwards. It was so like life and the picture it left behind it was so vivid.

What was the picture? Just this; but as plain to my eye as if presented to it by a motion-picture film. Orpha, standing by herself alone, staring at some object lying in her open palm. She was dressed in white, not black. This I distinctly remember. Also that her hair which I had never seen save when dressed and fastened close to her head, lay in masses on her shoulders. A picture of loveliness but of great mental perplexity also. She was intrigued by what she was looking at. Astonishment was visible on her features and what I instinctively interpreted as alarm gave a rigidity to her figure far from natural to it.

Such was my dream; such the picture which would not leave me, nor explain itself for days.

I had got well into the swing of work and was able, strange as it may seem, to hold my own in all business matters, notwithstanding the personal anxieties which devoured my mind and heart the moment I was released from present duty. I had received one or two letters from Mr. Jackson, which while encouraging in a general way, added little to my knowledge of how matters in which I was so concerned were progressing in C— . Edgar was no longer there. In fact, he was in the same city as myself, but for what purpose or where located he could not tell me. The press had ceased covering the first page with unmeaning headlines concerning a tragedy which offered no new features; and although there was a large quota of interested persons who inveighed against the police for allowing me to leave town, there were others, the number of which was rapidly growing, who ventured to state that time and effort, however aided by an inexhaustible purse, would fail to bring to light any further explanation of their leading citizen's sudden death, for the very good reason that there was nothing further to bring out,—the doctor's report having been a mistaken one, and the death simply natural,—that is, the result of undue excitement.

"But there remain some few things of which the public is ignorant."

In this manner Mr. Jackson ended his last letter.

CHAPTER 41

There remain some few things of which the public is ignorant. This was equally true of the police, or some move would have been made by them before this.

The clew afforded by the disappearance simultaneously with that of the will and of a key considered of enough importance by its owner to have been kept upon his person had evidently led to nothing. This surprised me, for I had laid great store by it; and it was after some hours of irritating thought on this subject that I had the dream with which I have opened this account of a fresh phase in my troubled life.

Perhaps, the dream was but a natural sequence of the thought which had preceded it. I was willing to believe so. But what help was there in that? What help was there for me in anything but work; and to my work I went.

But with evening came a fresh trial. I was walking up Broadway when I ran almost into the arms of Edgar. He recoiled and I recoiled, then, with a quick nod, he hurried past, leaving behind him an impression which brought up strange images. A blind prisoner groping in the dark. A marooned sailor searching the boundless waste for a ship which will never show itself above the horizon. A desert wanderer who sees the oasis which promises the one drop of water which will save him fade into ghastly mirage. Anything, everything which bespeaks the loss of hope and the approach of doom.

I was struck to the heart. I tried to follow him, when, plainly before me—as plainly as he had himself appeared a moment previous, I saw her standing in a light place looking down at something in her hand, and I stopped short.

When I was ready to move on again, he was gone, leaving me very unhappy. The gay youth, the darling of society, the beloved of the finest, of the biggest-natured, and, above all, of the tenderest heart I knew—come to this in a few short weeks! As God lives, during the days while the impression lay strongest upon me, I could have cursed the hour I left my own country to be the cause, however innocently, of such an overthrow.

That he had shown signs of dissipation added poignancy to my distress. Self-indulgence of any kind had never been one of his failings. The serpent coiled about his heart must be biting deep into its core to drive one so fastidious into excess.

Three days later I saw him again. Strange as this may seem in a city of over a million, it happened, and that is all there is to it. I was passing down Forty-second Street on my way to the restaurant I patronized when he turned the corner ahead of me and moved languidly on in the same direction. I had still a block to walk, so I kept my pace, wondering if he could possibly be bound for the same eating-place, which, by the way, was the one where we had first met. If so, would it be well for me to follow; and I was yet debating this point when I saw another man turn that same corner and move along in his wake some fifty feet behind him and some thirty in front of me.

This was a natural occurrence enough, and would not even have attracted my attention if there had not been something familiar in this man's appearance—something which brought vividly to mind my former encounter with Edgar on Broadway. What was the connection? Then suddenly I remembered. As I shook myself free from the apathy following this startling vision of Orpha which, like the clutch of a detaining hand, had hindered my mad rush after Edgar, I found myself staring at the face of a man brushing by me with a lack of ceremony which showed that he was in a hurry if I was not. He was the same as the one now before me walking more and more slowly but still holding his own about midway between us two. No coincidence in this. He was here because Edgar was here, or— I had to acknowledge it to myself— because I was here, always here at this time in the late afternoon.

I did not stop to decide on which of us two his mind was most set—on both perhaps—but pursued my course, entering the restaurant soon after the plain clothes man who appeared to be shadowing us.

Edgar was already seated when I stepped in, but in such a remote and inconspicuous corner that the man who had preceded me had to look covertly in all directions before he espied him. When he did, he took a seat near the door and in a moment was lost to sight behind the newspaper which he had taken from his pocket. There being but one empty seat, I took it. It, too, was near the door.

It seemed a farce to order a meal under these circumstances. But necessity knows no law; it would not do to appear singular. And when my dinner was served, I ate it, happy that I was so placed that I could neither see Edgar nor he me.

The man behind the newspaper, after a considerable wait, turned his attention to the chafing-dish which had been set down before him. Fifteen minutes went by; and then I saw from a sudden movement made by this man that Edgar had risen and was coming my way. Though there was some little disturbance at the time, owing to the breaking up of a party of women all seeking egress through the same narrow passage, it seemed to me that I could hear his footsteps amid all the rest, and waited and watched till I saw our man rise and carelessly add himself to the merry throng.

As he went by me, I was sure that he gave me one quick look which did not hinder me from rising, money in hand, for the waiter who fortunately stood within call.

My back was to the passage through which Edgar must approach, but I was sure that I knew the very instant he went by, and was still more certain that I should not leave the place without another encounter with him, eye to eye.

But this was the time when my foresight failed me. He did not linger as usual to buy a cigar, and so was out of the door a minute or two before me. When I felt the pavement under my feet and paused to look for him in the direction from which he had come, it was to see him going the other way, nonchalantly followed by the man I had set down in my mind as an agent of police.

That he really was such became a surety when they both vanished together around the next corner. Edgar was being shadowed. Was I? I judged not; for on looking back I found the street to be quite clear.

CHAPTER 42

That night, the vision came for the third time of Orpha gazing intently down at her open palm. It held me; it gripped me till, bathed in sweat, I started up, assured at last of its actual meaning. It was the key, the missing key that was offered to my view in my darling's grasp. She had been made the repositor of it—or she had found it—and did not know what to do with it. I saw it all, I was practical; above all else, practical.

However, I sent this letter to Mr. Jackson the next morning: "What have the police done about the key? Have they questioned Miss Bartholomew?" and was more restless than ever till I got the reply.

Nothing doing. Clarke acknowledges that Mr. Bartholomew carried a key around with him attached to a long chain about his neck. He had done so when Clarke first entered his service and had continued to do so ever since. But he never alluded to it but once when he said: "This is my secret, Clarke. You will never speak of it, I know."

Asked when he saw it last, he responded in his blunt honest way, "The night he died. It was there when I prepared him for bed." "And not when you helped the undertaker's men to lay him out?" "No, I think I would have seen it or they would have mentioned it if it had been."

Urged to tell whether he had since informed any one of the existence and consequent disappearance of this key, his reply was characteristic. "No, why should I? Did I not say that Mr. Bartholomew spoke of it to me as his secret?" "Then you did not send the letter received in regard to it?" His eyes opened wide, his surprise appeared to be genuine. "Who—" he began; then slowly and repeatedly shook his head. "I wrote no letter," he asserted, "and I didn't know that any one else knew anything about this chain and key." "It was not written," was the retort; at which his eyes opened wider yet and he shook his head all the more vigorously. "Ask some one else," he begged; "that is, if you must know what Mr. Bartholomew was so anxious to have kept secret." Still loyal, you see, to a mere wish expressed by Mr. Bartholomew.

I have given in detail this unofficial examination of the man who from his position as body servant must know better than any one else the facts about this key. But I can in a few words give you the result of questioning Miss Bartholomew and the woman Wealthy,—the only other two persons likely to share his knowledge. Miss Bartholomew was astonished beyond measure to hear that there was any such key and especially by the fact that he had carried it in this secret way about with him. Wealthy was astonished also, but not in the same way. She had seen the chain many times in her attendance upon him as nurse, but had always supposed that it supported some trinket of his dead wife, for whom he seemed to have cherished an almost idolatrous affection. She knew nothing about any key.

You may rely on the above as I was the unofficial examiner; also why I say "Nothing doing" to your inquiries about the key. But the police might have a different story to tell if one could overcome their reticence. Of this be sure; they are working as they never have worked yet to get at the core of this mystery and lift the ban which has settled over your once highly reputed family.

CHAPTER 43

So! the hopes I had founded upon my dream and its consequent visions had all vanished in mist. The clew was in other hands than Orpha's. She was as ignorant now as ever of the existence of the key, concerning which I had from time to time imagined that she had had some special knowledge. I suppose I should have been thankful to see her thus removed from direct connection with what might involve her in unknown difficulties. Perhaps I was. Certainly there was nothing more that I could do for her or for any one; least of all for myself. I could but add one more to the many persons waiting, some in patience, some in indignant protest for developments which would end all wild guessing and fix the blame where it rightfully belonged.

But when it became a common thing for me to run upon Edgar at the restaurant in Forty-second Street, sometimes getting his short nod, sometimes nothing but a stare, I began to think that his frequent appearance there had a meaning I could safely associate with myself. For under the obvious crustiness of this new nature of his I observed a quickly checked impulse to accost me—a desire almost passionate to speak, held back by scorn or fear. What if I should accost him! Force the words from his lips which I always saw hovering there? It might precipitate matters. The man whom I had regarded as his shadow was no longer in evidence. To be sure his place might have been taken by some one else whom I had not yet identified. But that must be risked. Accordingly the next time Edgar showed himself at the restaurant, I followed him into his corner and, ignoring the startled frown by which I was met, sat down in front of him, saying with blunt directness which left him no opportunity for protest.

"Let us talk. We are both suffering. I cannot live this way nor can you. Let us have it out. If not here, then in some other place. I will go anywhere you say. But first before we take a step you must understand this. I am an honest man, Edgar, and my feeling for you is one from which you need not shrink. If you will be as honest with me—

He laughed, but in a tone totally different from the merry peal which had once brought a smile from lips now buried out of sight.

"Honest with you?" He muttered; but rose as he said this and reached for his overcoat, to the astonishment of the waiter advancing to serve us.

Laying a coin on the table, I rose to my feet and in a few minutes we were both in the street, walking I knew not where, for I was not so well acquainted with the city as he, and was quite willing to follow where he led.

Meantime we were silent, his breath coming quickly and mine far from equable. I was glad when we paused, but surprised that it was in the middle of a quiet block with a high boarded fence running half its length, against which he took his stand, as he said:

"Why go further? You have seen my misery and you want to talk. Talk about what? Our uncle's death? You know more about that than I do; and more about the will, too, I am ready to take my oath. And you want to talk! talk! You—"

"No names, Edgar. You heard what I said at the inquest. I can but repeat every word of denial which I uttered then. You may find it hard to believe me or you may be just amusing yourself with me for some purpose which I find it hard to comprehend. I am willing it should be either, if you will be plain with me and say your say. For I am quite aware, however you may seek to hide it, that there is something you wish me to know; something that would clear the road between us; something which it would be better for you to speak and for me to hear than this fruitless interchange of meaningless words which lead nowhere and bring small comfort."

"What do you mean?" He was ghastly white or the pale gleam from the opposite lamp-post was very deceptive. "I don't know what you mean," he repeated, stepping forward from the closely boarded fence that I might not see how he was shaking.

"I am very sorry," I began; then abruptly, "I am sure that you do know what I mean, but if you prefer silence,—prefer things to go on as they are, I will try and bear it, hoping that some of these mysteries may be cleared up and confidence restored again between us, if only for Orpha's sake. You must wish that too."

"Orpha!" He spoke the word strangely, almost mechanically. There was no thought behind the utterance. Then as he looked up and met my eye, the color came into his cheeks and he cried:

"Do not remind me of all that I have lost. Uncle, fortune, love. I am poorer than a beggar, for he—"

He pulled himself up with a jerk, drew a deep breath and cast an uneasy look up and down the street.

"Do you know," he half whispered, "I sometimes think I am followed. I cannot seem to get away all by myself. There is always some one around. Do you think that pure fancy? Am I getting to be a little batty? Are they afraid that I will destroy myself? I have been tempted to do so, but I am not yet ready to meet my uncle's eye."

I heard this though it was rather muttered than said and my cold heart seemed to turn over in my bosom, for despair was in the tone and the vision which came with it was not that of Orpha but of another woman—the woman he had lost as he had lost his fortune and lost the man whose gaze he dared not cross death's river to meet.

I tried to take his hand—to bridge the fathomless gulf between us; but he fixed me with his eye, and, laughing with an echo which caused the two or three passers-by to turn their heads as they hurried on, he said in measured tones:

"You are the cause of it all." And turned away and passed quickly down the street, leaving me both exhausted and unenlightened.

CHAPTER 44

Next day I received a telegram from Mr. Jackson. It was to the effect that he would like some information concerning a man named John E. Miller, who had his office somewhere on Thirty-fifth Street. He was an attorney and in some way connected with the business in which we were interested.

This, as you will see, brings us to the incident related in the first chapter of this story. Having obtained Mr. Miller's address from the telephone book, I was searching the block for his number when the gentleman himself, anxious to be off to his injured child and, observing how I looked this way and that, rushed up to me and making sure that I answered to the name of Edgar Quenton Bartholomew, thrust into my hands a letter and after that a package containing, as he said, a key of much importance, both of which were obviously meant for Edgar and not for me.

Why, in the confusion of the moment, I let him go, leaving the key and letter in my hand, and why, after taking them to my hotel, I had the struggle of my life deciding what I should do with them, should now be plain to you. (For I felt as sure then as later, that the key which had thus, by a stroke of Providence, come into my possession was the key found by some one and forwarded by some one, without the knowledge of the police, to this Mr. Miller who in turn supposed he had placed it in Edgar's hands.

Believing this, I also believed that it was the only Open sesame to some hitherto undiscovered drawer or cupboard in which the will might be found. If passed on to Edgar what surety had I that if this will should prove to be inimical to his interests it would ever see the light.

There is a devil in every man's soul and mine was not silent that night. I wanted to be the first to lay hands on that will and learn its contents. Would I be to blame if I kept this key and made use of it to find what was my own? I would never, never treat Edgar as I felt sure that he would treat me, if this advantage should be his. The house and everything in it had been bequeathed to me. Morally it was all mine and soon would be legally so if I profited by this chance. So I reasoned, hating myself all the while, but keeping up the struggle hour in and hour out.

Perhaps the real cause of my trouble, the furtive sting which kept me on the offensive, was the fear—shall I not say the belief—that the unknown person who had thus betrayed her love and sympathy for Edgar was Orpha. Had I not seen her in my dream with a key lying in her hand? That key was now in mine, but not by her intention. She had meant it for him;—to give him whatever advantage might accrue from its possession—she, whom I had believed to be so just that she would decline to favor him at my expense.

Jealousy! the gnawing fiend that will not let our hearts rest. I might have gathered comfort from the thought that dreams were not be relied upon; that I had no real foundation for my conclusions. The hand-writing was not hers either on packet or letter; and yet the human heart is so constituted that despite all this; despite my faith, my love, the conviction remained, clouding my judgment and thwarting my better instincts.

But morning brought me counsel, and I saw my duty more clearly. To some it may seem that there was but one thing to do, viz: to hand over packet and letter to the police. But I had not the heart to place Orpha in so compromising a position, without making an effort to save her from their reprobation and it might be from their suspicion. I recognized a better course. Edgar must be allowed to open his own mail, but in my presence. I would seek him out as soon as I could hope to find him and, together, we would form some plan by which the truth might be made known without injuring Orpha. If it meant destruction to him, I would help him face it. She must be protected at all hazards. He was man enough still to see that. He had not lost all sense of chivalry in the debacle which had sapped his courage and made him the wreck I had seen him the night before. But where should I go? Where reach him?

The police knew his whereabouts but as it was my especial wish to avoid the complication of their presence, this afforded me small help. Mr. Miller was my man. He must have Edgar's address or how could he have made an appointment with him. It was for me to get into communication with this attorney.

Hunting up his name in the telephone book, I found that he lived in Newark. Calling him up I learned that he was at home and willing to talk to me. Thereupon I gave him my name and asked him how his child was, and, on hearing that she was better, inquired when he would be at his office. He named what for me, in my impatience, was a very late hour; and driven to risk all, rather than lose a possible advantage, I told him of the mistake we had made, he in giving and I in receiving a package, etc., belonging, as I now thought to my cousin of the same name, and assuring him that I had not opened either package or letter, asked for my cousin's address that I might immediately deliver them.

Well, that floored him for the moment, judging from the expletive which reached my ear. No one could be ignorant of what my name stood for with the mass of people. He had blundered most egregiously and seemed to be well aware of it.

But he was a man of the world and soon was explaining and apologizing for his mistake. He had never seen my cousin, and, being in some disorder of mind at the time, had been misled by a certain family resemblance I bore to the other Edgar as he was presented to the public in the newspapers. Would I pardon him, and, above all, ask my cousin to pardon him, winding up by giving me the name of the hotel where Edgar was to be found.

Thanking him, I hung up the receiver, put on my hat and went out.

I had not far to go; the steps I took were few, but my thoughts were many. In what mood should I find my cousin? In what mood should I find myself? Was I doing a foolish thing?—a wrong thing?—a dangerous thing? What would be its upshot?

Knowing that I was simply weakening myself by this anticipatory holding of an interview which might take a very different course from any I was likely to imagine, I yet continued to put questions and answer them in my own mind till my arrival at the hotel I was seeking put a sudden end to them.

And well it might; for now the question was how to get speech with him. I could not send up my name, which as you will remember was the same as his; nor would I send up a false one. Yet I must see him in his room. How was this to be managed? I thought a minute, then acted.

Saying that I was a messenger from Mr. John E. Miller with an important letter for Mr. Bartholomew, I asked if that gentleman was in his room and if so, whether I might go up.

They would see.

While I waited I could count my own heart-beats. The, hands of the clock dragged and I wondered how long I could stand this. Finally, the answer came: he was in and would see me.

He had just finished shaving when I entered and for a moment did not turn. When he did and perceived who it was, the oath he uttered showed me what I might expect.

But the resolution with which I faced him calmed him more quickly than I had any reason to anticipate. Evidently, I had not yet found the key to his nature. Edgar at that moment was a mystery to me. But he should not remain so much longer.

Waiting for nothing, I addressed him as brother to brother. The haggard look in his eye had appealed to me. Would to God there was not the reason for it that I feared!

"Edgar, the message I sent up was a correct one. I come as an agent from Mr. John E. Miller with a letter and a package addressed to your name which you will remember is identical with my own. Do you know any such man?"

"I have heard of him." Why did his eyes fall and his cheek take on a faint flush?

"Have you heard from him?"

"Yes, I got a message from him yesterday, asking me to call at his office, but—but I did not go."

I wanted to inquire why, but felt it unwise to divert his attention from the main issue for the mere purpose of satisfying my curiosity.

"Then," I declared, "these articles must belong to you. They were handed to me under the supposition that I was the man to whom they were addressed. But, having some doubts about this myself, I have brought them to you in the same state in which I received them—that is, intact. Edgar, there is a key in this package. I know this to he so because Mr. Miller said so particularly. We are both interested in a key. If this is the one our uncle wore about his neck I should be allowed to inspect it as well as yourself."

I had expected rebuff—an assertion of rights which might culminate in an open quarrel. But to my amazement the first gleam of light I had discerned on his countenance since the inquest came with that word.

"Give me it," he cried. "I am willing that you should see me open it."

I laid down the package before him, but before he had more than touched it, I placed the letter beside it, with the intimation that perhaps it would be better for him to read that first.

In an instant the package was pushed aside and the letter seized upon. The action and the glance he gave it made my heart stand still. The fervor and the devouring eagerness thus displayed was that of a lover.

Had his affection for Orpha already reached the point of passion?

Meanwhile, he had thrust the letter out of sight and taken up the small package in which possibly lay our mutual fate. As he loosened the string and pulled off the wrappers, I bent forward, and in another moment we were gazing at a very thin key of the Yale type he held out between us on his open palm.

"It is according to description," I said.

To my astonishment he threw it down on the table before which we were standing.

"You are right," he cried. "I had better read the letter first. It may enlighten us."

Walking off to a window, he slipped behind a curtain and for a few minutes the earth for me stood still. When he reappeared, it was with the air and presence of the old Edgar, a little worse for the dissipation of the last few weeks, but master of himself and master of others,— relieved, happy, almost triumphant.

"It was found by Orpha," he calmly announced. (It was not like him to be calm in a crisis like this.) "Found in a flower-pot which had been in Uncle's room at the time of his death. She had carried it to hers and night before last, while trying to place it on a shelf, it had fallen from her hands to the floor, breaking apart and scattering the earth in every direction. Amid this debris lay the key with the chain falling loose from it. There is no doubt that it is the one we have been looking for; hidden there by a sick man in a moment of hallucination. It may lead to the will—it may lead to nothing. When shall we go?"

"Go?"

"To C— . We must follow up this clew. Somewhere in that room we shall find the aperture this key will fit."

"Do you mean for us to go together?" I had a sensation of pleasure in spite of the reaction in my spirits caused by Edgar's manner.

With an unexpected earnestness, he seized me by the arm and, holding me firmly, surveyed me inquiringly. Then with a peculiar twitch of his lips and a sudden loosening of his hand he replied with a short:

"I do."

"Then let us go as quickly as the next train will take us." He nodded, and, lifting the key, put it in his pocket. Ungenerously, perhaps, certainly quite foolishly, I wished he had allowed me to put it in mine.

CHAPTER 45

We went out together. I did not mean to leave him by himself for an instant, now that he had that precious key on his person. I had had one lesson and that was enough. In coming down the stairs, he had preceded me, which was desirable perhaps, but it had its disadvantages as I perceived when on reaching the ground floor, we passed by a small reception room in which a bright wood-fire was burning. For with a deftness altogether natural to him he managed to slip ahead of me and enter that room just as a noisy, pushing group of incoming guests swept in between us, cutting off my view. When I saw him again, he was coming from the fireplace inside, where the sudden blaze shooting up showed what had become of the letter which undoubtedly it would have been very much to my advantage to have seen.

But who can say? Not I. It was gone; and there was no help for it. Another warning for me to be careful, and one which I should not have needed, as I seemed to see in the eye of a man standing near us as we two came together again on our way to the desk.

"There's a fellow ready to aid me in my work, or to hinder according to his discretion," I inwardly commented.

But if so, and if he followed us and noted our several preparations before taking the train, he did it like an expert, for I do not remember running upon him again.

The chief part which I took in these preparations was the sending of two telegrams; one to the office and one to Inspector Redding in C— . Edgar did not send any. The former was a notification of absence; the latter, a simple announcement that I was returning to C— and on what train to expect me. No word about the key. Possibly he already knew as much about it as I did.

CHAPTER 46

Edgar continued to surprise me. On our arrival he showed gratification rather than displeasure at encountering the Inspector at the station.

"Here's luck," he cheerfully exclaimed. "This will save me a stop at Headquarters. I hear that my cousin has found a key, presumably the one for which we have all been searching. Quenton and myself are here to see if we cannot find a keyhole to fit it. Any objections, Inspector?"

His old manner, but a little over-emphasized. I looked to see if the Inspector noticed this, but he was a man so quiet in his ways that it would take one as astute as himself to read anything from his looks.

Meantime he was saying:

"That's already been tried. We've been all the morning at it. But if you have any new ideas on the subject I am willing to accompany you back to the house."

The astonishment this caused me was hard to conceal. How could they have made the trial spoken of when the key necessary for it was at that very moment in Edgar's pocket? But I remembered the last word he had said to me before leaving the train, "If you love me—if you love yourself—above all, if you love Orpha, allow me to run this business in my own way;" and held myself back, willing enough to test his way and see if it were a good one.

"I don't know as I have any new ideas," Edgar protested. "I fear I exhausted all my ideas, new and old, before I went to New York. However, if you—" and here he drew the Inspector aside and had a few earnest words with him, while I stood by in a daze.

The end of it all was that we went one way and the Inspector another, with but few more words said and only one look given that conveyed any message and that was to me. It came from the Inspector and conveyed to me the meaning, whether true or false, that he was leaving this matter in my hands.

And Edgar thought it was in his!

One incident more and I will take you with me to Quenton Court. As we, that is, Edgar and myself, turned to go down the street, he remarked in a natural but perfectly casual manner:

"Orpha has the key."

As the Inspector was just behind us on his way to the curb, I perceived that this sentence was meant for his ear rather than for mine and let it pass till we were well out of hearing when I asked somewhat curtly:

"What do you mean by that? What has your whole conduct meant? You have the key—"

"Quenton, do you want the police hanging over us while we potter all over that room, trying all sorts of ridiculous experiments in our search for an elusive keyhole? Orpha has a key but not the right one. That is in my pocket, as you know."

At this I stopped him short, right there in the street. We were not far from Quenton Court, but much as I longed to enter its doors again I was determined not to do so till I had had it out with this man.

"Edgar, do you mean to tell me that Orpha has lent herself to this deception?"

"Deception? I call it only proper circumspection. She knew what this key meant to me—to you—to herself. Why should she give up anything so precious into hands of whose consequent action she could form no opinion. I admire her for her spirit. I love—" He stopped short with an apologetic shrug. "Pardon me, Quenton, I don't mean to be disagreeable." Then, forcing me on, he added feverishly, "Leave it to me. Leave Orpha to me. I do not say permanently—that depends—but for the present. I'll see this thing through and with great spirit. You will be satisfied. I'm a better friend to you than you think. Will you come?"

"Yes, I will come. But, Edgar, I promise you this. As soon as I find myself in Orpha's presence I am going to ask her whether she realizes what effect this deception played upon the police may have upon us all."

"You will not." For the first and only time in all our intercourse a dangerous gleam shot from his mild blue eye. "That is," he made haste to add with a more conciliatory aspect, "you will not wish to do so when I tell you that whatever feelings of distrust or jealous fear I once cherished towards you are gone. Now I have confidence in your word and in the disinterestedness of your attentions to our uncle. You have expressed a wish that we should be friends. I am ready, Quenton. Your conduct for the last two days has endeared you to me. Will you take my hand?"

The old Edgar now, without any question or exaggeration. The insouciant, the appealing, the fascinating youth, the child of happy fortunes! I did not trust him, but my heart went out to him in spite of all the past and of a future it took all my courage to face, and I took his hand.

CHAPTER 47

Haines' welcome to us at the front door was a study in character which I left to a later hour to thoroughly enjoy.

The sudden flush which rose to his lank cheek gave evidence to his surprise. The formal bow and respectful greeting, to the command he had over it. Had one of us appeared alone, there would have been no surprise, only the formal greeting. But to see us together was enough to stir the blood of even one who had been for years under the discipline of Edgar Quenton Bartholomew, the one and only.

Edgar did not notice it but stepped in with an air which left nothing for me to display in the way of self-assertion. I think at that moment as he stood in face of the unrivalled beauties of the leaping fountain against its Moorish background he felt himself as much the master of it all as though he already had in his hand the will he was making this final attempt to discover. So rapidly could this man of quick impulses pile glorious hope on hope and soar into the empyrean at the least turn of fate.

As I was watching him I heard a little moan. It came from the stairway. Alarmed, for the voice was Orpha's, we both turned quickly. She was looking at us from one of the arches, her figure swaying, eyes wide with alarm. She, too, had felt the shock of seeing us together.

Above, in strong contrast to her pathetic figure, Lucy Colfax stood waiting, elegant in pose and attire, but altogether unmoved in face and bearing and, as I thought, quite without feeling, till I saw her suddenly step down and throw her arm about Orpha. Perhaps it was not possible for her naturally composed features to change except under heart-breaking emotions. But it was not upon her, interesting as she was at that moment, that my glances lingered, but upon Orpha who had rapidly regained her poise and was now on her way down.

We met her as she stepped down into the court and I for one with a smile. All my love and all my confidence had returned at the sight of her face, which, if troubled, had never looked more ingenuous.

"What does this mean?" she asked, a little tremulously, but with a growing courage beaming in her eye. "Why are you both here? Do the police know?"

"Yes, and approve," Edgar assured her. "We have come to test the key which was such a failure in their hands." And in his lordly way he took possession of her, leading her across the court to the library, leaving me to follow with Miss Colfax, who gave me her first smile as she graciously consented to join me. He had got the better of me at the start; but in my determination that he should not retain this advantage, I proceeded to emulate the sang froid of the glowing creature at my side whom I had once seen with her soul bared in a passionate parting from the man she loved, and who now, in close proximity to that man moving ahead of her with the woman he hoped to claim, walked like a goddess in anticipation of a marriage which might bring her prestige but no romance.

What we said when we were all four collected in the library is immaterial. It was very near the dinner hour and after a hurried consultation as to the manner and time of the search we had come there to undertake, Edgar and I went upstairs, each to our several rooms to prepare for the meal awaiting us, as if no interval of absence had occurred and we were still occupants of the house.

I had rather not have walked down that third story hall up to and past the cozy corner. I did not want to see Wealthy's rigid figure rise from her accustomed seat, or hear the well-remembered voices of the maids float up the spiral staircase. But I might have spared myself these anticipations. I met nobody. That end of the hall was silent. It was even cold; like my heart lying so heavily in my despairing breast.

CHAPTER 48

A gloomy evening. I am speaking of its physical aspects. A lowering sky, a pelting rain with a wind that drove the lurching branches of the closely encircling trees against windows reeking with wet.

Every lamp in the electroliers from the ground floor to the top was alight. Edgar would have it so. As he swung into Uncle's room, that too leaped vividly into view, under his hand. It was as of old; every disturbed thing had been restored to order; the bed, the picture; ah, the picture! the winged chair with its infinite memories, all stood in their proper places. Had Uncle been entering instead of ourselves, he would have found everything as he was accustomed to see it. Could it be that he was there, unseen, impalpable but strong as ever in love and purpose?

We were gathered at the foot of the bed.

"Let me have the key, Orpha,"

She put up her hand to her neck and then I perceived there the encircling glint of a very finely linked chain. As she drew this up a key came with it. As she allowed this to fall to the full length of the chain, it became evident that the latter was long enough to be passed over her head without unclasping. But it was with an indifferent eye I watched her do this and hand key and chain to Edgar, for a thought warm with recovered joy had come to me that had she not believed the key thus cherished to be the very one worn by her father she would never have placed it thus over her heart.

I think Edgar must have recognized my thought from the look he cast me as he drew the key from the chain and laid the latter on the table standing in its corner by the fire-place. Instantly I recognized his purpose; and watched his elbows for what I knew would surely take place before he turned around again. Always an adept at legerdemain it was a simple thing for him to substitute the key he had brought from New York for the one he had just received from Orpha; and in a moment he had done this and was facing us as before, altogether his most interesting self, ready for action and primed to succeed.

"Do you know," he began, taking us all in with one sweeping glance from his proud eye, "I have felt for years, though I have never spoken of it, that Uncle had some place of concealment in this room inaccessible to anybody but himself. Papers which had not been sent to the bank and had not been put away in his desk would disappear between night and morning only to come into view again when wanted, and this without any explanation. I used to imagine that he hid these things in the drawer at the back of his bed, but I soon found out that this was not so, and, losing all interest in the matter, scarcely gave it another thought. But now its importance has become manifest; and what we must look for is a crack in or out of this room, along which we can slip the point of this key. It will find its home somewhere." And he began to look about him.

I remained where I was but missed not one of his movements whether of eye or hand. The girls, on the contrary, followed him step by step, Lucy with an air of polite interest and Orpha eagerly if not hopefully. But the cracks were few in that carefully paneled room, and the moments sped by without apparent accomplishment. As Edgar's spirits began to give way before repeated disappointment, I asked him to grant me a momentary trial with the key.

"I have an idea."

He passed it over to me, without demur. Indeed, with some relief.

It was the first time I had held it in my hand and a thrill ran through me at the contact. Was my idea a good one?

"Uncle was a large man and tall. He wore the chain about his neck. The chain is long; I doubt if he found it necessary to take off the key in using it. The crack, as you call it, must have been within easy reach of his hand. Let us see."

Taking up the chain, I ran it through the hole in the end of the key and snapping the clasp, threw the chain over my head. As I did so, I chanced to be looking at Orpha. The change in her expression was notable. With eyes fixed on the key dangling at my breast, the color which had enlivened her cheeks slowly died out, leaving her pale and slightly distraught as though she were struggling to revive some memory or settle some question she did not quite understand.

"Let me think," she murmured dreamily. "Let me think."

And we, lost in our own wonder, watched her as the color came creeping back to her cheeks, and order took place in her thoughts, and with hands suddenly pressed against her eyes, she cried:

"I see it all again. My father, with that chain hanging just so over his coat. I am in his arms—a hole—all dark— dark. He draws my head down—he stoops . . . The rest is gone from me. I can remember nothing further."

Edgar stared. Lucy glanced vaguely about the walls. Orpha dropped her hands and her glance flew to my face and not to the key this time—when with a crash! A burst of wind rushed upon the house, shaking the windows blinded with wet, and ripping a branch from the tree whose huge bulk nestled against the western wall.

They shuddered, but not I. I was thinking as I had never thought before. Memories of things said, of things done, were coming back to match the broken and imperfect ones of my confused darling. My reasoning faculties are not of the best but I used what I had in formulating the theory which was fast taking on the proportions of a settled conviction. When I saw that I had them all expectant, I spoke. I had to raise my voice a little for the storm just then was at its height.

"What Orpha has said"—so I began—"has recalled the surprise which I felt on first entering this room. To you who have been brought up in it, its peculiarities have so long been accepted by you as a matter of course that you are blind to the impression they make on a stranger. Look at this wall."

I laid my hand on the one running parallel with the main hall—the one in which was sunk the alcove holding the head of the bed.

"You are used to the two passageways connecting the wall of this room with that of the hall where the staircase runs down to the story below. You have not asked why this should be in a mansion so wonderful in its proportions and its finish, or if you have, you have accounted for it by the fact that a new house with new walls had been joined to an old one, whose wall was allowed to stand, thus necessitating little oddities in construction which, on the whole, were interesting and added to the quaintness of the interior. But what of the space between those two walls? It cannot have been filled. If I see right and calculate right there must run from here down to the second floor, if no further, an empty space less than one yard in width, blocked from sight by the wall of this room, by that of the hall and"— here I pulled open the closet door—"by that of this closet at one end and by the wall holding the medicine cabinet at the other. Isn't that so, Edgar? Has my imagination run away with me; or is my conclusion a reasonable one?"

"It—it looks that way," he stammered; "but—but why—"

"Ah! the why is another matter. That may be buried in Uncle's grave. It is the fact I want to impress upon you that there is a place somewhere near us, a place dark and narrow, down which Orpha, when a child, was once carried and which if we can reach it will open up for us the solution of where Uncle used to hide the papers which, according to Edgar, never went to the bank and not into any of the drawers which this room contains."

"Oh," exclaimed Orpha, "if I could only remember! But all is blank except what I have already told you. The dark—my father stooping—and a box—yes, I saw a box— he laid my hand upon it—but where or why I cannot say. Only, there is no suggestion of fear in these strange, elusive memories. Rather one of happiness,—of love,—of a soft peace which was like a blessing. What does it all mean? You have got us thus far, take us further."

"I will try." But I hesitated over what I had to say next. I was risking something. But it could not be helped. It was to be all or nothing with me. I must speak, whatever the result.

"Orpha, did you ever think, or you, Edgar, that there was some grain of truth in the tradition that this house held a presence never seen but sometimes felt?"

Orpha started, and, gripping Edgar by the arm, stood thus, a figure of amazement and dawning comprehension. Edgar, whom I had always looked upon as a man of most vivid imagination, appeared on the contrary to lack the power—even the wish to follow me into this field of suggestion.

"So, that's coming in," he exclaimed in a tone of open irony.

"Yes," I answered, "that is coming in; for I have had my own experience with this so-called Presence. I was coming up the stairs outside one night when I felt— Well, a little peculiar and knew that the experience of which I had heard others speak was about to be mine. But when it came, it came with a difference. I heard a cough. A sight—a sound may be supernatural,—that is from the romanticist's standpoint,—but not a cough. I told Uncle about it once and I am sure he flushed. Edgar, there is a second staircase between these walls, and the Presence was Uncle."

"It may be." His tone was hearty; he seemed glad to be convinced. "And if so," he added, with a gesture towards the key hanging over my breast, "you have the means there of reaching it. How do you propose to go about it?"

"There is but one possible way. This closet provides that. Somewhere along these shelves, among these shoes and hats we shall find the narrow slit this key will fit."

Turning the bulb in the square of ceiling above me, the closet was flooded with light. When they were all in, the narrow space was filled and I was enabled to correct an impression I had previously formed. Miss Colfax was so near me I could hear her pulses beat. For all her lofty bearing she was as eager and interested as any one could be whose fortunes were not directly wrapped up in the discoveries of the next few minutes.

Calling attention to a molding running along the edge of one of the shelves, I observed quite boldly: "To my eyes there is a line there dark enough to indicate the presence of something like a slit. Let us see." And lifting the key from my breast I ran its end along the line I had pointed out till suddenly it came to a stop, entered, and, yielding to the turn I gave it, moved the lock cunningly hidden beyond and the whole series of shelves swung back, revealing an opening into which we were very nearly precipitated in our hurry and surprise.

Recovering our equilibrium, we stood with fascinated gaze fixed on what we beheld slanting away into the darkness of this gap between two walls.

A series of iron steps with a railing on one side—ancient of make, but still serviceable, offered us a means of descent into depths which the light from the closet ceiling, strong as it was, did not entirely penetrate.

"Will you go down?" I asked Edgar; "or shall I? The ladies had better remain where they are."

I was quite confident what his answer would be and I was not disappointed.

"I will go down, of course. You can follow if you wish: Lucy, Orpha, not one step after me, do you hear?"

His tone and attitude were masterful; and instinctively they shrank back. But my anxiety for their safety was equal to his. So I added my appeal.

"You will do as Edgar says," I prayed. "We must go down, both of us; but you will remain here?"

"Unless you call us."

"Unless you are gone too long."

"I will not be gone too long." And I hurried down, Edgar having got the start of me by several steps.

As I went, I noticed what settled a question which had risen in my mind since I became assured of the existence of this secret stairway.

My uncle was an unusually tall man. How could he with so many inches to his credit manage to pass under the bridge between the two walls made by the flooring of the intervening alcove. It must have caused effort—an extraordinary effort for a man so weakened, so near to being moribund. But I saw that it could be done if he had the strength and knew just when to bend his body forward, for the incline of the stairway was rapid and moreover began much further back from the alcove than I had supposed in measuring the distance with my eye. Indeed the whole construction, as I noted it in my hasty descent, was a remarkable piece of masonry built by an expert with the evident intention of defying detection except by one as knowing as himself. The wall of the inn, which had been a wooden structure, had been reinforced by a brick one into which was sunk the beams of the various bridges upholding the passage-ways and the floor of the alcove already alluded to. Hundreds of dollars must have been spent in perfecting this arrangement, but why and to what end was a question which did not then disturb me, for the immediate mystery of what we should find below was sufficiently engrossing to drive all lesser subjects from my mind.

Meanwhile Edgar had reached a small wooden platform backed by a wall which cut off all further descent, and was calling up for more light. As the stairs, narrowed by the brick reinforcement of which I have spoken, were barely wide enough to allow the passage down of a goodly sized man, I could not but see that it was necessary for me to remove myself from his line of vision for him to get the light he wanted. So with a bound or two I cleared the way and stood in a sort of demi-glow at his side.

A bare wall in front,—nothing there, and nothing at the right; but on the left an old-fashioned box clamped to the wall at the height of a man's shoulder. It was indeed an ancient box, and stained brown with dust and mold. There was a lid to it. This lid was half wrenched away and hung over at one side, leaving the box open. From the top of this box protruded the folded ends of what looked like a legal document.

As our eyes simultaneously fell on this, we each made a movement and our glances clashed. Then a long deep breath from him was answered by the same from my own chest heaving to suffocation.

"We have found it," he muttered, choking; and reached out his hand.

But I was quicker than he.

"Wait," said I, pulling him back. "Before either of us touch it, listen to me. If that is the will we are looking for and if it makes you the master here, I here swear to recognize your rights instantly and without question. There will be no legal procedure and no unpleasantness so far as I am concerned."

With this I loosened my clasp.

Would he respond with a like promise? No, he could not. It was not in his nature to do so. He tried,—I felt him make the struggle, but all that resulted were some choked words in recognition of my generosity, followed by a quick seizure of the paper and a rush up the first half dozen steps. But there he stopped, his silhouette against the light making a picture stamped indelibly upon my memory.

"I've got it; I've got it!" he shouted to those above, waving the paper over his head in a triumph almost delirious.

I could not see their faces, but I heard two gasping cries and dashed up, overtaking him just as he emerged into the full light.

He was unfolding the document, all eagerness and anticipatory delight. He could not wait to reach the room itself; he could not wait even to reach the closet; he must see now —at once—while the woman he loved was within reach.

A minute lost was so much stolen from the coming rapture.

I was at his shoulder eager to know my own fate, as his trembling fingers threw the covering leaf back. I knew where to look—I endeavored to forget everything but the spot where the name should be,—the name which would tell all; I wished to see it first. I wished—

A cloud came over me, but through it as if the words blazed beyond the power of any mist to hide them I read: Edgar Quenton Bartholomew, son of James—

Myself!

CHAPTER 49

He had not seen it yet. But he would. In one more moment he would. I waited for his cry; but as it delayed, I reached over and put my finger on the word James. Then I drew back, steadying myself by a clutch on the rail running up at my side.

Slowly he took it in. Slowly he turned and gave me one look; then with a moan, rather than a cry he flung himself up and dashing by the two girls who had started back at his wild aspect, threw himself into the great room where he fell headlong to the floor.

I stood back while they ministered to him. He had not fainted for I heard him now and then cry out, "Wealthy! call Wealthy." And this they finally did. As Orpha passed me on her way to ring the bell communicating with the cozy corner, I saw her full face for the first time since Edgar's action had told her the truth. It was pale, but as I looked the blush came and as I looked again it was gone. I felt myself reeling a trifle, and seeing the will lying on the floor where he had dropped it, I lifted it up and folding it anew, put it in my pocket. Then I walked away, wondering at the silence, for even the elements warring without had their hushed moments, and creaking panes and wrestling boughs no longer spoke of tumult.

In this instant of quiet we heard a knock. Wealthy was at the door.

As Orpha stepped to unlock it, I turned again. Edgar had leaped to his feet, his eyes blazing, all his features working in rage. Lucy had withdrawn into the background, the only composed one amongst us. As the old nurse entered Edgar advanced to meet her.

"I am ill," he began. "Let me take your arm to my room, I have no further rights here unless it is a night's lodging." Here he turned towards me with a sarcastic bow. "There is your master," he added, indicating me with one hand as he reached with the other for her arm. "The will has been found. He has it in his pocket. By that you may know what it does for him and"—his voice falling—"what it does for me."

But his mood changed before he reached the door. With a quick twist of his body he took us all again within the sweep of his vision. "But don't any of you think that I am going to yield my rights without a struggle. I am no hypocrite. I do not say to my cousin, 'No litigation for me.' I dare him to meet me without gloves in an open fight. He knew that the will taken from the envelope and hidden in the box below there was the one favoring himself. How did he know it?"

For a moment I forebore to answer. Evil passions raged within me. The Devil himself seemed whispering in my ear; then I remembered Uncle's own admonition and I turned and looked up at Orpha's picture and that old hour came back and my heart softened and, advancing towards him, I replied:

"I did not know it; but I felt confident of it because our uncle told me what to expect and I trusted him."

"You will never be master here," stormed Edgar, livid with fury.

"Yes, I will," I answered mildly, "for this night." Wealthy drew him away. It would have been hard to tell which was trembling the most, he or the nurse.

They left the door open. I was glad of this. I would have been gladder if the whole household had come trooping in. Orpha standing silent by the great bed; Lucy drawn up against my uncle's old chair—and I wishing the winds would blow and the trees crack,—anything to break the deathly quiet in which we could hear the footfalls of those two disappearing up the hall.

Lucy, marking my trouble, was the first to move.

"I am no longer needed here," she said almost sweetly. "Orpha, if you want to talk, come to me in my room."

At that I started forward. "We will all go." And I closed the closet door and seeing a key in the lock, turned it and, drawing it out, handed it to Orpha, together with the one hanging from my neck.

"They are yours," I said; but did not meet her eyes or touch her hand. "Go with Lucy," I added, "and sleep; I pray you sleep. You have suffered enough for one night."

I felt her leave me; felt every light step she took through the passage-way press in anguish upon my heart. Then the storm rushed upon us again and amid its turmoil I shut the door, dropped the hangings and sat down with bursting heart and throbbing head before her picture.

Another night of sleeplessness in this house which I had once entered in such gayety of spirits.

CHAPTER 50

At an early hour I summoned Haines. He came quickly; he had heard the news.

But I ignored this fact, apparent as it was. "Haines," said I, "you see me here. That is because my uncle's will has been found which grants me the right to give orders from this room. But I shall not abuse the devotion you feel for my cousin. I have only one order to give and that will please rather than disturb you. My cousin, Mr. Edgar, is not satisfied with things as they are. He will contest this will; he has told me so. This being so, I shall await events elsewhere. You have a mistress. See that she is well cared for and that everything goes on as it should. As for myself, do not look for me at breakfast. I am going to the hotel; only see that this note is delivered to Miss Bartholomew before she leaves her room. Good-by, Haines; trust me."

He did not know what to say; or what to do. He looked from me to the note which he held, and from the note back to me. I thought that his lip quivered. Taking pity on his indecision, I spoke up more cheerfully and asked him if he would be good enough to get my bag for me from my old little room, and as he turned in evident relief to do this, I started down the stairs, presently followed by him to the front door, where he helped me on with my coat and handed me my hat. He wanted me to wait for the car, but I refused, acceding only to his request that I would allow him to send a boy to the hotel with my bag. As I passed down the walk I noticed that he closed the door very slowly.

The few lines I had left for Orpha were very simple, though they came from my heart. I merely wrote:

For your sake I leave thus unceremoniously. You are to be considered first in everything I do. Have confidence in me. All I seek is your happiness.

Quenton.

BOOK IV

LOVE

By night the whole town rang with the extraordinary news that I have just endeavored to convey to you. I had visited Mr. Jackson at his office and had a rather serious talk with the Inspector at the Police Station while I myself had many visitors, to all of whom I excused myself with the exception of one. That one was an elderly man who had in his possession an old picture of the inn which had been incorporated in the Bartholomew mansion. He offered to show it to me. I could not resist seeing it, so I ordered him sent up to my room.

At the first glimpse I got of this picture I understood much that I had been doubtful about before. The eighteen or twenty steps we had discovered leading down from Uncle's closet, were but the upper portion of the long flight originally running up from the ground to the large hall where entertainments had been given. The platform where we had found the box made the only break in the descent. This was on a level with the floor of the second story of the inn and from certain indications visible in this old print I judged that it acted as the threshold of a door opening into this story, just as the upper one now represented by the floor of Uncle's closet opened into the great hall. The remaining portions of the building had been so disguised and added to by the clever architect, that only from the picture I was now studying could one see what it had originally been.

I thanked the man and seeing that for a consideration he was willing to part with this picture, made myself master of it at once, wishing to show it to Orpha.

Orpha! Would I hear from her? Was my letter to her little more than a pebble dropped into a bottomless well?

I tried not to think of her. How could I with the future rising before me an absolutely blank wall? Both the Inspector and Mr. Jackson advised me to keep very quiet—as I certainly wished to do—and make no move till the will had been offered for probate and the surrogate's decision obtained. The complications were great; time alone would straighten them out. The murder charge not made as yet but liable to fall any day like a thunderbolt on one or the other of us—Edgar's violent character hidden under an exterior so delightful—the embarrassing position of Orpha—all combined to make it wise for me to walk softly and leave my affairs to their sole manipulation. I was willing, but—

And instantly I became more than willing. A note was handed in. It was from Orpha and vied with mine in its simplicity.

To trust you is easy. It was because my father trusted you that he laid his great fortune in your hands.

Orpha

During the days which now passed I talked to no one, but I read with avidity what was said in the various journals of the discovery of the will under the bizarre circumstances I have already related, and consequently was quite aware that public opinion was as much divided over what bearing this latest phase had upon the main issue as it had been over the main issue itself and the various mystifying events attending it.

Gaining advocates in one quarter, I lost them in another and my heart frequently stood still with dismay as I realized the strength of the prejudice which shut me away from the sympathy and understanding of my fellow creatures.

I was waiting with all the courage possible for some strong and decisive move to be made by Edgar or his lawyers, when the news came that he was ill. Greatly distressed by this, I begged Mr. Jackson to procure for me such particulars as he could gather of the exact condition of things at Quenton Court. He did so and by evening I had learned that Edgar's illness dated from the night of our finding the will. That an attempt had been made to keep this fact from the public, but it had gradually leaked out and with it the rumor that nobody but those in attendance on him had been allowed to enter his part of the house, though no mention of contagion had been made nor any signs perceived of its being apprehended. That Orpha was in great distress because she was included amongst those debarred from the sick room—so distressed that she braved the displeasure of doctor and nurse and crept up to his door only to hear him shouting in delirium. That some of the servants wanted to leave, not so much because the house seemed fated but because they had come to fear the woman Wealthy, who had changed very markedly during these days of anxious nursing. She could not be got to speak, hardly to eat. When she came down into the kitchen as she was obliged to do at times, it was not as in the old days when she brought with her cheer and pleasant fellowship to them all. She brought nothing now but silence and a face contorted from its usual kindly expression into one to frighten any but the most callous or the most ignorant.

For the last twenty-four hours Edgar had given signs of improvement, but Wealthy had looked worse. She seemed to dread the time when he would be out of her hands.

All this had come to Mr. Jackson from private sources, but he assured me that he had no reason to doubt its truth.

Troubled, and fearing I scarcely knew what, I had another of my sleepless nights. Nor was I quite myself all the next day till at nightfall I was called to the telephone and heard Orpha's voice in anxious appeal begging me to come to her.

"Wealthy is so strange that we none of us know what to do with her. Edgar is better, but she won't allow any of us in his room, though I think some one of us ought to see him. She says the doctor is on her side; that she is only fulfilling his orders, and I'm afraid this is so, for when I telephoned him an hour ago he told me not to worry, that in a few days we could see him, but that just now it was better for him to see nobody whose presence would remind him of his troubles. The doctor was very kind, but not quite natural—not quite like his old self, and— and I'm frightened. There is certainly something very wrong going on in this house; even the servants feel it, and say that the master ought to be here if only to get the truth out of Wealthy."

The master! Dear heart, how little she knew! how little any of us knew how much we should have to go through before either Edgar or myself could assume that role. But I could assume that of her friend and protector, and so with a good conscience I promised to go to her at once.

But I would not do this without notifying the Inspector. A premonition that we were at a turn in the twisted path we were all treading which might offer me a problem which it would be beyond my powers to handle under present auspices, deterred me. So I telephoned to Headquarters that I was going to make a call at Quenton Court; after which, I proceeded through the well-known streets to the home of my heart and of Orpha.

I knew from the relieved expression with which Haines greeted me that Orpha had not exaggerated the situation.

He, however, said nothing beyond the formal announcement that Miss Bartholomew awaited me in the library; and there I presently found her. She was not alone (had I expected her to be?), but the lady I saw sitting by the fire was not Miss Colfax this time but the elderly relative of whom I have previously spoken.

Oh, the peace and quiet look of trust which shone in Orpha's eyes as she laid her hand in mine. It gave me strength to withhold my lips from the hand I had not touched in many, many weeks; to face her with a smile, though my heart was sad to bursting; to face anything which might lie before us with not only consideration for her but for him who ever held his own in the background of my mind as the possible master of all I saw here, if not of Orpha.

I had noticed that Haines, after ushering me into the library had remained in the court; and so I was in a degree prepared for Orpha's first words.

"There is something Haines wants to show you. It will give you a better idea of our trouble than anything I can say. Will you go up with him quietly to—to the floor where—"

"I will go anywhere you wish," I broke in, in my anxiety to save her distress. "Will you go, too, or am I to go up with him alone?"

"Alone, and—and by the rear stairs. Do you mind? You will understand when you are near your old room."

"Anything you wish," I repeated; and conscious of Haines' impatience, I joined him without delay.

We went up to the second floor by the Moorish staircase, but when there, traversed the hall to the rear which, with one exception, is a replica of the one above. It had no cozy corner, but there was the same turn to the right leading to the little winding stairway which I knew so well.

As we reached the foot of this, Haines whispered:

"I hope you will pardon me, sir, for taking you this way and for asking you to wait in the small hall overhead till I beckon you to come on. We don't want to surprise any one, or to be surprised, do you see, sir?" And, with a quick, light movement, he sprang ahead, beckoning me to follow.

There was not much light. Only one bulb had been turned on in the third story hall, and that was at the far end. As I reached the top of the little staircase and moved forward far enough to see down to the bend leading away from the cozy corner, I could only dimly discern Haines' figure between me and the faintly illuminated wall beyond. He seemed to be standing quietly and without any movement till suddenly I saw his arm go up, and realizing that I was wanted, I stepped softly forward and before I knew it was ensconced in Wealthy's old place behind the screen, with just enough separation between its central leaves for me to see through.

Haines was at my side, but he said nothing, only slightly touched my elbow as if to bid me take the look thus offered me.

And I did, not knowing what to expect. Would it be Edgar I should see? Or would it be Wealthy?

It was Wealthy. She was standing at the door of Edgar's bedroom, with her head bent forward, listening. As I stared uncomprehendingly at her figure, her head rose and she began to pace up and down before his door, her hands clenched, her arms held rigid at her side, her face contorted, her mind in torture. Was she sane? I turned towards Haines for explanation.

"Like that all the time she is not in the room with him," he whispered. "Walking, walking, and sometimes muttering, but most often not."

"Does the doctor know?"

"She is not like this when he comes."

"You should tell him."

"We have tried to; but you have to see her."

"How long has she been like this?"

"Only so bad as this since noon. Miss Orpha is afeard of her, and there being nobody here but Mrs. Ferris, I advised her to send for you to comfort her a bit. I thought Dr. Cameron might heed what you said, sir. He thinks us just foolish."

"Miss Colfax? Where is she?"

"Gone to New York to buy her wedding-clothes."

"When did she go?"

"To-day, sir."

I looked back at Wealthy. She was again bending at Edgar's door, listening.

"Is his case so bad? Is this emotion all for him? Is she afraid he will die?"

"No; he is better."

"But still delirious?"

"By spells."

"Has she no one to help her? Does she remain near him night as well as day, without rest and without change?"

"She has a helper."

"Ah! Who?"

"A young girl, sir, but she—"

"Well, Haines?"

"Is in affliction, too. She is deaf—and she is dumb; a deaf mute, sir."

"Haines!"

"The truth, sir. Miss Wealthy would have no other. They get along together somehow; but the girl cannot speak a word."

"Nor hear?"

"Not a thing."

144

"And the doctor?"

"He brought her here himself."

The truth was evident. Delirium has its revelations. If one should listen where I saw Wealthy listening, the mystery enveloping us all might be cleared. Was it for me to do this? No, a thousand times, no. The idea horrified me. But I could not leave matters where they were. Wealthy might develop mania. For as I stood there watching her she suddenly started upright again, presenting a picture of heart-rending grief,—wringing her hands and sobbing heavily without the relief of tears.

She had hitherto remained at the far end of the hall close by Edgar's rooms; but now she turned and began walking slowly in our direction.

"She is coming here. You know her room is just back of this," whispered Haines.

I took a sudden resolution. Bidding him to stay where he was, I took a few steps forward and pulled the chain of the large electrolier which lighted this portion of the hall.

She started; stopping short, her eyes opening wide and staring glassily as they met mine. Then her hands went up and covered her face while her large and sturdy form swayed dizzily till I feared she would fall.

"Wealthy!" I cried, advancing hurriedly to her side. "Are you ill? Is my presence so disagreeable to you? Why do you look at me like this?"

She broke her silence with a gasp.

"Because—because"—she moaned—"I—I—"

With a despairing cry, she grasped me by the arm. "Let us go somewhere and talk. I cannot keep my secret any longer. I—I don't know what to do? I tried to injure you—I have injured you, but I never meant to injure Miss Orpha. Will—will you listen?"

"Yes, I will listen and with sympathy. But where shall we go? Into my uncle's room?"

"No, no." She shrank back in sick distaste. "Into my little cozy corner."

"That is too far from Edgar's room," I protested. "He is alone, is he not?"

"Yes, yes; but he is sleeping. He is well enough for me to leave him for a little while. I cannot talk in the open hall."

I felt that I was in a dilemma. She must not know of Haines' near presence or she would not open her mouth. I thought of my own room, then of Clarke's, but I dared not run the risk of her passing the cozy corner lest she might for some reason pause and look in. Impulsively, I made a bold suggestion.

"Edgar has two rooms. Let us go into his den; you will be near him and what is better, We shall be undisturbed." Her mouth opened, but she said nothing; she was wholly taken aback. Then some thought came which changed her whole aspect. She brightened with some fierce resolve and, acceding to my request, led me quickly down the hall.

At the furtherest door of all she stopped; it was the door from which Edgar had looked out on that fatal night to see if I were still lingering in the hall opposite. It had been dark there then; it was bright enough now.

With finger on lip she waited for an instant while she listened for any sounds from within. There were none. With a firm but quiet turning of the knob, she opened the door and motioned me to enter. The room was perfectly dark; but only for an instant. She had crossed the floor while I was feeling my way, and opening the door communicating with the bedroom, allowed the light from within to permeate the room where I stood. As it was heavily shaded, the result was what one might call a visible gloom, through which I saw her figure in a silhouette of rigid outline, so tense had she become under the influence of this daring undertaking.

Next moment I felt her hand on my arm, and in another, her voice in my ear. This is what she said:

"I thought he loved Orpha. Before God I thought he loved her as much as he loved fortune. Had I not, I would have let things alone and given you your full chance. But —but—listen."

Edgar was stirring in the adjoining room, throwing his arms about and muttering words which soon took on emphasis and I heard:

"Lucy! Lucy! how could I help it? I had to do what Uncle said. Every one had to. But you are my only love, you! you!"

As these words subsided into moans, and moans into silence, I felt my arm gripped.

"That's what's killing me," was breathed again into my ears. "I did what I did and all for this. He will fight for the money but not to spend on Orpha, and you, you love her. We all know that now."

"Be calm," I said. "It is all coming right. Miss Colfax will soon be married. And—and if Edgar is innocent—"

"Innocent?"

"Of anything worse than planning to marry one woman while loving another—"

"But he is not. He—"

I stopped her in time. I was not there to listen to anything which would force me to act. If there was action to be taken she must take it or Edgar.

"I don't want to hear anything against Edgar," I admonished her as soon as I could get her attention. "I am not the one to be told his faults. If they are such as Justice requires to have made known, you must seek another confessor. What I want is for you to refrain from further alarming the whole household. Miss Bartholomew is frightened, very much frightened by what she hears of your manner below stairs and of the complete isolation in which you keep your patient. It was she who sent for me to come here. I do not want to stay,— I cannot. Will you promise me to remain quiet for the rest of the night? To think out your problem quietly and then to take advice either from the doctor who appears to understand some of your difficulties or from—"

"Don't say it! Don't say it," she cried below breath, "I know what my duty is, but, oh, I had rather die on the spot than do it. "

"Remember your young mistress. Remember how she is placed. Forget yourself. Forget your love for Edgar. Forget everything but what you owe to your dead master whose strongest wish was to see his daughter happy."

"How can she be? How can she be? How can any of us ever be light-hearted again? But I will remember. I —will—try." Then in a burst, as another cry of "Lucy" came from the other room, "Do you think Miss Orpha's heart will go out to you if—if—"

I shrank away from her; I groped for the door. That question here!—in this semi-gloom—from such lips as these! A question far too sacred and too fraught with possibilities of yea and nay for me to hear it unmoved, bade me begone before I lost myself in uncontrollable anger.

"Do not ask me that," I managed to exclaim. "All I can say is that I love my cousin sincerely and that some day I hope to marry her, fortune or no fortune."

I thought I heard her murmur "And you shall," but I was not sure and never will be. What I did hear was a promise from her to be quiet and to keep to the room where she was.

However, when I had rejoined Haines and we had gone to the floor below, I asked him if he would be good enough to relieve me for the night by keeping a personal watch over his young mistress. "If only I could feel assured that you were sitting here somewhere within sight of her door I should rest easy. Will you do that for me, Haines?"

"As I did that last night on my own account, I do not think it will be very hard for me to do it to-night on yours. I am proud to think you trust me, sir, to help you in your trouble."

And this was the man I had dared to stigmatize in my own thoughts as a useful but unfeeling machine!

CHAPTER 53

I left Orpha cheered, and passing down the driveway came upon a plain clothes man awaiting me in the shadow of the high hedge separating the extensive grounds from the street.

I was not surprised, and stopping short, paused for him to speak.

He did this readily enough.

"You will find a limousine waiting in front of one of the shops halfway down on the next block. It's the Inspector's. He would be glad to have a word with you."

"Very good. I'll be sure to stop."

It could not be helped. We were in the toils and I knew it. Useless to attempt an evasion. The lion had his paw on my shoulder. I walked briskly that I might not have too much time for thought.

"Well?" was the greeting I received, when seated at the Inspector's side. I turned to see what mood he was in before we passed too far from the street lamp for me to get a good look at his features. "Anything new?"

"No." I could say this conscientiously because I had not learned anything new. It was all old; long thought of, long apprehended. "Miss Bartholomew was concerned over the illness in the house. She is young and virtually alone, her only companion being an elderly relative with about as little force and character as a jelly fish. I felt that a call would encourage her and I went. Mrs. Ferris was present—"

"Never mind that. I've been young myself. But—" We were passing another lamp, the light was on my face, he saw my eyes fall before his and he instantly seized his advantage—"Are you sure," he asked, "that you have nothing to tell me?"

I gave him a direct look now, and spoke up resolutely.

"Have pity, Inspector. You know how I am situated. I have no facts to give you except—"

"The young fellow talks in his sleep; we know that. I see that you know it, too; possibly you have heard him—"

"If I have I should not feel justified in repeating a man's ravings to an officer of the law intent on official business. Ravings that spring from fever are not testimony. I'm sure you see that. You cannot require—"

"No, not to-night." The words came slowly, reluctantly from his lips.

I faced him with a look of gratitude and real admiration. This man with a famous case on his hands, the solution of which would make his reputation from one end of the continent to the other, was heeding my plea—was showing me mercy. Or perhaps, he was reading in my countenance (why, we were in business streets, the best lighted in the city!) what my tongue so hesitated to utter.

"Not to-night," he repeated. "Nor ever if we can help it. I am willing you should know that it is a matter of pride with me to get at the truth of this matter without subjecting you to further inquisition. Your position is a peculiar one and consideration should be shown you. But, mark me, the truth has got to be reached. Justice, morality, the future of your family and of the innocent girl who is its present representative all demand this. I shall leave no stone unturned. I can only say that, if possible, I shall leave your stone to be attended to last."

"Inspector, you shall have this much from me. If you will wait two days, I think—I am almost certain—that a strand will be drawn from this tangle which will make the unravelling of the rest easy. It will be by another hand than mine; but you can trust that hand; it is an honest one."

"I will wait two days, unless circumstances should arise demanding immediate action."

And with no further talk we separated. But he understood me and I understood him and words would have added but little to our satisfaction.

CHAPTER 54

The phone in my room rang early on the following morning. Haines had promised to let me know what kind of a night they had had, and he was promptly keeping his word.

All had gone well, so far as appeared. If he learned to the contrary later he would let me know. With this I had to be content for some three hours, then the phone rang again. It was Haines calling and this time to the effect that

Nurse Wealthy was going out; that she had demanded an hour off, saying that she must have a breath of air or die. Miss Orpha had gladly given her the leave of absence she desired, and, to Haines' own amazement, he had been put in charge of the sick room till her return, Mr. Edgar being much better this morning. No one knew where she was going but the moment she came back I should hear of it.

This was as I expected. But where was Wealthy going? Could she possibly be coming to see me in my hotel or was her destination Police Headquarters?

Strangely neither guess was correct. A third ring at the phone and I was notified that my presence was urgently desired at Mr. Jackson's office, and upon hastening there I found her closeted with the lawyer in his private room. Her veil—a heavy mourning one,—was down and her attitude one of humility; but there was no mistaking her identity, and Mr. Jackson made no attempt at speaking her name, entering at once upon the momentous reason for which I had been summoned.

"I am sorry to have made you this trouble, Mr. Bartholomew," said he, after having given orders that we were to be left undisturbed. "But this woman whom I am sure you recognize would not speak without your presence; and I judge that she has something important to tell."

"Yes," she insisted, moving a trifle in her restlessness. "I thought that nothing would ever make me talk; but we don't know ourselves. I have not slept and do not think I shall ever sleep again unless I tell you—"

"Don't you remember what I insisted upon in our talk last night, Wealthy? How it was not to me you must tell your story, but to—"

"I know whom you mean," she interrupted breathlessly. "But it's not for the police to hear what I have to say; only yourself and lawyer. I did you a wrong. You must know just what that wrong was. I have a conscience, sir. It's troubled me all my life but never so much as now. Won't you listen? Tell him to listen, Mr. Jackson, or I'll leave this place and keep silence till I die."

It was no idle threat. If she had been motherly and sweet in the old days, she was inflexible and determined in these. Under the kindliness of an affectionate nature there lay forces such as give constancy to the martyr. She would do what she said.

Looking away, I encountered the eye of Mr. Jackson. Its language was unmistakable. I felt myself in a trap.

But I would not yield without another effort. Smiling faintly, I said:

"You have never liked me, Nurse Wealthy; why, then, drag me into this? Let me go. Mr. Jackson will be a sympathetic listener, I know."

"I cannot let you go; but I can go myself," she retorted, rising slowly and turning her back upon me. She was trembling in sheer desperation as she took a step towards the door.

I could not see her go. I was not her sole auditor as on the night before. My duty seemed plain.

"Come back," I called to her. "Speak, and I will listen."

She drew a deep breath, loosened her veil, but did not lift it; then quietly reseated herself.

"I loved the Bartholomew family, all of them, till— You will excuse me, sir, I can hide nothing in telling my story—till you came to visit us and things began to go wrong.

"It was not liking I felt for them, but a passionate devotion, especially for Mr. Edgar, whose like I had never seen before. That he would marry Miss Orpha and that I should always live with them was as much a settled fact in my mind as the knowledge that I should some day die. And I was happy. But trouble came. The night which should have seen their engagement announced saw Mr. Bartholomew stricken with illness, and the beginning of changes, for which I blamed nobody but you."

She was addressing me exclusively.

"I felt that you were working against us—against Mr. Edgar I mean,—and my soul turned bitter and my hatred grew till I no longer knew myself. That Mr. Edgar could do anything wrong—that he could deceive himself or Miss Orpha or the uncle who doted on him you could not have made me believe in those days. It was you, you who did all the harm, and Mr. Bartholomew, weakened by illness, was your victim. So I reasoned as I saw how things went and how you were given an equal chance with Mr. Edgar to sit with him and care for him, nights as well as days.

"Then the lawyers came, and though I am not over bright, it was plain enough to me that something very wrong was being done, and I got all wrought up and listened and watched to see if I could get hold of the truth; and I saw and heard enough to convince me that Mr. Edgar's chance of fortune and happiness with Miss Orpha needed guarding and that if worst came to worst, I must be ready to do my part in saving him from losing the property destined for him since he was a little child.

"I said nothing of this to any one, but I hardly slept in my eagerness to know whether the two documents your uncle kept in the little drawer near his head were really two different wills. I had never heard of anybody keeping two wills ready to hand before. But Mr. Bartholomew was not like other men and you could not judge him by what other men do. That I was right in thinking that these two documents were really two wills I soon felt quite sure from his actions. There was not a day he did not handle them. I often found him poring over them, and he always seemed displeased if I approached him too closely at these times. Then again he would simply lie there holding them, one in each hand, as if weighing them one against the other,—his eyes on the great picture of Miss Orpha and a look of sore trouble on his face. It was the same look with which I saw him in the last few days glance from your cousin Edgar to yourself, and back again, when by any chance you were both in the room at the same time.

"I often wanted to have a good talk with Miss Orpha about these strange unnatural doings; but I didn't dare. I knew she wouldn't listen; and so with a heart eaten into by anxiety, I went on with my nursing, loving her and Mr. Edgar more than ever and hating you almost to the point of frenzy.

"You must pardon me for speaking so plainly, but it is necessary for you to know just how I felt or you would never understand what got into me on that last night of your uncle's life. I could see long before any of the rest of you that something of great importance was going to happen in the house before we slept. I had watched him too long and too closely not to draw certain conclusions from his moods. When he ordered his evening meal to be set out near the fireplace and sent for Clarke to dress him, I felt confident that the great question which was driving him into his grave was on the eve of being settled. But how? This was what I was determined to find out, and was quite prepared if I found things going against Mr. Edgar to do whatever I could to help him.

"You will think this very presumptuous in a woman in my position; but those two motherless children were like my own so far as feeling went, and if there is any excuse for me it lies in this, that I honestly thought that your uncle was under an influence which might force him to do in his present condition what in his right mind he would never dream of doing, no, not if it were to save his life."

Here she paused to catch her breath and gather strength to proceed. Her veil was still down, but her breast was heaving tumultuously with the fierce beating of her heart. We were watching her carefully, both Mr. Jackson and myself, but we made no move, nor did we speak. Nothing must check her at this point of her narrative.

We showed wisdom in this, for after a short interval in which nothing could be heard but her quick gasps for breath, she spoke again and in the same tone and with the same fervor as before.

"The supper cleared and everything made right in the room, he asked for Clarke, and when he came bade him go for Mr. Edgar. I could not stay after that. I knew his wishes. I knew this, too, that the prospect of doing something, after his many days of worriful thinking, had brought him strength;—that he was in one of those tense moods when to cross him meant danger; and that I must be careful what I said and did if I was to serve him, and that I must urge Mr. Edgar to be careful, too.

"But no opportunity was given me to speak to him. He came up, with Clarke following close behind, and went directly to your uncle's room just as I stole away to the cozy corner. When he came out my eye was at the slit in my screen. From the way he walked I knew that things had gone wrong with him and later when you came out, I saw that they had gone well with you. Your head was high; his had been held low.

"I like Clarke, and perhaps you think, because we were sitting there together waiting for orders that I took him into my confidence. But I didn't. I was too full of rage and fear for that. Nobody must know my heart, nobody, at least not during this uncertainty. For I was still determined to act; to say or do something if I got the chance. When after going to your uncle's room, he came back and said that Mr. Bartholomew was not yet ready to go to bed, —that he wanted to be left alone for a half hour and that I was to see from the place where I was that no one came to disturb him, I felt that the chance I wanted was to be mine, and as soon as Clarke went on to his room, I got up and started to go down the hall.

"I am giving a full story, Mr. Quenton, for I want you to know it all; so I will not omit a little thing of which I ought to be ashamed, but of which I was rather proud at the time. When I had taken a few steps I remembered that a half hour was a long time, and that Clarke might find it so and be tempted to take a look to see if I was keeping watch as he had bid me. Not that he seemed to doubt me, but because he was always over particular in every matter where his master was concerned. So I came back and going to my room brought out a skirt like the one I had on and threw it over a chair behind the screen so that a little bit of the hem would show outside. Then I went to your uncle's door and with a slow turn of the knob opened it without a sound and stepped into the passage-way. To my great satisfaction the portieres which separated it from the room itself were down and pulled closely together. I could stand there and not be seen, same as in the cozy corner.

"Hearing nothing, I drew the heavy hangings apart ever so slightly and peered through the slit thus made at his figure sitting close by the fireside. He was in his big chair with the wings on either side and placed as it was, only his head was visible. I trembled as I saw him, for he was too near the hearth. What if he should fall forward!

"But as I stood there hesitating, I saw one of his hands come into view from the side of his chair—the side nearest the fire. In it was one of the big envelopes and for an instant I held my breath, for he seemed about ready to toss it into the fire. But he soon drew it back again and I heard a moan, then the low cry, 'My boy! my boy! I cannot.' And I knew then what it all meant. That there were really two wills and that he was trying to summon up courage to destroy the one which would disinherit his favorite nephew. Rebelling against the act and determined to stop it if I could, I slipped into the room and without making any noise, for I had on my felt slippers, I crept across the floor nearer and nearer till I was almost at his back. His head was bent a little forward, but he gave no sign of being aware of my presence. I could hear the fire crackle and now and then the little moan which left his lips, but nothing else. The house was like the house of the dead; not a sound disturbed it.

"Taking another step, I looked over his shoulder. He was holding those two documents, just as I had frequently seen him in his bed, one in each hand. He seemed to be staring at them and now one hand would tremble and now the other, and I was so close that I could see a red cross scrawled on the envelope he held in his right—the one he had stretched out to the fire and drawn back again a few minutes before.

"Dared I speak! Dared I plead the cause of the boy I loved, that he loved? No, I didn't dare do that; he was a terrible man when he was roused and this might rouse him, who could tell. Besides, words were leaving his lips, he was muttering aloud to himself and soon I could understand what he was saying and it was something like this:

" 'I'm too old—too weak—some one else must do it— Orpha, who will not know what she is doing, not I,—not I. There's time yet—I asked the doctor— two weeks was what he said—Edgar! my boy, my boy.' Every murmur ending thus, 'My boy! my boy!'

"All was well then; I need not fear for to-night. Tomorrow I would pray Edgar to exert himself to some purpose. Better for me to slide back to my place behind the portiere; the half hour would soon be up— But just then I heard a different cry, his head had turned, he was looking up at his daughter's picture and now a sob shook him, and then came the words:

" 'Your mother was a just woman; and she says this must be done. I have always heeded her voice. To-morrow you shall burn—'

"There he stopped. His head sank back against the chair top, and, frightened out of my senses, I was about to start forward, when I saw the one will—the one with the red mark on it slip from his hand and slide across the hearth close to the burning logs.

"That was all I needed to make me forget myself and rush to the rescue of

Edgar's inheritance. I was on my knees in front of the fire before I realized what I had done, and clutching at the paper, knelt there with it in my hand looking up at your uncle.

"He was staring straight at me but he saw nothing. One of the spells of brief unconsciousness which he sometimes had had come upon him. I could see his breast rise and fall but he took no note of me, and, thanking God in my heart, I reached up and drew the other will from his unresisting hand and finding both of the envelopes unsealed, I changed the will in the marked one for that in the other and laid them both in his lap.

"I was behind his chair again before I heard the deep sigh with which he woke from that momentary trance; and I was already behind the portiere and watching as before when I heard a slight rattle of paper and knew that he had taken the two wills again into his hands.

"But he did nothing further; simply sat there and as soon as I reckoned that the half hour was nearly up and that Clarke would be coming from his room to attend him, I stole out of the door and into my cozy corner in time to greet Clarke when he showed himself. I was as tired as I had ever been in my life, and doubtful as to whether what I had done would be helpful to Edgar or the reverse. What might not happen before the morrow of which he spoke. I was afraid of my own shadow creeping ahead of me along the wall as I hurried to take my place at your uncle's bedside.

"But I was more doubtful yet and much more frightened when upon asking him if I should not put away the documents I saw on the stand at his side (a pile such as I had often taken from his little drawer in the bed-head with the two I was most interested in on top) he said that he wanted me for another purpose and sent me in great haste downstairs on a foolish little errand to Miss Orpha's room. He was again to be left alone and for a long while, too.

"I wanted to call Clarke, but while your uncle looked at me as he was looking then, I knew that it would be madness to interfere, so I sped away on my errand, conscious that he was listening for the opening and shutting of the door below as proof that I had obeyed him.

"Was it a whim? It could easily be that, for the object he wanted had belonged to his dead wife and men as sick as he have such whims. But it might just as well be that he wanted to be alone so as to look at the two wills again, and if that was his purpose, what would happen when I got back?

"The half hour during which I helped my poor, tired young lady to hunt through drawers and trunks for the little old-fashioned shawl he had sent for was one of great trial to me. But we found it at last and when I saw it in her hand and the sweetness of her face as she stooped to kiss it, I wanted to take her in my arms, but did not dare to, for something stood between us which I did not understand then but which I know now was my sin.

"There was a clock on her dresser and when I saw how late it was I left her very suddenly and started on my way back. What happened to me on my way up you've already heard me tell;—the Presence, which was foolishness, and afterwards, on reaching the stair-head, something which was not foolishness,—I mean the hearing of the two doors of your uncle's room being unlocked, one after the other, in expectation of my coming. What had he been doing? Why had he locked himself in? The question agitated me so that it was quite a few minutes before I could summon up courage to enter the room.

When I did, it was with a sinking heart. Should I find the two wills still lying where I had last seen them, huddled with the other papers on the little stand? If they were, I need not fret; but if they were in his hands or had been hidden away somewhere, the fear and anxiety would be insupportable.

"But my first glance towards the little stand reassured me. They were still there. There was no mistaking those stiff dark envelopes; and, greatly heartened, I stepped to the bedside and took my first look at him. He was lying with closed eyes, panting a little but otherwise peaceful. I spoke his name and held out the little shawl. As he took it he smiled. I shall never forget that smile, never. Had it been meant for me I would have fallen on my knees, and told him what I had done, but it was for that young wife of his, dead for some seventeen years now; and the delight I saw in it hardened rather than softened me and gave me courage to keep silent,

"He was ready now to have those papers put away, and drawing the key to the little drawer from under the pillow, he handed it to me and watched me while I lifted the whole pile of business documents and put them back in the place from which they had been taken, and as nothing in his manner showed that he felt the least suspicion that any of these papers had been tampered with, I was very glad to see them put away for the night. I remember thinking as I gave him back the key that nothing must hinder me from seeking an early opportunity to urge Mr. Edgar to exert himself to win his uncle's favor back. I knew that he could if he tried; and, satisfied so far, I was almost happy.

"Now we know that your uncle himself had tampered with them while I was gone that good half hour after the little shawl. He had taken out one of the wills from its envelope and carried it—he who could hardly stand—down that concealed stairway to the box dangling from one of the walls below. But how could I dream of anything so inconceivable as that—I who had been in and out of that room and up and down the main staircase for fifteen years without a suspicion that the Presence which sometimes haunted that spot was actual and not imaginary. I thought that all was well for the night at least and was bustling about when he suddenly called me.

"Running to his bedside, I found him well enough but in a very earnest mood. 'Wealthy,' he said, 'I am old and I am weak. I no longer trust myself. The doctor said when he left to-day that I had two full weeks before me; but who knows; a whiff of air may blow me away at any minute, and the thing I want done might go undone and infinite trouble ensue. I am resolved to act as though my span of life was that of a day instead of a fortnight. Tomorrow morning we will have the children all in and I will wind up the business which will set everything right. And lest I should not feel as well then as I do now, I will tell you before I sleep just what I want you to do. And then he explained about the bowl and the candles which I was to put on the stand when the time came and made it all so clear that I was now thoroughly convinced that it was really his intention to have Miss Orpha burn the will he had not had the courage to burn himself, and this speedily, —probably in the early morning.

"I stared at him, stupefied. What if they looked at the will before they burned it. This, Mr. Edgar would be likely to do, and give himself away in his surprise and so spoil all. I must hinder that; and when Mr. Bartholomew fell into a doze I crept to Mr. Edgar's room, putting out the lights as I went, and, finding him awake, I told him what I had done and said that he need not worry if we found his uncle in the same mind in the morning as now and ordered the will burned which was in the marked envelope, for that was the one which should be burned and which he would himself burn if he were the man he used to be and had not been influenced by a stranger. Meaning you, sir, of course. God forgive me."

"So he knew!" I burst forth, leaping to my feet in my excitement. "That's why he took it all so calmly. Why from that day to this he has found it so difficult to meet my eye. Why he has followed me, seeming to want to speak— to tell me something—"

I did not go on—a thousand questions were rising in my mind. I cast a quick glance at Mr. Jackson and saw that he was startled too and waited, with every confidence in his judgment, for him to say what was in his mind.

"At what time was this?" he asked, leaning forward and forcing her to meet his eye.

"I don't know." She tried to shun his gaze; her hands began to tremble. "I didn't take any notice. I just ran to his room and back; I had enough to think of without looking at clocks."

"Was it before you heard the glass set back on the shelf?"

She gave a start, and pressing the two arms of her chair with those trembling hands of hers tried to rise, but finding that her knees would not support her, fell back. In the desperation of the moment she turned towards me, putting up her veil as she did so. "Don't ask me any more questions," she pleaded. "I am all unstrung; I've had no sleep, no rest, no ease for days. When I found that Mr. Edgar —you know what I would say, sir—I don't want to repeat it here—"

"Yes, we know," Mr. Jackson broke in. "You cannot bridle the curiosity of servants. We know that he loves another woman than your young mistress with all her advantages. You may speak plainly."

"Oh, but it hurts!" she moaned. Then, as if no break had occurred, "When I found that he was not the man I thought him—that nothing I could do would ever make good the dream of years, I hated myself and what I had done and above all my treatment of you, Mr. Quenton. I did not succeed in the wrong I planned,—something happened— God knows what—to upset all that, but the feeling was there and I am sorry; and now that I have said so, may I not go? I have heard that you are kind; that none of us knew how kind; let me go—"

She paused, her lips half closed, every sense on the alert. She was no longer looking at me but straight ahead of her though the danger was approaching from the rear. A door behind her was opening. I could see the face of the man who entered and felt my own heart sink. Next moment he was at her side, his finger pressing on her shoulder.

"Let us hear your answer to the question which Mr. Jackson has just put to you. Was your visit to Mr. Bartholomew's room before or after you heard the setting down of the medicine glass on the shelf?"

"Before."

She spoke like one in a dream. She seemed to know who her interlocutor was though she did not turn to look at him.

"You lied when you said that you saw this gentleman here hurrying down the hall immediately after you had heard some one carefully shutting the door next to the medicine cabinet?"

"Yes, I lied."

Still like one in a dream.

"Did you see him or his shadow pass down the hall at any time that night?"

"No."

"Why these stories then? Why these lies?"

She was silent.

"Was it not Edgar Bartholomew you heard or saw at that door; and did you not know it was he?"

Again silence; but now a horrified one.

"Are you sure that he did not come in at that door you heard shut? That the only mistake made that night was that the dose was not strong enough—that your patient did not die in time for the will in this gentleman's favor to be abstracted and destroyed, leaving the other one as the final expression of Mr. Bartholomew's wishes and testamentary intentions? You need not answer. It is a law of this country that no one can be compelled to incriminate himself. But that is how it looks to us, Mrs. Starr. That is how it looks."

With this he lifted his finger; and the breath held back in all our throats broke from us in a simultaneous gasp. She only did not move, but sat gazing as before, cheek and brow and even lips growing whiter and whiter till we all shrank back appalled. As the silence grew longer and heavier and more threatening I covered my face with my hands. I could not look and listen too. A vision of Edgar in his most buoyant mood, with laughter in his eye and winsome bonhomie in every feature flashed before me and passed. I could hardly bear it. Then I heard her voice, thin, toneless, and ringing like a wire which has been struck:

"Edgar is innocent. He never entered the room. No one entered it. That was another lie. I alone mixed the dose. I thought he would die at once and let me do what you said. It came to me as I sat there waiting for the morning—the morning I did not feel myself strong enough to face."

CHAPTER 55

We believed her. I, because it lifted a great load from my heart; Lawyer Jackson and the Inspector because of their long experience with criminal humanity. Misery has its own voice! So has conscience; and conscience, despite the strain she had put upon it during these last few evil days was yet alive within her.

Notwithstanding this, the Inspector would not let the moment pass without a warning.

"Mrs. Starr," said he, "it is my duty to tell you that you will be making a great mistake in taking upon yourself the full burden of this crime if you are simply its accessory before or after. The real culprit cannot escape by any such means as that, and you will neither help him or yourself by taking such a stand."

The dullness which had crept into her eyes, the loose set of her lips, the dejection, with every purpose gone, which showed in the collapse of her hitherto firmly held body offered the best proof which had yet been given that she had not exaggerated her position. Even her voice had changed; all its ringing quality was gone; it sounded dead, utterly, without passion, almost without feeling:

"I did it myself when I was alone with—with my patient and this—this is why. If I must tell all, I will tell all, though the shame of it will kill me. When I got back from Mr. Edgar's room, I took another look at Mr. Bartholomew. He was still sleeping and as much of his face as I could see for the little shawl, was calmer than before and his breath even more regular. I should have been happy, but I was not, and stood looking at him, asking myself again and again what he had been doing while I was below and if I were right in thinking that he had not looked into the envelopes. If he had and had changed the wills back where should we be? Mr. Edgar would lose his inheritance and all my wicked work would go for nothing. I could not bear the thought. If only I dared open that little drawer, and have a peep at those documents. I had not the least suspicion that one of them had been withdrawn from its envelope. The full one was on top and I was so nervous handling them under his eye that the emptiness of the under one had escaped me. So I had not that to worry about, only the uncertainty as to which was in the marked envelope—the envelope he had held over the fire and drew back saying that Orpha must do what he could not.

"I knew that if he should wake and detect me fumbling under his pillow for his key that I should fall at his bedside in shame and terror; yet I was putting out my hand, when he moved and turned his head, disarranging the shawl, and I saw projecting from under the pillow not the key but his eye-glasses and started back and let the curtain fall and sank into the chair I always had near, overcome by a certainty which took away all my strength just when I needed it for fresh thought.

"For there was no mistaking now what he had been doing in my absence. He could not read without his glasses, though he could see other things quite well. He had risen to get them—for I remembered only too clearly that they had been lying on his desk when I left the room. I can see them now, just where they lay close against the inkstand; and having got them, and being on his feet, he had locked the doors so that he would not be interrupted while he satisfied himself that the will he had resolved to destroy was in the marked envelope. That he had done more than this—taken the will he wished kept and carried it out of the room, was not within the mind of a poor woman like me to conceive. I was in a bad enough case as it was. He knew in which envelope was the will which would give Edgar his inheritance and I did not. Should I go and consult Edgar as to what we should do now? No; whatever was to be done should be done by me alone; he should not be dragged into it. That is how I felt. But what to do? I did not know. For an hour I sat there, the curtain drawn between us, listening to his breathing. And I thought it all out. I would do just what you said here a little moment ago. Open the drawer and take out the will I hated and burn it to ashes in the fireplace, leaving only the one which would make everything right. But to be free to do this he—must—first—die. I loved Edgar; I was willing to do anything for him but meet his uncle's accusing eye.

That would take bravery I did not possess. So I rose at last, very determined now my mind was made up, and moving quietly around the foot of the bed, crept stealthily to the medicine cabinet, and lifting out the phial I wanted, set it on a lower shelf and then returning for the glass of soothing mixture already prepared, dropped into it what I thought was a heavy dose, and putting back the medicine phial, carried the glass to the bedside where I put it on a chair close to his hand; for he had turned over again by this time and lay with his face toward the windows.

"The light from the fire added to that of the lamp on the other side of the bed made the room bright enough for me to do all this; but when I got back and had seated myself again, the lamp-light seemed an offense and I put it out. The glow from the fire was enough! He could see to reach the glass—and I waited—waited—till I heard a sigh—then a movement—then a quietly whispered Wealthy?—and then, a slight tinkle as though the button at his wrist had touched the glass—and then—

"Oh, God! will I ever forget it? Or how I waited and waited for what must follow, watching the shadows gather on the ceiling, and creep slowly down the walls till they settled upon my head and about the bed where I still heard him moving and muttering now and then words which had no meaning. Why moving? Why muttering? I had expected silence long before this. And why such a chill and so heavy a darkness? Then I realized that the fire he so loved was out for the first time since his illness,—the fire that was to destroy the will I had not yet touched or even sought out, and I rose to rebuild it, when he suddenly cried out, 'Light!' and shaken by the tone, subdued in one instant to my old obedient self, I turned on the lamp and pulled back the curtain.

"He was looking at me, not unkindly, but in the imperious way of one who knows he has but to speak to have his least wish carried out.

"He was ill. I was to rouse the house—bring the bowl— the candles—no waiting,—I knew what I was to do; he had told me the night before.

"And I did each and every thing just as he commanded. Alive to seeming failure, to possible despair, I went about my task, hoping against hope that all would yet go right; that Fate would step in and make my sin of some avail at this terrible crisis. Though the hands I wrung together in my misery as I ran through the hall were like ice to the touch, I was all on fire within. Now there is no more fire left here"—her hand falling heavy on her breast—"than on the stones of the desolated hearth;—only ashes! ashes!" The Inspector moved, and was about to speak, but ceased as her voice rose again in that same awful monotone.

"I loved my Mr. Edgar then." She spoke as though years had intervened instead of a few flitting days. "I used to think that in return for one of his gay smiles I would put my hands under his feet. But to-day, I do not seem to care enough for him to be glad that he is not guilty. If he were, and had to face what I have to face—shame, when I have always prided myself on my good name—isolation, when to help others has been my life—death, when—" She paused at that, her head falling forward, her eyes opening into a wide stare, as though she saw for the first time the abyss into which she was sinking,—"I should not now be so lonely."

The Inspector drew back, Mr. Jackson turned away his head. I could not move feature or limb. I was beholding for the first time the awakening of a lost soul to the horror of its own sin.

"I don't know why it is," she went on, still in that toneless voice more moving than any wail or even shriek. "It did not seem such a dreadful thing to do that night. It was but hastening his death by a few days, possibly by only a few hours. But now—now—" Suddenly to our amazement she was on her feet, her eyes roaming from one face to the other of us three, all signs of apathy gone, passion restored to her heart, feeling restored to her voice, as she cried out: "Will Miss Orpha have to know? I wish I could see her before she knows. I wish—I wish—"

It was my turn now. Leaping to her side, I held her while the sobs came in agony from her breast, shaking her and distorting her features till in mercy I pulled down her veil and seated her again in her chair.

As I withdrew my arm she managed to press my hand. And I heard very faintly from behind that veil:

"I am glad something happened to give you what you wanted."

CHAPTER 56

I thought I had only to go now, and leave her to the Inspector who I felt would deal with her as mercifully as he could. But Mr. Jackson shook his head as I was about to depart, and stepping up to the Inspector said a few earnest words to him after which the former sat down at his desk and wrote a few lines which he put in the official's hands. Then he drew me apart.

"Wait," he said; "we may want your signature."

It was a written confession which the Inspector took upon himself to ask her to sign.

She was sitting back in her chair, very quiet now, her veil down, her figure immovable. The slow heaving of her chest bespoke life and that was all. The Inspector bent down as he reached her and after a minute's scrutiny of her veiled features said to her not unkindly:

"It will save you much mental suffering if you will sign these words which I first ask you to listen to. Are you ready to hear them?"

She nodded, her hands which were clasped about a little bag she was carrying, twitching convulsively.

"Water, first," she begged, turning up her eyes till they rested on his face.

He made me a motion, but did not stir from where he stood before her. Instead, he directed his full glance at her hands, and unclasping them gently from the bag she was clutching, opened them out and took away the bag which he laid aside. Then he raised her veil, and handed her the glass which I had brought and watched her while she drank. A few drops seemed to suffice to reinvigorate her, and giving back the glass, she waited for him to read.

The words were mercifully few but they told the full story. As she listened, she sank back into her old pose, only that her hands missing the little bag clutched the arms of the chair in which she sat, and seemed to grow rigid there. But they loosed their grasp readily enough as the Inspector brought a pad and a pen and laying the pad in her lap with the words she had listened to plainly before her, handed her the pen and asked her to sign them.

She roused herself to do this, and when he would draw her veil again she put up her hand in protest, after which she wrote somehow, almost without seeing what she did, the three words which formed her name. Then she sank back again and as he carried away the pad, and, laying the signed confession on the desk for Mr. Jackson and myself to affix our signatures to it as witnesses, she clutched again the arms of her chair and so sat as before, without further word or seeming interest in what was being done.

Should I go now without a word to her, without asking if she had any message to send to Edgar or to Orpha? While I was hesitating, whether or not to address her, I saw the Inspector start and laying his hand on Mr. Jackson's arm point to her silent figure. A coldness, icy and penetrating struck my heart, I saw them hurriedly advance, I saw the Inspector for the second time slowly lift her veil, give one look and drop it again. And I saw nothing more for a minute, then as my senses cleared, I met the eyes of the two men fixed on me and not on her, and summoning up my strength I said:

"It is better so."

They did not answer, but in each man's eye I saw that had they spoken it would have been in repetition of my words:

"It is better so."

CHAPTER 57

My first duty, now as ever, was to Orpha. Before rumor reached her she must know, and from no other lips than mine, what had happened. Then, —I did not get much beyond that then, for mortal foresight is of all things most untrustworthy, and I had fought too long with facts to wish to renew my battle with delusive fancies.

To shut out every imagining which might get the better of my good sense, I forced myself to recall the foolish reasoning in which I had indulged when the possibility of Uncle having been the victim of Edgar's cupidity was obsessing my brain. How I had attributed to him acts of which he had been entirely guiltless. How in order to explain our uncle's death by poison I had imagined him going to the sick room upon seeing Wealthy leave it, and winning the old gentleman to his mind, had carried off the will whose existence threatened his rights, and burned it, with our uncle's consent, in his own room. All this, while uncle was really behind locked doors making his painful journey down between the walls of his house, in order to place in safe keeping,—possibly from his own vacillation, —the will which endowed myself with what had previously been meant for Edgar alone.

That I had thus allowed my imagination to run so far away from facts was another lesson of the danger we incur in trusting to fanciful reasoning where our own interests are involved; and that I should have carried my futile deductions further, even to the point of supposing that after the question of poisoning was mooted he had taken Orpha and Wealthy upstairs in order to confuse his former finger-prints with fresh ones of his own and theirs, brought me a humiliation in my own eyes now that I knew the truth, which possibly was the best preparation I could have for the interview which now lay before me.

That I was not yet out of the woods,—that I was still open to the attack of vituperative tongues I knew full well; but that could not be helped. What I wanted was to square myself with my own conscience before I faced Orpha and turned another leaf in our heavy book of troubles.

CHAPTER 58

Haines, for all his decorum, showed an anxious face when he opened the door to me. It changed, however, to one of satisfaction as he saw who had come.

"Oh, sir!" he cried, as I stepped in, "where is Wealthy? Mr. Edgar has been asking for her this half hour. The girl is no good and he will have none of the rest of us in his room."

"I will go to him. Is Miss Bartholomew in?"

"Yes, sir; he won't see her either."

"Haines, I have something serious to say to Miss Bartholomew. You may tell her that I should be very glad to have a few words with her. But first I must quiet him; and while I am in the third story, whether it be for a few minutes or half an hour, I rely on you to see that Miss Bartholomew receives no callers and no message from any one. If the phone rings, choke it off. Cut the wire if necessary. I am in earnest, Haines. Will you do as I ask?"

"I will, sir."

I could see how anxious he was to know what all this meant, but he did not ask and I should not have told him if he had. It was for Edgar first, and then for Orpha to hear what I had to relate.

CHAPTER 59

When I entered Edgar's room he was sitting propped up in bed, a woeful figure. He had just flung a book at the poor mute who had vainly tried to find for him the thing he wanted. When he saw me he whitened and slid down half out of sight under the bed-clothes.

"Where is Wealthy?" he shouted out. "I want her and nobody else." But before I could answer, he spoke again and this time with a show of his old-time lightness. "Not but what it is good of you to come and see a poor devil like me."

"Edgar," I said, advancing straight to his bedside and sitting down on its edge, "I have come, not only to see what can be done for you to-day, but to ask if you will let me stay by you till you are well enough and strong enough to kick me out."

"But where is Wealthy?" he cried, with a note of alarm in his voice. "She went out for an hour. She should be back. I—I must have Wealthy, glum as she is."

Should I shock him with the truth? Would it prove to be too much for him in his present feverish state? For a moment I feared so, then as I noticed the restlessness which made his every member quiver, I decided that he would be less physically disturbed by a full knowledge of Wealthy's guilt and the events of the last hour, than by a prolonged impatience at her absence and the vexation which any attempt at deception would occasion him.

"Won't I possibly do for a substitute?" I smiled. "Wealthy cannot come. She will not come any more, Edgar. Though you may not have known it she was a great sufferer—a great sinner—a curse to this house during the last few weeks. It was she—"

"Ah!"

He had me by the arm. He had half raised himself again so that his eyes, hot with fever and the horror of this revelation burned close upon mine. His lips shook; his whole body trembled, but he understood me. I did not need to complete my unfinished sentence.

"You must take it calmly," I urged. "Think what this uncertainty has done to the family. It has almost destroyed us in the eyes of the world. Now we can hold up our heads again; now you can hold up your head again. It should comfort you."

"You don't know," he muttered, turning his head away. Then quickly, violently, "I can never get away from the shame of it. She did it for me. I know that she did it for me and people will think—"

"No," I said, "they will not think. She exonerates you completely. Edgar, I have to tell this news to Orpha. She must not hear it first from one of the servants or from some newspaper man. Let me go down to her. I will come back, but not to weary you, or allow you to weary yourself with talk. When you are better we will have it all out. What you have to do now is to get well, and I am going to help you."

I started to rise but he drew me back again.

"There is something I must confess to you before you undertake that. I have not been fair—"

I took him by both hands.

"Let us forget that. It has come between us long enough. It must not do so any longer."

"You know—"

"I had to listen to Wealthy's story."

Letting go of his hands, I again tried to rise; but for the second time he drew me back.

"You are going to tell Orpha. Are you going to tell Lucy, too?"

"Miss Colfax is not in the house; she left this noon for New York."

He stiffened where he lay. I was glad I had let go of his hands. I could affect more easily a nonchalant manner. "She has an aunt there, I believe. Is there anything you want before I go down?"

Oh, the hunger in his stare! "Nothing now, nothing but to get well. You have promised to help me and you shall." Then as I crossed to the door, "Where have they put her? Wealthy, I mean. I ought to do something."

"No, Edgar, she is being cared for. She confessed, you know, and they will not be too harsh with her. I will tell you another time all that I have failed to say to-day. For two days we will not speak her name. After that you may ask me anything you will."

With that I closed the door behind me. The greater trial was to come.

CHAPTER 60

So I thought, but the first view I had of Orpha's face reassured me. Haines had successfully carried out the role I had assigned him and she was still ignorant of what had occurred to change the aspect of all our lives. Her expression was not uncheerful, only a little wistful; and we were alone, which made the interview both easier and harder.

"How is Edgar?"

Those were her first words.

"Better. I left him in a much calmer mood. He has been worrying about Wealthy. Have you been worrying, too?"

"Not worrying. I think she has been a long time gone, but she was very tired and needed a change and the air."

"Orpha, how much faith do you put in this woman who has been so useful here?"

"Why, all there is in the world. She has never failed us. What do you mean?"

"You have found her good as well as useful?"

"Always. She has seemed more like a friend than a housekeeper. Why do you ask? Why are we discussing her when there are so many other things we ought to talk about?"

"Because this nurse of Edgar concerns us more than any one else in the world to-day. Because through her we nearly came to grief and now through her we are to see the light again. Will you try to understand me? Without further words, understand me?"

I could see the knowledge coming, growing, flaming in her face.

"Wealthy!" she cried. "Wealthy! Not any one nearer and dearer! I could never bring myself to believe that it was. But not to know! I could not have borne it much longer."

And I had to sit there, with her dear hand so near and not touch it. To explain, counsel and console, with that old adjuration from lips whose dictates still remained authoritative over me, not to pass the line from cousinship to lover till he had taken off the ban or was dead. He was dead, but the ban had not yet been removed, for there were some things I must be sure of before love could triumph; one of which I was resolved to settle before I left Orpha's presence.

So when we had said all there was to say of the day's tragedy and what was to be expected from it, I spoke to her of the odd little key which had opened the way to the hidden stairway and asked her if she had it about her as I greatly desired to see it again.

"I am wearing it for a little while," she answered and drawing the chain from her neck she laid both that and the key in my hand.

I studied the latter closely before putting the inquiry:

"Is this the key you found in the earth of the flower-pot, Orpha?"

"Yes, Quenton."

"Is it the one you gave to the police when they came the next day?"

"Of course. It was still on the chain. But I took it off when I gave it to them. They had only the key."

"Did you know that while they were working with that key here, another one—the one which finally found lodgment in the slit in the molding upstairs was traveling up from New York in Edgar's pocket?"

Oh, the joy of seeing her eyes open wide in innocent amazement! She had had nothing to do with that trick! I was convinced of it before; but now I was certain.

"But how can that be? This key opens the way to the secret staircase. I know because I have tried it. How could there be another?"

"If Wealthy were still living I think she could tell you. At some time when you were not looking, she slipped the one key off and slipped on the other. She was used to making exchanges and her idea was to give him a chance to try the key, and, if possible, find the will unknown to you or the police. She had a friend in New York to whom she sent the key and a letter enclosing one for Edgar; and had not Providence intervened and given them both into my hands—"

Orpha had shaken her head in protest more than once while I was speaking but now she looked so piteously eager that I stopped.

"Am I not right?" I asked.

"No, no. Wealthy never knew anything about the key till the police came to try it. I told nobody but—"

The change in her countenance was so sudden and so marked that I turned quickly about, thinking that some one had entered the room. But it was not that; it was something quite different—something which called up more than one emotion—something which both lifted her head and caused it to droop again as if pride were battling with humiliation in her dismayed heart.

"Won't you finish, Orpha?" I begged. "You said that you had told only one person about it and that this person was not Wealthy. Who, then, was it?"

"Lucy," she breathed, bringing her hands, which had been lying supine in her lap, sharply together in a passionate clutch.

"Lucy! Ah!"

"She was with me the night I dropped the flower pot and picked up the chain and key from the scattered dirt. I had brought the pot from Father's room the morning he died, for the flower in it was just opening and it seemed to speak of him. But I did not like the place where I had put it and was carrying it to another shelf, when it slipped from my hands. If I had left it in Father's room the key might have been found long before; for I noticed on first watering it that the soil on top gave evidences of having been lately stirred up—something which made no impression on me, but which might have made a decisive one on the Inspector. Who do you think hid the key there? Father?"

"I wish I knew, Orpha; there are several things we do not know and never may now Wealthy is gone. But Miss Colfax? Tell me what passed between you when you talked, about the key?"

It was a subject Orpha would have liked to avoid; which she would have avoided if I had not been insistent. Why? Had she begun to suspect the truth which made it hard for her to discuss her friend? Had some echo from the cry which for days had filled the spaces of the overhead rooms drifted down to her through the agency of some gossiping servant? It was likely; it was more than likely; it was true. I saw it in the proud detached air with which she waited for me to urge her into speech.

And I did urge her. It would not do at a moment when the shadows surrounding the past were so visibly clearing to allow one cloud to remain which might be dissipated by mutual confidence. So, gently, but persistently, I begged her to tell me the whole story that I might know just what pitfalls remained in our path.

CHAPTER 61

Thus entreated, she no longer hesitated, though I noticed she stammered every time when obliged to speak the name of the woman who had shared with her—so much more than shared with her—Edgar's affection.

"The flower-pot lay broken on the floor and I was surveying with the utmost surprise the key which I had picked up from the mold lying all about on the rug, when Lucy came in to say good night. When she saw what I held in my hand, she showed surprise also, but failed to make any remark,—which was like—Lucy.

"But I could not keep still. I had to talk if only to express my wonder and obtain a little sisterly advice. But she was in no hurry to give it, and not till I reminded her how lonely I was for all my host of so-called friends, and had convinced her by showing the chain, that this was the very key my father had worn about his neck and for which we had all been looking, did she show any real interest.

" 'And if it were?' she asked. To which I answered eagerly, 'Then, perhaps, we have in our hands the clew to where the will itself lies hidden.' This roused her, for a spot of red came out on her cheek which had been an even white before; and glad to have received the least sign that she recognized the importance of my dilemma, I pressed her to tell me what I should do with this key now that I had found it.

"Even then she was slow to speak. She began one sentence, then broke it off and began another, ending up at last by entreating me to let her consider the subject before offering advice. You will acknowledge that it was a difficult problem for two ignorant girls like ourselves to solve, so I felt willing to wait; though I could not but wonder at her showing all at once so much emotion over what concerned me so much and herself so little—our cold Lucy always so proper, always so perfectly the mistress of herself whatever the occasion. Never had I seen her look as she was looking then nor observed in her before that slow moving of the eye till it met mine askance; nor heard her speak as she did when she finally asked:

" 'Who do you want to have it?' "

Orpha shot me a sudden glance as she repeated this question of Lucy's, but did not wait for any comment, rather hastened to say:

"I am telling you just what she said and just how she looked because it means something to me now. Then it simply aroused my curiosity. Nor did I dream what was in her mind, when upon my protesting that it was not a question of what I wanted, but of what it was right for me to do, she responded by asking if I needed to be told that. The right thing, of course, for me to do was to call up the police and get from them the advice I needed.

"But, Quenton, I have a great dread of the police; they know too much and too little. So I shook my head, and seeing that Lucy was anxious to examine the key more closely, I put it in her hands and watched her as she ran her fingers over it remarking as she called my attention to it that she had never seen one quite so thin before—that she could almost bend it. Then in a quick low tone altogether unlike her own, added, as she handed it back that we had somebody's fate in our hands, whose, she would not say. But this much was certain, mine was indissolubly linked with it. And when I shuddered at the way she spoke, she threw her arms about my neck and begged me to believe that she was sorry for me.

"This gave me courage to ask,"—and here Orpha's lip took a sarcastic curve more expressive of self-disdain than of any scorn she may have felt for her confidant— "whether she thought Dr. Hunter would be willing to act as my advisor; that I did not like Mr. Dunn and never had, and now that my two cousins were away I could think of no one but him.

"But she rejected the idea at once—almost with anger, saying that it was a family matter and that he was not one of the family yet. That we must wait; come to no decision to-night, unless I was willing to try what we two could do with the key. Perhaps we might find the lock it fitted somewhere in my father's room.

"But I refused, remembering that some member of the police is always in or near the grounds ready to remark any unusual lighting up of the third story windows. She did not seem sorry and, begging me to put the whole matter out of my mind till the next day, stood by while I dropped the chain and key into one of my bureau drawers, and then kissing me, went smilingly away.

"Quenton, I thought her manner strange,—at once too hurried and too affectionate to seem quite real—but I never thought of doubting her or of— of— Tell me if you know what I find it so difficult to say. Have the servants—"

"Yes, Orpha, I know through them what I have long known from other sources." And waited with a chill at my heart to see how she took this acknowledgment.

Gratefully. Almost with a smile. She was so lovely that never was a man harder put to it to restrain his ardor than I was at that moment. But my purpose held. It had to; the time was not yet.

"I am glad," fell softly from her lips; then she hurried on. "How could I doubt her or doubt him? We have been a thousand times together—all three, and never had I seen—or felt— Perhaps it is only he, not she. Listen, for I'm not through. Something happened in the night, or I dreamed it. I do not really know which. From what you say, I think it happened. I didn't then, but I do now."

"Go on; I am listening, Orpha."

"I was very troubled. I slept, but only fitfully. My mind would be quite blank, then a sudden sharp realization would come of my being awake and seeing my room and the things in it with unusual distinctness. The moon would account for this, the curtains being drawn from one of the western windows, allowing a broad beam of unclouded light to pour into the room and lie in one large square on the floor. I once half rose to shut it out, but forgot myself and fell asleep again. When I woke the next time things were not so distinct, rather they were hazy as if seen through a veil. But I recognized what I saw; it was my own image I was staring at, standing with my hand held out, the key in my open palm with the chain falling away from it. Dazed, wondering if I were in a dream or in another world—it was all so strange and so unreal,—I was lost in the mystery of it till slowly the realization came that I was standing before my mirror, and that I was really holding in my hand the chain and key which I had taken from my bureau drawer. What is the matter, Quenton? Why did you start like that?"

"Never mind now. I will tell you some other time."

She looked as if she hated to lose the present explanation; but, with a little smile charming in its naïveté, she went bravely on:

"As I took this quite in, I started to move away, afraid of my image, afraid of my own self, for I had never done anything like this before. And what seems very strange to me, I don't remember the walk back to my bed; and yet I was in my bed when the next full consciousness came, and there was daylight in the room and everything appeared natural again and felt natural, with the one exception of my arm, which was sore, and when I came to look at it, it was bruised, as if it had been clutched strongly above the elbow. Yet I had no remembrance of falling or of hitting myself. I spoke to Lucy about it later, and about the image in the glass, too, which I took to be a dream because—”

“Because what, Orpha?”

“Because the chain and key were just where I had put them the night before,—the same chain and what I supposed to be the same key or I would never have said so when Lucy asked me about it.”

“Orpha, Miss Colfax has a streak of subtlety in her nature. I think you know that now, so there is no harm in my saying so. She was in the room when you laid by that key. She was watching you. It was she who helped you into your bed. She had a key of her own not unlike the one belonging to your father. She went for this and while you slept put it on the chain you may have dropped in crossing the floor or which she may have taken from your unresisting hand. And it was she who carefully restored it to the place it had occupied in the bureau drawer, ready to hand, in case the police should want it the next day. The other one—the real one, she mailed to Edgar. Did you ever hear her speak of a New York lawyer by the name of Miller?”

“Oh, yes; he is her aunt’s husband. It is to them she has gone. She is to be married in their house. They live in Newark.”

I own that I was a little startled by this information. In handing me the key and his letter two days before in Thirty-fifth Street he had taken me for Edgar. This he could not have done had he ever met him. Could it be that they were strangers? To settle the question, I ventured to remark:

“Edgar goes everywhere. Do you suppose he ever visited the Millers?”

“Oh, no. Lucy has not been there herself in years.”

“Then you do not think they are acquainted with him?”

“I have no reason to. They have never met Dr. Hunter. Why should they have met Edgar?”

Her cheek was aglow; she seemed to misunderstand my reason for these questions; so I hastened to explain myself by relating the episode which had had such an effect on all our lives. This once made clear I was preparing to consult with her about my plans for Edgar, when she cast a swift glance towards the door, the portieres of which were drawn wide, and observing nobody in the court, said with the slightest hint of trouble in her voice:

“There is something else I ought to speak about. You remember that you advised me to make use of my first opportunity to visit the little stairway hidden these many years from everybody but my father? I did so, as I have already told you, and in that box, from which the will was drawn I found, doubled up and crushed into the bottom of it, this.”

Thrusting her hand into a large silken bag which lay at her side on the divan on which she was seated, she drew out a crumpled document which I took from her with some misgiving.

“The first will of all,” I exclaimed on opening it. “The one he was told by his lawyer to destroy, and did not.”

“But it is of no use now,” she protested. “It—it—”

“Take it,” I broke in almost harshly. The sight of it had affected me far beyond what it should have done. “Put it away—keep it—till I have time to—”

“To do what?” she asked, eyeing me with some wonder as she put the document back in the bag.

"To think out my whole duty," I smiled, recovering myself and waving the subject aside.

"But," she suggested timidly but earnestly as well, "won't it complicate matters? Mr. Dunn bade Father to destroy it." And her eye stole towards the fireplace where some small logs were burning.

"He would not tell us to do so now," I protested. "You must keep it religiously, as we hope to keep our honor. Don't you see that, cousin mine?"

"Yes," came with pride now. But from what that pride sprung it would take more than man to tell.

And then I spoke of Edgar and won her glad consent to my intention of taking care of him as long as he would suffer it or need me. After which, she left me with the understanding that I would summon all the remaining members of the household and tell them from my personal knowledge what they would soon be learning, possibly with less accuracy, from the city newspapers.

CHAPTER 62

Night again in this house of many mysteries. Late night. Quiet had succeeded intense excitement; darkness, the flashing here and there of many lights. Orpha had retired; even Edgar was asleep. I alone kept watch.

To these others peace of a certain nature had come amid all the distraction; but not to me. For me the final and most desperate struggle of all was on,— that conflict with self which I had foreseen with something like fear when I opened the old document so lately found by Orpha, and beheld Edgar's name once more in its place as chief beneficiary.

Till then, my course had seemed plain enough. But with this previous will still in existence, signed and attested to and openly recognized as it had been for many years as the exact expression of my uncle's wishes, confusion had come again and with it the return of old doubts which I had thought exorcized forever.

Had the assault been a feeble one—had these doubts been mere shadows cast by a discarded past, I might not have quailed at their onslaught so readily. But their strength was of the present and bore down upon me with a malignancy which made all their former attacks seem puerile and inconsequent.

For the events of the day previous to Orpha's production of the old will had shown to my satisfaction that I might yet look for happiness whether my claim would be allowed or disallowed by the surrogate. If allowed, it left me free to do my duty by Edgar, now relieved forever in my eyes of all complicity in our uncle's tragic death. If disallowed, it left Orpha free, as heiress and mistress of her own fortunes, to follow her inclination and formulate her future as her heart and reason dictated.

But now, with this former will still in existence, the question was whether I could find the strength to carry out the plan which my better nature prompted, when the alternative would be the restoration of Edgar to his old position with all the obligations it involved.

This was a matter not to be settled without a struggle. I must fight it out, and as I have said, alone. No one could help me; no one could advise me. Only myself could know myself and what was demanded of me by my own nature. No other being knew what had passed between Uncle and myself in those hours when it was given me to learn his heart's secrets and the strength of the wish which had dominated his later life. Had Wealthy not spoken—had she not cleared Edgar from all complicity in Uncle's premature death,—had I possessed a doubt or even the shadow of one, that in this she had spoken the whole unvarnished truth, there would have been no question as to my duty in the present emergency and I should have been sleeping, at this midnight hour just as Edgar was, or at the most, keeping a nurse's watch over him, but no vigil such as I was holding now.

He was guilty of deception—guilty of taking an unfair advantage of me at a critical point in my life. He did not rightly love Orpha, and was lacking in many qualities desirable in one destined to fill a large place in civic life. But these were peccadilloes in comparison to what we had feared; and remembering his good points and the graces which embellished him, and the absolute certainty which I could not but feel that in time, with Lucy married and irrevocably removed from him, he would come to appreciate Orpha, I felt bound to ask myself whether I was justified in taking from him every incentive towards the higher life which our uncle had foreseen for him when he planned his future—a future which, I must always remember, my coming and my coming only had disturbed.

I have not said it, but from the night when, lying on my bed I saw my uncle at my side and felt his trembling arms pressing on my breast and heard him in the belief that it was at Edgar's bedside he knelt, sobbing in my ear, "I cannot do it. I have tried to and the struggle is killing me," I had earnestly vowed and, with every intention of keeping my vow, that I would let no ambition of my own, no love of luxury or power, no craving for Orpha's affection, nothing which savored entirely of self should stand in the way of Edgar's fortunes so long as I believed him worthy of my consideration. This may explain my sense of duty towards Orpha and also the high-strung condition of my nerves from the day tragedy entered our home and with it the deep felt fear that he did not merit that consideration.

I was aware what Mr. Jackson would say to all this— what any lawyer would say who had me for a client. They would find reason enough for me to let things take their natural course.

But would that exonerate me from acting the part of a true man as I had come to conceive it?

Would my days and nights be happier and my sleep more healthful if with a great fortune in hand, and blessed with a wife I adored, I had to contemplate the lesser fortunes of him who was the darling of the man from whom I had received these favors?

I shuddered at the mere thought of such a future. Always would his image rise in shadowy perspective before me. It would sit with me at meals, brood at my desk, and haunt every room in this house which had been his home from childhood while it had been mine for the space only of a few months. Together, we had fathomed its secret. Together, we had trod its strangely concealed stairway. The sense of an unseen presence which had shaken the hearts of many in traversing its halls was no longer a mystery; but the by-ways in life which the harassed soul must tread have their own hidden glooms and their own unexpectedness; and the echoes of steps we hear but cannot see, linger long in the consciousness and do not always end with the years. Should I brave them? Dare I brave them when something deep within me protested with an insistent, inexorable disclaimer?

The conflict waxed so keen and seemed destined to be so prolonged—for self is a wily adversary and difficult to conquer—that I grew impatient and the air heavy with the oppression of the darkness in which I sat. I was in Edgar's den and comfortable enough; but such subjects as occupied me in this midnight hour call for light, space and utmost freedom of movement if they would be viewed aright and settled sensibly. Edgar was sleeping quietly; why not visit Uncle's old room and do what he once told me to do when under the stress of an overwhelming temptation—sit within view of Orpha's portrait and test my wishes by its wordless message.

But when I had entered the great room and, still in solitude though not in darkness, pulled the curtain from before that breathing canvas, the sight of features so dear bursting thus suddenly upon me made me forget my errand — forget everything but love. But gradually as I gazed, the purity of those features and the searching power they possessed regained its influence over me and I knew that if I would be true to her and true to myself,—above all, if I would be true to my uncle and the purpose of his life, I should give Edgar his chance.

For, in these long hours of self-analysis, I had discovered that deep in the inmost recesses of my mind there existed a doubt, vitiating every hope as it rose, whether we were right in assuming that the will we had come upon at the bottom of the walled-in stairway was the one he meant us to find and abide by. The box in which it was thrust held a former testament of his manifestly discarded. What proof had we that in thus associating the two he had not meant to discard both. None whatever. We could not even tell whether he knew or did not know which will he was handling. The right will was in the right envelope when we found it, he must therefore have changed them back, but whether in full knowledge of what he was doing, or in the confusion of a mind greatly perturbed by the struggle Wealthy had witnessed in him at the fireside, who could now decide. The intention with which this mortally sick man, with no longer prospect of life before him than the two weeks promised him by the doctor, forced himself to fit a delicate key into an imperceptible lock and step by step, without assistance, descend a stairway but little wider than his tread, into depths damp with the chill of years for the purpose of secreting there a will contradictory to the one he had left in the room above, could never now be known. We could but guess at it, I in my way, and Edgar in his, and the determining power—by which I mean the surrogate's court—in its.

And because intention is all and guessing would never satisfy me, I vowed again that night, with my eyes fixed on Orpha's as they shone upon me from her portrait, that come weal, or come woe,

Edgar should have his chance.

CHAPTER 63

The next day I took up my abode in Edgar's room, not to leave him again till he was strong enough to face the importunities of friends and the general talk of the public. The doctor, warned by Orpha of my intention, fell into it readily enough after a short conversation we had together, and a week went by without Edgar hearing of Wealthy's death or the inevitable inquest which had followed it. Then there came a day when I told him the whole story; and after the first agitation caused by this news had passed, I perceived with strengthening hope that the physical crisis had passed and that with a little more care he would soon be well and able to listen to what I had to say to him about the future.

Till then we both studiously avoided every topic connected with the present. This, strange as it may appear, was at his request. He wanted to get well. He was bent upon getting well and that as quickly as it was in his power to do so. Whether this desire, which was almost violent in its nature, sprang from his wish to begin proceedings against me in the surrogate's court or from a secret purpose to have one last word with Lucy Colfax before her speedily approaching marriage, the result was an unswerving control over himself and a steady increase in health.

Miss Colfax was in Newark where the ceremony was to take place. The cards were just out and in my anxiety to know what was really seething in his mind—for his detached air and effort from time to time at gayety of manner and speech had not deceived me—I asked the doctor if it would he safe for me to introduce into my conversation with Edgar any topic which would be sure to irritate, if not deeply distress him.

"Do you consider it really necessary to broach any such topic at this time?"

"I certainly do, Doctor; circumstances demand it."

"Then go ahead. I think your judgment can be depended upon to know at what moment to stop."

I was not long in taking advantage of this permission. As soon as the doctor was gone, I drew from my pocket the cards which had come in the morning's mail and handed them to Edgar, with just the friendly display of interest which it would be natural for me to show if conditions had been what they seemed to be rather than what they were.

I heard the paper crunch under the violent clutch which his fingers gave it but I did not look at him, though the silence seemed long before he spoke. When he did, there was irony in his tone which poorly masked the suffering underlying it.

"Lucy will make a man like Dr. Hunter a model wife," was what he finally remarked; but the deliberate way in which he tore up the cards and threw the fragments away—possibly to hide the marks of his passion upon them—troubled me and caused me to listen eagerly as he went on to remark: "I have never liked Dr. Hunter. We could never hit it off. Talk about a crooked stick! She with all her lovers! What date is it? The seventeenth? We must send her a present!"

I sat aghast; his tone was indescribable. I felt that the time had come to change the subject.

"Edgar," said I, "the doctor has assured me that so far as symptoms go your condition is satisfactory. That all you need now is rest of mind; and that I propose to give you if I can. You remember how when we two were at the bottom of that stairway with the unopened will between us that I declared to you that I would abide by the expression of our uncle's wishes when once they were made plain to me? My mind has not changed in that regard. If you can prove to me that his last intention was to recur—"

"You know I cannot do that," he broke in petulantly, "why talk?"

"Because I cannot prove that he did not so intend any more than you can prove that he did."

I felt a ghostly hand on my arm jerking me back. I thought of Mr. Jackson and of how it would be like him to do this if he were standing by and heard me. But I shook off this imagined clutch, just as I would have withdrawn my arm from his had he been there; and went quietly on as Edgar's troubled eyes rose to mine.

"I am not going to weary you by again offering you my friendship. I have done that once and my mind does not easily change. But I here swear that if you choose to contest the will now in the hands of the surrogate, I will not offer any defense, once I am positively assured that Orpha's welfare will not suffer. The man who marries the daughter of Edgar Quenton Bartholomew must have no dark secret in his life. Tell me—we are both young, both fortunate enough, or shall I say unfortunate enough, to have had very much our own way in life up to the difficult present—what was the cause of your first rupture with Uncle? It is not as a father confessor I ask you this, but as a man who cannot rightfully regulate his own conduct till he has a full knowledge of yours."

With starting eyes he rose before me, slowly and by jerks as though his resisting muscles had to be coerced to their task. But once at his full height, he suddenly sank back into his chair with a loud shout of laughter.

"You should have been a lawyer," he scoffed. "You put your finger instinctively on the weakest spot in the defense." Then as I waited, he continued in a different tone and with a softer aspect: "It won't do, Quenton. If you are going to base your action on Orpha's many deserts and my appreciation of them, you had better save yourself the trouble. I"—his head fell and he had to summon up courage to proceed—"I love her as my childhood's playmate, and I admire her as a fine girl who will make a still finer woman, but—"

I put up my hand. "You need not say it, Edgar. I will spare you that much. I know—we all know where your preference lies. You shouted it out in your sickness. But that is something which time will take care of if—"

"There is no if; and time! That is what is eating me up; making me the wretch you have found me. It is not the fortune that Uncle left which I so much want," he hurried on as his impulsive nature fully asserted itself. "Not for myself I mean, but for its influence on her. She is a queen and has a queen's right to all that this world can give of splendor and of power. But Orpha has her rights, too; Lucy can never be mistress here. I see that as well as you do and so thanking you for your goodness, for you have been good to me, let us call it all off. I am not penniless. I can go my own way; you will soon be rid of me."

Why couldn't I find a word? Now was the time to speak, but my lips were dumb; my thoughts at a standstill. He, on the contrary, was burning to talk— to free himself from the bitterness of months by a frank outpouring of the hopes and defeats of his openly buoyant but secretly dissatisfied young life.

"You asked me what came between Uncle and myself on that wretched night of the ball," he hurried on. "I have a notion to tell you. Since you know about Lucy—" His tongue tripped on the word but he shook his head and began volubly again. "I am not a fellow given to much thought unless it is about art or books or music, so I was deep in love before I knew it. She had come back from school— But I cannot go into that. You have seen her, and perhaps can understand my infatuation. I had supposed myself happy in the prospects always held out to me. But a few days of companionship with her convinced me that there was but one road to happiness for me and that was closed against me. That was when I should have played the man—told Uncle, and persuaded him to leave his fortune directly to Orpha. Instead of which, I let Uncle dream his dreams while Lucy and I met here and there, outwardly just friends, but inwardly— Well, I won't make a fool of myself by talking about it. Had Orpha been older and more discerning, things might have been different; but she was a child, happy in the pleasures of the day and her father's affection. When he, eager to see his plans matured, proposed a ball and the announcement of our engagement at this ball, she consented joyfully, more because she was in love with the ball than with me. But to Lucy and me it was quite another matter. We woke to the realities of life and saw no way of opposing them. For me to be designated as my uncle's heir and marry Orpha had been the expectation of us all for years. Besides, there is no use in my concealing from you who know me so well, I saw no life ahead of me without fortune. I was accustomed to it and it was my natural heritage; nor would Lucy have married a poor man; it was not in her; there are some things one can never accept.

"I am speaking of affairs as they were that week when Lucy and I virtually parted. Before it was over she had engaged herself to Dr. Hunter, in order, as she said, to save ourselves from further folly. This marked the end of my youth and of something good in me which has never come back. I blamed nobody but I began to think for myself and plan for myself with little thought of others, unless it was for Lucy. If only something would happen to prevent that announcement! Then it might be possible for me to divert matters in a way to secure for me the desires I cherished. How little I dreamed what would happen, and that within a short half hour!

"I have asked the doctor and he says that he thinks Uncle's health had begun to wane before that day. That is a comfort to me; but there are times when I wish I had died before I did what I did that night. You have asked to know it and you shall, for I am reckless enough now to care little about what any one thinks of me. I had come upon Uncle rather unexpectedly, as, dressed for the ball, he sat at his desk which was then as you know in the little room off his where we afterwards slept. He was looking over his will—he said so—the one which had been drawn up long before and which had been brought to the house that day by Mr. Dunn. As I met his eye he smiled, and tapping the document which he had hurriedly folded, remarked cheerfully, 'This will see you well looked after,' and put it back in one of the drawers. With some affectionate remark I told him my errand—I forget what it was now—and left him just as he rose from his desk. But the thought which came to me as he did this went with me down the stairs. I wanted to see that will. I wanted to know just how much it bound me to Orpha— Don't look at me like that. I was in love, I tell you, and the thought which had come to me was this; he had not locked the drawer.

"Uncle was happy as a king as he joined us below that night. He looked at Orpha in her new dress as if he had never seen her before, and the word or two he uttered in my ear before the guests came made my heart burn but did not disturb my purpose. When I could—when most of the guests were assembled and the dance well under way —I stole through the dining-room into the rear and so up the back stairs to Uncle's study. No one was on that floor; all the servants were below, even Wealthy. I found everything as we had left it; the drawer still unlocked, and the will inside.

"I took it out—yes, I did that—and I read it greedily. Its provisions were most generous so far as I was concerned. I was given almost everything after some legacies and public bequests had been made; but it was not this which excited me; it was that no conditions were attached to my inheriting this great fortune. Orpha's name was not even mentioned in connection with it. I should be free—

"My thoughts had got thus far—dishonorable as they may appear—when I felt a sudden chill so quick and violent that the paper rattled in my hands; and looking up I beheld Uncle standing in the doorway with his eyes fixed upon me in a way no man's eyes had ever been before; his, least of all. He had remembered that he had not locked up his desk and had come back to do so and found me reading his will.

"Quenton, I could have fallen at his feet in my shame and humiliation, for I loved him. I swear to you now that I loved him and do now above every one in the world but—but Lucy. But he was not used to such demonstrations, so I simply rose and folding up the paper laid it between us on the desk, not looking at him again. I felt like a culprit. I do yet when I think of it, and I declare to you that bad as I am, when, as sometimes happens I awake in the night fresh from a dream of orchestral music and the tread of dancing feet, I find my forehead damp and my hands trembling. That sound was all I heard between the time I laid down the will and the moment when he finally spoke:

" 'So eager, Edgar?'

"I was eager or had been, but not for what he thought. But how could I say so? How could I tell him the motive which had driven me to unfold a personal document he had never shown me? I who can talk by the hour had not a word to say. He saw it and observed very coldly:

" 'A curiosity which defies honor and the trust of one who has never failed you has its root in some secret but overpowering desire. What is that desire, Edgar? Love of money or love of Orpha?'

"A piercing thrust before which any man would quail. I could not say 'Love of Orpha,' that was too despicable; nor could I tell the truth for that would lose me all; so after a moment of silent agony, I faltered:

" 'I—I'm afraid I rate too high the advantages of great wealth. I am ashamed—'

"He would not let me finish.

" 'Haven't you every advantage now? Has anything ever been denied you? Must you have all in a heap? Must I die to satisfy your cupidity? I would not believe it of you, boy, if you had not yourself said it. I can hardly believe it now, but—'

"At that he stumbled and I sprang to steady him. But he would not let me touch him.

" 'Go down,' he said. 'You have guests. I may forget this, in time, but not at once. And heed me in this. No announcement of any engagement between you and Orpha! We will substitute for that the one between Lucy and Dr. Hunter. That will satisfy the crowd and please the two lovers. See to it. I shall not go down again.'

"I tried to protest, but the calamity I had brought upon myself robbed me of all initiative and I could only stammer useless if not meaningless words which he soon cut short.

" 'Your guests are waiting,' came again from his lips as he bent forward, but not with his usual precision, and took up the will.

"And I had to go. When halfway down the stairs I heard him lock the door of his room. It gave me a turn, but I did not know then how deeply he had been stricken —that before another hour he would be really ill. I had my own ordeal to face; you know what it was. My degeneration began from that hour. Quenton, it is not over. I—" He flung his hands over his face; when he dropped them I saw a different man—one whom I hardly understood.

"You see," he now quietly remarked, "I am no fit husband for Orpha."

And after that he would listen to nothing on this or any other serious topic.

CHAPTER 64

Two flights of stairs and two only, separated Edgar's rooms from the library in which I hoped to find Orpha. But as I went down them step by step they seemed at one moment to be too many for my impatience and at another too few for a wise decision as to what I should say when I reached her. As so frequently before my heart and my head were opposed. I dared not yield to the instincts of the former without giving ear to the monitions of the latter. Edgar had renounced his claim, ungraciously, doubtless, but yet to all appearance sincerely enough. But he was a man of moods, guided almost entirely by impulses, and to-morrow, under a fresh stress of feeling, his mood might change, with unpleasant if not disastrous results. True, I might raise a barrier to any decided change of front on his part by revealing to Orpha what had occurred and securing her consent to our future union. But the indelicacy of any such haste was not in accord with the reverent feelings with which I regarded her; and how far I would have allowed myself to go had I found her in one of the rooms below, I cannot say, for she was not in any of them nor was she in the house, as Haines hastened to tell me when I rang for him.

The respite was a fortunate one perhaps; at least, I have always thought so; and accepting it with as much equanimity as such a disappointment would admit of, I decided to seek an interview with Mr. Jackson before I made another move. He was occupied when I entered his office, but we ultimately had our interview and it lasted long enough for considerable time to have elapsed before I turned again towards home. When I did, it was with the memory of only a few consecutive sentences of all he had uttered. These were the sentences:

"You will get your inheritance. You will be master of Quenton Court and of a great deal besides. But what I am working for and am very anxious to see, is your entrance upon this large estate with the sympathy of your fellow-citizens. Therefore, I caution restraint till Edgar recovers his full health and has had time to show his hand. I will give him two weeks. With his head-long nature that should be sufficient. You can afford to wait." Yes, I could afford to wait with such a prospect before me; and I had made up my mind to do so by the time I had rung the bell on my return.

But that and all other considerations were driven from my mind when I saw a renewal of the old anxiety in Haines' manner as he opened the door to admit me.

"Oh, sir!" was his eager cry as I stepped in. "We don't know how it happened or how he was ever able to get away; but Mr. Edgar is gone. When I went to his room a little while ago to see if he wanted anything I found it in disorder and this—this note, for you, sir."

I took it from his hand; looked at it stupidly, feeling afraid to open it. Like a stray whiff of wind soaring up from some icy gulf, I heard again those final words of his, "You will soon be rid of me." I felt the paper flutter in my hand; my fingers were refusing to hold it. "Take it, and open it," I said to Haines.

He did so, and when he had drawn out the card it held and I had caught a glimpse of the few words it contained, my fear became a premonition; and, seizing it, I carried it into the library.

Once there and free to be myself; to suffer and be unobserved, I looked down at those words and read:

Do not seek me and do not worry about me. I have money and I have strength. When I can face the world again with a laugh you shall see me. This I will do in two weeks or never.

Two weeks! What did he mean by two weeks. Mr. Jackson had made use of the same expression. What did he mean? Then it came to me what Edgar meant, not what Mr. Jackson had. Lucy Colfax was to be married in two weeks. If he could face the world after that with a smile—

Ah, Edgar, my more than brother! Weak, faulty, but winsome even when most disturbing,—if any one could face a future bereft of all that gives it charm, you can. But the limit may have been reached. Who knows? It was for me to follow him, search him out and see.

"Haines," I called.

He came with a rush.

"Has Miss Bartholomew returned?"

"No, sir, not yet. She and Mrs. Perris are out for a long ride."

"When she does come back, give her this note." And I scribbled a few lines. "And now, Haines, answer me. Mr. Edgar could not have left on foot. Who drove him away?"

"Sammy."

He mentioned a boy who helped in the garage.

"In what car?"

"The Stutz. Mr. Edgar must have come down the rear stairs, carrying his own bag, and slipped out at the side without any one seeing him. Bliss is out with Miss Orpha and Mrs. Ferris and so he could have every chance with Sammy, who is overfond of small change, sir."

"Has Sammy shown up since? Is the car in the garage?"

"No, sir."

"Haines, don't give me away. Understand that this is to be taken quietly. Mr. Edgar told me that he was going to leave, but he did not say when. If he had, I would have seen that he went more comfortably. The doctor made his last call this morning and gave him permission to try the air, and he is doing so. We don't know when he will return; possibly in two weeks. He said something to that effect. This is what you are to say to the other servants and to every inquirer. But, Haines, to Clarke— You know where Clarke is?"

"Yes, sir."

"Can you reach him by telephone?"

"Easily, sir."

"Then telephone him at once. Go to my room to do it. Say that I have need of his services, that Mr. Edgar, who is just off a sick bed, has left the house to go we don't know where, and that he and I must find him. Bid him provide for a possible trip out of town, though I hope that a few hours will suffice to locate Mr. Bartholomew. Add that before coming here he is to make a few careful inquiries at the stations and wherever he thinks my cousin would be apt to go on a sudden impulse. That when he has done so he is to call you up. Above all, impress upon him that he is to give rise to no alarm."

"I will, sir. You may rely upon me." And as though to give proof of his sincerity, Haines started with great alacrity upstairs.

I was not long in following him. When I reached my room I found that he had got into communication with Clarke and been assured that all orders received by him from me would be obeyed as if they had come from his old master.

This relieved me immensely. Confident that he would perform the task I had given him with much better results than I could and at the same time rouse very much less suspicion, I busied myself with preparations for my own departure in case I should be summoned away in haste, thankful for any work which would keep me from dwelling too closely on what I had come to regard with increasing apprehension. When I had reached the end, I just sat still and waited; and this was the hardest of all. Fortunately, the time was short. At six o'clock precisely my phone rang. Haines had received a message from Clarke and took this way of communicating it to me.

No signs of the Stutz at either station, but Clarke had found a man who had seen it going out Main Street and another who had encountered it heading for Morrison. What should he do next?

I answered without hesitation. "Tell him to get a fast car and follow. After dinner, I will get another somewhere down street and take the same road. If I go before dinner, questions will be asked which it will be difficult for me to answer. Let me find a message awaiting me at Five Oaks."

Five Oaks was a small club-house on the road to Morrison.

CHAPTER 66

When at a suitable time after dinner I took my leave of Orpha, it was with the understanding that I might not return that night, but that she would surely hear from me in the morning. I had not confided to her all my fears, but possibly she suspected them, for her parting glance haunted me all the way to the clubhouse I have mentioned.

Arriving there without incident, I was about to send in the man acting as my chauffeur to make inquiries when a small auto coming from the rear of the house suddenly shot past us down the driveway and headed towards Houston.

Though its lights were blinding I knew it at a glance; it was Edgar's yellow Stutz. He was either in it and consequently on his way back home, or he was through with the car and I should find him inside the club-house.

Knowing him well enough to be sure that I could do nothing worse than to show myself to him at this time, I reverted to my first idea and sent in the chauffeur to reconnoiter and also see if any message had been left for James E. Budd—the name under which I thought it best to disguise my own.

He came back presently with a sealed note left for me by Clarke. It conveyed the simple information that Edgar had picked up another car and another chauffeur and had gone straight on to Morrison. I was to follow and on reaching the outskirts of the town to give four short toots with the horn to which he would respond.

It was written in haste. He was evidently close behind Edgar, but I had no means of knowing the capacity of his car nor at what speed we could go ourselves. However, all that I had to do was to proceed, remembering the signal which I was to use whenever we sighted anything ahead.

It was a lonely road, and I wondered why Edgar had chosen it. A monotonous, stretch of low fences with empty fields beyond, broken here and there by a poorly wooded swamp or a solitary farmhouse, all looking dreary enough in the faint light of a half-veiled gibbous moon.

A few cars passed us, but there was but little life on the road, and I found myself starting sharply when suddenly the quick whistle of an unseen train shrilled through the stagnant air. It seemed so near, yet I could get no glimpse of it or even of its trailing smoke.

I felt like speaking—asking some question—but I did not. It was a curious experience—this something which made me hold my peace.

My chauffeur whom I had chosen from five others I saw lounging about the garage was a taciturn being. I was rather glad of it, for any talk save that of the most serious character seemed out of keeping with these moments of dread—a dread as formless as many of the objects we passed and as chill as the mist now rising from meadow and wood in a white cloud which soon would envelop the whole landscape as in a shroud.

To relieve my feelings, I ordered him to sound the four short blasts agreed upon as a signal. To my surprise they were answered, but by three only. There was a car coming and presently it dashed by us, but it was not Clarke's.

"Keep it up," I ordered. "This mist will soon be a fog." My chauffeur did so,—at intervals of course—now catching a reply but oftener not, until from far ahead of us, through the curtain of fog shutting off the road in front, there came in response the four clear precise blasts for which my ears were astretch.

"There are my friends," I declared. "Go slowly."

At which we crawled warily along till out of the white gloom a red spark broke mistily upon our view, and guided us to where a long low racing machine stood before a house, the outlines of which were so vague I could not determine its exact character.

Next minute Clarke was by my side.

"I shall have to ask you to get out here," he said, with a sidelong glance at my chauffeur. "And as the business you have come to settle may take quite a little while, it would be better for the car to swing in beside mine, so as to be a little way off the road."

"Very good," I answered, joining him immediately and seeing at the same time that the house was a species of tavern, illy-lit, but open to the public.

"What does it mean?" I questioned anxiously as he led me aside, not towards the tavern's entrance, but rather to the right of it.

"I don't know, sir. He is not inside. He drove up here about ten minutes ago, dismissed the car which brought him from the club-house, went in,—which was about the time I appeared upon the scene—and came out again with a man carrying a lantern. As I was then on my feet and about where we are standing now, I got one quick look at him as he passed through the doorway. I didn't like his looks, sir; he must be feeling very ill. And I didn't like the way he carried himself as he went about the turn you see there at the rear of the building. And I wanted to follow, though of course he is safe enough with the man he is with; but just then I heard your signal and ran to answer. That is all

I have to tell you. But where is he going in such a mist? Shall I run in and ask?"

"Do," I said; and waited impatiently enough for his reappearance which was delayed quite unaccountably, I thought. But then minutes seem hours in such a crisis.

When he did come, he, too, had a lantern.

"Let us follow," said he, not waiting to give me any explanations. And keeping as closely to him as I could lest we should lose each other in the fog, I stumbled along a path worn in the stubbly grass, not knowing where I was going and unable to see anything to right or left or even in front but the dancing, hazy glow of the swinging lantern.

Suddenly that glow was completely extinguished; but before I could speak Clarke had me by the arm.

"Step aside," he whispered. "The man is coming back; he has left Mr. Edgar to go on alone."

And then I heard a hollow sound as of steps on an echoing board.

"That must be a bridge Mr. Edgar is crossing," whispered Clarke. "But see! he is doing it without light. The man has the lantern."

"Where is your lantern?" I asked.

"Under my coat."

We held our breath. The man came slowly on, picking his way and mumbling to himself rather cheerfully than otherwise. I was on the point of accosting him when Clarke stopped me and, as soon as the man had gone by, drew me back into the path, whispering:

"The steps on the bridge have stopped. Let us hurry."

Next minute he had plucked out his lantern from under his coat and we were pressing on, led now by the sound of rushing water.

"It's growing lighter. The fog is lifting," came from Clarke as I felt the boards of the bridge under my feet.

Next minute he had the lantern again under his coat, but for all that, I found, after a few more steps, that I could see a little way ahead. Was that Edgar leaning against one of the supports of the bridge?

I caught at Clarke's hand.

"Shall we go forward?" I asked.

His fingers closed spasmodically on mine, and as suddenly loosened.

"Let me," he breathed, rather than whispered, and started to run, but almost instantly stopped and broke into a merry whistle. I thought I heard a sigh from that hardly discerned figure in front; but that was impossible. What did happen was a sudden starting back from the brink over which he had been leaning and the sound of two pairs of feet crossing the bridge to the other side.

Clarke's happy thought had worked. One dangerous moment was passed. How soon would another confront us?

I was on and over that bridge almost as soon as they. And then I began to see quite clearly where we were. The lights of a small flagging station winked at me through the rapidly dissolving mist, and I remembered having often gone by it on the express. Now it assumed an importance beyond all measurement, for the thunder of an approaching train was in the air and Edgar poised on the brink of the platform was gazing down the track as a few minutes before he had gazed down at the swirling waters under the bridge.

Ah, this was worse! Should I shout aloud his name? entreat him to listen, rush upon him with outstretched arms? There was not time even for decision—the train was near—upon us—slackening. It was going to stop. As he took this in I distinctly heard him draw a heavy breath. Then as the big lumbering train came to a standstill, he turned, bag still in his hand, and detecting me standing not a dozen steps behind him, uttered the short laugh I had come to know so well and with a bow of surpassing grace which yet had its suggestion of ironic humor, leaped aboard the train and was gone before I could recover from my terror and confusion.

But it was not so with Clarke. As the last car went whizzing by I caught sight of him on the rear platform and caught his shout:

"Home, sir, and wait for news!"

All was not lost, then. But that station with the brawling stream beyond, and the square and ugly tavern overlooking it all, have a terror for me which it will take years for me to overcome.

CHAPTER 67

I did not tell Orpha of this episode, then or ever. Why burden her young heart with griefs and fears? I merely informed her when I met her the next morning at breakfast that having seen Edgar take a late train for New York my anxieties were quelled and I had returned to tell her so before starting out again for the city on an errand of my own.

When I came to say good-by, as I did after receiving a telegram from Clarke—of which I will say more later—I told her not to be anxious or to worry while I was away; that being in New York, I should be able to keep a watch over Edgar and see that he was well looked after if by any chance he fell ill again; and the smile I received in return, though infinitely sad, had such confidence in it that I would not have exchanged it for the gayest one I had seen on her lips on that memorable night of the ball.

The telegram I have mentioned was none too encouraging. It had been sent from New York and ran thus:

> Trouble. Man I want has escaped me. Hope to pick him up soon. Wait
> for second telegram.
>
> C.

It was two hours before the second one came. It was to the point as witness:

> Sick. Safe in a small hospital in the Bronx. Will await trains at the
> Grand Central Station till you come.
>
> C.

This sent me off in great haste without another interview with Orpha. On reaching the station in New York I found Clarke waiting for me according to promise. His story was short but graphic. He had had no difficulty on the train. He had been able to keep his eye on Edgar without being seen by him; but some excitement occurring at the short stop made at One Hundred and Twenty-fifth Street—a pickpocket run down or something of that kind— he had leaned from his window to look out and in that instant Edgar had stepped from the train and disappeared in the crowd.

He had tried to follow but was checked in doing so by the quick starting up of the train. But he had a talk with the conductor, who informed him that the man to whom he probably referred had shown decided symptoms of illness, and that he himself had advised him to leave the train and be driven to a hospital, being really afraid that he would break out in delirium if he stayed. This was a guide to Clarke and next morning by going the rounds of upper New York hospitals he had found him. He had been registered under his own name and might be seen if it was imperative to identify him, but at present he was in a delirious condition and it would be better for him not to be disturbed.

Thankful that it was not worse, but nevertheless sufficiently alarmed, a relapse being frequently more serious than the original attack, I called a taxi and we rode at once to the hospital. Good news awaited us. Edgar had shown some favorable symptoms in the last hour and if kept quiet, might escape the worst consequence of a journey for which he had not had the necessary strength. The only thing which puzzled the doctors was his desire to write. He asked for paper and pen continually; but when they were brought to him he produced nothing but a scrawl. But he would have this put in an envelope and sealed. But he failed to address it, saying that he would do that after he had a nap. But though he had his nap he did not on waking recur to the subject, though his first look was at the table where the so-called letter had been laid. It was there now and there they had decided to let it lie, since his eyes seldom left it and if they did, returned immediately to it again as if his whole life were bound up in that wordless scrawl.

This was pitiful news to me, but I could do nothing to save the situation but wait, leaving it to the discretion of the doctors to say when an interview with my cousin would be safe. I did not hesitate to tell them that my presence would cause him renewed excitement, and they, knowing well enough who we were, took in the situation without too much explanation. They succeeded in startling me, however, with the statement that it would probably be two weeks before I could hope to see him.

Two weeks again! Why always two weeks?

There was no help for it. All I could do was to settle down nearby and wait for the passing of those two weeks as we await the falling of a blow whose force we have no means of measuring. Short notes passed between Orpha and myself, but they were all about Edgar, whose condition was sensibly improving, but hardly so rapidly as we had hoped. Clarke had been given access to him; and as Clarke had wisely forborne from mentioning my name in the matter, simply explaining his own presence there by the accounts which had appeared in the papers of his former young master's illness, he was greeted so warmly that he almost gave way under it. Thereafter, he spent much time at Edgar's bedside, reporting to me at night the few words which had passed between them. For, Edgar, so loquacious in health, had little to say in convalescence; but lay brooding with a wild light coming and going in his eyes, which now as before were turned on that table where the unaddressed letter still lay.

For whom was that indecipherable scrawl meant? We knew; for Lucy.

CHAPTER 68

I think that it was on the tenth day of my long wait,—I know that it was just two before Miss Colfax's wedding—that Clarke came in looking a trifle out of sorts and said that he had done something which I might not approve of. He had mailed the letter which Edgar had finally addressed to Miss Colfax. A few words in explanation, and I perceived that he could hardly have helped it; Edgar was so appealing and so entirely unconvinced by what the nurse said concerning the incoherence of its contents. "I know what I have written," he kept saying; and made Clarke swear that he would put it in the first box he saw on leaving the hospital.

"What harm can it do?" Clark anxiously inquired. "It may perplex and trouble Miss Colfax; but we can explain later; can we not, sir?"

I thought of the haughty self-contained Lucy, with a manner so cold and a heart so aflame, receiving this jumble of words amid the preparation for her marriage,—perhaps when her bridal veil was being tried on, or a present displayed,—and had nothing to say. Explanations would not ease the anguish of that secretly distracted heart.

"Shall we do anything about it, sir? I know where Miss Colfax lives."

"No, we can do nothing. A matter of that sort is better left alone."

But I was secretly very uneasy until Clarke came in from the hospital the following day with the glad story that Edgar had improved so much since the sending of this letter that he had been allowed to take an airing in the afternoon. "And to-morrow I am to go early and accompany him to a jeweler's shop where he proposes to buy a present for the bride-to-be. He seemed quite cheerful about it, and the doctors have given their consent. He looks like another man, Mr. Bartholomew. You will find that when this wedding is over he will be very much like his old self."

And again I said nothing; but I took a much less optimistic view of my cousin's apparent cheerfulness.

"He sent me away early. He says that he is going to rest every minute till I come for him in one of Jones' fine motor cars."

"It's a late hour for sending presents," I remarked. "Three hours before the ceremony."

"I am to bring him back to the hospital and then take the car and deliver it."

"Very well, Clarke; only watch him and don't be surprised if you find us on the road behind you. There is something in all this I don't understand."

CHAPTER 69

But when on the following morning I actually found myself riding in the wake of these two and saw Edgar alight with almost a jaunty air before one of the smallest, but most fashionable jeweler shops on the Avenue, I could not but ask myself if my fears had any such foundation as I had supposed. He really did look almost cheerful and walked with a perfectly assured air into the shop.

But he went alone; and when quite some little time had elapsed and he did not reappear, I was ready to brave anything to be sure that all was right. So taking advantage of a little break in the traffic, I ordered my chauffeur to draw up beside the auto waiting at the curb; and when we got abreast of it, I leaned out and asked Clarke, who hastily lowered his window, why he had not gone in with Mr. Bartholomew.

"Because he would not let me. He wanted to feel free to take his own time. He told me that it would take him at least half an hour to choose the article he wanted. He has been gone now just twenty-seven minutes."

"Can you see the whole length of the shop from where you sit?"

"No, sir. There are several people in front—"

"Get out and go in at once. Don't you see that this shop is next to the corner? That it may have a side entrance—"

He was out of the car before I had finished and in three minutes came running back.

"You are right, sir. He did not buy a thing. There is no sign of him in the shop or in the street. I deserve—"

"We won't talk. Pay your chauffeur and dismiss him. Then get in with me, and we will drive as fast as the law allows to that house in Newark where he said the present was to go. If we do not find him there we may as well give up all hope; we shall never see him again."

CHAPTER 70

It was a wild ride. If he had been fortunate enough to secure a taxi within a few minutes after reaching the street, he must have had at least twenty minutes the start of us. But the point was not to overtake him, but to come upon him at Mr. Miller's before any mischief could take place. I was an invited guest, though probably not expected; and it being a house-wedding, I felt sure of being received even if I was not in a garb suited to the occasion.

There were delays made up by a few miles of speeding along the country roads, and when we finally struck the street in which Mr. Miller lived, it lacked just one hour of noon.

What should we do? It was too soon to present ourselves. The few autos standing about were business ones, with a single exception. Pointing this out to Clarke, I bade him get busy and find out if this car were a local or a New York one.

He came back very soon to the spot where we had drawn up to say that it belonged to some relative of the bride; and satisfied from this and the quiet aspect of the house itself that nothing of a disturbing character had yet occurred, I advised Clarke to hang about and learn what he could, while I waited for the appearance of Edgar whom we had probably outridden in crossing the marshes.

We had a place on the opposite side of the street, from which I could see the windows of Mr. Miller's house. I took note of every automobile which drove up before me, but I took note also of those windows and once got a glimpse in one of the upper ones of a veiled head and a white face turned eagerly towards the street.

She was expecting him. Nothing else would account for so haggard a look on a face so young; and with a thought of Orpha and how I would rather die than see her in the grip of such despair, I nerved myself for what might come, without a hope that any weal could follow such a struggle of unknown forces as apparently threatened us.

The house in which my whole interest was centered at this moment was of somewhat pretentious size, built of brick painted brown and set back far enough from the sidewalk to allow for a square of turf, in the center of which rose a fountain dry as the grass surrounding it. From what conjunction of ideas that fountain with its image of a somewhat battered Cupid got in my way and inflicted itself upon my thoughts, I cannot say. I was watching for Edgar's appearance, but I saw this fountain; and now when the memory of that day comes back, first and foremost before anything else rises a picture of that desolate basin and its almost headless Cupid. I was trying to escape this obsession when I saw him. He had alighted by that time and was halfway up the walk, but I entered the door almost at his heels.

He was stepping quickly, but I was close behind and was looking for an opportunity to speak to him when he took a course through the half-filled hall which led him into a portion of the house where it would have been presumptuous in me to follow.

We had been asked to go upstairs, but with a shake of the head and the air of one at home, he had pressed straight on to the rear and so out of my sight. There was nothing left for me to do but to mount the stairs in front which I did very unwillingly.

However, once at the top and while still in the shadow of a screen of palms running across this end of the hall, I heard his voice from behind these palms asking for Miss Colfax. He had come up a rear staircase.

By this time there were others in the hall besides myself making for the dressing-rooms opening back and front, and I saw many heads turn, but nobody stop. The hour for the ceremony was approaching.

What to do? The question was soon answered for me. Edgar had stepped from behind the palms and was rapidly going front in the direction of the third story staircase. She was above, as I knew, and any colloquy between them must be stopped if my presence would prevent it.

Following in his wake, but not resorting to the leaps and bounds by which he reached the top of the stairs in a twinkling, I did not see the rush of the white-clad figure which fell into his arms with a moan which was more eloquent of joy than despair. But I was in time to hear him gasp out in wild excitement:

"I am here. I have come for you. You shall never marry any one but me. Sickness has held me back—hospital—delirium. I cannot live without you. I will not. Lucy, Lucy, take off that veil. We do not need veils, or wedding guests or orchestra or luncheon. We only need each other. Do you consent? Will you take me weakened by illness, deprived of my inheritance but true to you when the full realization came."

And listening for her answer I heard just a sigh. But that sigh was eloquent and it had barely left her lips when I heard a rush from below and, noting who it was, I slipped quickly up to Edgar and touching him on the arm, said quietly but very firmly:

"Dr. Hunter."

They started apart and Edgar, drawing back, cried under his breath:

"You here!"

"Would you wish it otherwise?" I asked; and stepped aside as Dr. Hunter, pale to the lips, but very dignified and very stern, advanced from the top of the stairs followed by a lady and gentleman who, as I afterwards learned, were Lucy's aunt and uncle. There was a silence; which, repeated as it was below stairs, held the house in a hush for one breathless moment. Then I took the lead, and, pointing to an open door in front, I addressed the outraged bridegroom with all the respect I felt for him.

"Pardon me, Dr. Hunter. As the cousin and friend of Edgar Bartholomew, allow me to urge that we say what we have to say behind closed doors. The house is rapidly filling. Everything said in this hall can be heard below. Let us disappoint the curiosity of Mrs. Miller's guests. Miss Colfax, will you lead the way?"

With a quick gesture she turned, and moving with the poise of a queen, entered the room from which I had seen her looking down into the street, followed by the rest of us in absolute silence. I came last and it was I who closed the door. When I turned, Dr. Hunter and Edgar were confronting each other in the middle of the room. Lucy was standing by herself, an image of beauty but cold to the eye as the marble she suggested. Mr. and Mrs. Miller stood aghast, speechless, and a little frightened. I hastened to put in a word.

"Edgar left a hospital bed to be here this morning. Have a little care, Dr. Hunter. His case has been a serious one."

The doctor's lips took a sarcastic curve.

"I have a physician's eye," was his sole return. Then without a word to Edgar, he stepped up to Lucy. "Will you take my arm?" he asked. "The clergyman who is to marry us is waiting."

The image moved, but, oh, so slightly. "I cannot," she replied. "It would be an outrage to you. All my heart goes out to the man behind you. It always has. He was not free—not really free—and I thought to help him do his duty by marrying you. But I cannot—I cannot." And now all the fire in that woman's soul flamed forth in one wild outburst as she cried aloud in undisguised passion, "I cannot so demean you, and I cannot so discourage Edgar. Free me, or—or I shall go mad." Then she became quiet again, the old habit of self-restraint returned, the image resumed its calm, only her eyes steady and burning with the inner flame she sought to hide, held his with an undeviating demand.

He bowed before it, wincing a little as she lifted her arms and with a slow, deft movement, took the veil from her head and as slowly and deftly began to fold it up. I see her now as she did this and the fascination which held those two men in check—the one in a passion of rejoicing, the other in the agitation of seeing, for the first time, doubtless, in his placid courtship, the real woman beneath the simulated one who had accepted his attentions but refused him her love.

When she had finished and laid the veil aside, she had the grace to thank him for his forbearance.

But this he could not stand.

"It is for me to thank you," said he. "It were better if more brides thought twice before bringing a loveless heart to their husband's hearthstone." And always dignified; always a man to admire, he turned towards the door.

Mr. Miller sought to stop him—to hold him back until the guests had been dismissed and the way prepared for him to depart, unseen and uncommiserated. But he would have none of that.

"I have been honest in my wish to make your niece happy and I need not fear the looks of any one. I will go alone. Take care of the sick man there. I have known great joy kill as effectually as great pain."

Lucy's head fell. Edgar started and reached out his hand. But the door was quickly opened and as quickly shut behind the doctor's retreating form.

A sob from Lucy; an instant of quiet awe; then life came rushing back upon us with all its requirements and its promise of halcyon days to the two who had found their souls in the action and reaction of a few months of desperate trial and ceaselessly shifting circumstances.

And what of myself, as, with peace made with the Millers and arrangements entered into whereby Edgar was to remain with them till his health was restored, I rode back to New York and then—

Home! As the bee flies, home!

CHAPTER 71

When I entered C— in the late afternoon I was met by a very different reception from any which had ever been accorded me before.

It began at the station. News travels fast, especially when it concerns people already in the public eye, and in every face I saw, and in every handshake offered me, I read the welcome due to the change in my circumstances made by Edgar's choice of a wife. The Edgar whom they had held in preference above all others was a delightful fellow, a companion in a thousand and of a nature rich and romantic enough to give up fortune and great prestige for love; but he was no longer the Edgar of Quenton Court, and they meant me to realize it.

And I did. But there was one whose judgment I sought—whose judgment I awaited—whom I must see and understand before I could return these amenities with all the grace which they demanded. There was nothing for me in this open and unabashed homage, rendered after weeks of dislike and suspicion, if the welcome I should not fail to receive from Orpha's courtesy should be shot through with the sorrow of a loss too great for any love of mine to offset.

So I hastened and came to Quenton Court, and entering there found the court ablaze with color and every servant which the house contained drawn up in order to receive me. It was English, but then by birth I am an Englishman and the tribute pleased me. For their faces were no longer darkened by distrust and some even were brightened by liking; and were I to remain master here—

But that was yet to be determined; and when they saw with what an eager glance I searched the gallery for the coming of their youthful mistress, they filed quickly away till I was left alone with the leaping water and the rainbow hues and the countless memories of joy and terror with which the place was teeming.

Orpha had a favorite collie which from the first had shown a preference for my company that was sometimes embarrassing but oftener pleasing, since it gave me an opportunity to whisper many secrets in his ear. As I stood there with my eyes on the gallery, he came running to me with so many evidences of affection that I was fain to take it as an omen that all would be well with me when she who held him dear would greet me in her turn.

When would she come? The music of the falling drops plashing in their basin behind me was sweet, but I longed for the tones of her voice. Why did she linger? Dare I guess, when at last I heard her footfall in the gallery above, and caught the glimpse of her figure, first in one opening of its lattice work and then in another as she advanced towards the stairs which were all that now separated us, unless it were the sorrow whose ravages in her tender breast she might seek to hide, and might succeed in hiding from every eye but mine?

No, I would guess at nothing. I would wait; but my heart leaped high, and when she had passed the curve marking the turn of the great staircase, I bounded forward and so had the sweetest vision that ever comes to love—the descent, from tread to tread of the lady of one's heart into the arms which have yearned for her in hope and in doubt for many weary days.

For I knew before she reached me that she loved me. It was in her garb of white, filmy and virginal, in her eager, yet timid step, in the glow of youth—of joyous expectation which gave radiance to her beauty and warmth to my own breast. But I said not a word nor did I move from my position at the foot of the stairs till she reached the last step but one and paused; then I uttered her name.

Had I uttered it before? Had she ever heard it before? Surely not as at that moment. For her eyes, as she slowly lifted them to mine, had a look of wonder in them which grew as I went on to say:

"Before I speak a word of all that has been burning in my heart since first I saw you from the gallery above us, I want you to know that I consider all the splendor surrounding us as yours, both by right of birth and the love of your father. I am ready to sign it all over—what we see and what we do not see—if you desire to possess it in freedom, or think you would be happier with a mate of your own choosing. I love you. There! I have said it, Orpha—but I love you so well that I would rather lose all that goes with your hand than be a drag upon your life, meant as you are for peace and joy and an unhampered existence. Do you believe that?"

"Yes, I believe that. But—" Oh, the delicious naïveté of her smile, bringing every dimple into play and lighting up into radiance the gravity of her gaze, "why should you think that I might want to be free to live in this great house alone? For me, that would be desolation."

"Desolation because you would be alone or because—" even now I hardly dared to say it—"because it would be life without reality—without love? Orpha, I must know; —know beyond the shadow of a doubt. I cannot take the great gift bequeathed me by your father, unless with it I receive the greatest gift of all—your undivided heart. You are young and very lovely—a treasure which many men will crave. I should never he satisfied for you to be merely content. I want you to know the thrill—the ecstasy of love—such love as I feel for you—"

I could not go on. The pressure of all the past was upon me. The story of the days and nights when in rapture and in tragedy she was my chief thought, my one unfailing inspiration to hold to the right and to dare misapprehension and the calumny of those who saw in me an interloper here without conscience or mercy, passed in one wild phantasmagoria through my mind, rendering me speechless.

With that fine intuition of hers—or perhaps, because she had shared alike my pains and my infinite horrors— she respected my silence till the time came for words and then she spoke but one:

"Quenton!"

Had she ever spoken it before? Or had I ever heard it as it fell at this moment from her lips? Never. It linked us two together. It gave the nay to all my doubts. I felt sure now, sure; and yet such is the hunger of a lover's heart that I wanted her assurance in words. Would she grant me that?

Yes; but it came very softly and with a delicate aloofness at first which gave me the keenest delight.

"When you spoke of the first time you saw me and said it was from the gallery above us, you spoke as if life had begun for you that night. Did you never think that possibly it might have begun for me also? That content had revealed itself as content, not love? That I was happy that what we had expected to take place that night did not take place—that—that—"

Here her aloofness all vanished and her soul looked through her eyes. We were very near, but the collie was leaping about us, and the place was large and the gorgeousness of it all overpowering; so I contented myself with laying my hand softly on hers where it pressed against the edge of the final pillar supporting the lattice work.

"Let us go into the library," I whispered.

But she led me elsewhere. Quieting the dog, she drew me away into a narrow hall, the purpose of which I had never understood till I had learned the secret of the hidden stairway and how this hall denoted the space which the lower end of the inn's outside stairway had formerly occupied. Pausing, she gave me an earnest look, then, speaking very softly:

"It was here—on the steps which once united the ground with those still remaining above, that my father and my mother pledged themselves to each other in a love that has survived death. Shall we—"

She said no more: I had her in my arms and life had begun for us in very truth.

CHAPTER 72

Lovers have much to say when the barriers which have separated them are once down, and I will not hazard a guess at the hour when after a moment of delicious silence I ventured to remark:

"We have talked much about ourselves and our future. Shall we not talk a little now about Edgar?"

"Oh, yes; tell me the whole story. I've only heard that he arrived in time to prevent the marriage. That Dr. Hunter generously released her from all obligation to him and that she and Edgar will be united very soon."

I was glad to comply. Glad to throw light into that darksome corner none of us had ever penetrated, our Lucy's heart. When I had finished, we sat a moment in awe of the passionate tale, then I said:

"We must do something for Edgar. He will have no wedding, but he must have a wedding present."

"Let it be much."

"It shall be much."

"But not too much. Edgar is reckless with money and even queens in these days sometimes come to grief. Shall we not put by a fund for the time when we see the sparkle leaving his eye and anxiety making Lucy's pale cheeks still more pallid?"

"You shall do just as you wish, Orpha."

"No; just as Father would wish."

Ah! my beloved one!

CHAPTER 73

I have one more memory of that night. As I was leaving—for I was resolved to remain at my hotel until our marriage, which, for many reasons, was to be an immediate one without preparation and with but little ceremony,—I asked my love why in the months of her father's illness, and during the time when perplexities of various kinds were in all our hearts, she never allowed herself to remain alone with me or to go where I went even with her father's permission.

And her answer, given with a smile and a blush was this:

"I did not dare."

She did not dare! My conscientious darling.

And I had not dared. But my fears were not her fears. I had feared to be presumptuous; of building up a fairyland out of dreams; of yielding to my imagination rather than to my good sense. And yet, deep down in some inner consciousness, a faint insidious hope had whispered to itself that if I showed myself worthy, perhaps—perhaps—

And now perhaps had become reality, and all doubt and mistrust a vanished dream.

But though I had walked in clouded ways and had not known my Orpha's heart, there had been one in the household who had. I learned it that night from a few words uttered by Clarke on my return to the hotel.

I was not surprised to find him waiting for me in the lobby; we had come into such close contact during the strenuous days that had just passed, that it would have seemed unnatural not to have found him there. But what did astonish me was to see the wistful look with which he contemplated me as I signified to him my wish for him to follow me upstairs. But once together in my room, I understood, and letting the full joyousness of my heart to appear, I smilingly said:

"You may congratulate me, Clarke. My good fortune is complete."

And this is what he uttered in response, greatly to my surprise and possibly to his own:

"I thought it would all come right, sir."

But it was not till he was on the point of leaving me for the night that I learned his full mind.

His hand was on the knob of the door and he was about to turn it, when he suddenly loosened his hold and came back.

"Excuse me, sir, but I shan't feel quite right till I tell you all the truth about myself. Did you, when things looked a little dark after the terrible news the doctors gave us, get a queer looking sort of note hidden in your box of cigars?"

"Yes, I did, Clarke; and I don't know yet who took that much compassion on me?"

"It was I, Mr. Bartholomew." (Never had he called me that before. I wonder if it came with a long dreaded effort.) "But it was not from compassion for you, sir— more's the pity; but because I knew my young lady's heart and felt willing to help her that much in her great trouble."

"You knew—"

"Not by any words, sir; but by a look I saw on her face one day as she stood in the window watching you motor away. You were to be gone a week and she could not stand the thought of it. I hope you will pardon me for speaking so plainly. I have always felt the highest regard for Miss Bartholomew."

Oh, the pictures that came back! Pictures I had not seen at the time but which now would never leave me.

Perhaps he saw my emotion; perhaps he only realized it, but an instant of silence passed before he quietly added: "A man thinks he's honest till he comes to the point of trial. When they asked me if I wrote anything to anybody about that key, I said No, for I didn't write anything as you must know who read the printed letters I pasted in such crooked lines on a slip of paper."

I smiled; it was easy to smile that night.

"You know where the key was found. How do you think it got there?"

"In the flower-pot? Of course, I can't say for certain, but this is how I've figured it out. On the morning he died, you found him, as you must remember, in the same flannel robe which he had worn while sitting up. This was because he would not allow me as he had always done before to remove it. That robe was buttoned close to his neck when we left him, but it was not so buttoned in the morning, and we know why. He had wanted to use the key he wore strung on a chain about his neck, and that key hung under his pajama jacket. To get it he had first to unfasten his dressing-gown and then his pajama jacket, or if he did not want to go to that trouble, to simply pull it up into his hand by means of the chain which held it. He probably did the latter, being naturally impatient with buttons and such like and letting it fall within reach, went about the business he had planned.

"So far excitement had kept him up, but when, after an act which would have tired a well man, he came back into his room— Well! that was different. He could draw into place the shelves which had hidden the secret stairway, and he could put out the light in his closet; for all this had to be done if he did not want to give away his secret. And he could manage, though not without difficulty, I'm sure, to reach and unlock his two doors; but that done, the little job of unbuttoning his jacket, throwing the chain over his head and rearranging his whole clothing so that the key would be invisible to his nurse when she came in, was just a little too much. But the key had to be hidden, and hidden quickly and easily, and he being, as there is every reason to believe on the further side of the bed where he had gone to unlock the upper door, he was at this time of failing strength within a foot of the potted plant standing in the window, and this gave him his idea.

"Gathering up the chain and key in his hand, he made use of the latter to push aside the soil in the pot sufficiently to make a hole large enough to hold anything so thin and slight as that chain and key. A flick given by his fingers to the loose mold and they were covered. That's how I've reasoned it out; and if it is not all true some of it is for his slippers were found lying on that side of the bed, instead of under the stand by the closet where I had placed them on taking them off. What do you think, sir? Doesn't that answer your question?"

"Yes, Clarke, as well as it ever will be answered. Have you given this explanation to Miss Bartholomew, or to any one else in fact?"

"No, sir. I'm not quick to talk and I should not have said as much to you if you had not asked me. For after all it is only my thoughts, sir. We shall never know all that passed through the mind of your uncle during those last three hours."

It was after our return from a very short wedding journey, during which we had seen Edgar married to Lucy, that one evening when life seemed very sweet to us, Orpha put into my hands a sheet of discolored paper, folded letter-wise, saying softly:

"My last secret, Quenton. That is an old, old letter written by my father and found by me at the same time I found the early will in the old box at the foot of the hidden stairway. It was lying underneath the will and would have escaped my notice if the box had not fallen from its peg while I was pulling at the crumpled-up document in my effort to get it out. It is a treasure and the time has come for you to share it with me. Read it, Quenton."

And this is what I read:

* * * * * * * *

Some day, my darling child, you will find this letter. When you do, you will wonder why in building this house, I took such pains to retain within its walls a portion of the old iron stairway belonging to the ancient inn against which I chose to rear this structure.

I am going to tell you. You are a child now, thirteen last Tuesday. I hope you will be a woman when you read these lines, and a fine one, as just and as generous-hearted as your mother. You will understand me better so, especially if that great alchemist, Love, has wrought his miracle in your heart.

For Love is my theme, dear child, the love I felt for your mother. The stairway down which you have stepped in such amazement was our trysting place in those days. At its base was the spot where we pledged our young love. She lived within with her father and mother, but there were moments when she could steal out under the stars,—moments so blessed to me, a thoughtless lad, that their influence is with me yet though the grave has her sweet body, and Immortal Love her soul.

You will be like her. You will be to Edgar what your mother has been to me. When you are that—when a woman is a guiding star to her husband—she may face the ills of life without fear, for the blessing of Heaven is upon her.

As is that of your father,

Edgar Quenton Bartholomew.

THE END